MESOPOTAMIA//TIAMAT

The Tribes of Typhi

Ashley Wrigley

To Rob, for the countless ways you make my dreams come true every day.

Part One

"The death of God left the angels in a strange position."
Donald Barthelme

The newswoman's voice was accompanied with horrific images of smoldering streets in Tonatti Haan and a sea of dead stacked outside MAAR headquarters. Every wired-connect—comm-units, imagers, datapads, slates, and vidscreens—were tuned into the report. The people of Anshar gaped at the news, splintered with fear.

"The sanctioned attack on the recently discovered enclave of the mysterious Keepers left Tonatti Haan in ruin. The unexpected explosion that followed the angel infiltration unit left no one alive, not even the angels dispatched. Though MAAR refuses to make a solid statement concerning the sensitive details surrounding the explosion, it is clear to many that it was an unanticipated and suicidal counter-attack.

"Days later, the Keepers retaliated, leaving a bloody wake of indescribable carnage. Over two hundred angels were slaughtered in the assault, executed by one woman codenamed Dreadknight by Mirax authorities. Skeptical as it may seem, footage shows this woman single-handedly marched into Mirax headquarters and, room by room, slaughtered every angel she came to with a dark kind of magic. Official representatives call it witchtech, the street name for a powerful form of superscience. Though imaging claims this woman acted solo, other leads concerning a much larger operation assisted by fellow Keepers is being investigated.

"The Keeper fled the tower with a man in custody—a man whose significance is being kept under wraps. They vanished somewhere in the Tonatti Haan district, followed closely by an ordered attack on the site, burning a hole into Tonatti's once-beautiful city proper. The terrorists are said to have been annihilated in the attack, but official channels are closed.

"In the wake of such terror, an indefinite number of refugees has already started returning from the Mine, wreaking havoc wherever they go. The people of Anshar join in with the Haan cities, crying for their dead and for the destruction of their homes, wondering why this is happening to them. The attack on MAAR has left Anshar volatile, and representatives are asking the people to prepare." The woman paused for a moment and her face appeared on the screen. "An invasion army from Kishar is amassing beneath our streets and an attack is imminent. A war with the Mine is coming."

"Shade!"

Knick coughed in the cloud of debris filling the small space. Her body was limp in his arms. He shook her once, twice, over and over, but she did not wake. He coughed again.

"Shade!"

They were in utter darkness. He squinted as if it would help. He could not see her, only groped blindly for her, for a grip to hold her and carry her, for the walls, for a foothold.

"Shade! Wake up!"

He stumbled, his ankle twisting around. They fell down a slope. There was a sharp pain in his back when he landed. He scrambled in the dark, patting her arms and legs and neck to make sure nothing had broken.

Someone else touched his forearm, gripped it tightly.

"Get up!" the familiar voice said.

"Lethan?" Knick coughed. "How did you—"

"No time! Get up!" Lethan's and Whiskey's blue eyes were the only thing he could see in the blackness. "I will lead you. Now come."

The back room was quiet. It was always quiet. Oil lamps burned in the corners, softening the edges with a blend of light and shadow. Befitting, Knick thought for the thousandth time, how the shadows came to her as though called, hugging her form like pups huddled up to their wounded mother. He had seen with his own two eyes the command she had over them and wondered if they were now heeding an unconscious call for aid; he wondered if they sensed her close to death and could not help but come to her side. Were they mending her, too? Or were they merely a presence to comfort their beloved master and hope that she would wake up? Like him.

"She's bleeding!"

He could feel the wetness all over her. It compromised his grip when he carried her, dragged her, held her. She had been bloody when she'd found him, but this felt warm, felt fresh.

There was a second pair of hands on her suddenly and Lethan's blue eyes were looking down. Knick looked down, too, but couldn't see anything. Whiskey's large eyes were near his hand that cradled her head, staring intently.

3

"She is bleeding," Lethan confirmed.

"Where?"

"Everywhere. She has many wounds."

"Fuck!" Knick screamed, panicky and helpless. "Shade." It was a desperate plea, but to who? Begging her subconscious to save her? "Shade!"

He was going to lose her. She was going to die. Her pulse was weak and she wasn't responding to any of the harsh treatment she'd been forced to endure as she was hauled through a steep decent of mostly stomach-turning drops and rough slides. She had already been in terrible condition when she'd found him at the Halo—covered in blood, shaking, wild, filled with fury. Now she was going to die. There was nothing he could do. He was blind.

"I will treat these wounds as best I can," Lethan said calmly, the only voice in the impenetrable darkness. "But Knick. She is dying. I cannot promise I can save her, or that this journey will not undo all that I might accomplish."

"Do it!" he screamed.

Knick reached out and took Shade's hand. It was cold. It had been cold for two weeks but she had a pulse and it was stronger than it had been when they first brought her to the *Mermaid*. In that darkness, Lethan had not lied to him or sugarcoated his words to soften the hard reality of the situation—that Shade was dying. And as Knick floundered down the tunnel, unsure of where to put his foot next much less how to attend to the person he cared for most, Lethan had been there to save her, to save them both.

"She will live for now, but we must hurry or she will die."

Those worse had scared him and angered him, but those words had afforded them an unexpected bond.

In the cold black, Knick moved her limp body in the way that Lethan instructed so as not to reopen any of her wounds or upset her system into fresh bleeding. Isis and the others were there with them, quiet and shivering and weak. He knew they wondered the same thing he did: will I live through this? Will I see the light of day ever again?

He tightened his arms, pulling Shade a little closer than before. He lowered his ear to her lips, listened for her shallow breath. Her dry, rough mouth brushed his ear, warning him that she was dehydrated.

"Whiskey," Lethan said.

There was the sound of scurrying. Suddenly a furry hand grabbed his and tiny fingers placed a water canister in his palm then pushed it toward his face. He took two sips and passed it back to the lehn, expecting the creature to immediately scamper off to the others. Instead, Whiskey took his hand again and placed a sopping wet rag over his fingers. He stared in the direction he thought it was, wondering what purpose it had.

Whiskey chirped, took his hand in both of his tiny paws, and guided him toward his other hand—the hand that cradled Shade's head. Whiskey squeezed Knick's fingers around the rag and then it all clicked. He was trying to give Shade water. Knick suddenly sat up, let his fingers seek out her mouth. Her lips were now damp. Excitedly, he bundled the cloth into a point and fitted it just between her lips. He squeezed gently, heard the squish of water.

Whiskey patted his hand and shuffled away.

Lethan came over soon after. Knick was suddenly very aware of the sound of chewing.

"She is doing better," Lethan told him. There was a pause in the chewing, another sound—like a bite—and then Lethan's arm brushed Knick as he reached to inspect one of her wounds. "She is still very weak. If we do not reach the Obeahani soon, we will lose her."

"What are you doing?"

"Applying a paste. The fungi grows in the tunnels the Krueh-jin wander. My people call it a miracle plant. It heals our wounds and speeds our recovery but we have only used it for simple gashes and cuts, never for some-thing this extreme. I do not know if it can help her."

"It can't hurt her…"

"No, Knick Coltin, it cannot."

In those innumerable hours, Lethan had been the only person in the entire world that Knick could trust. He was the only way any of them would survive. He had been like the gentle god in the darkness guiding them toward safety. And then they hit something hollow and felt wood slats instead of stone beneath their fingers. There was a hatch in the far side of the floor that opened up and flooded the attic with light.

"Where are we headed?" His voice sounded strange in the silence.

"To a healing house called The Bright Mermaid," Lethan explained. "The Obeahani will be able to help us."

"You mentioned them before. Who are they?"

"The wise women of the Mermaid are a tribe of spirithealers kin to the Nabari. Their ways are beyond understanding, but there are very few that they have lost to Death's fierce grip." Lethan paused for a long moment. *"When they come for her, you must let her go."*

But he had refused to let Shade go. He had fought them, swore he wouldn't leave her side. They had won, enlisting his friends to help restrain him. He was shut out—door slammed and locked in his face. Otto, Antion, and Shade disappeared into the back of the healing house and all became quiet. A few hours later, the women attending to Antion emerged. A day later, they departed Otto's room. Three days later, they left Shade's. She would live, they promised him, but she was very weak and would need time to rest.

"You're so stupid," he muttered, running his thumb across her pale knuckles. "Who told you to violate the Balance, huh? What happened to stealth and subterfuge? You need to work on that, you know. Violence isn't always the answer. That's your problem—you're too violent. Always charging into a fight." He clenched the muscles in his jaw. "You're the one who dragged me into this. Don't you think it's time to wake up and let me know what's next? I'm not doing this without you. You can forget it."

Suddenly there were footsteps in the hallway so he released her fingers and mentally backed away, running his hands over the short, wild hair on his head as he prepared for the interruption. There was a gentle knock on the door and then it opened. Slot poked her head inside.

"Knick," she said. "Someone's here to see you."

He got up and shut the door so softly that it didn't make a sound. The narrow, wooden-walled corridors he navigated made him feel trapped in a maze—an unusually accurate metaphor considering his current plight. One sharp turn after another in a labyrinth with no viable markers, just brown slabs for doors and darker brown slabs of walls. The wood was nicked and knocked, but all of the scars blended together and there was no way to discern one blemish from the next—not enough to turn it into a dependable guide. And while the back rooms were not really a maze at all, sometimes, if he wasn't paying attention, he really did get lost.

Out in the front of the healing house, the lobby was mostly empty. Only the High Healer Etrusca, Lethan with his lehn Whiskey, Jilk, and now he were present—that is, aside from the stranger, whose scrawny form was pale and knobby. With her back to him, he observed stringy, white-blond hair randomly banded in various places that fell to her lower back; blue veins protruded under the flexed muscles of her calves and thighs as she turned to face him. Terrifying scars wormed across her face and peculiar, turquoise eyes seemed to glow in the dim light. She wore a single, unique earring of jingling coins carved of bone.

"Knick Coltin?" she asked with a disarmingly kind and soothing voice.

"So far," he replied.

"My name is Caleigh of the Bloodsworn. I was asked by a fellow Sworn to deliver this to you." She held out a delicately wrapped package.

"Hezara?" he asked as he took it; he could tell by the weight that it was the statue she'd been sent to investigate. The woman nodded. "Why didn't she deliver it herself?"

"Hezara was afraid she was being followed and did not wish her delivery compromised," she answered.

"Did she say anything else?"

"Asgard must fall," the woman replied. "That is the only message she had for you." Caleigh paused and considered him for a moment. "There's something else you might want to know. Hezara's tracker went offline a few days ago."

"Tracker?" he echoed, looking up from the statue.

"Every Sworn has one installed to locate their remains should anything happen to them during a delivery so someone could be dispatched to finish their job."

"What does that mean then?" he asked, frowning.

"She's dead," Caleigh replied darkly.

Knick stared blankly at her for a few moments, quietly exhaling as his shoulders slumped. He hadn't known Hezara long but their journey together had built up enough familiarity for him to not want something bad to happen to her. He felt guilty. It was true the ex-Keepers were already after her, but would she still be dead if he hadn't gotten involved with her? Wouldn't she still be alive today if she knew nothing about the Keepers and the turmoil in the Order? The idea made him sick to his stomach.

"I hope whatever that package is means something. She

certainly believed it was worth dying for," Caleigh mumbled and walked out.

Knick slowly unwrapped the statue and held it away from him as though it were cursed. It felt heavier than it had the first time he'd held it. Hezara's life was in it now, and it carried that burden rolled up in his guilt.

"Asgard must fall?" Jilk said, interrupting the silence Knick hadn't even realized had crept in.

"Huh?" He snapped out of the trance. "Yeah, right. Wonder what that means."

"Asgard has already fallen," Lethan pointed out, gingerly fingering Whiskey's fuzzy head. "Doesn't that make the statue worth-less now?"

"Perhaps there's more to it," Etrusca offered.

He stared at the carved representation of Yggdrasil, turning it over in his palm. He hadn't really talked to Isis about anything that had happened. Shade had to wake up first—he insisted upon it. Surprisingly, Isis had agreed. So the days were filled with stretched out quiet. Antion had recovered completely, left with a nasty scar on his face; between studying the old books the Obeahani possessed and worshipping Isis as the Enoch, he didn't have time to think about his updated appearance. Otto was faring only slightly better than Shade. He was awake and slowly retaining some strength. His arm had been infected and—as the healers had said—a couple more days and it would've had to come off. Fortunately for him, he was inside the limit and was able to keep his limb.

Knick mentally shook his head and tried to get back to his thoughts on the relic when a woman of the Mermaid poked her head into the room.

"Sahi Knick," she called. "She is waking up."

Without even asking or thinking, he pushed past her and darted through the halls, stopping only to compose himself before he entered the room. Shade was stirring, not yet awake. He noticed out of the corner of his eyes that others tried to enter the room and were promptly yanked out, allowing him privacy.

"Shade?" he began, moving to her side. He dumped the statue on the bed, no longer interested, and sat on the edge. "You awake?"

"Knick," she grunted with a raspy voice of vulnerability

he wasn't used to hearing from her. "Where am I?"

"A healing house in Gehrs, Mine side," he replied.

"OT?"

"Surprisingly, we're still in the Cradle. Low on cogs, though, so you don't have to worry." He brushed some hair away from her forehead. "Otto led us out a secret tunnel to the Mine. We barely escaped Mirax—they dropped a strike right on our ass minutes before we got down that hatch."

"I…don't remember."

"It's no wonder," he muttered. "You blacked out after the hit." He put his arm on the other side of her body and leaned into it so that he could get closer to her face. "You know, Shade, twice now you've wound up dying in my arms. That's a sign, don't you think?"

"Yeah, to stay the hell away from you!" Slot exclaimed from the hallway, promptly followed by, "Ow!" He glared up at the empty doorway. Weak laughter beneath him brought his gaze back to the pale woman lying under him.

"She's right," Shade mused. "What kind of sign is that?"

"You tell me," he mumbled. "You're the one who took on the angels to save me." He grinned when a little color flushed her cheeks. "Oh, now you're embarrassed?"

"Only because you're so stupid," she muttered, but it lacked the usual curtness she wielded whenever she insulted him. It was a good sign, he decided.

"While we're on the topic, I guess I should say thanks." Knick cleared his throat. "I don't think I would've gotten out of Heaven if you hadn't shown up."

Shade shifted uncomfortably and the muscles in her face tightened. Her gaze moved away from him. The implications of her actions were undeniable, but he had no intention of letting her panic under pressure and shoot him down. Though he really wanted to talk about it—really wanted some kind of answer—he recognized the flash of fear in her eyes. He knew he had to back off.

"What did you find out when you were gone?" he asked, bringing her eyes back to him.

"Your prophecy," she replied. "You *are* the One, Knick. And I can see you now…" She lifted her hand and touched his forehead. It was only for a moment, because soon after she gritted her teeth and her hand dropped like a weight onto her chest.

Just then, several of the Obeahani shuffled into the room, wide and thick skirts swishing about their feet. They began checking Shade's vitals, forcing him to move away so that they could work.

"She is in much pain," one of the women said. "Shade, you should tell us you suffer so."

"I'm fine," she growled.

"You are not fine. You barely move without pain," the same woman retorted gently, her voice lathered with a strange accent. "I will give you this for your pain." And the woman lifted a syringe to Shade's arm. "You will sleep heavily and feel nothing."

"No," Knick protested. "Don't make her go back to sleep. She's been sleeping all this time. She just woke up. What if she doesn't wake up again?"

"She will, sahi. She will," the woman assured him, injecting the medicine into her patient. She then held her hand over Shade's chest and neck, eyes closed, and a soft glow emanated under Shade's skin. "Good... Very good sign." She opened her eyes and smiled. "You are healing so quickly, sana. Remarkable, the dark ones come and they stay with you, heal you."

And then she and the other Obeahani shuffled out of the room, leaving Knick and Shade alone once more. He moved back to the bed.

"Shade?" he asked, but the drug was working too quickly. Her eyes were drifting closed but she still stretched her arm out to touch his forehead. He leaned in close so that she wouldn't have to reach very far.

"You are the turning point, Knick Coltin, and I will protect you," she mumbled lazily. "As an angel...a cogwheeler...a *Keeper*..." Shade swallowed and drowsily looked from one eye to the next. "As a...man..." she whispered, and his heart started beating a little more noticeably.

Suddenly Shade tilted her head up and kissed him. It was gentle, soft, barely a touch, but it was enough to snap whatever restraint he had. He scooped her neck up with his palm and pulled her into his mouth, kissing her harder and deeper. She responded for a split second and then she went limp in his grasp. He cautiously lowered her back to the bed, slightly confused, and then realized she had passed out.

"Don't bother," Jilk said from the door, leaning against the frame with his arms crossed over his chest. "It's the drugs talking."

Knick glared at his friend, embarrassed at being caught and agitated that he was probably right.

"Shut up," he snapped, "or I'll tell Solo you peeped on Slot when she was in the shower."

"Hey, man," Jilk exclaimed and started to back away. "That shit's not funny! Evil. You're evil." He disappeared from view. "Try to give a friend advice and what does he do?" He poked his head around the door only to add, "Something evil!"

Knick flipped the vacant space the bird and then looked back at Shade sleeping serenely. He chewed his inner lip while staring at hers. Did that really happen? Yes. Yes it did. He had a witness. How could she kiss him first? Wasn't that supposed to be his job? Worse than unfair, she kissed him and passed out, leaving him to ponder it, leaving him frustrated as hell, leaving him with a rapidly beating heart.

"Damn," he muttered, tearing his gaze away from her.

The holding was called Hojo, one of the oldest settlements since before the Lotus Merge—the original Chinatown. Layers and layers of buildings were built on top of one another, red and gold paifang arches lording over bridges, streets, and tall, narrow staircases snaking through the city. The color scheme was rustic warmth with muted browns, grungy golds, and muddy whites painted alongside burnt orange, faded scarlet, and brick red. From a distance, Hojo looked like a beautiful blur of red and gold—traditional, in the only remaining sense of the word, Chinese architecture—but in the thick of it, it was old and dusty. And most of the population did not realize that they had an almost direct link to the Mine.

Kallo and Delia stood out front of a noodle shop, spying their fellow Kur hidden among the colorful yukata and dingy street clothes—a dichotomy that blended surprisingly well. They counted fifteen Keepers, noted the last five were scouting, and were satisfied that the city had not yet been infiltrated.

"Do we think they would try something so covert?" Kallo

asked his sister, brow creased in thought.

"The shaft connects with the OT. There are only riotous civilians in those parts, and little Black Tuesday presence. There are no organized cogwheeler outposts in that zone."

"We can expect a flood of anger and violence."

"If we can expect retaliation at all."

"We can." He tilted his head, watching the colorful people flutter alongside the grungy sloths. "Do we know that it's a shaft?"

"The Krueh-jin use this line as a trading route. If it is a shaft, it would need to be larger than the riser the cogwheelers built to Gomorra," Delia said.

"For trade," Kallo agreed. "A cargo elevator."

"Or a tunnel."

"But the outlet?"

"We don't know," Delia surmised. "Where would they hide it?"

"Where?" Kallo echoed.

Kallo and Delia were twins, thoughts synced in such a way that sometimes they were "I" and sometimes "we". They both had the same shade of dark brown skin and amber eyes but Kallo's dreadlocks were longer than Delia's. They wore matching body suits—his the color of pitch, hers the color of mud—and dark alloy armor pieces strapped to their chests, legs, and arms. On the breastplate, over the heart, was carved a two-tailed fox—their symbol, though its origin and meaning were a secret only they knew.

Far across the forum, a shadow appeared between two shops, lingering among the garbage. Kallo pushed off of the wall.

"Delia," he began.

"I see it," she replied, tilting her head and narrowing her gaze on the spot. "The little mouse looks lost." She grinned and looked at her brother. "He shouldn't be here."

"A scout. They are more organized than we thought. Delia, I believe it's your turn."

"It is." She pulled a black wrap over her nose and her amber eyes sparkled. "Minu ga hana." And then Delia darted off into the crowd and disappeared among the throng.

The chaos in Sanctuary had reached an all-new high

since the attack on Mirax headquarters. As soon as Dr. Basset pronounced one of the injured "not dying", the man was armored and armed and sent out into the world. The swell from the Mine was merely the few drops of rain before the storm, so he had been told; those who had surfaced were vagrants, punks, thugs, and crazies out for revenge and trouble-making. They were not so challenging to stop as they were an unusual brand of anarchy that Anshar was not used to fighting. Thus, the Keepers had to step in; rather, what was left of them.

Therefore, Dr. Basset's patient list grew, as many that had been sent out into the field returned in dire need of medical attention. Then there were those who still remained from the Asgard attack, and they were either close to recovery or never would. Many had died under his hands and it was beginning to add up. No matter how many times his wife told him that he did all he could and couldn't be blamed, he still felt responsible, as though the dead men's souls were stacking on top of his, clinging to him, wondering why he hadn't saved them. Had he done something differently, would they still be alive? Had he left them well alone, would they eventually have pulled through on their own?

He put his forehead in his hand and rubbed at the wrinkles that had taken up permanent residence. Basset was tired. Very tired. And more than that, he was beginning to wonder what he was fighting for. The Keepers had saved him and his family and he was grateful, but eventually he would run out of soldiers to tend—or they would never stop coming—and he would need to face reality. The reality was that he and his family were homeless fugitives. Where would they go? Where could they go? The Mine? What would happen to his daughters there? The horror stories of that realm made it seem like a cesspit of utter wickedness, that it lacked civilization in its entirety. He knew that couldn't be entirely true. Somehow, those criminals had found the civility to organize Black Tuesday and keep it functioning, so perhaps all the stories were utter fiction.

Basset sighed. Believing that was true was hard. Optimism, his wife kept saying, but optimism was nearly impossible to hold on to. He reached over to the family water canister on his bedside table and lifted it for a sip. Empty. He carefully removed his wife's arm from his chest and hoisted himself out of his bed, immediately groaning as his back spasmed painfully. He took a few deep breaths to steady himself then shuffled out to Sanctuary's cantina.

There were people sleeping in the hallways, the sick and the stitched up, and Basset felt guilty that he and his family had their own room and some beds to share. The few that were awake gave him nods and half-smiles; they respected him, valued him because he had done what he could to heal them. They all treated his family with absolute kindness and gratefulness. Not one complained that he had a warm bed to return to. He ducked his head in shame and quickly refilled his water canister.

He stopped outside of his family's room and stared at his wife and daughters as they slept. He took quiet sips of water and listened to the groaning in the background, to the shuffle of soldiers preparing to leave Sanctuary, at the distant clamor of the returned as they shed their armor and bit down on rags to stifle their screams. He watched the gentle rise and fall of his wife's chest, saw how her night-shirt was twisted around her— she would hate that if she were awake. For the thousandth time, he admired just how beautiful she was. His gaze shifted to his children, to their angelic faces. Casey was clearly trying to escape her younger sister's hostile takeover of the cot and Clara was sprawled out, one leg over Casey's hip and an arm across her head.

There was suddenly a hand on his shoulder. His head snapped up and he tensed. Was something wrong with one of his patients? Had someone taken a turn for the worse? But Eros was smiling at him and so he relaxed his shoulders. Somehow, this man before him was able to calm those around him, set them at ease. Basset was probably old enough to be Eros' father—older brother, at most—and yet he felt vastly inferior to the Baron, as though his young face were a lie and beneath that youth lay a lifetime's worth of wisdom.

"You look troubled," the Baron said.

"Yes," Basset agreed, rubbing his forehead, "but by nothing new, I assure you."

"Tell me anyway."

Basset eyed the Baron again—at his pale skin and blue eyes and the jet black hair tied at the nap of his neck. He was tall, even taller than him. His voice was deep and gentle, but he spoke with authority. Even the offer to listen to a troubled old man came with a sense of command, prompting Basset to speak even if he didn't feel he had a right to.

He took a swig of water to calm his nerves. "My wife," he began, "my little girls...they're homeless fugitives. We cannot return to Molatta or Isali. Even if we could find some place in Anshar that we'd be out of MAAR's reach, it isn't safe anymore. I have no idea where to take my family that they'll be safe, that they'll have a future. I can do nothing for them. I'm the head of this family. I'm supposed to protect them, provide for them. I can't even do that much."

"You have helped us." Eros looked straight ahead. "You have protected and provided for the Keepers by nursing our wounded back to health and helping the hopeless to quick peace. They have watched you do this. They admire you for it. They find strength in your selflessness. And if it is time for you to move on, I understand. You have done far more than we could have asked for."

"I was happy to do it. You saved my family and my life." Basset rubbed his eyes and then pushed his hands through his hair, exhaling a deep breath. His arms dropped to his sides with a loud smack of resignation. "If I thought the horror-stories about the Mine were just stories, then maybe..."

"They are stories," Eros confirmed. "Though Kishar is certainly different than in Anshar, you could find a suitable life there; the most civilization lies in the bigger cities, but certainly more guild presence. In the smaller towns outside of the Cradle, you'll find life harder but quieter. Many of those places are in desperate need of someone like yourself."

"I'm not a real doctor—"

"You are a man willing to help. That is far more valuable, don't you think?" Eros smiled.

Dr. Basset nodded slowly, smoothing down his wrinkled sleeves before rolling them up. The Baron was right. It may not have been what he wanted for his family, but it was a start. Maybe a temporary one. Maybe one day, they could return to Anshar. But he couldn't think in maybes. Life was ever-changing and he couldn't be the fool that thought his niche in the universe was untouchable. He had once ignorantly lived as though it was true, and then MAAR had come knocking on his door.

"I just never imagined this day would come. I never thought I'd be faced with this kind of future," Basset said quietly. He looked over at the man next to him and, much to his surprise, saw that the Baron's face was pulled tight in serious regret.

"Trust me when I say that we didn't either." Eros turned to go. "Get some sleep, Doctor."

"I have patients—"

"They can wait until you've had your rest."

"Can they?"Basset asked. "I don't know that I can rest on that."

Eros nodded and walked away. With one last sip of water and a quick kiss to Laura's forehead, he quietly closed the bedroom door and went out to see just how bad the damage was.

Knick rapped once on the door then opened it and stepped inside. Isis was sitting next to Otto's bed, looking over her shoulder to see who was entering, and the boy was propped up by a mountain pillows. They smiled when they saw him.

"Hey, man." He nodded in Otto's direction. "You look better."

"Thanks," Otto replied in a raspy voice as Knick crossed to the other side of the bed, pulled a chair up, and straddled the back of it.

The truth was Otto did look better but not really good. His skin had gone from sallow to just pale and he had only gained a couple of pounds in the few weeks he'd been resting. His arm had greatly improved, wrapped with colorful papers called sutras and hung in a sling. The Obeahani claimed the sutras had powerful healing words, like spells. It was part of their healing practices and Otto seemed to be getting better, not worse, so who was he to judge? As for the dark circles around Otto's eyes, they had faded from purple to brown, but the progress was slow.

"How are you feeling?" Knick asked.

"Same as yesterday," Otto replied.

"That's not bad, right? Yesterday was a good day for you," Knick mused and Otto nodded, one corner of his mouth tipping up in a smile.

"I heard Shade woke up today," Isis began. Knick furrowed one brow, narrowing his gaze on her.

"Speaking of which, I'm surprised you weren't there."

She smiled. "It is not time."

"They just put her back to sleep anyway," he mumbled, disappointed.

"But this is good news," Isis told him. "She's already so much better. She will be back to normal soon."

"You just want to put her to work," Knick said as he picked some jerky off the food tray next to Otto's bed and began chewing. He offered Otto a stick but he declined.

"Shade has a destiny. So do you."

"Yeah but," Knick leaned forward, "what if we don't believe in that?" He intercepted her look. "Okay, what if I don't?"

"You don't have to believe. You just have to *be*. You can leave if you like, that very well may be one of your paths in the great Weave. But I don't think you will go, because you returned to Heaven for Shade—"

"For the Oracle."

"For Shade, so that she wouldn't have to. And if you were willing to go that far, I doubt you would abandon her now. If you intended to leave, you would have the moment we arrived in Gehrs. But you didn't. You are waiting for her to wake up." She tilted her head to the side. "Do you think you can take her away to some ignored corner of the earth and live together, hidden from the eyes of the world?"

Knick thought of her kiss and felt his face get hot. "No," he snapped, suddenly wanting to change the subject. "Like hell she'd go anyway. Whatever, it doesn't matter. You got my help." He nodded to Otto. "Sorry, man."

"Yeah," Otto mumbled, amused. He'd heard the two of them argue plenty since he'd woken up and had gotten used to tuning out the bickering, so he said.

Knick reached into his jacket pocket and pulled out the statue. "Bloodsworn dropped this off earlier."

Isis reached across the bed and gently took the statue from him, carefully turning it over in her small and delicate hands.

"Asgard," she said regretfully and there was no missing the sadness in her voice. She looked up at Knick with her crystalline green eyes; those eyes always shocked him with how vivid and clear they were, as though a shadow never crossed them. "This is the statue you told me about. Did your friend find out anything?"

"Something," he replied. "And it got her killed."

Isis frowned. "I'm sorry."

"Yeah." Knick rubbed his hand across his mouth. "Me, too. All she said was 'Asgard must fall.' I don't know how that helps us since Asgard has already been knocked over."

Isis handed the statue back to Knick and he dumped the heavy thing back in his jacket. She pushed her blond hair away from her face, silent in thought for several minutes. Knick grabbed more jerky, once again offered it to Otto only to be turned down, and chewed.

"We'll wait for Shade," Isis instructed.

"Now you want to wait for her? Before it was all state-of-emergency with the Oracle missing, and now you're content to idle out?"

"There are things that must happen. It may seem senseless to you. You may not understand the reason behind every choice. But they must happen. You were meant to be trapped in Heaven so that Shade could go to you."

"So you're saying there's no pointless action in the world? That's fucked up. And bullshit."

"Everything is a reaction to something else, some purpose unseen. Do not waste your time questioning everything, measuring it for value or waste. Just move forward."

"Don't question?" Knick balked. "Just do it, is that right? Go through life like an angel? Fuck that. I've been down that road before. I won't go down it again."

"There is always an Operations, Knick, just as there is always a rebel—even if they exist within the same individual." Isis tilted her head. "Even if I were to send you on some journey now, you would not go. You would wait for Shade. Why fight me when I am in agreement with you? Let us wait."

Knick thought about arguing but she was right—there was no point. "Fine," he said with a shrug. He patted Otto's shoulder and stood up. "Isis. Otto." He nodded to each of them respectively, grabbed a few more small pieces of jerky, and then held a fist out to Otto who banged his knuckles against Knick's.

"See you," Otto said.

Knick left the room and made his way through the confusing corridors to the front of the healing house. He pushed through the warped wooden door to the outside and the darkness of night pressed in with the cavern lights dimmed.

Damn Isis was nothing but trouble. Oracle, Enoch—whatever. If he didn't know firsthand the Keeper hocus pocus was legit, he would've put the kid in a corner a long time ago. And it's not that he wanted to be stubborn for difficulties' sake, but after breaking from the Hive Mind, after living a life of do's and don'ts with no real accountability, he wasn't going to go through life blindly following anyone else's orders. Or maybe he had when he joined up with the Cogs, but somehow it seemed different. He was in control of his mind, at least, and if it was fear that motivated him, at least it wasn't good, old-fashioned brainwashing.

He pulled a cigarette pack out of his jacket, tapped one out, and lit up. He inhaled, held it in for longer than usual, and then exhaled a satisfied cloud of gray. He couldn't get it out of his head the idea that everything was destiny, and that his horrific three days back in Heaven had been so that Shade could get him out. How could that be destiny? It sure as hell seemed to him like Isis had set them up and they had walked into the trap. And how could he believe that every pathetic existence was fate? What about the poor SOBs in the Mine? Was their tragic existence just destiny, too? So life wasn't fair, but believing in destiny seemed just damn cruel. Not to mention a shitty justification for making mistakes or doing some good.

"It's destiny you put that rial in that guy's cup," he mumbled, mimicking Isis' voice. "It's destiny you got drunk and put your arm in that sawblade." He shook his head. "Yeah right…"

That's when he noticed a pair of big, round, blue eyes peering over at him, the figure crouched on the other side of the old building.

"Lethan," Knick greeted.

"Knick," he replied.

"You don't like it inside much, do you? In the weeks we've been here, I think I've seen you in there maybe twice."

As Lethan stood, Whiskey hopped up onto his shoulder. Knick handed the lehn a piece of jerky that the creature nibbled quietly.

"I was born under cavern ceilings. We drifted, always drifted. Tents, at times...but otherwise, it's low, raw ceiling. Tunnel-tops. Being inside is strange," Lethan explained, turning his blue eyes toward Knick. "Like being in another world."

Knick regarded the Krueh-jin behind his cigarette. "Lethan, let me ask you something," he began. "Why did you steal Hezara's package?"

"Because she told me to," he replied solemnly.

"Who?"

"Sabal."

"The crone?" Knick asked and Lethan confirmed with a nod. "Why?"

"So that I could be saved by you and indentured into your service."

"Why?" But Lethan did not respond. He tried a different approach. "Why you? Why not some other Krueh-jin?"

"It is my right. This job is for no one but Whiskey and I."

If he asked "why" again, he'd only get more silence, so that line of questioning had successfully come full circle. Knick leaned back against the front of the building and tilted his head against the wall.

"The crone said you were special—you and Whiskey. That's why you were sent with me isn't it?"

Lethan stared at the ground. "Yes," he finally replied.

Knick sucked on his cigarette. "Your eyes, right?"

"Our eyes," Lethan confirmed, nodding. "We were born with special eyes—eyes that see in the dark but can also withstand the light. They slip into all spectrums with ease, suffering no penalties of change. Toshi-shi, that's what we're called. 'To see everything', that is what it means." Lethan reached back and rubbed at Whiskey's head. He smiled as he considered the lehn perched on his shoulder and the animal affectionately touched his master's face. His blue eyes then cut to Knick in an intense stare. "We will follow you, Knick Coltin. Our sight will be your sight, until death takes us."

Knick just stared at him, uncomfortable with the pledge. He didn't deserve their lives, but he knew it would be impossible to convince them to leave. He'd tried before to no avail. But if he had, Shade would probably be dead and he would still be lost in the pitch black tunnels beneath *The Dark Mermaid*.

He owed Lethan, not the other way around.

"What if I hadn't saved you? You ever think about that?" Knick blurted.

"There was no question. You would save me. And you did."

"But *what if*, huh? You don't know me! What if I had just let Hezara kill you? I didn't have to interfere."

"The law made you uncomfortable."

"I didn't have to like it but I didn't need to stop it, either. I was an angel, for fuck's sake. I witnessed far worse and did it myself. Cogwheeler's no different on the morality scale. Weren't you afraid that I just wouldn't care? That you would die for nothing?"

Lethan looked at Whiskey. "For a moment," he admitted, "I was afraid. But that fear was misplaced. Sabal would never mislead me, and you," he cut his gaze to Knick, "are not for me to second-guess. I am sorry for doubting you, even for just a moment."

"You *should* doubt me," Knick hissed. "You should doubt me at every turn. I don't even know why I did it."

Lethan shrugged. "To know or not know, it doesn't matter. That will come in time. You acted, and that is who you are. An action without thought is a movement in the dark— that is instinct. Your instinct was to spare me. That same instinct led you to sever ties with the angels." The blue-eyed man smiled. "Maybe it is you who should not doubt yourself."

Knick just stared dumfounded as his cigarette slowly burned.

Ross held his breath and peaked through the rusty garbage tins at Lotus Street, the main road cutting through Hojo—wide compared to the rest of the streets but still not very large. The crowd of buildings at every angle cast a dark shadow across the depths of the town, aided by the never-lifting veil of fog caused by the constant storms in the neighboring waterfront holding of Tarsus. Thousands of lanterns—paper lanterns, glass lanterns, bowls of burning wood, even oil lamps—had been strung up at every place imaginable, casting a strange, orange glow through the haze. The tall, red and golden arches towered over the colorful mass of meandering people, reminding him of giant red lords on a chessboard of innumerable pawns.

Ross looked left and right, giving each direction a long, careful stare. So far, so good. No angels in sight. There were bright kimonos and grungy hoodies but not a soul was wearing white. He pushed away from the garbage and took a deep, raspy breath. The Mine never spelled like roses, but whatever these people were cooking and dumping in these cans could be weaponized.

He gave Lotus Street one last glance and then pushed the button on his locater device, sending off his quarter-hour update to let his friends know he was alive. Then he scampered off through the alleys, picking his way with all the grace of an expert scout. Growing up in the OT, he had made it his business to map the trainways from Kettle Kot to Gypsy. He was just eight years old the first time he navigated a coal maze. So with his arm reached out and his fingers twitching against the buildings he passed like a snake's flickering tongue, he mapped the alleyways of Hojo.

Ross stopped suddenly, his fingertips resting barely a quarter-inch from mossy brick. The air in his space had changed, felt heavier. He looked back but there was no one sharing the alley with him. Ross began tapping the brick, eyes focused straight ahead. He waited, tap-tap-tapping patiently; the longer he tapped, the more certain he became that he was not alone. His heart began to beat hard in his chest, adrenaline pumping thunderously through his system. But his feet did not move and his middle finger just kept tapping against the brick.

The presence was elusive, but he couldn't detect any movement. It was as though curtains were being blown back and forth, covering the creature in one moment and revealing it in the next, but every time it was concealed, it seemed to cease to exist. How was that possible? Tap, tap, tap. There were eyes on him, studying him. He was being sized up, but for what? This was purposeful gazing; he was being scouted as much as he had been scouting the city. But this kind of stare, it felt broad and all-knowing, as if Hojo itself was looking back at him. Tap, tap, tap. This presence was not a scout. It was a hunter. He was prey. Tap, tap. He knew where the predator would strike from.

Ross suddenly twisted around and looked up. High above him, crouched on a gutter, was a black silhouette, seemingly human, but all he could focus on were the reflective, wide, yellow eyes gazing at him—eyes that looked like an animal's. Ross' foot shuffled back as his heart leapt into his throat, fingers frozen over the bricks. He couldn't move, struck with paralysis at the very sight of his stalker. The staring contest seemed to go on forever. For every second that passed, his heart had hammered a thousand times in his chest.

And then the predator moved—a slight stretch and then it's back arched. Was it human or animal? He couldn't tell anymore. But it was preparing to pounce. He wasn't going to wait around to find out what it was. He wasn't going to get caught. Ross whirled around and took off, sprinting as fast as he could through uncharted alleyways. He reached out and began tapping quickly on the walls he passed but the mapping was incomplete. He was going to get lost, he was going to run into a dead end, he was going to die!

Ross risked a glance back and saw nothing but that didn't stop him from running, or even slow him down. He hooked a hard right and slammed his heels into the concrete. The creature stood tall, like a man, and those animals eyes stared at him. Without ever fully stopping, Ross reversed his trajectory and propelled himself back the way he came only, instead of making a turn, he just went straight. And as he passed through the intersecting alleys, he thought he glimpsed the creature peering down at him from another gutter.

Ross cried out in terror, tapping the bricks out of instinct rather than conscious thought, but the map in his head was getting jumbled. A black shadow scampered across a junction ahead of him and he screamed, sliding to the ground as he hit his breaks. He scrambled back to his feet, legs slipping in the sludge, and blindly chose a new path to run down. Any path, he didn't care. He just wanted to get away from whatever it was that stalked him, whatever creature it was that could lurk behind him and, at the same time, be two steps ahead.

He risked a glance back and saw the stalker was coming up behind him. He lost all train of thought, a need for survival overwhelming even his most basic scouting instincts. He was taking turns without tapping, racing through alleys he couldn't mark, and then he hit what he feared the most: a dead end. Ross threw himself at the stone trapping him, wheezing as he panted. He stumbled, turning this way and that, desperately searching for a door, a window, latticework, anything to aid his escape. There was nothing but rusty trashcans and piles of garbage bags. Ross stared at the mouth of the alley, wide-eyed and senses alert to any sound or touch. There was nothing waiting for him. But it would come. Any minute now, the beast-like man would fill the void of his only escape and close in for the kill.

Ross tapped so furiously on the wall that his finger began to bleed. Nothing came. In a brief moment of lucidity amidst his panic, Ross realized he could not detect another presence. He glared at the alley and then charged, desperate with hope that he could clear it. As he drew closer, he expected the creature to step out. It did not come. He cleared the alley and almost smiled, but as he turned the corner, he saw his stalker standing there, arms folded across its chest, back against the wall. It had been waiting for him.

Something reached out and grabbed him from behind as those bestial, yellow eyes stared at him. Ross opened his mouth to scream but no sound came out. Whatever had him was not his stalker, but the grip was like iron as it lifted him off of his kicking feet and slammed him against the wall where the creature leaned. He gaped at those yellow eyes and then turned to face who had pinned him, whose fingers clamped tight around his throat. Another set of reflective eyes glared at him. He shut his eyes tight.

Two. He had not imagined there had been two of them. He had not detected two in his tapping. He had never stood a chance. They had toyed with him. He was going to die.

Ross screamed and flailed with all his might, and groaned when he hit the ground and smacked his head against the wall. When he opened his eyes, a man and a woman were looming over him—twins, with dreadlocks and armor. The man had swords. Who the hell used swords anymore? He winced, head snapping left and right in search of the monsters that had captured him. There was nothing, only these two. He kicked away from them, but the pain in his head lit up his nervous system and he grunted, clutching the bump on his skull.

"Who are you?" the man asked.

"Where did you—" Ross stammered. "Did you see—?"

"Your name," the woman said.

"R-Ross," he replied. "R-R-Ross R-R-Racoon."The twins exchanged glances. "Call me Roscoon," he mumbled numbly.

"And what is a scout from the Mine doing in Hojo, Ross?" the woman asked him.

"How did you—?" he started to ask but snapped his jaw shut as she crouched down in front of him. She had very pretty amber eyes.

"Ross." Her voice was commanding. "Why are you in Hojo?"

He swallowed the lump in his throat and tried to figure out what was going on. He leaned toward her and whispered, "Did...did you scare away those things chasing me?"

"Did you imagine something strange?" she asked with a smile. "We only want to talk to you, Ross."

"There is nothing to fear so long as you cooperate," the man told him.

Ross nodded hesitantly. "Y-you're the boss."

"Why are you in Hojo?" he asked.

"Scoutin'."

"For what?" the woman asked.

"Angels."

"Why?" It was the man again.

"To know whether it was safe."

"For what?" the woman persisted.

"A raid."

They were suddenly quiet, staring at him with blank expressions. Even though they were looking at him, they didn't seem to see him. It unnerved him and he shifted under their gaze. His head throbbed at the movement.

"A raid for supplies," the man said and Ross gave a jerk of a nod.

"Who brought you to the surface?" the woman asked.

"Reinhardt."

She suddenly stood up and stared at her twin. They seemed to be silently discussing something. He could tell by the look they shared that they were piecing the story together.

"Who are you?" he asked, but they ignored him. "The

Cogs are prepping for war," he mumbled, "and harvesting all the meds, weapons, and food they can get—even from the OT. Shipments are doubly protected, and people are suffering. So Reinhardt figured we'd get it from the only other source available: the surface. S'not like these people need it anyway, the spoiled shits."

The twins looked at him.

"You know nothing of the lives here," the woman said to him, "and neither does Reinhardt."

"How did you access Hojo?" the man asked.

"What's it matter? We need the supplies! We aren't leavin' without it."

"War will make us all suffer, Ross," she said. "Anshar is to be the battlefield. What happens to those who live on that field?"

Ross swallowed another lump and shifted uncomfortably. "I mean...I don't..."

"There is a way to proceed, a way to kill or be killed," the man told him. "Tell us where the tunnel is and when the raid is going down."

"Reinhardt would never—" He froze. "Oh no." Ross dug into his jacket pocket and pulled out his locator. The signal light was beeping red. He jammed the button but it never turned green. "Uh oh..."

"What is it?" she asked.

"I didn't check in," he replied numbly.

"And what does that mean to the people on the other side?"

"Angels."

The woman looked to her brother again, and this time he nodded.

"Retaliation," he said.

And just then, an explosion rocked the earth beneath them.

Otto stared at Isis after Knick left and wondered, for the thousandth time, if she was real. Every time Knick or the High Healer or any of the others had walked in and spoken to her, her existence had been validated. The dream girl had been real. She had needed his help and he had really saved her. And the strangest part about it? He had survived. He barely remembered their escape into the Mine. It was all a blur—everything happening so fast, everything hurting so much. But when he woke up in a warm, fluffy bed and saw her staring down at him with such a gentle smile on her face, he was so awed that he thought he was still dreaming, that he still needed to save her.

Otto bashfully stared at his lap. He hadn't had the courage to talk to her about what had happened. It had taken him almost a week to believe the last few months were even real and not just him in a coma having crazy dreams—he'd read somewhere that kind of thing happened to people in comas. So by the time he figured it all out, he was presented with a new dilemma: how to approach the topic? He wanted to make a good impression. And she had been patient, waiting quietly at his bedside every day. It was enough to just have her there, watching over him.

"Isis," he began, picking at threads in the sheets. "I'm really glad...you're okay."

"Otto," she said in such a way to pull his gaze to hers, "I never thanked you properly." She smiled but there was no joy in it, only sorrow. Maybe even guilt. "I plagued your dreams and stole your sleep so that you would come find me. You suffered and never once did you resent me for it. I nearly killed you and all you wished for was to save me before you died. There is no other man like you in this world. That is why I chose you. That is why it had to be you."

Otto stared dumbly, awed by her words. No girl had ever said something so kind to him. But Isis was more than just a girl. She was the goddess in his dreams. Maybe that had been the point—to be the goddess he couldn't resist—but somehow he didn't care, and it didn't change anything. She was Isis. She was perfect.

"Please forgive me, Otto," she whispered. "And know that you have my eternal gratitude and the deepest thanks of the Oracle."

"I'm just a garbage guy," he mused. "I kind of feel... honored you picked me." He attempted to smile without looking completely flustered. He had never been entirely comfortable around beautiful women, but with Isis he found himself even more unprepared than normal. It wasn't like he met her in line at the coffee shop or through a friend of a friend. She had appeared in his dreams. And when he had come face to face with her, she was lying comatose hooked up to a massive machine. She was both high on a pedestal of his own devising that he would never be able to reach and a woman he felt he knew better than anyone he'd ever known in his entire life. "Kind of nice to know that you could trust me to help you. No one else ever did."

"Otto, I'm so sorry," she said again, "that your part in all of this is not yet ended. I must ask more from you."

"That's okay," he mumbled. "I'll do whatever you need me to."

"I know." One tear slipped out of her regret-filled eyes. "That is why I chose you. That is why it had to be you. I'm so sorry, Otto." She suddenly buried her face in her arms and cried into his bed. "Please forgive me."

Otto reached out and touched her arm. Her hand slipped out from beneath her blond tresses and tightly grasped his knuckles with her tiny fingers. He laid his head back onto the pillow and closed his eyes. At this point, he didn't have any words; he didn't even have any thoughts. He was holding her hand and it was enough.

Rexis reached out for any steel used in the construction of the healing house but *The Bright Mermaid* was made almost entirely of wood. He closed his eyes and concentrated. When he focused, he could sense every nail and screw, but there was nothing of substance that would allow him to transfer his consciousness into the healing house—not with those wards the Obeahani had sealed the foundation with.

Donovan bumped his arm, breaking his concentration and severing his ties to the alloy. He cut a glare at his companion. The Sovereign of Frost grinned and his pronounced canines caught the light, giving the appearance of fangs. Donovan was a sharp man, everything about him seemingly ready to cut. His hair stood up in spikes, his teeth were like fangs, and even his eyes were icy slits like razorblades. Before the fall of Asgard, he had been considered the most menacing among the Interim, but something about his betrayal had brought out the sinister side of him. Now he acted the part he had looked for so long.

But Rexis did not fear him.

"I need concentration if this is going to work," the Sovereign of Steel snapped.

"My bad," Donovan said, but nothing in his tone was apologetic. "You need quiet for your voodoo mind tricks, huh?"

"I need you to shut up and stay still, ay."

"It's just so fucking boring, man."

"You could stab yourself. A quick shot of ice would keep you still."

Donovan peered coolly at him, arms behind his head and back propped against a rock. After a moment, he nudged Rexis with his foot.

"So tell me again, man, how it was that you escaped Sanctuary."

"Shade isn't the only one who figured out a few old Interim tricks," was all he replied with. He turned back to his sword laid out in front of him and closed his eyes again. Donovan's boot toed his arm. "What?" he snapped, annoyed.

"That isn't an answer and you know it. You turncoat twice over, Rex?"

"You know I'm not. I got out the same way Shade got away from you that day you failed to kill her." He felt a sense of satisfaction at Donovan's scowl; his hatred of Shade was no secret, and Rexis liked to use his inferiority to her to push his buttons. He would never forgive Donovan for trying to kill her, and would return the favor someday. "Now shut up and let me work."

Donovan said nothing so Rexis took a deep breath and tried once again to connect to the synergy of his sword but something was disrupting his concentration. He could sense the unrest—the tiny shifting of his partner, the anxious clicks of his tongue and tapping of his fingers, the irritable sighs. Try as he might, he couldn't block it. Finally, he snapped his gaze back at the Interim.

"What?" Rexis hissed.

"I'm just so damn bored. Can't you hurry up? We could just go in there and find out the truth the easy way."

"This is the easy way, Donovan."

"Okay, the *fun* way."

"No."

"You just don't want her to know you're a turncoat like

me." He smirked. "You're scared what she'll do when she finds out."

"Aren't you the once who's scared?" Rexis narrowed his eyes on him. "You remember the look on her face when she stormed Heaven. You remember how the angels kept coming, how she kept killing. She manipulated the shadows without her bells. We were all scared shitless." Rexis grinned victoriously. "And so were you."

"Fuck you."

"I think you're the one too scared to go in there, because no matter how she may hate me, we already know you're on her hit list, ay. She takes one look at you, she will end you."

"She's probably half-dead from that little stunt she pulled."

"Maybe. Or maybe she's waiting for the next fight."

Donovan kicked Rexis' sheath to emphasize his anger as he stood up and walked off, a string of curses under his breath. Rexis went back to concentrating. He let his fingers glide over the steel of his blade, felt himself slipping into the fluid synergies of the aegis. It was like going down a slide—effortless, and with the elements rushing up to meet you. Only these elements weren't air or dirt, but carbon and iron.

Ever since Shade had explained to him how she had moved—quite accidentally—through the shadows, he had begun to think of his sword in ways that the others didn't: not as a weapon, but a conduit. The bells reached a frequency that activated the synergies of the aegis, but the power was there all along—in him or the weapon, he wasn't sure. So he had practiced and practiced until he had finally been able to teleport through the steel. That was the true secret behind his escape from Sanctuary, but he did not want Donovan to know. He didn't want anyone to know these ancient Keeper secrets. He had no intention of opposing Shade—only the traitors and blasphemers.

Rexis found *The Bright Mermaid* again and began scouring the structure for something useful. He crept room to room, nail to nail, screw to bolt to washer, doorknob to lock. It was a long process as it took all of his focus to project his energy that far. He had claimed a quiet alcove in the rocky slope above the healing house no more than thirty meters away but it was still far enough to drain him. When he had teleported away from

Sanctuary, he had moved no farther than a hundred meters. How Shade had managed to go all the way to the Mine—and drugged—boggled his mind.

There was suddenly a pull nearby so Rexis steered his consciousness in its direction. Then he felt it—the ether of an aegis. And not just any aegis. It was Shade's. The ether was nethergy, unique to darkblades—weapons that fed off a life force. The nethergy of her weapon consumed the essence of its target, unlike the other interim weapons, which merely manipulated forces that already existed within the world. He crept closer to it, combating the will of the Shadow Sword. He could not bend or break this steel—it was imbued with ether too powerful to corrupt—so he couldn't transport himself through it...but he could reflect off it. Leaving his physical form completely vulnerable, he quietly closed his mind and bounced his consciousness off of her blade.

An image of him appeared in the room.

Shade was lying on a bed. He could not perceive color in this state, but even so he could see that she was deathly pale. *Shade*, he thought, for he could not speak. *What happened to you?* He moved closer to her—floating more than walked—and reached down to touch her hand but his flesh sunk slightly into hers. He felt nothing. He was just an image, after all, a ghost in the room; it was taking all of his effort to keep himself there.

Shade frowned. Her head jerked a little. A bad dream? He watched her sleep, thought of how one day he would save her. Shade was his best friend. Though it was hard to penetrate her frigid shell, he had discovered a very kind person beneath the steely mask she wore. More than that, Shade was loyal—fiercely loyal. He had never felt alone in her company. She had been consistent, a virtue unto the Order. Shade had seen the world and everyone in it, every ideal and belief, and every decision in black and white. It was impossible to shake her. She was incorruptible, and he had believed in her, believed that he, too, could be so steadfast and true. She gave him hope.

And that was why he would have to kill Knick Coltin, the man who had made her see the gray in the world. Morality could not be gray and neither could the Keepers. She was the only true Keeper and he would preserve that. When he had destroyed Muriel and the rest of the defectors, and when he had killed Knick, she would be able to restart the Keeper Order as it was meant to be. There could only be black and white, two weighing platforms on a scale, two truths to balance. And she could balance them. The reason the Keepers had failed was because they had seen the gray.

I'll save you, he thought. *Just wait. I'll rid the world of gray.*

The door suddenly opened and his image dispersed. The last thing he saw before fading out was Knick Coltin's face and the statue once carried by Hezara, the Bloodsworn. Then Donovan was kneeling over him, shaking him, calling to him but Rexis couldn't hear any sounds. He shook his head, lifted his fingers to his forehead. His skin was clammy. Suddenly there was a high-pitched ringing in his ears. As it faded, Donovan helped him sit up.

"Are you all right?"

Rexis was gasping, soaked with sweat. "What?" he rasped.

"You look half-dead. What happened? What'd you see?"

"She's there…they have it…"

"Good. Let's go back."

Donovan helped him to his feet. After a moment, he was able to walk on his own. As they neared the tunnel out to the old train ways, a beggar hobbled in front of them.

"Rials for the poor," he croaked with a toothless grin. His breath smelled rotten. "You have the change, kids. Don't play cheap." He took a swig of alcohol. "Help a man out. It'll do your soul some good, make you feel better for it."

Donovan's blade suddenly flashed and sliced the beggar's throat open. Rexis glared at him.

"What the hell was that for?" he exclaimed.

"I helped him on his way to hell," Donovan answered. "He was right." The Interim smiled. "I do feel better."

Slot looked up when Jilk walked in the door and he could tell by the look on her face that she'd been waiting a while. She pushed out of the chair she was sunk into and crossed over to him in an amazing three bouncy steps.

"Where've you been?" she exclaimed with suppressed concern. "It's been two days."

Jilk tilted his head up to try to hide his embarrassment. Ever since he was released from Cogclock and Slot had hung on him, he had become very aware of her femininity. He wondered if it was the sudden affection that made him feel tingly inside whenever she came around. In his whole life, he had never been the talk of the town and, every time he looked into her eyes, past those ridiculously long eyelashes, he didn't want the tinglies to be because he was lonely.

"The Cogs," he replied, stuffing his hands into his pockets to warm them up. "Shit, its cold out there."

She fished something out of her back pant pocket, reached up, and yanked a sock hat over his head. It was awkwardly warm and he realized she must've been sitting on it. That made the heat creep into his face even more.

"What's up?" she asked, crossing her arms over her chest.

"Bad news," he replied. "Big news. Where's Knick?"

"Guess." Slot struggled not to smile. "He really looks after her, y'know?"

"Heard you looked after me when I was under," Jilk mumbled casually.

"A'course. It's not the same without you." She shrugged. "Who else is gonna tease me all the time? Solo's my brother; he can't do it cause he's always looking out for me. Knick's too busy chasing you-know-who. I mean, you're the only one always telling me when I do something dumb." She grinned. "Like picking up russells with my bare hands."

He laughed, embarrassed. "You remember that?" He barely remembered that.

"Sure," she said. "I remember a lot of things."

Jilk suddenly felt really nervous. Just how many things did she remember? He couldn't ask, but now he had a desperate desire to know. Knick entered the room with Solo right behind him and spared him his indecision.

"Thought I heard you come in," Knick began. "What's down?"

"You heard me come in?" Jilk asked in disbelief.

"Heard Slot barking at you. Same thing," Solo replied.

"Yeah." Jilk wondered if he'd ever have any privacy with them. He had never noticed a need for it before, but the tinglies were making him notice all sorts of things these days. "Word down the vine is that Black Tuesday's waging war on MAAR."

"What?" Slot gasped as they all gaped in shock.

"It's true," he confirmed. "The Cogs are all set to march,

so to speak. Every spare's being called in from all the provinces—OT, everywhere. Rumors say volunteers," he began counting out on his fingers, "escapist militias, refugees, uh, freelancers—all the baddies are coming out. It's going from Black Tuesday versus MAAR to Kishar versus Anshar real quick."

"Shit," Knick cursed, and a heavy silence hung in the aftermath of Jilk's revelation.

"Knick," he finally said, and his next words dropped like stones in water. "This is our fault." More silence. "What are we going to do about it?"

"I don't...I don't know yet," he confessed.

"We're running out of time, Knick. We need a plan. The Cogs are calling."

Everyone tensed.

"Jilk," Solo began. "You sure we should be answering that call?"

"You should go," Knick said. "Tell 'em I ditched. Tell 'em I'm dead. Tell 'em whatever, but don't put your neck out there for me."

"Knick—" Solo began, but his sister interrupted him.

"Not your call, Knick!" she snapped then looked pointedly at her boss. "Jilk. I don't rally for the cogs. I rally for you. Solo's right. Is this what we need to be doing?"

"Thought you might say that," he said. "I didn't answer the call." He saw them visibly ease. "But that flags us deserters. And you know how the Cogs feel about deserters..."

The warning weighed heavily in the group. Deserters were more than dead, they were made examples of. To call it torture and public humiliation was being kind. Knick glanced back at Jilk and nodded to let him know he got the message.

"I'll talk to the healers," he assured him, and then he left.

Solo, Slot, and Jilk all exchanged unsteady looks.

A flood of people poured out of the newly opened hole in the belly of the dragon statue centered in Hojo. As Kallo and Delia exited the alleys, they took a moment to stare in stunned silence; a secret passage in the great beast had been the last idea in their heads. And yet the freedom fighters had emerged, armed with guns and knives and decades of anger.

Kallo ripped his swords off his back—a khopesh in one

hand, a sabre in the other. Delia held two throwing knives in her fists with an arsenal of shuriken and kunai attached to her armor, and even a kpinga belted onto her thigh.

"What are you gonna to do?" Ross exclaimed. "You can't hurt them! They're just here for the supplies!"

"Supplies stolen to ensure this town starve instead?" Delia asked as her brother pointed across the way to where some of the civilians were turning to face the intruders.

"Tell me, Ross," Kallo began, "what people do when they are threatened." When there was no answer, he said, "They fight back."

Just then, the boy was racing down the alleyway. Delia called after him once then twice, but he never looked back.

"Forget him," Kallo said.

"We must stop this from attracting Heaven's eye," Delia agreed.

Kallo gave the signal to the Keepers hidden around the plaza. They leapt from their perches and darted from their alcoves, threading among the fleeing citizens to target the attacking Miners. Delia loosed two knives with lightning-fast reflexes that pierced their targets between the eyes.

"Minu ga hana," Kallo said to her and then leapt into the fray.

Everywhere, people were screaming. Colorful kimonos scattered like bright fish in a pond darting away from a pebble dropped into the water. Only the pebble was a grenade of anger and desperation, shrapnel exploding out in every direction. The Keepers had no trouble slipping between the chaos, expertly navigating the zigzagging flight of the frightened to get at the heart of the invasion.

Delia's daggers cut through the air between the heads of citizens to sink deep in chests and skulls of the enemy. She did not wish to kill the Miners but they had crossed a line with their hostility. Should the angels come, many more would die as a result. Kallo shared her sentiment, fighting hard and fast. He used his khopesh to disarm his opponents of their guns and clubs and the sabre to cut the jugular before moving on to the next.

But there were so many of them. If it was one thing the Mine had in abundance, it was people—desperate people that had grown up on the streets. Only some knew how to fight, but none of them were strangers to survival, each capable of clawing another man's eyes out if it meant one more day to live.

As the Miners spread further into the plaza, Delia ripped the wind-and-fire wheels hooked to the back of her armor from their hold and gripped them tightly. As the masses rushed up to meet her, she launched into a beautiful ballet of combat, using the momentum of one blow to bounce her to the next enemy—back and forth between targets. Slice, kick, slice, spin, slice, sweeping leg, slice. Her martial combat had given her the nickname the Black Butterfly because watching her fight was like watching a butterfly fluttering about, leaving a trail of blood.

Kallo was just as graceful, just as quick. He wielded his weapons like extensions of his arms. His khopesh lashed out, hooking onto a weapon and ripping it from the enemy's grasp. It was not limited to disarming, however, but to place his enemies where he wanted them. He would strike, digging into flesh, into muscle, hooking around bones, and then he would drag them into his sabre's bite. He was the Iron Serpent.

The twins fought together, sometimes changing places, sometimes fighting back to back. Even with their wide range and sometimes acrobatic movements, they never once risked harming the other. They fought as though they shared bodies; Delia's arms were Kallo's arms, his feet were her feet, and their minds were linked indefinitely. A force to be reckoned with.

The world was made of shale and shadow. A bottomless chasm severed the land surrounding a thick, steadfast stone wall that blockaded the gray isle. Shade stared at the black gate that stood tall and wide before her, the only possible point of penetration for miles. On either side of the intricately carved doors, a giant golem stood watch. They had no eyes that she could see, but she sensed they were looking at her, silently measuring her—but for what, she did not know. Their hulking masses slowly pulsed up and down as though the stone guardians were breathing. She thought she heard a low growl in what she imagined to be an exhaled breath.

Then the gate was grinding open.

She was cloaked in living shadow that clung to her naked form and took the shape of a simple, sleeveless dress; smoke-like vapors were rising off the wispy garment. Then she was moving toward the gate, and the shadow clung to her, stretched, flowed out from her body like silk dragging the ground. The guardians stood passively at their posts as she passed.

Before her stretched a grand city built in another age. The ziggurat was easily five times the size of any of the other structures, towering over the city from its foundation on the hillside, the center of the massive expanse. Shade glimpsed out of her peripherals empty streets and dark windows. She could see no sign of life, but she could feel it. There were eyes on her, thousands of spirits crowding around her.

There was a pulse in the earth and Shade felt it in the core of her being. A faraway sound, like a kettle whistling—faintly heard at first—was slowly growing louder. She stared at the ziggurat. There was something within, something dark, something powerful. Though she saw nothing, she felt it seeping out of those black openings, slithering down the steps. The shadow that clung to her changed from a dress to a set of armor. The whistling grew louder, as though it rode a wave heading straight for her, and she stood there waiting to be overtaken. Her heart started pounding as she realized the noise was a scream. She reached for her sword.

"Don't!" a voice cried out just as the scream overcame her.

Isis gasped as she awoke in the stiff, wooden chair where she had fallen asleep, bent over Otto's bed. The chair skittered backward as she pushed out of it but Otto did not wake, still dreaming peacefully.

"Shade is awake!" she tried to yell but a muted croak was all that came out. She pushed her hair from her face and cleared her throat as she made for the door. "Shade," she cried as she hobbled down the hallway and cursed her fragile body.

Isis had only considered herself human for a short while— ever since Otto had woken her from the Theatre—and was not used to the weaknesses of her own body. When she was simply Sight, there was only the Weave; she had not even been aware of her physical body or all of the machinery hooked into her just to keep her alive and from degeneration. She had been immortal, omniscient. She had not even been a "she", just Sight. Now, every moment of every day, she was reminded of her mortality.

"Shade," Isis called as pain tingled in her legs. "Shade is awake!"

Etrusca came around the corner and grasped the small woman's shoulders. The pain in her legs had turned into an almost overwhelming tickle spreading through her calves and thighs. She collapsed into the High Healer's firm grasp.

"My lady Isis," the woman exclaimed in her breathy whisper of a voice. "Are you well?"

"My legs...something's wrong..." Every move seemed to overwhelm her nerve endings. The High Healer knelt down to examine her skinny limbs, allowing Isis to use her shoulders for support. "It tingles."

"My dear girl," Etrusca began, "it seems your legs merely fell asleep. When you were sleeping in the chair, the wood applied pressure to your nerve pathways so that they could not properly transmit the signals your brain sends to the rest of your body."

"Is it permanent?" Isis asked, hoping her voice did not give away her fear.

"Not at all." Etrusca laughed. "This is quite common. The tingle you feel is the sign that the electrochemical pulses from your brain are once again reaching your legs. The feeling will go away soon."

Isis flushed with embarrassment. Already, the pins-and-needles feeling was subsiding. She had just had a brush with terror over something that was "quite common". *Once, I was godlike,* she thought. *Now, I'm not even a very impressive mortal.*

"Thank you, High Healer," Isis whispered. "Forgive my ignorance."

"There is nothing to forgive," she replied as she stood up straight. "We are all of us babes in this world, ignorant of many things."

"Ignorance," Isis began thoughtfully as they began walking down the hall. "Knowledge is a sign of growth."

"Knowledge is power," Etrusca said with a smile. "But then, strength is power. One of us can overtake the other under any given circumstance. It really takes all kinds to survive in this world."

As they rounded the corner, Antion came into view. The scar on his cheek was still red; there was nothing, the Obeahani had said, that could be done about it after so much time had passed. When his eyes met hers, he immediately dropped to his knees and bowed his head.

"Most holy Enoch," he murmured.

"Antion," she said stiffly. "Get up. Please. Do not worship me. I am only Isis now."

"You are the Enoch, the great archive. You are knowledge. You are everything we scholar's hold precious—nothing more so…except for the Balance, of course."

"Then please consider me as you consider yourself." She knelt in front of him. "The archive is in my head, true, but I can no longer access it as I could when I was the Enoch. I have to delve into the shelves of my mind just as you once had to inside the walls of Asgard. We are equals now. Remember that."

"I…I will try," Antion mumbled while avoiding meeting her eyes.

Isis sighed.

Muriel and the delegates looked up when the door to their secret chamber swung open with a resounding clang. Donovan and Rexis swept into the room with a different sense of urgency than usual. When they reached the dais, both dropped to their left knee and planted their right fist on the floor.

"You're late," Muriel croaked, the heavy wrinkles in his face shaping his brow so that his eyes were irritated slants. The Sovereigns stood. "Where have you been?"

"Apologies. We were…held up." Rexis flicked his eyes at Donovan, pure disgust read on his face.

"The man won't hold up anyone ever again," was all Donovan said with a nonchalant shrug.

"Since when did you have such a vicious streak? We were Interim, once. Not murderers."

"Once!" For a moment, the Sovereign of the Sword of Frost glared, his fang-like teeth flashing in the dim light. And then he smiled. "It's liberating, isn't it, Rex?"

"Is that how you explain it, ay?" Rexis smirked. "It's not insanity, just mental freedom?"

"Something like that."

"Enough!" Muriel barked. "What have you found?"

"They're holed up in a healing house in the Mine," Rexis explained, adjusting his stance to one of crisp attention. "They were visited by a Bloodsworn, one called on by the Sworn Donovan was tracking—" he glanced at the other "—and killed."

"Did you question her?" the Regent wanted to know.

"No, my lord," Donovan replied and bowed his head. "There were others. We would have risked exposing ourselves. We were, however, able to confirm that both Shade and the statue are within."

Muriel's brows gathered together, his eyes darkening into slits so small that one could barely see his beady irises under the wrinkle of skin. He was thinking, plotting, reworking years upon years of planning to fit into his ultimate scheme. Finally, he spoke.

"Shade's unpredictability has centered around one thing: the emergence of her curiosity. Before Knick Coltin perverted the Keeper in her, she would merely have returned to the fold. Now, we can count on her seeking answers. They have the statue…let them explore the mysteries on their own. We still have our wild card"—his eyes focused on Rexis—"and other concerns."

"Eros and the Keepers," Rexis concluded.

"Exalted Regent," Donovan began, "would you have us go to Sanctuary?"

"Not yet," he replied. "Though the scouts report many Kur being sent forth, Eros remains within and he keeps the other Interim close at hand. I do not wish to sacrifice so many when patience is a far more effective plan of attack."

"We will kill Eros and destroy the remnants of the old Order!" Donovan exclaimed. There was a bark of laughter that sounded more like a cough from the Regent's wheezing lungs.

"Such bloodlust is as commendable as it is foolish, Donovan. Do not underestimate the Baron. It will be your last mistake." He chuckled—a low, gravelly sound. "I have waited decades for my plans to unfold. I do not intend to throw them away on rash decisions and anxious actions. Fear not, my vicious child. We will deal with Eros and name a new Baron when the time comes. But first, there are things you must do—things you both must do. You've been held back by customs, by the thinning of power. It is time to unbind those wards and reclaim what was lost with time."

"You're talking about unlocking the true potential of the Interim," Rexis said. "Like Shade."

"Yes." Muriel frowned again. "Shade... I do not know how she unlocked the power. She has always been a special child. She always had a gift the others did not. Eros hid it well. I subdued her as I could and she was committed. But I underestimated her. The severing and Coltin's influence have triggered that which was much better left hidden. I blame myself. I should have brought her into the fold."

"My lord, we do not need her," Donovan spat.

"Your jealousy is tiresome and irrelevant. We must focus on unlocking that ancient power, and then even the Baron will fall before you."

"And Shade?" Donovan asked.

"Yes, she, too, must needs removing. She is a powerful obstacle, but against Malkira, she is but dust at your feet." He narrowed his gaze on them. Donovan grinned, flashing his fangs in Rexis' direction. "In due time."

"Yes, Regent," both Donovan and Rexis replied, bowing stiffly with their right arms crossed over their chests.

Those that did not litter the street dying or dead quickly fled into the city or back into the hole from which they came. The battle was ending, as Kallo observed, as he made quick work of his last opponents, expending more energy in a few quick and precise moves than he would have had he expected the fighting to continue. He slammed his khopesh into a rifle, feeling it catch in the rail, and ripped it out of the Miner's grasp with such force that the barrel dislodged. He immediately swooped in with the sabre, arcing his arm in front of him to slice the man's throat open. He let the momentum of the move turn him around where he plunged the khopesh up through the last assailant's stomach. The man dropped his rusted axe as the weapon hooked into his ribcage then spit blood when he was yanked forward into the sabre where it pierced his breastbone and cut through his heart.

Kallo found his sister not too far away and watched as she loosed two daggers at runaways then whipped her wind-and-fire wheels through the three men attacking her. He saw streams of red as her razor-sharp wheels flashed through the air. He managed to catch her eyes amid the blur and nodded; she immediately disengaged, allowing those she was fighting to run or die. Two of them hobbled away, the third just slumped onto the ground. Delia slung the blood from her weapons and locked them back into place on her armor as she joined her brother to survey the damage.

There was a moment of silence as the patter of escapees faded and the only creatures left standing on the killing field was Keepers. Then the groaning of the wounded and wailing for the lost arose like a chorus, and the painful aftermath of battle filled the streets of Hojo. Kallo signaled to the Kur to hunt down those that had fled deeper into the city and they quickly dispersed as the citizens scrambled out of their houses to collect their dead and tend to the injured.

Kallo and Delia made their way through the crowd toward the great statue where the freedom fighters had breached the city. Delia picked through the bodies, retrieving her daggers and returning them to their sheaths and loops. Near the great dragon's belly, they found Ross slumped next to a woman in a bloody and burned kimono, two bullet holes erasing much of her face. He looked up to them, pale and dirty, with tear stains on his cheeks.

"Are you hurt?" Kallo asked gently. Ross just stared. He knelt down and placed his hand firmly on the boy's shoulder. "Are you hurt?"

Ross shook his head as if to say "no", but once he got started, he couldn't stop. "We just wanted supplies. S'what Reinhardt said. Just supplies. No one needs to get hurt. Am I stupid? I'm so fucking stupid. I'm stupid—I believed that. But it's a lie. Someone always gets hurt."

"Ross," Delia softly said, "there are still things you can do to help us. Tell us about the breach. Where does it connect? Will more Miners come through?"

Ross stared at her with a gaping, uncertain expression on his face, as though he were seeing her for the first time, as though the words were banging on the doors of his ears but they remained closed. Delia reached down and opened her hand to him. He blinked at it, gawked at her fingers, and then met her gaze once more. The doors had opened and he was hearing her.

"G-Gypsy," he stammered. "The tunnel leads to Gypsy.

That's in the OT. There aren't any more down there, but once Reinhardt hears about it, he's gonna retaliate to keep the angels from coming through." He suddenly seemed panicked. Kallo looked at his sister. She nodded. Ross' gaze bounced from one to the other. "You're gonna blow it, right?" he asked. "You'll blow the tunnel."

"Yes. We're going to seal it," Kallo confirmed.

"You're the boss," Ross said, taking Delia's outstretched hand. "Tell me what to do."

"Ross," Delia began as she hoisted the boy to his feet. "If you wish to return home, you should go now to ensure you clear the blast radius."

"I brought 'em here," Ross said. "I'm a scout, boss. I found this tunnel. I let Reinhardt talk me into it. I'll go, but…lemme help first. Lemme do something to make this right."

"You cannot make things right," Kallo told him. "What's done has been done. You can only do right things in the wake of the wrong."

Ross looked down at his shoes and then nodded. "You're the boss, boss."

Knick frowned when he entered Shade's room and saw the bed was empty. When his eyes found her, she was wearing the pajama pants the Obeahani had given her and nothing else, caught with the bandage across her torso half unwrapped as she examined her healing wounds.

"Shit," he cursed, immediately averting his gaze. At just that moment, her kiss popped into his head and he felt his face getting hot. He turned away. Stopped. Walked out, drawing the door closed. Stopped. Went back in. Risked a glance at her. She had finished wrapping herself up—she was bandaged up like it was a fucking fashion statement—and was pulling on a shirt.

"Stay in or get out," she snapped.

"Shouldn't you be in bed?"

"I'm fine." She reached for the pajama shirt. "Where are my clothes?"

"You're fine, just like that? You spend weeks unconscious and then just like that you're fine?"

"I'm fine. You don't sound happy I'm awake."

"Well, I don't know." He grinned. "You're kind of cute

when you're sleeping, Shade."

She rolled her eyes and then went searching through the dresser drawers. "Where are my clothes?"

"You going somewhere?" He stuffed his hands inside his jacket pockets. "Running back to the Keepers?"

She stilled and looked back at him. "I can't go back," she said and, for once, Knick didn't have a smartass retort. "I violated the Balance when I went into Heaven and came back out alive. They wouldn't have me now. I would be executed." Her gaze fell to the ground and she quietly added, "I would deserve it."

"Hey, I wouldn't go that far. I'm pretty thrilled with your choices seeing as how I'd be dead if you'd picked otherwise. I mean I only went there for you—your Oracle in the first place."

"I started a war."

Knick was momentarily taken aback. "How did you know that?"

"It isn't hard to deduce. I showed the world how vulnerable Mirax can be. Now the Black Hand will be out for blood, and the Keepers aren't the only ones with ways through the Grey." She frowned. "I don't even know if I could do what I did again. It will be a slaughter on all sides."

"You can't blame yourself. You made a choice. Shit happens."

"I made a choice that will lead to the inevitable death of thousands. How can I not take responsibility for that?"

"So you regret it?" he balked.

"I don't. I would do it again. That does not mean I can forget the repercussions."

"You can't let yourself worry over that anymore. There are more important things we have to do."

"I still have my mission. I'm still a Keeper."

"What mission? What Keeper? You said yourself they won't have you back, and you threw your mission out the window when you came for me—isn't that what we just established?"

Shade glared at him. "Do you want to fight?"

"Only if we can make it more physical," he said with a smirk and she started to move away from him. He stepped after her. "Look, Shade, I'm not saying forget the Keepers forever, just that we have more important things to do right now — things that may help your Keepers in the long run. I mean it's your Enoch giving the orders here, not mine."

Shade nodded and then hung her head. A sad expression crossed her face — one he had never seen before. He wasn't sure what it was for, but he felt the urge to go over and put his arm around her shoulder or something — an urge he denied. He was so caught up in the moment that he didn't even noticed Slot come to the door, jump in surprise to see them there, then push Solo out of view as he caught up to her.

"Asgard is gone. So many are dead... I vowed to protect them. Gobol and Nico, all of them. I swore on my aegis to protect them and the Balance. I forsook that vow."

"You didn't," he insisted with an urgency that surprised even him. "That was the traitors and the angels. You can't blame yourself for not knowing what would happen."

"Bartimaeus is dead. One of my brother's is dead!" She met his gaze, eyes raw with pain and anger. "I defied Eros when I left Asgard that night. I left the walls I was ordered to protect to save a man who died anyway! And you saw how I defiled Heaven! If I had not disobeyed, could I have not saved Asgard as well?"

"I don't know," he replied quietly, honestly. "Maybe." Knick rubbed his face with a deep sigh and slowly walked over to her. "I'm sorry," he whispered. "If you need some time, I won't tell anyone you're up just yet." He hesitantly reached out and touched her shoulder, rubbed his thumb back and forth, then pulled her into a hug. "Thank you... Thanks for coming for me. Next time, try not to nearly kill yourself doing it."

"Knick," she began, slowly reaching up to touch his back. He felt her lean into the hug. "I'm going to protect you."

"I was going to say the same thing to you," he mumbled then leaned back to look at her face. "Ecstatic," he said and she frowned in confusion. "I'm ecstatic that you're awake."

Shade suddenly blushed and it made his heart beat like crazy.

"Get a room!" Slot yelled and the two of them jumped apart.

"They're in a room," Solo pointed out.

Knick glanced back to see his cogwheeler friends, Lethan

with Whiskey, Etrusca, and Isis all gathered outside the door. He hoped his face didn't look as hot as it felt.

"Assholes," he muttered. "Can't a person get some privacy?"

"Shouldn't leave the door open," Slot countered.

"Shade," Isis began. "I am glad to see you're well. There is much we must discuss."

High Healer Etrusca, who easily towered over them all, pushed into the room and went straight to Shade's side.

"Allow me to check your condition, sana," she said. Shade nodded and the High Healer stretched out her arms and roved her hands over the Sovereign's form. She placed a sutra on Shade's chest, chanting softly under her breath.

"The King's Way is long and treacherous," Isis began as the Obeahani worked. "We must pool our intellect to discover the true path. Knick," she nodded in his direction, "discovered this artifact after he departed Asgard." Knick pulled the statue out of his pocket and handed it to Shade as Isis continued to explain. "A Bloodsworn was delivering it to a man named Roskolniv in the Mine. He was lover to a woman called Red who died twenty-five years ago."

"A letter," Knick said, "came with the statue telling of how Muriel or Hermes killed her. Muriel," Knick repeated, "as in the ex-Regent."

Shade studied the statue, carefully turning it over in her hands. After a moment, Etrusca smiled at her and bowed, gently backing away from them. She positioned herself on the far side of the room to quietly listen. Clean bill of health, Knick supposed.

"Asgard…" Shade mumbled sadly.

"The Bloodsworn I traveled with—Hezara—took it to a friend of hers that did some research or something. She died getting this back to me. She had just one message: Asgard must fall."

"It is the only clue we have," Isis finished. "Any thoughts, Shade?"

The Sovereign of Shadows looked at them with sharp, violet eyes and then hurled the statue to the ground. It hit with a loud crash, causing everyone but her to jump in surprise. They gawked at what she'd done in utter shock and horror.

"There," she said bitterly. "Asgard has fallen."

"Shade," Isis whispered, eyes deadlocked on the ruin of stone on the floor. Amid the chunks and pebbles was an age-old piece of canvas wrapped around a small, bronze object.

For Bit and Tad, running trains was a thrill of adulthood. For Charlie and Sampson, it was an art. All the older kids were gathered on either side of the track pit, shouting and hollering as Charlie came racing down the rafters. The majority of the crowd had started with him up at L-Pole and ran along the station platforms to witness the full array of his show; the rest hung out at the end for the grand finale. Bit and Tad were sitting on the South Crossing wood bridge with their legs through the crooked rungs, swinging over the track. A crowd was clustered at their backs, drinking and celebrating and occasionally spilling their beers on the two boys' heads.

"You got it, man!" Sampson yelled and everyone went on alert, perking up and straining to see down the tunnel where Charlie would soon appear.

"Here he comes!" squealed a girl on the bridge. Three other girls joined in the pointless screaming, sloshing more beer onto Bit and Tad.

"Bitches," Bit muttered.

"Bitches," Tad agreed.

Charlie finally appeared to those at South Crossing, racing up the sides of the track pit, kicking off to the other side, and toe-touching the track about a second before the EM pulse popped on the railing. One wrong step and he was rail-cooked; the timing was critical. There at the final stretch, he added spins and flips to his jumps. Everyone started screaming in glee. The charge crept ever closer, nipping at his heels as he dove into a series of rolls leading up to the flak-trap.

"Jump th' deck!" a few people in the crowd exclaimed, but Charlie was fearless; he'd never jump the deck.

In one final move, he jumped the flak-trap and somersaulted, landing in a hand-stand. Just as the pop-pop of electricity connected with the rung he balanced on, he pushed off and propelled his body over the pulse so that flesh and energy moved parallel. For a moment, everyone held their breath. And then the charge was gone and Charlie was pulling himself up the rubber rope and swinging onto the bridge.

The girls went crazy, emptying most of their drinks onto the wooden slats and the two boys as they gathered around Charlie's sweaty form. Bit twisted back to look up at his older brother, at the tight, honed muscles on his bare chest and the wide grin on that square jaw; he looked at him in part awe and part jealousy, hoping he looked as cool when he grew up—and was just as tall, or taller.

"Showoff," he muttered as Sampson flew into the crowd to congratulate his best friend. Sampson was just as tall as Charlie and just as cool. All the girls flocked to them. "Sam acts like he donno Charlie's whole damn act when he'sus one who dun help him marked it."

"S'all a show," Tad reminded him. "Nice one, Charlie!"

The two young boys went largely unnoticed by everyone present, including Charlie, even though they had helped the two older boys time the performance long hours into the night every day for six weeks. Grumbling, they crawled between the crowd's legs until they freed themselves from the throng on the other side of South Crossing, heading away from Newyard. They sauntered down the rocky incline toward Kettle Kot, taking a detour down the slate ridges to get away from the noise.

"Charlie says in just-a few years, I'll's be ables-ta run a style," Bit told his best friend.

"Shit, Bit, you run it just fine now. Thinkin' prolly by summer," Tad said, kicking stones as he walked. "I been workin'-a style a-my own. Y'know, just'n walls'n stuff, but it gots potential."

Bit nodded and mumbled his agreement. After a moment, Tad tapped his buddy on the shoulder and pointed out across the way to the old mine shaft. A black retriever with long, shaggy fur was sniffing around the stones.

"Is that Mol?" Bit asked.

"Think so," Tad said. "What's she doin' alla way out there?"

The dog looked over at them and sat, as if waiting. The two boys scrambled over dirt inclines and slid down rocky slopes, picking their way across the abandoned quarry. The dog stood up when they came close and darted down into the tunnel. The boys went in after her, arms waving through cobwebs and feet slipping in loose dirt.

"Shit, Mol, whachu want down here, anyhow?" Tad cursed.

"Ain't no'un been down here in years," Bit said. "Can't see a damn shittin' thing."

They walked for what seemed like forever in utter darkness with only the dog's bark and nudges with her nose to lead the way. When they finally saw light, they found themselves in a large cavern with a ruin of old buildings crumbled into a misshapen pile of rubble. Streams of ghost-light—pale light seeping in from side tunnels and cracks in the ceiling, reflecting off crystal and glass—barely lit the room. The dog went straight to a particular spot, turned one circle, and plopped down.

"Whoa," Bit gasped. "Whachu think thisus?"

"Donno. Ol' mine camp?"

The boys inched around the outside of the collapsing town, careful not to get too close. The shadows moved eerily— as in they shouldn't have moved at all with the low light source—and gave them the creeps. When a chunk of stone fell off one of the roofs and crashed, producing a dusty cloud, they backed off, officially spooked.

"C'mon, Mol," Tad called to the dog. "Lesgo. S'dangerous down here."

"Prolly needle-fested," Bit groaned.

The dog got up and moved to the boys' sides, revealing a strange carving where she had been laying. The boys crept closer and squinted through the dust cloud.

"Whachu think that is?" Tad whispered.

"Itsus scales," Bit replied.

"Scales?" Tad echoed in disbelief, instantly thinking of reptiles.

"Scales," Bit said again. "Like for weighin' shit'n shit." He held out his hands and seesawed them in large, reckless movements. "Seen'a copycat at Sam's once."

"Whasat good for?"

"Y'know, balancin' stuff," Bit explained, trying to sound smart.

"Whatsat good for?" he asked again. Bit shrugged, out of answers. "Whatever," Tad grumbled. "C'mon, Mol. Lesgo."

The two boys and the shaggy, black dog made their way back through the dark tunnel.

Part Two

"…the clock is ticking, the hours are going by. The past increases, the future recedes. Possibilities decreasing, regrets mounting."

Haruki Murakami

The circulet was empty save for Muriel. He sat stone-still on his throne and stared deadpan at the Oracle. The ex-Regent was a patient man, but he could feel that he was dying. He could taste the rot on his tongue. He could no longer afford the long years of waiting that came with careful planning.

"Oracle," he croaked.

"You have promised the dissenters Malkira," the wraith-like voice of the Oracle hissed, water churning royal blue in the lapis lazuli bowl.

"You will tell me the location," he demanded. A terrifying sound gurgled in the pool that mimicked laughter. "Do not test my patience."

"False kings and true make no demands of me," it rasped.

"You will tell me what I wish to know or I will empty you into the drain."

More otherworldly laughter filled the chamber, louder and more sinister than before. The water in the bowl changed from blue to deep purple.

"Do it," the Oracle hissed. "I have seen more time than you can fathom, Pretender. I serve the Keepers that serve the Balance only. I am bound by no ancient word. Spill me. I will answer none of your questions."

The gurgling stopped, the lightshow subsided, and the chamber was utterly silent. Muriel glared at the sacred bowl as another idea suddenly surfaced in his mind. The Oracle spoke only when it wanted, it was true, but there was one other creature that could not only see inside the Oracle but could speak to it, speak for it, and be forced to speak.

The Enoch was the key.

Vox stood in front of the mirror and stared at her naked, pregnant form. She had grown so much in so little time and soon there would be no hiding her stomach or breasts beneath wisps of cloth. She looked at her hair, at the wavy, orange spikes standing up on her head. Would the child have her orange hair or would it be black like Dimitri's? What about the eyes? She had amber eyes. Dimitri had deep, endless pools of blue—she loved those eyes, they had drawn her to him in the first place. She hoped their child had eyes like his, beautiful drops of deep sea.

Vox smiled a small and secret smile, finding pride in a child not yet born, in features unknown. Whatever the child looked like, she would love him more than anything. Or her. A boy or a girl? How long before she could know? Perhaps Dr. Basset could tell her.

"Whatever you are, you will have eyes like your father," Vox whispered then reached out for her dress and tied herself into it.

A surge of pain suddenly ripped through her and she cried out, doubled over, and protectively wrapped her arms around her stomach. She immediately clenched her jaw shut to hide her exclamations. When the tremor subsided, Vox slid to the ground and held her swollen tummy, panting from the strain. It had felt as though her gut was being ripped apart. She had told Basset she was feeling some discomfort but nothing more than could be expected, and yet the sudden tremor was beyond discomfort—it had been excruciating. What was happening to her? Was the child in danger? Vox's brow wrinkled in fear.

The door opened and Dimitri slipped inside, forcing her to wipe the stress off her face. When he saw her on the floor, he raced to her side in panic and those beautiful, blue eyes could have drowned her in sorrow.

"Vox, are you all right?" he hissed, reaching out to her. "What happened?"

"I was just feeling a bit dizzy," she lied, and then forced a smiled. "I wasn't sure I'd make it to the bed so I sat where I was."

He sighed, visibly relieved. "Yes, better safe than sorry." He reached out to stroke her cheek. "Do you need anything? Something to eat, something to drink—"

"Dimitri," she gently interrupted him, "it was just a spell. Please don't worry, love."

"I'm sorry. I'm just…terrified."

"Why?"

"I love you so much."

"Love shouldn't terrify you, Dimitri," she whispered, placing her hands on either side of his face. "Love should embolden you to the impossible."

"On any other day," he began quietly, pausing to kiss her palm, "it would. But Interim have never had children before and—"

"Sh. We talked about this, love. If it's me or the child, we choose the child."

"I know." He nodded. "I know, but I don't want to lose you. Either of you." He kissed her forehead and hugged her. "I love you so much. I just want to keep you safe. Both of you." He kissed her temple. "I would give my life for you, you know that."

"That is not something you can do." She brushed his hair away from his face. "Sometimes there is nothing you can do, and you must accept life as it unfolds." And even though she said it, she all but shook with terror herself; she was afraid to die, afraid to lose him, afraid that somehow she could not protect their child. "But I love you. And together we can survive anything."

He scooped her up effortlessly and carried her to the bed. He kissed her over and over again and she wrapped her arms around him and held him close. There was a soft knock at the door and the couple broke apart, passion momentarily quelled as they quickly composed themselves.

"Come in," Vox called and Dr. Basset poked his head inside and smiled.

"I will leave you to it, then," Dimitri said and, with one last loving glance at Vox, he slipped out of the room.

"How are you feeling, Vox?" Basset asked.

"Fine," she lied.

"I'm afraid there isn't much time these days, but I had a spare moment and thought we should proceed with your examination."

"Of course. How are your other patients, Doctor? How are my brothers and sisters?"

He sighed and rubbed his face tiredly. "They are…as they were. Some are healing, some are dying, and others I haven't even had the chance to look at."

Vox lowered her head and the conversation concluded as he set to work. Dr. Basset asked her all the routine questions as he carried on with his examination and she answered them all honestly. As he finished up and began packing up his equipment, Vox felt another prick of pain inside her stomach.

"Everything looks good," Basset was telling her, his back to her as he sterilized his tools and put them in his bag. "Everything looks normal. There has been a lot of fetal activity. That's a good sign." She tried to hold in her gasp but it escaped when the pain doubled. Basset whirled around, wide-eyed. "Vox!"

Basset was immediately by her side, leaning over her. She tried to push him away but there was no strength in her arms. She kept them coiled protectively around her stomach, folded over in agony. Tears leaked out of her eyes as she momentarily lost track of what was happening around her. Basset was saying something but she didn't know what. His words were distant, drawn out noises that she could not decipher. He was doing something, but what? She felt nothing, only pain. And fear. And then her vision was going white.

When she came to, Basset was standing over her with a frown.

"The baby is fine," he said hoarsely, "as far as I can tell. I am not a real doctor—I didn't finish the schooling—so there is a point when my assessments become guesses and you could be at risk."

Vox nodded but said nothing.

"Have you experienced this before?" he asked. She just stared at her hands folded over her swollen stomach. "I see. Why didn't you tell me?" Again nothing. "This is serious, Vox. I understand you are in a challenging predicament, but failure to act could cost you your life, the child's life. You must be completely honest with me."

"Eros cannot know."

"Do you think he will sacrifice you for your sins?" he asked quietly. Vox's gaze snapped up to meet his and he held her eyes with hard determination. "After awhile, I won't be able to help you anymore," he whispered. "I implore you to trust those around you. I know nothing of your Keeper society or how it worked before all of this happened, but I know something of it now. And it's lying in ruins out there in those halls, bleeding out. All you have is each other, the trust that binds you. Tell them. Tell *him*. Let him help you. Let him find you someone who can look after you properly."

Vox looked at her hands again. "I will consider it," she

said at long length.

Everyone was huddled inside Shade's room—Jilk and the siblings, the three Keepers, and Lethan with Whiskey perched on his shoulder—everyone except Otto who was still asleep in his own bed. Antion had suddenly appeared in the doorway at the sound of the statue crashing on the floor. Knick folded his arms over his chest and leaned against the far wall, pretending to be interested in the proceedings but he couldn't keep his attention off of Shade. She was staring at the ruin of the statue of Asgard with a completely unreadable expression. Was she angry? Sad? He couldn't tell. She just stared at it.

"What happened?" Antion asked but no one answered him.

Isis went to the ruin and pulled the scrap of canvas and bronze object from the shards. She gently unfolded the delicate cloth and stared hard at the faded words scrawled across it. Antion came to her side, bowed and extended his hands, silently asking for permission. Isis handed the canvas to him.

"This is Sumerian," he marveled.

"Sumerian," Etrusca exclaimed. "The old tongue of Babylon?"

"You know of it?" Antion asked.

"The women of the Mermaid are taught many ancient things, which are the basis of our techniques, though they are passed down through generations. No one can read or speak Sumerian any longer. At least that is what we were taught."

"Yes, you're right. There are none who speak it now. The High Counselor, once. Yes. He could read it, even speak some. Scholar Nico," his voice wavered sadly, "he read a little of it. He promised to teach me some day."

Knick watched Shade's expression darken. There was pain in her eyes and the lines of her face.

"The Tongue of Babylon?" Jilk asked. "I'm guessing you don't mean the strip club on Tieks Street."

Antion only smiled. "It was the last unified language before the languages dispersed and became many, before the scattering of the five tribes. Did you know that it is in recent history that language was unified again? People spoke many languages across the earth for thousands and thousands of years."

"What does that have to do with anything?" Knick wanted to know. "You can't read it. We're fucked."

"There's more," Isis said, extending the bronze object in her palm. She held a five-pointed star with a pyramid at its heart.

"Oh, the Balance," Antion whispered in awe. "I can't believe it. It's Etemenanki, the ziggurat that scattered the five tribes—the Tribes of Typhi. This is their ancient symbol."

"*The* Tribes of Typhi," Slot echoed. "You mean the *legendary* Tribes that're supposedly responsible for the rogue dialects still floatin' 'round after the language unification?"

"They aren't legend," Antion told her. "They were real, once."

"Tell me," Shade said.

"When Asgard was attacked, the High Counselor and I were trapped together. Before he died, he bid me read from a book he carried with him. It was about the Tribes. I didn't understand then." Antion stared at the piece of cloth in his hands where the faded ancient scribbling was scrawled. "The Tribes of Typhi were the original five tribes of ancient Mesopotamia. There was a great temple that stood at the heart of the city, a six-sided ziggurat—the greatest ever built if the text is to be believed. And in the shadows of five sides, extending far throughout the land, were the five tribes who dwelled in the darkness and light of their great king. And the sixth side faced the rising sun so that glorious light flooded the stairwell to the height of the ziggurat, the topmost level where the holy temple resided. And below the temple sat the king's throne and he ruled in the path of light. And it was this sixth road that they called the King's Way."

"The King's Way?" Knick echoed in disbelief.

"Let me show you." Antion scrambled around for paper and a writing utensil. Shade ripped a sutra off her arm bandage for him to write on and Jilk passed him a pen. "Look." He drew a hexagon. "Here is the ziggurat—if you were looking down on it." He scribbled a circle in the center of it. "The temple." He drew five lines leading away from the temple. "See? That is the star representing the five Tribes. And then," he drew wavy lines through the last, empty side of the hexagon, "the King's Way."

"The King's Way," Isis whispered as she gingerly picked

up the drawing and examined it.

"And this ziggurat," Knick began, "is Etemenanki?"

"No. Well, yes. But no, not this," Antion explained. "This ziggurat was something else. You see, the land fell into darkness. And the city was lost. And I say lost because I truly mean it. There is no record of what happened to it, of war touching it—nothing. It just vanished. But the tribes survived. They were cast out, some believe—deserted, others believe. Or maybe they were all that was left of the great kingdom—but either way, they persevered. They joined with the other humans—or, or maybe they *were* the other humans. We don't know. But they tried to build a new temple. Etemenanki. But something happened and the Tribes were scattered forever, never again to be one people. This five-pointed star with the ziggurat in its heart is the symbol of the Tribes, the symbol of who they became after Etemenanki."

"Five-pointed star," Lethan murmured in shock. "Ziggurat?" He pushed to the center of the room where Isis stood. She held out the object for him to see. "The Tribes…they *are* real," Lethan said, gingerly picking up the star. "I know this symbol. It is worn by our Chief, Sabal."

"The Crone," Knick said. Lethan nodded. "When Zara and I came to you guys, she told me I was not yet meant to come to the Krueh-jin. That she would put me on the road that led back to them. It's like she knew I would be coming back."

"We must go to the Krueh-jin," Shade concluded. "This Crone knows something."

"I can lead you there," Lethan said and Whiskey chirped in agreement.

"Good," Shade said. "Let's prepare. We can leave within the hour."

"I'm afraid not all of your company is ready for travel," Etrusca announced.

"Doesn't matter. We need to leave," she said as a matter-of-fact, "and that doesn't include him." She looked at every face in the room. "Any of you."

"Now wait just a minute," Slot began.

"What do you mean 'any of us'?" Antion asked.

"Don't you understand?" Shade exclaimed, raspy voice booming over the rest. Knick watched the shadows darken around her as though summoned to her side. "The Keepers were the last line of defense between Anshar and Kishar, and they are gone now! Ex-Keepers hunt Knick, the Keepers hunt me, and a war is breaking out between two vile corporations that urge the masses to act. We cannot be a traveling caravan and bring attention to ourselves. Some of you can fight, some of you can't, and I can't waste precious effort protecting you every time we meet a roadblock or we might never get to where we're going! Knick, the Jin, and I go. The rest of you stay."

"She's right," Knick said. "Jilk, Slot, Solo—it'd be best if you guys got the rest of them to safety somewhere. Hunker down out of bounds and keep out of this war as long as you can."

"And you," Shade pointed to Antion, "I want you to find me answers."

"What answers?"

"About Mesopotamia, about King Malikiel, about the Tribes, about the One, about everything."

"I-I'll do my best. But how?"

"However you can, Monk." Shade looked at the cogwheelers and then over at Knick, as if to say, *they are your friends, they are your responsibility.* "Knick."

"Right," he said with a nod. He walked over to his cogwheelers friends and brought them into a private circle, placing his arms around Jilk and Solo's shoulders. They all huddled together. "If you're in, you're in. If you're not, go now." None of them moved. "Good. When Otto is okay to travel, you take those three and get the hell out of here. Find a hole, crawl in it, and stay there. We'll find you as soon as we know something."

"I get it, man," Jilk said, "but I still don't know if I like the idea."

"I don't really think there's anything to like about what's happening right now," Knick told him.

"Except you gettin' some alone-time with Gothic," Solo said with a smirk.

"Fuck you," Knick grumbled.

"Remember that job we had out in Britz?" Jilk asked them. They nodded. "That's way out there on the edge of the Cradle. There's a bar there."

"The *Toxic Ox,*" Knick said, remembering. It was where

he'd first met Shade. "I know the place."

"It's run by an old friend of mine. Duke. We'll meet up there. If we have to bail for any reason, I can trust Duke'll keep the secret until you come calling."

"Deal."

And the cogwheeler huddle was over.

Since Hojo was neither a blasting town nor on the edge of one, finding explosives was like finding Keepers— before they had been found, at any rate. Ross had rummaged through half-a-dozen hardware stores and half-of-half warehouses and so far all he'd found was the materials to rebuild what had already been damaged in the raid, not anything that could further destroy it.

He sighed and walked out of the store, one hand shoved into his pants pocket and the other idly tapping on the buildings as he strolled down the street. He knew how to make a bomb from kitchen scratch and it was beginning to look like Ross' only option. It was going to take time—time the Keepers may not have—but if it was the only way...they'd have to understand, right?

He found them by the dragon tunnel discussing something with a scout. He waited some distance away, idly tapping some rubble and wondering how the Keepers were going to react to the news. As bosses went, the twins weren't all that bad. Ross had been under someone's thumb ever since he was a squalling babe and none had ever been so nice as them. Still, they were Keepers, and they had done some weird beast-hunt trick on him—he was sure it was them—when they'd first met. He was wary. But more than anything, he was determined. Maybe it was like they said. Maybe things couldn't ever be set right. But he had to do something to make up for the fool he'd been believing Reinhardt.

Ross was snapped out of his thoughts when he noticed Kallo and Delia were approaching him. He straightened up to his full height and cleared his throat.

"Boss," he began, nodding at Kallo. "Boss," he said again, nodding at Delia. "Got some not so good reports. Seems there it'n a drop of explosives in this town. I think we're gonna have to make our own. Could take some real time, but my buddy Zapho taught me how."

The twins exchanged looks, privately discussing the situation; Ross had figured that one out, how the twins communicated with each other without ever speaking. It was kind of cool and kind of scary at the same time.

"How long will it take?" Kallo asked.

"I figure we need a pretty long chain going down the tunnel so we get a good cave-in—something not easy to dig through on either side. Powerful pop, too. Could be…twenty, thirty bombs? Mmmmm, let's double that on account of I'm not sure just how potent I can make them until I see the mats I got to work with."

"How long, Ross?" Delia asked patiently. He kicked the dirt.

"By myself? Few days…weeks?"

A warning horn sounded seconds before a rush of white suits flooded the paths between the buildings. Ross paled, backing into the dragon statue as the Keepers hidden among the shadows leapt out to meet the intruders.

"Angels!" one of the civilians exclaimed, inciting panic among those still on the streets.

Ross was one of those panicking. He had never seen an angel in real life, only pictures in Black Tuesday's headquarters. He had heard all the stories, though, and his heart was pounding so hard that he thought it might easily pound out of his chest. The fear worming in his gut was crawling inside of him, crawling into his brain, into his arms and legs—he couldn't move.

"Kallo," Delia said. Her brother pulled his mask over his face.

"Minu ga hana," he told her and was gone.

"Ross!" Delia exclaimed, grabbing him firmly by his shoulder, but he wasn't hearing her. "Ross!" she shouted again, snapping his wide-eyed gaze onto her. "Build that chain. We will keep the angels away from you."

But how could he build anything? He couldn't move. He couldn't think. He was going to die. The angels…the angels were going to kill him.

"Ross!"

Suddenly her whole face filled up his vision. Her amber eyes were inches from his and all he could see was Keeper and animal and woman all fused as one. He wasn't sure why or how but his heartbeat began to slow, his frantic breathing calmed down, and feeling returned to his limbs. Her voice echoed between his ears, soothing his spirit, though he didn't know what she was saying. He just knew there were amber eyes looking at him, drawing him in.

And then the hypnotic bubble burst.

"Build the chain," she said. "We will protect you."

Ross nodded over and over again, feeling strangely empowered. "You're the boss," he said. She smiled, pulled on her mask, and ran off to fight.

Knick stood at the end of the bed, leaning on the footboard, and stared at Otto as he slept, letting the soft sound of his breathing fill his ears. His mind was jumbled. What was he doing? Chasing some fantasy with some crazy Keeper and Krueh-jin, pretending he was the center of it all—the One. Was he out of his mind? All he had wanted when he escaped the angels was to disappear. The cogwheelers helped him do that. Maybe he had been numb working those shit jobs from shit town to shit town, but he had been surviving. He knew survival. He understood survival. So what was he doing saying "fuck you" to the cogs and running off with some merry band of crazies? Balance. Mesopotamia. Tiamat. King's Way. It was insane.

And yet there lay Otto, the garbage boy. He had simply had a dream—a crazy dream—and chased it. All reservations dropped, all logic discarded. Just got up and went. Didn't even know if it was real or not. He even lost his sense of survival in the pursuit of this dream. He was ready to die so long as he could find her. And he did. He found her. Because it had been real. And he had survived it.

Knick's jaw tightened and loosened, tightened and loosened as he stared at the frail boy softly snoring. The guy had shit for brains but he was brave. And admirable. More admirable than Knick was, because Otto never doubted himself, and Knick never stopped.

"See you around, kid," Knick mumbled as he pushed off the footboard. "Stay alive 'til I get back."

He met everyone in the sitting room in the front of *The Bright Mermaid*. He had changed into a fresh pair of black jeans and a white t-shirt, pulled on his leather jacket and street boots, and stuffed a pack of smokes into every pocket on his person. He handed Whiskey his last spare pack as the creature hopped onto Lethan's shoulder; the lehn tucked it into Lethan's sack, which presumably held the food, and began munching a nut.

Lethan was wearing his usual shades of gray and brown beneath leather armor of the same coloring and his weapons, a sickle and kukri, were strapped to the armor.

Shade's bandages had been changed, he noticed, and most of the sutras had been removed. Her hair hadn't gone back up in the tight ponytail but was tied at the nape of her neck. He studied her outfit; it was the most casual he'd ever seen her. She wore black fisherman pants tucked into boots and a black, long-sleeved shirt that wrapped around her torso. She looked like a warrior version of the Obeahani. And much, much sexier. She had nothing else but her sword and the light band—a bracer that covered wrist to mid-forearm and lit up in dark spaces. The Obeahani had given him one, too.

"Are you ready?" Lethan asked him.

"As I'll ever be," he replied nonchalantly.

"Balance protect you," Antion told Shade with a bow. He turned to Knick to say the same but he held up his hand to stop him.

"She protects me," he said, pointing at Shade, "so we're covered."

Isis said nothing, only stared passively at him. He didn't like that look in her eyes—the look that said she knew something he didn't. It made him uneasy. They finished their goodbyes to the Keepers and Obeahani, and the cogwheelers followed them outside to smoke.

"Take care, man," Jilk said, passing him a cigarette.

"You, too," he replied, lighting up.

"Make it back in one piece," Slot told him, "or I'll kick your ass into thirds."

He chuckled and mussed her hair. Solo clasped his shoulder, gave it a squeeze, and then clapped him on the back. He turned to see Shade waiting for him. With one last wave to his fellow cogs, he joined her.

"You will see them again," she promised.

"Yeah," he mumbled, "just hope it's with a pulse." There had been too many deaths lately. "We're going into the Grey, you know. Aren't you going to be cold in that? It's pretty thin."

"I'll be fine."

"I could keep you warm." He smirked and took a pull on his rette. She narrowed her gaze on him. "No need to by shy, Shade. After everything, it's only natural."

"Everything?" she echoed. "Your fantasies don't count."

"Still playing hard to get, huh? Even after you made the first move."

"I don't know what you're talking about. You've been acting strange."

"Well how am I supposed to act after what happened?"

"*What* happened?"

"You told me I was the turning point and you would protect me," he explained, "as a Keeper and as a man."

"You have some imagination, Knick Coltin," she mumbled.

Knick stopped dead in his tracks and watched her walk ahead of him. "Yeah?" he began, seeing her twist at the waist to look back at him. "You're a bad kisser." She blushed dark red but the confusion on her face was real. She really didn't remember. "Shit," he mumbled as she kept walking away. That's when he heard Jilk laughing. He glanced back at the cog. Jilk shrugged at him and laughed some more. "Hey, Slot, c'mere." Knick said and motioned to her. Jilk's smiled vanished. When she was next to him, he bent and whispered, "Wanna know a secret? Don't tell Solo."

"Knick," she mused, "I tell Solo everything."

"Good. Jilk was peeping on you in the shower yesterday."

"I didn't shower yesterday."

"Day before."

"Nope."

"A few days ago, then."

"Weeeell—"

"Geez, Slot. When the hell's the last time you bathed?"

"Solo says dirt builds character."

"I'll bet. Point is, Jilk was watching."

"Hmmm, wonder what he wanted."

"Donno. You could ask Solo. He might know."

"Sure." She hugged his neck. "Thanks for lookin' out for me."

He hugged her back. "Just keep those two in line, got it?"

"Got it."

She ran back to the group and Knick began his depressing trek to catch up to Shade. It burned him up that Jilk had been right. He knew deep down inside that it had made sense—that it was the drugs and nothing more. But some part of him had hoped beyond any logical reason that she would at least remember it, even if she hadn't meant to do it. And yet in spite of it all, he had the last string of hope that Shade's subconscious wanted to kiss him and that was what had made her act on it when under the influence.

That was a sign, right? He wasn't making that up. Or was he? Knick rubbed his forehead in frustration. Even though he hadn't been allowed to feel emotion as an angel, analyzing others' actions based on those emotions had always been easy, but now that he was in it, it was all so confusing. And difficult. He liked her. He didn't know what he wanted to do with that yet, just that he wanted to be near her.

"Hey, Knick," Jilk hollered, running to catch up with him. "Wait up a sec."

"I didn't say anything—" he began, but his boss cut him off.

"Before, when we were topside and Shade found out you were in Heaven...Isis told her not to go after you—"

"The hell?"

"—not to go after you *unless* she loved you. Because she would fail." Jilk shrugged one shoulder. "She went anyway. I don't know if that means what you want it to mean, but it means something. Thought you should know."

Knick looked back at Shade and then again at Jilk. "Hey, Slot!" he exclaimed. "About what I said earlier, I don't know what I was thinking. You can bump that."

She shrugged and shouted, "Okay."

"Thought you said you didn't say anything," Jilk pointed out. Knick grinned.

"Thought it should be a surprise."

The Baron was gathered with what were left of his Interim, Kur generals, and Dr. Basset in his office. A large, old map of Anshar was spread out on his desk with smaller, updated sector maps scattered on top of it.

"Mace's team reported the successful bombing of the

cogwheeler connector at Gomorra," Eros announced. "Kallo and Delia have suppressed an attack at Hojo and are working to seal the tunnel. Horne's team is holding down D-Water and Jiselli reports they are about to close the shaft at Alico. Katcha is at Pylos—"

"Katcha reported within the hour, Baron," General Gorric announced. "A fight broke out in Mercury; cogwheelers found another way through. He took his team out to deal with it."

Eros nodded. "Was Pylos taken care of?"

"He set the charges, sir, but there's no confirmation."

"Send Murray's team to confirm."

"Yes, sir."

"How many were lost at Pylos, General?"

"Katcha reported three men were killed."

Eros turned to the chart behind him and updated the information. They had lost two dozen men in preventive measures.

"Baron," Sonia began, "the cogwheelers are relentless. They are opening new holes into the city. Between them and miner raids, we will soon find ourselves outnumbered. We are losing too many trying to prevent a war we cannot stop from happening. There will be no one left to fight when the cogwheelers break through."

"We could not fight it now," Eros said. "I merely aim to delay it as long as possible. Scouts say the rumors of Asgard falling have not yet been confirmed in the Mine and many are still afraid it's an angel trick to lure them into a trap. If they meet enough Keeper resistance, perhaps they'll believe it's true."

"And if they don't?" Balthazar asked.

"Then we prolong the inevitable as long as we can. Between now and then, much could happen. And if nothing happens, then we are prepared for the worst."

"We will fail," Vox whispered dejectedly. "We are to protect the Balance of Life and we can no longer do it."

"We protect the Balance," Eros reminded her. "If that means to sabotage war efforts and give aid to certain armies, we will do it. The war will not last forever and we are all that stands between Lotus Maze and genocide."

"Of course," Vox agreed, bowing her head respectfully. Her face momentarily contorted with pain as a tremor shot up her gut. She instinctively reached for her stomach but stopped when she realized that doing so would draw attention to her condition. She returned her arms to her sides and looked up bravely. No one, it seemed, had noticed; no one save the doctor.

"Dr. Basset, how many men are ready to be sent back into the field?" the Baron asked. Basset cleared his throat and stepped up to the desk.

"Three dozen men have been treated and should be ready to fight within the week."

"Good. We have scouts in the northern sector—" Eros was interrupted when the datapad on the corner of the desk began to beep. He picked it up and answered the call. "Eros."

"Baron!" Delia cried, her voice crackling through static. The sound of gunfire and screams threatened to overtake her. "Angels have attacked Hojo in full force. We've lost four men already. They're overwhelming us!"

"I'm sending Interim to your position. Hold it," he commanded.

"Yes, sir!"

The call ended. Eros pointed to Dimitri and Vox. They bowed their heads and went for the door as Dr. Basset shook his head. Vox shot him a warning glare but he ignored it.

"Sir," Basset began, "I don't think it's wise to send Lady Vox."

The room went still and Eros looked up from his charts. He glanced from the doctor to the Sovereign of the Sword of Flame and back again.

"No?" he began. "And why is that?"

"She…wasn't well earlier. I am concerned the illness could be something much more serious than what it seems, at present."

"Is it contagious?"

"No."

"Is her life in danger?"

"Possibly."

"Vox," Eros said seriously, focusing his dark gaze on her. "Are you fit?"

"Yes, Baron," she replied. "I am fit."

"Then go. Dimitri, watch out for her."

"Of course, Baron," the Water Sovereign replied. Basset

looked back at Dimitri and shook his head, eyes begging him not to let this happen, but the Interim had to behave as though nothing were wrong. They departed the office.

"What was that all about?" Dimitri asked her when they were walking down the hallway.

"Nothing," she replied. "He feels a pregnant woman has no place on a battlefield."

"He is not wrong."

"Would that I was so fortunate. It was sooner or later that Eros sent us all into battle. I would rather be fighting at your side."

"And me at yours," he said with a smile, grasping her hand tightly.

Rexis and Donovan headed deep into the bowels of the hideout to the lower levels where Muriel's collected scholars were pouring through the thousands of tomes that had been copied and stored during a darker age in the Order, an age when Keepers had been weaker and hunted. The Order was itself subject to the Balance, meaning sometimes the Keepers were too powerful and had to be culled. The Keepers were a cap on power to any would-be aspirant to world domination, so every king and emperor and president and CEO that had learned of their existence had tried to destroy them. Sometimes their efforts had been more successful than they realized, for even Keepers could be killed.

Or so the stories had gone. Such tales were from days Rexis had never known, all before the foundation of Lotus Maze. Until, of course, betrayal brought Mirax right to their doorstep. In every story of the old days he had ever heard, the Keepers had never been betrayed by one of their own. And though he knew his actions were for the best, the bitter taste in his mouth would not be washed away. He blamed Muriel for it.

"What do you think Malkira means?" Donovan asked, breaking the silence.

"Sounds like a name, not a thing."

"Like a person rather than an object or a power."

"Yeah."

"Do you think he's found a new recruit?" Donovan sounded disappointed. He wanted power and he wanted to wield it, not witness it; he'd had enough of seeing others' power watching Shade grow up.

"Who knows?"

When they reached the Oubliette—the massive, domed chamber where the books were kept, named for the single, small exit within a trap of knowledge—they were bombarded with a new type of silence; this was the silence of learned men deep in their research, filling the air with a tension that warned others not to break the quiet.

They obeyed the unspoken law and crossed the library. It was an open room with many tiers surrounding the lowest point, the arena-like center called "the pit". Wooden stairs connected these various levels and quite often the most direct route from one side to the other was a weaving path up and down. When they reached the pit, they found the man they were looking for peering over his glasses and long, hooked nose into a thick book. He was a young scholar with dull brown hair, tired eyes, and a wiry frame.

"Tate," Donovan began, flashing his fangs in a grin. The young man jumped, as though he hadn't realized they were there until Donovan had spoken. "You have something for us."

"My lords Interim," he said in a scratchy voice, bowing his head respectfully. When he lifted his head, he smiled, showing off a few of his crooked teeth. "You wanted to know about Malkira."

"Have you learned anything?" Rexis asked.

"Yes."

"What is it? Or who?" Donovan wanted to know.

"The nature of Malkira's original form is up to debate. Some say she was a powerful warrior, others say a goddess, a princess, a queen—most agree she was an angel."

"An angel?"

"Yes. The Talmud suggests that Malkira—originally Malkirel, beloved by God—was the angel of death and destruction."

"How sweet," Rexis muttered sarcastically.

"Malkirel only acted by divine decree to destroy the enemies of God," Tate explained. "Many believed Malkirel to be male, but that was her twin brother Samael; the two were thought to be the same being, but they were not. Where she was the angel of death and destruction, he was the venom of

God, accuser and seducer."

"You don't expect me to believe Malkira was really an angel, do you?" Donovan said, folding his arms across his chest and leaning against a bookshelf.

"I don't expect you to believe or disbelieve," Tate replied with a casual shrug. "Malkirel fell from grace when Lucifer defied God. Her brother betrayed God and fought for Lucifer, and though she fought for God, she could not raise her sword against her own brother, vile as he was. She was cast out of Heaven and henceforth called Malkira, which means King of the Wicked."

"Wicked?" Rexis echoed.

"The wicked were those that fought unholy battles. Since she failed to strike down God's enemies, she was cursed. But her power as the angel of death was immense, and the call to vanquish enemies could not be ignored. Blood stained the sands of the East until she was struck down by her Creator for the violation of her once-sacred duty. Angels, however, are said to be immortal, so her soul would live on."

"That's fascinating," Donovan droned. "But what about the real Malkira?"

"Well, likely Malkira was the powerful priestess known as the Sword of Babylon. The Sword, they say, slew thousands of men and guided one hundred swords to slay as many as hers. She often attacked her enemies with the rising sun at her back to blind them, and she wore spiked shoulder mounts that—scholars theorize—when hit by the rising sun gave the appearance of wings, hence the angel rumor. She was a fearsome warrior with power unnatural, and none knew from where it derived. Eventually, she was struck down...but her soul, they say, was eternal."

"So angel or not, her soul's eternal," Rexis said. "Got it."

"Her soul was bound within her sword-arm's mighty gauntlet. Whoever wore it wielded her power. More Malkira, however, was not what the world needed. The would-be Swords of Babylon were cut down far easier than the real priestess. The gauntlet was hidden away by ancient protectors to never again be used by the unworthy."

"Unworthy?" Rexis began. "It seems Malkira herself wasn't *worthy*."

"You sense the conflict, yes," Tate agreed. "Our

knowledge is assembled from various texts, but it is true that the way Malkira is spoken of suggests false report. It could be that someone was trying to hide her truth."

"Who cares?" Donovan scoffed. "You're saying I could be immensely powerful if I used the gauntlet."

"Yes. Malkira's gauntlet would quadruple your power."

Donovan grinned one of his sinister grins and pushed off of the bookshelf. "So where is it?"

"We are looking for its location, my lord Interim," Tate promised. "Those ancient protectors, you see, were none other than the Keepers." He smiled at the surprise on the Sovereigns' faces. "There are records of ancient relics being transported to the various Keeper strongholds over time. It is just a matter of figuring out where they hid Malkira when they brought her to what would become Lotus Maze."

"That's very good news, Tate," Donovan said as he smiled. "You'll let me know as soon as you find something." It wasn't a question, but a command. Tate bowed in acknowledgement. Rexis hung back as his companion walked away.

"My lord Interim?"

"What do *you* think, Tate?" Rexis asked. "Was Malkira an angel or just some renowned warrior?"

"I do believe Malkira was the Sword of Babylon, though it could just as easily be the given name of the angel of death. As for angels or demons, I've come to know only one true source of the use of superscience—or magic—on earth. And that is the Keepers."

Rexis frowned. "Malkira…could have been a Keeper?"

Tate shrugged. "Now that," the young man said, "is a sound theory."

Casey rolled up her sleeves for what felt like the hundredth time that morning then tucked some stray wisps of hair behind her ear. She rinsed out the bloody rags, grinding them over the washboard and wringing them out until they were clean. She couldn't believe this medieval form of cleaning still existed but if it helped her father then she wouldn't fuss about it.

She looked around at she washed, watching women that she had heard referred to as naga scrub rags and clothes and linens over washboards as well. These women also assisted her father with the patients—retrieving supplies, holding someone down, cleaning bedpans, stitching. They never asked questions or talked back or complained about their work. In fact, now that she was thinking about it, she was pretty sure she had never heard them speak at all.

She let the idea ferment as she finished up the bloody rags then hoisted up her basket of soapy wet cloths and carried it over to one of the clean water buckets to rinse them out. How could someone go through life without talking? Not that she was a big gabber herself but communication was vital to one's sanity. Sharing your thoughts and feelings with another person, the consolation of being agreed with, the challenge of being opposed—how could anyone willingly give that up? Another thought stuck her suddenly. What if it hadn't been willing? She had heard the rumors about the Keepers—mostly that they were powerful and dangerous. All the sinister details that had rumored through society had not proved true, however. She wanted to believe what she witnessed, not what she had been told. Though one thing about the Keepers had proved to be true: they were secretive. Secrets made trusting hard.

Casey finished rinsing out the soapy rags and went to pick up the basket to take them to the drying rack when a long, swishing skirt appeared in front of her. She recognized this once-white skirt, noted how the bottom was stained brown and red and black. The naga wore simple white drapes but the head of the order—the Cleric, they called her—wore a wide, swishing skirt that touched the ground. Casey looked up into the cherubic face of Camilla. She had personally helped her father in healing the soldiers that came through, deferring to his knowledge in spite of how Dr. Basset was convinced this woman knew more about healing than he did. Another mystery, another secret. But Camilla's smile was kind, and that couldn't be a lie.

Camilla held a basket of dry rags, all neatly folded, that she offered to Casey. "Let's trade," she said gently.

Casey hoisted the wet basket up, passed it to the Cleric, and took the dry ones. Camilla smiled again and they headed off down the corridor together.

"It's so admirable the way you help your father," Camilla

said, "and I want you to know that the Keepers are extremely grateful for everything your family has done to assist us."

"The Keepers saved my family. It's the least we can do," Casey replied. It was something she had said over and over again.

"I know, but your family has gone above and beyond. I just want you to know, we are simply grateful." Camilla smiled. "I am sorry for the pain you have seen. Such a young woman should be enjoying life, discovering the pursuits that stimulate her mind, activities that make her heart beat hard. You shouldn't be here, tending dying men, witnessing the ugliness of a war you have nothing to do with."

The thought had crossed her mind more than once on the really long, really hard days, but to agree would sound selfish and bitter, so she said nothing.

"Your clothes have become a bit worn in all of this chaos," Camilla continued. "I found some spares that would suit your size. I left them with your mother."

"Thank you."

As they reached the junction in the hallway, Camilla smiled and went right while Casey turned left. She brought the basket of rags to several naga standing near her father who was bent over a screaming man. The woman who took the basket bowed in thanks, whipped several cloths out, and pressed them against a mass of tattered, bloody flesh.

Casey quickly moved on. She went about her duties with numb thoughts, changing sheets, folding linens, washing, washing, washing, until she was eventually told to take a break. She found herself alone in the kitchen, pulling the band out of her hair and shaking it out. It was long and straight, completely without volume—unlike her mother and little sister—and she ran her fingers through it several times to try to put some lift back in.

She caught a glimpse of her reflection on the door of the cold storage unit. She was tall and thin without a single curve to speak about. A model's figure, her friends used to tell her, but she was an arcball player, not a painted doll. Sure, she had the tanned skin for a doll, but she was blond, not brunette. Besides, Casey never considered herself a canvas. She was more of a painter. She was meant to do things that made people gasp in awe, not be the one people gasped at. Playing had been her fulfillment.

"Probably could've gone to sectors," she mumbled to herself as she reached for the storage handle. The sound of a large crowd shuffling in the main room made her abandon her quest for food and peek out of the kitchen. Two of the Interim were at the head of a group of soldiers, leading them to the door. They were the pregnant couple. Even the pregnant woman was being sent out? Casey ducked back inside and put her back to the wall. Everyone was leaving. Would there be anyone left when it was all done? People left, and only some of them came back, and always worse than before.

Casey sighed. More than hungry, she was tired. Whenever she had a chance to think about how bleak their chances were, she felt the energy drain out of her. She tried not to think about it—to put on a brave face for Clara and her mom—but sometimes she couldn't help it. What if so many Keepers left that Sanctuary became defenseless? She didn't know the difference in ranks but she knew that some were more powerful than others, and more and more of the powerful ones were going. Even the pregnant one!

Casey ducked out of the kitchen, heading toward her bedroom, and immediately collided with someone. Strong hands gripped her arms to steady her. She looked up into the lavender eyes of one of those men who were more powerful than all the others.

"Are you all right?" he asked. His voice was kind.

"I'm fine," she replied quietly. Daelus. His name was Daelus, she was almost positive. "Just a bit tired."

He smiled knowingly. "You and your family have been going since you got here. You have a lot of endurance."

"I play first setter in arcball," she mumbled, as if that explained it. Then she realized he had been talking about her family. "I mean—well they—I, uh—uhm…"

He laughed and she blushed, embarrassed. She ran her fingers through her hair, shaking it out, trying to distract herself.

"Casey, right?" he asked, and she was surprised he knew her name.

"Yeah."

"Tell me why you look so scared."

She stared at him with wide eyes. She was caught.

Shuffling from foot to foot, she played with her hair, trying to find the right words to explain.

"Everyone's leaving," she managed to say. "What's going to happen to us? To my family?"

"We will protect you and your family, Casey," he said seriously. "I promise you."

"But you can't even protect yourself," she heard herself say. "Something happened, right? This isn't how the Keepers I heard about operate. There wasn't just a few of you, battered and bloody, hiding out in Lotus Maze's basement! Dad said MAAR got to you. They got to you when no one else could! Why are we safe here? There is one way into Sanctuary. If that door closes, we're trapped. We're dead. Why are you still fighting?"

"Because no one else will. We could be hiding down here, licking our wounds. But a war is coming, and thousands upon thousands of people like you and your family will die. We want to prevent as much of that as possible. So we keep fighting." Daelus stared at her so intensely that she couldn't look away. "MAAR took us by surprise because we were betrayed by our own. We lost many of our brothers and sisters. We lost our home. They sent an army to take us down and we lost much, but we survived. One of us did to them what hundreds of them did to us. I promise you, we can protect you."

Casey just stared at him, a lump in her throat preventing her from speaking. Her face felt hot. Daelus offered her a small smile.

"You should get some rest," he said and walked around her. She turned with him.

"How can I trust in your promises?" she blurted. He stopped moving, started to turn his head back to look at her but hesitated.

"I can't teach you how to trust," he answered. She watched him walk away.

It had been two days since they had entered the Grey, into the network of dark, rusty, wet tunnels, and they were making good time. Lethan and Whiskey were scouting ahead, tracking the Krueh-jin; only fellow Jin, he had explained, could track the Kada. Shade was positive that, if necessary, she could track them as well; she had done so before with the smaller cells that operated away from the main tribe. She said nothing about that, however, glad for the reprieve. Her mind was weighted down by her choices and the lives that they had cost.

She thought of all the Keepers in the tower. She thought of Nico riddled with holes and felt unbelievable pain in her chest. She saw Bartimeaus' charred eyes staring up at her. No matter how many times she closed them, she always felt he was looking at her, begging for an answer she couldn't give. *Why?* he silently asked. *Why did you abandon us?* Eros had told her to remain in the tower but she had disobeyed. Her legacy had been one of unfailing loyalty, trust, and obedience...until she met Knick. The question looped in an endless circle in her mind: could I have saved them?

And yet she could not bring herself to regret her choices. If she had to choose all over again between Knick's life and starting a war between Anshar and Kishar, she would choose his life. Shade quickly glanced back at him. She couldn't explain her devotion to him, but it was a feeling deep inside of her, at the core of her body. When she was with him, she felt as though she were where she needed to be. Protecting him seemed to be the only thing she was meant to do. Yet the closer he came, the more unsettled she felt. When he hugged her, when he made careless passes at her, it made her squirm, and that made her angry. She didn't know what to do with these feelings, but she did know that she had to be with him. So Shade wandered her conundrum back and forth between undiscovered truths.

"Hey," Knick said, suddenly walking beside her. His bracer's light amplified hers, illuminating the tunnel almost completely. He held out his hand in front of her. "Thought you might want these back."

"My bells," she whispered in surprise, seeing the braided leather band and tiny silver bells wrapped around his fingers. "Keep them," she said. "If we are separated again, they will help me find you."

"You sure? Aren't these things the lifeline to your Keeper voodoo?"

"They are my lifeline to you," she told him. Knick seemed almost embarrassed as he shrugged and shoved the bells back into his leather jacket pocket.

"Yeah, I know," he muttered absently. "You've always been worried when we were separated, afraid of your mounting attraction to me, and it was all very tragic."

Shade felt herself squirming again, which naturally meant her agitation levels were raising. "If I was worried, it is only because you were right about the prophecy; we were meant to be together—the shadows and the one. It is fate."

"Let's get something straight," he snapped. "I make my own destiny. If someone says I'm going to do something and I do it, it's only because I felt like it was the right thing to do and not because some asshole 'pre-ordained' it. I'm not going to fall into the trap of justifying and excusing all my bad decisions by saying it was 'fate' and I certainly won't give all the credit for my *good* choices to this destiny-bullshit." He suddenly was standing in front of her, forcing her to stop walking. "I'm responsible for me. Get it?"

Shade just stared at him. What he said made sense but she had seen a lifetime of prophecy preserve the Balance. She could not easily dismiss what she had seen and even done because Knick had some romantic notions about controlling his own life. Yet there was some truth to what he had to say, truth to being responsible and taking responsibility. She had always believed in that.

She walked away from him and continued down the dingy, rusty pipe. Moisture was thick in the air. She retied her hair and felt tiny water droplets drip onto her hands. Another half-an-hour of walking and Lethan reappeared, motioning to them. Whiskey hopped up and down on the ground.

"Come, just up ahead," he said, leading them out of the tunnel and to a cavernous formation. Beyond were many more tunnels, some pipes and some natural hollows. "They are not far now."

The cavern floor was littered with red-capped mushrooms that grew so large and so rampant that they started to overtake the walls. Paths had been carved through the fungi, connecting all the tunnels. Whiskey leapt up onto the Jin's shoulder.

"Do not touch them," Lethan warned as they threaded their way through the mushroom field. "They are extremely toxic."

"What's the symptom?" Knick asked. "Hallucinations, fever, vomiting—"

"Death," Lethan answered. "A few hours after contact, your blood turns black and strange spots appear on your eyes."

"No shit," Knick mumbled. "Angels use this stuff." He made eye contact with Shade when she looked back at him. "They tried to kill you with it through your Keeper buddy."

"It only grows here in the Grey," Lethan told them. "Only in certain areas where the chemicals mix just right."

"There are angels in the Grey," Shade surmised.

"There are many monsters in the Grey," Lethan said. "You just have to know where to look."

"Or where not to look," Knick added. "I don't think we need to meet any more monsters."

"Are you afraid?" Shade asked, unable to resist smiling a little. She tapped the hilt of her sword. "I'll protect you."

"Maybe you've forgotten but, the first time we met, you tried to kick my ass and failed." He cracked his neck. "I'm not defenseless, sweetie."

They reached the other side of the mushroom field and exited into a natural tunnel. Lethan ushered them forward as Whiskey hopped down and raced ahead. Shade kept pace with Knick, walking side by side.

"You do know how to fight," she conceded. "The angels are well-trained. I could teach you more. Refine your technique."

"To be honest, I tried to forget it." His smile was sour. "I don't really like knowing how easy it is to kill someone. And for all the good it did me, anyway. Against Keepers, we're kind of like baddies in a bad movie."

"There aren't many who can stand up to the Keepers," she admitted, "which is why this will be so hard."

"What will?"

"Anshar and Kishar may be fighting one another, but our enemy is ex-Keepers. Whatever Muriel is after, he isn't going to stop until his plans are fulfilled. If he wanted you dead before, that will not have changed."

"And you? He tried to kill you, too. Remember?"

"He didn't want me to discover the sight stone in 119-A and figure out the trap he had laid." Shade thought back to what Gobol had said. *Shade, he knows now…he knows he made a mistake. He knows it's you.* She didn't want to worry Knick further so she kept that bit of information to herself. "Either way, we can expect to see them again."

"Great," he replied sarcastically. "Can't wait."

Shade studied him as they walked, thinking on what he had said. He didn't want to be a weapon. She found that idea both foreign and admirable. She had always been a weapon, though she had never considered herself such. The Sword of Balance, that was the identity Eros had given the Interim. Knick being the One, he should be the weapon, strength and power flowing out of his body. Yet he didn't want it. Perhaps that was why she was sent to him—to be his bodyguard, his soldier, his sword. Not because he couldn't fight, but because he didn't want to.

Shade was resolved. "Okay," she said. "If you don't want to fight, you don't have to. You don't have to be a weapon, Knick. I am one already, and I will be *your* weapon."

He got a strange look on his face. He stopped her again and turned her to face him. "Shade," he whispered intimately, causing her heart to beat hard in her chest. "That's kind of romantic. Is that like a proposal?"

Her stomach churned angrily. "Idiot," she mumbled. She jerked out of his grasp and walked away. Her skin felt hot, most of all in her face.

"I don't think Lethan's ordained or anything, but I'm sure the old Crone's authorized for this," he called after her. "And here I thought you said you didn't remember. Sly, Shade. That's very sly."

Remember. Remember what? He had told her she made the first move. The first move to what? And what was that nonsense about being a bad kisser? She had never, in her entire life, kissed anyone. And the idea of kissing him was... Shade grunted in frustration, wondering why she felt so hot in such a cold, damp place.

Her violet eyes were electric. They glared vividly in a way he had never seen before. A haunting stare. A terrifying glower. Her jet black hair whipped about her pale skin like sharp shadows slicing the air. Her moves were precise. She danced in a never-ending chain of action: parry-attack-parry-attack-block-block-attack. There was absolute focus not rippled with even an ounce of fear or uncertainty. She wore the undisturbed countenance of a warrior who controlled the battlefield in its entirety. It was mesmerizing. It was frightening. But those eyes...

One of us did to them what they did to us.

Daelus frowned behind his closed lids, head bowed and shoulders slumped. He sat with his back to the door in a room far away from the crowded main chamber. He claimed a cot and privacy to gather his thoughts but they did not assemble coherently for him. All he could think of was Shade and her shocking violet eyes vibrant with violence.

In her quest to save Coltin, she had stormed Heaven, forsaking the Balance in a single move. He knew there were Keepers considering it a betrayal, but he had always trusted her—trusted that she knew what she was doing. The other Interim were hesitant, not sure where they stood, and so they looked to Eros for guidance, but the Baron had remained silent.

Did Daelus want to believe in her because of how he felt about her? Or was it true that Shade was and always had been a steadfast Keeper? No matter how he questioned himself, he could not shake his trust in her.

At first, he had been terrified that Shade had not survived the encounter and Eros' tense demeanor had told him that the Baron shared his fears; the nightmare plagued his every thought. However, after a few days, Eros told them all that she was alive and not to worry; his connection to the Interim had allowed him to glean that much. So, slowly, Daelus' concerns shifted from her well-being to her actions and how they had changed everything.

One of us did to them what hundreds of them did to us.

What upset him most, he realized, was that the Shade who stormed Heaven was a Shade he did not know. She had risked everything for a man who... Daelus frowned, unable to finish the thought with any justified reasoning. Truthfully, she has risked everything for a man that was not him. That was what really bothered him. And he knew what it meant, though doubtless she did, and that he would have to give up his feelings for her. That he could never tell her the words he'd long to say for twenty-five years.

The idea that he would have to give up on her was more painful than it should have been. Love was forbidden in the

Keeper Order and he should not be upset to know that they could never be. Somehow, with the world crumbling around them, he had felt a spark of hope that the cruel fate web had spun a future for them. Somehow, Eros' indirect blessing had given him courage to believe in that dream.

Daelus felt an ironic stab in his chest and he opened his eyes to look at his boots, at the ground. Before he could dive deeper into his thoughts, he felt a presence sidle up silently and take a seat beside him. He did not have to look to know the presence was Eros.

"Let's talk about it," Eros said.

"There's nothing to say," he countered quietly.

"I don't believe that. You aren't good at hiding things, Daelus."

Daelus looked at his mentor with eyes that said, 'You're kidding, right?' Daelus barely had a memory of a time he wasn't hiding. "I've successfully hidden for twenty-three years, Eros. My feelings, my identity—what's the point in it now?"

"We still have work to do. We are still Keepers."

"Yes," Daelus agreed. "And now we're at war."

"Yes," Eros said with a small smile. "The attack on Mirax solidified that prospect. Once the world was shown the vulnerability of the great White Hand, Kishar was sure to respond."

"Then...if Shade had not attacked..." Daelus wondered, not liking the idea that the world at war could be blamed on her. Though she had made an outrageous move against the Balance, he still wanted to believe she hadn't forsaken it.

"No, I don't think this is Shade's fault. It was merely one final act in a complex web of events—something far beyond our control. The High Counselor knew what was coming but I don't think he realized it until it was too late."

"The mark on the wall," Daelus muttered, remembering. "He was terrified."

Eros nodded grimly. "I didn't realize it then but it is clear now. There's a prophecy out there that the Order at present was not aware of. We have to find out what it is. If we do, we can learn what will happen next, perhaps how to resolve this situation before too much damage is done."

"Where can we possibly start? Our libraries are destroyed

or raided."

"We can start with Shade," Eros replied solemnly. Daelus flinched back in surprise. "She did what she did for a reason. I admit, I"—Eros suddenly looked down, as though guilty—"I was worried she was influenced by the legend of the One and that it drove her actions. But now I see she must know something we do not. Something we were too proud to see—*I* was too proud to see." He finally looked up again. "I think if we're going to find answers, we should start with her."

"Send me," Daelus blurted. Eros eyed him warily.

"I know you want to see her," he began hesitantly, "but there have been a number of unexpected turns of events that make me even more cautious than before. After Rexis…who knows if Muriel has anymore Interim in his claws?"

Daelus frowned, wondering if Eros was implying that he could possibly betray the Order. He waited to see, reading his friend's face and the deep lines that had started to form since Muriel first betrayed them. Eros made eye contact and must've realized his line of thought because he suddenly shook his head.

"I don't mean you, Daelus. I mean the others. I want to trust in them…but Rexis has spoiled my trust. I need all the help I can get—and I need those I can trust by my side. I know you want to see her, Daelus…perhaps too much. Perhaps you will stay with her and not come back."

"I am still a Keeper, Eros. I will not betray you. I will find her and learn as much as I can." He leaned slightly forward. "And I will come back. I swear it."

Eros nodded. "All right. Then you will go." He nodded once more, this time to himself, as though confirming it was the right plan. "The last we know of Shade, she disappeared underground with Coltin and several others. She is in the Mine, likely somewhere beneath Tonatti Haan or Gomorra."

"I will find her," Daelus assured him.

Gunfire rattled the streets of Hojo in several sectors. The citizens had all retreated indoors, leaving an empty and twisted maze for a battlefield. As angel 92-99-03 observed the situation from his skyglider, a hovering deployment pad, he noticed a pattern. Rather than fight them in the open, the Keepers in teams of two would lure a group of angels into a trap and pick them off one by one. They kept the angels chasing shadows as long as they could, and sometimes a shadow was caught and killed but not before many angels had been sacrificed.

92-99-03 lifted his tattooed hand and touched the wire in his ear. "Stop pursuit," he said. "Force them into the open. Execute civilians."

And like a well-choreographed ballet, the angels turned around and retreated back through the alleys to the center streets, opened doors, ripped people from their homes, and shot them. As 92-99-03 floated over the city observing the carnage, he watched the Keepers immediately regroup.

"Attack incoming. Prepare yourself," 92-99-03 told them as his second-in-command simultaneously regurgitated tactical information—coordinates and enemy numbers—to the field agents below. The angels sorted through the chatter of the hive mind, immediately digesting what was pertinent to them, and prepared to spring their trap. 92-99-03 nodded to his second who then gave the command to deploy the second unit.

Green fire exploded in test shots from the second unit's flamethrowers as they marched through the city toward the square, the main point of contention. Two Keepers slipped out of the shadows and, like sly beasts, cut through the second unit, killing four men in one quick sweep. Then they were gone. The angels regrouped instantly and, forming a protective ring, continued to move toward the square. Another flash of darkness and, for just a second, their tight formation was disrupted. In that brief moment, chaos descended as several more angels dropped. The unit opened fire, shooting at every shadow and peripheral movement.

One of the firebug's tanks was pierced and he screamed as his back erupted in flame. His unit turned on him, kicking him away from the group. He stumbled toward the center of the street, tripped, and caught himself on the column of a magnificent red arch. The tank exploded. Massive splinters of wood flew in every direction, catching several angels and killing or wounding them. The pillar groaned as it swayed and the loud cracking sound of wood splitting drew the focus of everyone on the battlefield. The column pulled the golden latticework and connecting pillar down with it, smashing half of a building before it slammed into the square to hug what was left of the dragon statue, kicking up dust and crushing several angels under its weight.

99-92-03 tapped his silver sunglasses and the lenses cycled through spectrums to infrared. Through the massive cloud, he spotted all the heat signatures of the survivors. Most of his unit had cleared the landing and all of the Keepers were vacating the area, both teams regrouping even with wood chips still flying and dust kicked up so thick that neither side could see with the naked eye. He heard the gunfire, saw the Keepers as red and yellow shapes darting through the cloud, and watched them cut down the angels. The men still alive on the ground switched on the breathing apparatus installed in their nostrils and throats then activated the infrared on their glasses, ready to retaliate. Two bright red, beast-like shapes burst into their formation and cut them down.

99-92-03 watched the angels fall and launched the third unit. As the next wave of angels prepared to storm Hojo, a bright flare of green fire chewed up the great dust cloud and set several Keepers on fire. The rest of them scattered. Red concentrations of heat bloomed everywhere as the angels began to torch the square. The fallen arch was soon ablaze and 99-92-03 had to shift spectrums again. The Keepers were regrouping, he guessed, because even from his vantage point he could not find them. He communicated as much to the men on the ground. He filtered spectrums, one after the other, scanning the city. Then he saw it. Huddled against the dragon statue, masked by the heat of the fallen arch, was a large heat signature with two solid red figures among it.

"We've found them," 99-92-03 told the ground units as his second communicated the Keepers' coordinates. "Destroy them."

The fire team moved in as the rest followed with guns. The Keeper signature shrank against the dragon statue. 99-92-03 almost smiled.

And then a bright ball of yellow fire rained down from the sky, splattering his units and setting them alight. They immediately scattered like golden fireflies. 99-92-03 watched a white-hot figure drop out of the sky and land amid the flames. He knew who this Keeper was. Her codename was Flamefang. There was something different about her. A hole like a seed in her womb was a second signature, though it burned black like a void.

A second figure with barely any heat signature followed her out of the sky and landed near the Keepers huddled against the statue. 99-92-03 left the enhanced spectrum view and ordered the glider to move in closer.

Solo sat slumped in a chair in what had been designated his and Slot's bedroom. She was sprawled across the bed, mouth open, softly snoring. He watched her sleep, his little sister. He stared at her ratty clothes, at the dingy jeans too big for her tied on her hips with a belt unraveling at the ends and stuffed into scuffed street boots. She wore two layers of shirts that were ripped and faded, an old army-green jacket, fingerless gloves, and a sock hat. He had cut her hair like a boy's but extra fucked-up. Most people assumed she was a boy. That's what he had wanted when he stuffed her in his old clothes and chopped her hair off.

Growing up in an OT town like Cobbler, right next to the miner outpost of Biszler, he learned the lessons hard. Their dad had split before Slot was born and their mom gave up being a mom before Slot was even eight years old. Solo was the only one who could look after her and he kept her close. He saw how girls sometimes ended up. Many wound up working in the whore huts—a good career move considering the payoff. Occasionally, miners would get drunk and wander into town. Girls would get raped before the men wizened up and ran the fuckers out.

However, Slot had been spared the attention of men. As a child, she was a scrawny little thing that passed for a boy half the time since she was always covered in mud and grime. Her smile was bright and innocent, adding to the childish air that continued to revolve around her no matter how ugly the world got. And if it weren't for that long hair of hers, most people would never even second-glance to confirm her gender. And then she hit puberty. Suddenly she had breasts and hips and, even though she still wore Solo's hand-me-downs and played in the mud like a guy, she had all the attention of the men around town. He still got angry when he thought about that boy who once asked her if she had any slots for him to play in. He beat the kid so bad he suffered permanent brain damage. If Solo could do it again, he would kill him.

So when the rumors came in that cogwheelers were coming through Cobbler for recruits, he grabbed his sister up, chopped her hair off, wrapped her chest up, and buried her in layers of his clothes. The Black Hand did come through and, at ages 14 and 17, they became cogwheelers. It wasn't until she was much older that anyone realized she was a girl and by then the potential appeal had dried up entirely.

Solo's frown deepened as he stared at his sleeping sister. She rolled over, curled into a ball, and suddenly she looked like the girl she really was underneath all those baggy clothes and dirt. He wondered if deep down inside she would rather wear girl clothes and grow her hair out. What if she wanted a boyfriend one day? To get married and maybe even have kids? Solo shook his head, banishing the idea. She was still mentally a kid herself. Was that his fault? Did he keep her from growing up?

All he had ever done was try to protect her. He hid her away as a boy to keep her safe. And now the three of them—him and Jilk and her—were going to be killed on sight if any other cogs saw them. Maybe the best way to keep her safe now would be to change her appearance again. No one would be looking for a girl.

Solo stood up and went in search of an Obeheani. The first one he found, he stopped and asked, "Do you have any spare clothes?" She looked at him in confusion. "Girl clothes," he added as Jilk walked by.

"The big one might have something in your size," Jilk mumbled, making a height gesture to indicate the High Healer, who seemed to tower over everyone else. "You thinkin' of going girl, Solo? You'd make an ugly girl."

"Not for me," he muttered as the Obeheani rushed away. "For Slot."

Jilk snorted a laugh. "What for?"

"No one will recognize her if she's not covered in mud and wearing my jeans."

Jilk stared long and thoughtfully at him before nodding and casually walking over. "Look, you did a good job keeping her under the radar but Slot can take care of herself now. If she wants to wear a dress, she'll say something. Otherwise, leave it alone."

But Jilk didn't know how much influence Solo had over

his sister's decision-making. He told her dirt built character to keep her from bathing so often and giving herself away. After that, he had to tell her to take a bath before she did it. It was better than the alternative. He'd never seen his sister cry and he'd be damned if he ever would.

"Easy for you to say," Solo growled. "She's not your—"

"Not my what?" Jilk interrupted him with a glare. "Not my Heavy? Slot may be your sister, but she's been in my crew for years and I care about her as much as you do. I wouldn't let anything happen to her and I put my life on that."

"Why? Cause she hugged you a bit?"

Jilk's pale-as-ass face might've actually blushed—it was hard to tell. "No. Because she's my crew. And if it *bothers* you that she hugged me, take it up with her. But just so we're clear on something: you may have dressed her up like a boy but you couldn't gut her personality and it's pretty damn good. So unless you're prepared to lobotomize her, get used to the idea that *someone's* going to be looking."

Solo shoved his hands in his pockets and watched Jilk walk away. He guessed if anyone was okay to look at his sister, it was Jilk. Then again, maybe not. But if he put her in girl's clothes, he really couldn't contain the amount of looks that would be heading her way and he didn't really know if he could keep up with killing so many people.

When he walked back into the bedroom, he muttered, "Sorry, kid."

"For what?" she asked around a yawn.

"Nothing."

"There trouble?"

"No. Don't worry. I'm lookin' out. Go back to sleep."

She yawned again. "Kay." And did as he told her to.

Knick was hunched as he inched along the low-ceiling tunnel, hands pressed up against the rough roof for balance. Shade was ahead of him, crouched as well but managing to move much faster. He couldn't even see Lethan or Whiskey in the narrow, winding tunnel with its limited line of sight. It felt like they walked like that for hours until his neck and back was screaming in protest. Just when he thought he was going to have to call a break, Lethan shouted excitedly to them.

"We're here," he said. Knick hurried through to the end, emerging on the edge of a chasm. Below, he could see the Krueh-jin bustling like a great caravan. "We have found them."

Knick stretched, cracked his back and his neck, and shook the tension out of his limbs. He noticed Shade rubbing the back of her neck so he reached out and gently began massaging her shoulders. Her felt her tense beneath him and laughed.

"You're supposed to relax," he told her. After a moment, her shoulders slumped and he continued his work. He admired her slender, pale neck and the slope of her shoulders, wishing he could touch her more and knowing he didn't have a reason. He'd been in more compromising positions with her than this but somehow knowing how he felt made this simple gesture all the more intimate. When she groaned in the back of her throat, he leaned forward to whisper in her ear. "Better?"

"Yes," she replied quietly. Before he could say anything more, Lethan interrupted them.

"Knick," he began. "I cannot go into the camp. I will shadow the Kada and find you when you are done here."

"Wait, wait. Why can't you go in?"

"When I was exiled, I was forever cast out of the Kada. I cannot return."

"You're with me now, not the Kada, and I need you."

Lethan stared at him for a long moment with brows furrowed and his mouth in a hard line. Finally, he nodded that he understood. He signaled for them to extinguish their bracers and led the way down a winding, almost invisible path to the chasm floor. By then the Krueh-jin had spotted them and were waiting when he reached the bottom. Sabal was at the head of the group, arms folded across her chest and an amused expression on her wrinkled face.

"Knick Coltin," she said. "You return. And you bring a Keeper. Look, Kada," she announced to the Krueh-jin. "Ittori yo sansi Kada-Ka—*Knick Coltin*—todo iro se *Shada*." She pointed to Shade. The whole of the Kada gasped and muttered to one another, humbly bending in deep bows. Sabal's eyes softened when she looked at Lethan and then, in an instant, they were hard and narrow slits. "Lethan. He is not welcome among the Kada anymore."

"He isn't yours anymore, remember? Lethan is with me."

Knick raised his voice so everyone could hear, "Lethan is with me! Fuck with him? You fuck with me."

Sabal stared at him a long moment as if deliberating and then nodded. "Very well." She motioned them into the safety of the group.

As Knick came to stand next to her, he leaned in and whispered, "You can drop the act. I know you set him up."

"The act is not for you," she croaked quietly. "It is for them that do not understand." She led them toward the center of the gathering. "You have come to the Krueh-jin again," she said once they stopped. "Why?"

"To find Mesopotamia," he said as Shade tossed her the pendant they'd found in the statue of Asgard. Sabal caught it with trembling hands and stared at it like she might a ghost. "You're one of them, aren't you? One of the leaders of the Tribes of Typhi."

"Yes," she replied quietly. "We are the sons and daughters of Nippur. So you know who you are, Knick Coltin. I thought as much when I saw you with the Shada—the Keeper of Shadows. That is well. There is much you need to know and much more that needs doing."

"Information freely given, freely received, right?" he asked. Sabal grinned. "I'm listening."

"The five Tribes of Typhi were the original children of Meso-potamia, the first civilization. When the city was lost, the Tribes gathered together and tried to resurrect what had been 'buried beneath the secret sands'. They built Etemenenki, but were cursed and scattered."

"That much we do know."

Sabal regarded him for a drawn out moment and then spouted orders to the Kada in their strange language. Immediately, the Krueh-jin began to build wood fires and break out provisions. They did not set up tents or make camp in any other respect, just the fires, just the food. Sabal motioned for him to sit with her near the central bonfire burning blue and purple.

"The five Tribes," Sabal continued as several of her people put skinned animals on roasting sticks over the flames, "are the Krueh-jin, the Na Varen, Ka'djai, Skahradahn, and the Ataashvatan, who was the head of the Tribes even after the split. There are many stories to explain the evolution of the

Tribes and why we never came together again, but much was lost with the passage of time and much more was discarded as fable in new ages long passed that had no need for ancient stories. Today..." But she silenced herself and stared at the flames. When she shook her head and her eyes returned to Knick's, she continued. "I cannot speak for the others; I know them only in name. As for the Krueh-jin, only I know the stories and the truths—or what my people have perceived as truth. I have told the Kada what I can, what will not stretch the imagination too greatly. For now, we are gypsies, traveling the Grey, scouring the folds between overcity and undercity for relics of times we have almost completely forgotten. That is who we are now. That is our calling. Do you understand?"

Knick nodded. "You moved on," he surmised.

"Yes. But I knew I could not forget. The *stories*," she said, as though imploring him to understand, "the stories have been passed down through countless generations, lessons taught to the chiefs so that we would never forget."

"Forget what?" Knick asked.

"That the One would come, this One who 'will make secret those bottomless sands no more', who will 'open the gates to home, ancient and true', who will 'unite the Tribes under the shadow of Panghora, else release the binding of an ancient vow.' I don't know what this means, Knick Coltin." She tilted her chin up. "But I know that I am to send with you the best of us, to fight and die for you, to guide and protect you." She motioned to Lethan and Whiskey. "I knew that Lethan would be your light in the dark. That, too, was a story passed down. That the One—Kada-Ka—would come to the Krueh-jin before the appointed time and that Kada-Ka would never return if Shada was lost in the darkness. I sent Lethan with you, yes, forced him to go so that he could bring you back to us, so that I could fulfill the mission set to me thousands and thousands of years ago to guide you to the next Tribe so that the path would be revealed to you, the path home."

Knick stared long and hard at Sabal, not liking the humanity in her voice one bit. She had been deceptive at their last meeting, talking in riddles as though she knew something he did not, regarding him with an eye that held some great wisdom and truth—like she knew the mysteries of the universe and he was a fool. Now, she spoke open and freely, as though he was the reliever of her burdens. He didn't like it.

Knick's gaze went to Lethan. The mocha-skinned man stared at the dirt. What a compliment he had been paid, the best of them exiled and cast out. What was that worth? Then he looked at Shade who was frowning as she stared at the Crone, violet eyes seemingly glowing as they reflected the purple and blue fire.

"Why didn't you tell me this before?" he wanted to know, anger prickling inside of him. How much would have changed had he just known?

"Because what you needed to hear was not what you wanted to hear, and now what you want to hear and need to hear are the same," she replied. "Before, you among us was an accident. Now, you among us is because you came looking for us, to seek out what it is that you needed to know."

"Don't bullshit me!" he exclaimed, startling the woman who came to take the roast off the fire.

"I am not," Sabal replied smoothly. "You would not have received my words had I told you before you wanted to hear them. It is simple."

"It's not simple!" he insisted. "If I had known, I could have—"

"Could have what?" the Crone asked in challenge. "Saved the Sworn?"

Sabal snapped her fingers. The crowd parted, allowing several Krueh-jin through. They carried a litter with a long cloth stretched over a body. Knick stood up, eyes fixated on the covered lump. He slowly walked over and pulled the cloth away. Hezara's skin was dead-white aside from the tattoos and the deep bruise on her cheek. She still had all of her piercings except for the delicate chain. He could see where it had been ripped out of her ear and nose. There was a split in her lip, black with congealed blood. Thankfully, her eyes had been closed.

"Hezara," he muttered guiltily. "Did you—" he began, angrily turning to look at Sabal, but what he saw was Shade coming to stand next to him. She studied the corpse.

"Donovan," she said darkly. "This has traces of aegis all over it." She looked at Knick and he stared hard at her, frowning, quietly asking for some kind of answer. Shade's expression was so gentle that it sucked him out of his anger at this injustice and into the comfort of her presence. "I knew this woman," she told him. "I sent her to the Keepers the morning before you and I made our pact to help each other."

"We retrieved her body," Sabal told them, the fire popping noisily in the awkward silence between sentences.

Knick covered up the Bloodsworn and turned away. "Why?" he asked, remembering how the Krueh-jin had taunted her with their rules.

"She died serving and protecting the Keepers," the Crone answered. "We do not bury the dead but we pay our respects. Now you, too, may pay your respects to the Sworn."

Sabal motioned to the Krueh-jin and they carried Hezara away. The group sat back down and a woman served them each a plate of food. Knick didn't know what type of meat it was but it was surrounded with pul potatoes and some strain of mushroom. He stared numbly at the food for a long time, unsure if he could eat after having just seen the corpse of a friend—well, someone he used to know, at any rate. He didn't know if he considered Zara a friend. She wasn't an enemy; that was certain. She had worked his nerves almost every second they had traveled together, but she had had his back as long as she called him companion.

Knick looked up at Sabal and the other Krueh-jin. They were eating as though a corpse hadn't just been paraded through their camp. Even Lethan was clearing his plate, passing off pieces of potato and beef to Whiskey every so often. He glanced at Shade. She was eating slowly, purposeful. He remembered that back when he was an angel, it didn't bother him, either. But he didn't want to be like that anymore. He didn't think he could even if he tried. He was too connected, too involved with his emotions. That was the angel trick—the disconnect. *They* disconnected you, though, and once you reconnected…you were shit out of luck unless *they* disconnected you again.

Knick forked a potato and shoved it in his mouth, refusing to think about the angels. He knew the reason why the Krueh-jin and Shade could eat after seeing Hezara's body and it had nothing to do with the disconnect. It was because they had seen it before, seen it enough, and had come to peace with it.

"We waited so long," Sabal began, interrupting the quiet. "Generations and generations ago, they started to believe you would never come. But Red, she knew...she *knew* you were coming."

"Red," Knick echoed. "How do you know Red?"

"She was the leader of the Ataashvatan and of the Tribes. Once. Before she died. I don't know who took her place."

Knick wondered if Rosk ever knew. Red wasn't off on some adventure without him; she was following an ages-old destiny to help the Keepers. She was the leader of *the* Tribes of Typhi. And she was dead because of it. It was bullshit. He didn't believe in prophecy or destiny, but did believing in it make it real? How many people were going to die for something they couldn't possibly know was true? They had said Mesopotamia was the first civilization. How many civilizations had passed since then?

"What's all this for?" Knick asked in agitation. "Who the hell cares about Mesopotamia anyway? The first civilization, so what? I'm sure we've improved in the thousands and thousands of years it's been since then. What's so important that we need to go back—that people are dying for it?"

Sabal shrugged. "For that, you will need to ask Hermes."

Shade stopped eating and locked her eyes on the Crone. "Who?" she asked.

The Crone's moon-like eyes went from one to the other, back and forth, in perplexity. "Hermes," she repeated, this time more as a question. "The Keeper. You know him. You must."

"If there was a Hermes in the Order, he is dead now," Shade told her.

"No," Sabal whispered. "No. Hermes was supposed to prepare you. He was to tell you things you *must* know. He cannot be dead."

"Tell me what?" Shade asked in a hard tone.

"I don't know," she confessed. "He promised that when the One appeared, he would prepare the Shada. That is why he came to us, to the Tribes. He held Lethan at his birth, saw his eyes, said 'This boy is the one.' That is why he bid us uncover the statue. That is why he gave it to Red—"

"The statue? The statue of Asgard?" Knick interrupted.

"Yes. We found it for him—a clue for the One. He gave it to Red—"

"He *killed* Red," Knick insisted.

"No, he would never. It wasn't safe, you see. The statue. He gave it to Red for safekeeping. One of them had to survive, he said, her or the statue. She told me because she needed one of our Kada-Si to help her. I sent her Gru. I never saw him again."

Knick remembered the name from the letter. Parts of the story fit, but Red had written that Hermes or Muriel had killed her. Shade said Hermes was dead and corpses didn't count, which meant it had to be Muriel. So who the hell was Hermes?

"The world that hangs in the Balance is about to sway," the Crone said, passing her plate off to a nearby Krueh-jin. "Na Varen. You must go to the Na Varen, the Sirens of Uruk. To the Bleak Shores." She looked at her mocha-skinned, blue-eyed chosen. "Lethan knows the way. Now come," she said, standing. Someone doused the fire. "There is still some distance we must go."

Daelus stepped under the cleansing heat of the shower and let it run over him in steaming rivulets. In the haze and low light, he traveled back through his memories and replayed his life, the active moments and the passive ones, from the strong man he had once been to the meek character he had been forced to play. No, not forced. Chose. He braced his hands against the clay tile walls and bent into the water. He tried to remember all of those secrets he had hidden inside himself, banished to a box he locked and buried within. Perhaps it was time to open it again.

He dug it up. There, in the steam and water, he gingerly brushed off the dust and dirt and held the box of buried secrets in his hands. Suddenly, he was afraid. He had been waiting for this moment for over two decades and now he was too scared to go through with it. Shakily, he reached out and unlocked it. And then her face flashed in front of his eyes. Shade's face. The vision of her, not the real woman. The vision he saw all those years ago. The secrets held within the box were hard to remember, but the reason for the box was a thing he had never forgotten. The reason was Shade.

For one moment in time, he had seen her smiling brightly, laughing, eyes bright. And then reality came crashing back in. Those sharp, violet eyes and that hard expression flashed before him. *One of us did to them what they did to us.* Daelus tucked the box away. He had lost his nerve.

Daelus quickly finished his shower, toweled off, and dressed in his Keeper blacks. After a quick meal, he laced up leather boots and pulled on his trench coat, buckling the series of clasps down the front. He strapped his sword onto his back and made his way through Sanctuary's twisting hallways out to the main hall. Eros met him by the door.

"I will find her," Daelus promised the Baron. "I will learn what she knows and I will make sure she understands that we are still on the same side."

Eros nodded. "And give her these."

Daelus held out his hand as Eros gently handed him the braided leather bracelet with the tiny, silver bells. He looked up at Eros and nodded. The Baron smiled at him, clasped his shoulder, and squeezed it.

"Be safe, Daelus," he said.

"And you as well, Baron. For the Balance."

"For the Balance."

The Baron walked away. Daelus looked at the bracelet in his palm and felt his heart skip a beat. He was going to find Shade. He had to make her understand. He thought back to the last time he had seen her, to the hours following the destruction of Asgard. He had all but begged her to trust him, had held her in his arms for a brief second. But the moment that stood out most in his memory was when she pulled away, how empty he had felt. She had trusted him with one task and one task only, which meant she did not trust him entirely. Since when had she lost faith in him? He wished he knew.

"You're going, too," a girl said, pulling him out of his thoughts. He looked up at Casey's passive expression. "It seems before too long there won't be anyone left."

"Casey—"

"Be careful," she said. "I don't want Dad having to patch you up when you get back, do you hear?"

"I hear," he replied. She smiled at him.

"Good."

He watched her leave, this surprisingly strong young woman. Physically, she was the opposite of Shade in every way. Blond hair, tanned skin, and green eyes versus Shade's black hair, pale skin, and violet eyes. Their personalities were even different. What he knew of Casey was warm and friendly and caring. Shade was...guarded. And yet as he watched Casey walk away, he couldn't help but think of Shade. That strength that came from within—not from others or objects— was rare and both women possessed it.

Watching Casey, he couldn't help but admire her.

Red fire consumed green fire as waters pulled from the river extinguished them, and the angels that flooded Hojo were washed away. Seeing two Interim had joined their fight, the Kur that had been pushed back and cornered exploded out of their alcove and into the fight with renewed vigor. Dimitri and Vox led the charge and fire was the cleansing agent that drove them back.

The fanged aegis left scars in the sky from which the Sovereign ripped her fire. Those wispy, sheer layers she wore rippled and bounced and swayed in the created energy, dancing just out of reach of the flames every time she stepped through them. Fire could not burn Vox, not the angels' fire or her own.

They fought the angels there in the streets, closing the gap so tightly that the angels were forced to abandon their guns and fight with Nightwalkers. Metal rang against metal as the roar of fire circled the battlefield. Vox saw in her peripherals that Dimitri never strayed far from her, continuously checking her status. It was not an unwelcome gesture, but unnecessary. She hadn't felt this good in days. Energy vibrated within her, sloughed off of her in excess. She felt so alive.

Her scimitar ripped through one angel after another, heat from the fang cauterizing wounds as she inflicted them. The smell of burned flesh crowded the area. The bells on her wrist jingled as she parried several swings and plunged her weapon up into the chest of one of her attackers. He burst into flame and was wholly consumed, crunching when he fell to the ground as little more than a charred husk.

The others attacking her backed away in hesitation but the blank stare of their silver lenses told Vox that the Hive Mind would not accept that flicker of fear, immediately overriding the emotion the second it was felt. They rushed in again, as she anticipated. The bells on her wrist jingled again as she struck the ground with her weapon and sent out a shockwave of heat, propelling them backward. They landed in lumps, skin bubbling and burned.

A ring of fire closed the gap between her and the other Keepers. She could hear Dimitri calling out to her. There were more enemies for her to fight, however, and so she pressed on.

"I'm fine!" she told him over the roar of flame and chased the others toward the perimeter of the city, cutting down one after another.

And as though karma had caught up with her for her lies, she felt a tremor of pain in her gut. Vox stumbled, clutched her stomach, and waited still as stone for the feeling to pass. The remaining angels crowded around her, observing. They inched closer, assessing her weakness. Another pulse of pain ripped through her and she screamed. A protective flash of fire whipped around her like a storm, scorching everyone and everything near her. She dropped the fang and fell to her knees, crying out and holding her stomach tightly. Her whole body hurt in a way she had never felt before, originating in her womb, and she curled into a ball, kicked, flailed, clawed at the ground.

And then there was darkness.

They had been walking for hours through tunnel and burrow, uphill and down—they even got down on their stomachs and crawled like spelunkers in a two-foot, sometimes less, crawlspace under what he perceived as a million tons of rock. That was not Knick's favorite moment of the trip. He sincerely hoped they didn't have to go back that way when they left.

"How much farther is it?" he asked when the sewage pipe opened up to another pipe dead ahead and a blasted out tunnel on the right. Sabal motion to the sloping tunnel even as Krueh-jin filed into it.

"Not much further," she replied. "Tonight, we sleep under the sky."

Knick looked at Shade who appeared just as confused as he was. Under the sky? He was convinced they were closer to the core of the earth than the sky. But Lethan was smiling in excitement. He reached out and motioned for them to follow.

"Come," he said. "Quickly!"

They pushed through the people crowding inside the tunnel, almost jogging when it flattened out, sometimes sliding down when it sloped. Lethan continued to shout "Come" or "Hurry" whenever they fell behind. Knick kept muttering apologies to everyone he bumped into. The tunnel opening at the bottom of an incline came in sight. He reached out to brush the wall as he slid the rest of the way down, joining the Krueh-jin exiting the tunnel. Lethan was smiling, waving him into the cavern beyond.

Knick held his breath when he looked up. Shade gasped and came to stand next to him. The ceiling was encrusted with so many gems that the blackness above looked like a night sky littered with stars. A shimmer of color undulated above like an aurora underground. A pond with phosphorescent algae swayed in the water, bouncing light around the room. Below them in a basin around the central plateau were hundreds of crystal formations that sparkled.

"We're surrounded by stars," Shade whispered in awe.

Knick slowly reached out to touch her and gently touched her hand. She wrapped her fingers around his for just a moment and then she was wandering off, head craned to take in the breathtaking view. He watched her. She was beautiful under that jeweled sky, the shadows edging toward her wherever she walked, surrounding her like a dark, protective aura. She was a dark star in the sky.

"You love her," Sabal said, appearing beside him. Knick looked at her, back at Shade, and then shook his head.

"I don't know what you're talking about."

"I'm just old, boy, I'm not blind," she crooned smugly and walked away. Knick flipped his middle finger at the back of her head.

The Krueh-jin set up their camp on the plateau and chose the highest point for the funeral pyre. Knick watched the preparations with a knot in his stomach and a cigarette between his lips. *Even dogs care, so we'll say you're a dog,* Hezara had once told him. She was right. He was wandering here to there, fully caught up in something so important that the world was changing because of it, trying to be as uninvolved as possible. He ran after Shade and followed at her heels like a puppy but was perfectly content to refuse to commit. Hezara had asked for his help and he had shrugged at her. Shade had offered to teach him how a Keeper fights for his own safety and he had refused. So much for being the One. He was the one who no one could depend on, and yet all of his friends were out there putting their lives on the line for him.

Fuck, but it sounded crazy! The One, Mesopotamia, Tiamat, Keepers—all of it. It sounded like some fucked up digital he might stream late at night when he couldn't get to sleep. But this was real. And Jilk and the siblings had gone with him into enemy territory all because he was "family"—that word that said he belonged with them. They dumped the Cogs for him, because he was involved, and didn't once try to talk him out of believing he was some ridiculous prophecy's foretold special somebody. They didn't ask what he was smoking, just where it was they needed to go and what it was he needed them to do.

His friends were fighters. They had fought through the Keeper ambush and come back for more. Shade was a warrior like no one he had ever seen. Otto had nearly died chasing a dream. Even Hezara had done what she could with all of her strength, fighting to uncover the truth to save an organization she had nothing to do with. They were all fighting with very ounce of their being. So what was his excuse?

Knick exhaled tendrils of gray smoke as he watched the Krueh-jin lower Hezara on top of the pyre. Shade walked up to stand next to him.

"Teach me," he said, "how to fight like you do."

She looked at him for a long time before asking, "Are you sure that's what you want?"

"Yeah," he replied as the chanting to send Hezara's spirit to paradise began. "It's what I want." He would never forgive himself if something happened to Jilk or Slot or Solo because he wasn't man enough to commit. "I can't say this is my destiny but, whatever's happening, I'm involved. This is real. So I'm here. You shouldn't be the only weapon." He took a drag on his cigarette. "It's not like you like the killing either. I was just making excuses."

"I don't like the killing," she confirmed, "but I have been doing it a long time."

"So have I," he said, folding down his glove to show her the angel wing tattoo. Shade nodded.

"But my actions have been my choice," she reminded him. Well, she had him there.

"Okay," he agreed, "but *this* is my choice."

Shade studied him, violet eyes soft, expression almost gentle. The chanting finished and the Krueh-jin lit the pyre, drawing both of their gazes. A bonfire of blue and purple fire burned in eerie quiet, making the gems overhead shimmer beautifully. He took the last drag on his rette and tossed it into the flames, watching Hezara's pale, tattooed face disappear in the fire.

This would be the last friend he burned. He could almost make that vow. Almost.

Thick columns of black smoke rose high into the sky like fingers reaching for heaven. As the citizens of Hojo scrambled to put out the fires overtaking their city and people shouted for their friends and loved ones, angel agent 99-92-03 and his company stepped across the charcoal remains of some wooden structure, smoldering coals crunching beneath their shoes. They stopped in front of the unconscious form of a woman in orange sheers with fire-like hair. She was codenamed Flamefang by the angels, a high-ranking operative within the Order of the Keepers, wielder of a Dionysian artifact, and—most importantly—a child was growing in her womb.

Someone was calling out for someone named "Vox" and the shouts were coming closer. 99-92-03 motioned to his companions and they immediately sprung into perfectly choreographed action. Four gathered her up while two others used their gadgets to quickly create a field stretcher. When she was strapped onto it, 99-92-03 called the skyglider into range. It hissed as it lowered itself to their position, kicking up ash and coal with the deceleration jets. 99-92-03 let his company load her onto the skyglider and secure the stretcher into the base before he stepped on.

99-92-03 surveyed the scene one last time to make sure there were no witnesses, no other treasures left behind, and tapped the console to give the thrusters more power. They blew away any sign of life on the ground as the skyglider rose out of the city into the black smoke and set a course for the waiting shuttle. 99-92-03 touched his earpiece.

"Operations. This is 99-92-03. I have operative Flamefang in custody, alive and unconscious. I'm escorting her to Heaven immediately. Confirm."

The screech that came through the earpiece was one of great elation and high praise.

Part Three

"Great perils have this beauty, that they bring light to the
fraternity of strangers."

Victor Hugo

A storm was raging. Wind whipped wildly back and forth, tugging at every strand of hair on the old shaman's head, at every article of clothing that she wore. Swollen water droplets rained down in a harsh torrent, drowning everything the sea could not touch. And the sea was a violent void under a black sky, churning and crashing and breaking against the docks and piers, undulating like the measured heartbeat of the world racing toward its end. The thick masses of coal-dark clouds covered the sky for miles so that the whole of Lotus Maze seemed swallowed in the tempest. Lightning streaked in bright, bold veins as though the gods were throwing bolts, not electrostatic discharges connecting earth and sky. Thunder cracked and roared, overtaking the surges of the sea.

The shaman stood on the sodden wooden planks that stretched across the raging Karnak Sea, bare feet awash with salt water. She hummed to herself, a melody that somehow could not be drowned by the storm. The tune bonded with the crashing waves and thundering flashes of light, transforming the storm into a transmitter of the eerie song. And as the shaman hummed, she rattled bones between her bony fingers. At the next peal of lightning, she cast them at her feet and they fell like stones from her hands. They rolled along the planks and settled, and not even the rushing water could sway them from their place, not even a fraction of an inch.

The shaman slowly lowered her aged bones to the dock and knelt before the sign, still humming. Another woman's voice joined in the song and then another and another until a group of women hummed and sang, and their voices were carried through the stormy night. The sirens crowded around the shaman, some walking barefoot onto the dock and others emerging from the raging sea. They stared at her with large, bright, watery eyes and waited for the message of the bones.

The shaman tilted her head up to look at her sirens, wrinkled and thin eyelids barely sheltering her cloudy eyes from the rain, and all at once their voices ceased the song.

"They are coming," the shaman told them. A young woman with pink hair tied into wet braids and twisted into locks stepped through the crowd to look at the old woman and the shaman stared into the girl's cyan eyes. "The Shadows bear the One. Your time has come, Tikal."

The sirens gasped and cooed and sighed in happiness,

crowding around their sister in congratulatory praise and comfort. And the one known as Tikal smiled, knowing her destiny was at hand. Once more, the sirens hummed and sang all as one, each a precious part of a greater melody, a perfect and beautiful and eerie sound. The sound of the beginning and of the end.

The sound of Panghora's Chant.

The world was made of shale and shadow. Shade stood with her back to the bottomless chasm that severed the land and stared at the massive black gate and giant golems that blocked her entry into the fortified wall. Those eyeless golems stared at her—she could sense it. They were waiting. They were all of them waiting, the whole of the city, the golems and the gate and the wall, and everything beyond.

Living shadow clung to her, cascaded down her frame to form the folds of a dress, and it trained behind her as she walked forward. Smoky vapors misted from the garment and excess shadow sloughed off and dissipated. As she walked, a grinding sound filled the still air and the gate opened. A grand city of another age stretched out before her. Flat-topped buildings of varying heights clustered as far as the eye could see. The windows were black and the streets were empty; there wasn't a single sign of life but she could feel the eyes on her, thousands of eyes all focused on her from every direction.

She slowly walked down those dusty streets and studied the blocky buildings. None were more than a few stories high with square windows and doors. Pottery clustered here and there, in window sills and door stoops and hanging from wooden pegs that lined the roofs. She stepped through one of the doorframes and walked through a black corridor to the center of the structure. A dead garden was soft beneath her footsteps. Above her, a square hole in the ceiling let in bleak light. Shade continued through the house and walked out onto another street.

She found herself on another main road that ran straight to the ziggurat that stood at the heart of the city on a hilltop, towering over everything. She stopped to stare at it, her skin prickling in alarm. Suddenly, a pulse rocketed through the earth and shook her to the core. The shadowy dress changed form and became a set of armor to shield her. Shade stared hard at the black opening of the ziggurat, felt the dark thing inside stirring. She could not see it but she could feel it seeping out of the temple and slithering down the steps. A loud whistling sounded in the distance and grew louder, racing toward her.

Shade's heart began pounding as she recognized the whistle was a scream. She drew her sword and prepared to meet whatever was coming at her.

"Don't!" a voice whispered in alarm. She felt someone reaching out to her. "Run!"

Shade snapped up in her bedroll with Knick leaning over her, brow pressed in concern.

"Are you all right?" he whispered.

"I'm fine," she replied. "It was a dream."

"Some dream," he muttered.

Shade looked at him for a long moment, at the backdrop of glittering gems that looked like stars, at his black, messy hair, at how dark his eyes looked in the lowlight, at his skin caressed by faint blue and purple firelight. Most of all she saw the concern in his expression and the way he pretended he was too hard to care. She found herself clinging to his sleeves as he supported her, found herself centered in his gravity. For so long, she had been following her instincts into this crazy turning of the Balance and those instincts had led her back and back again to Knick.

It wasn't until she stared up at him in that intimate darkness, with the universe seemingly surrounding him, that she realized something very important: Knick *was* her center of gravity. She had gone into Heaven to save him because she could do nothing else.

"Are you sure you're okay?" he asked, snapping her out of her thoughts. "Not that I don't enjoy you clinging onto me like this but, if you wanted to cuddle, you just have to say so." Shade let go of him and he grinned. "I thought so. C'mon. Lethan says it's time to go."

Shade watched him walk away before slipping out of her blankets and lacing up her boots. Almost all of the Krueh-jin were still asleep, except for those who stood watch and a few mothers nursing hungry babies. Sabal waited with Lethan, Whiskey, and Knick at the mouth of a tunnel. The Crone put her hands on Shade and muttered some kind of prayer. Shade looked at Knick who rolled his eyes, giving away the fact that it had happened to him as well. She almost smiled. When Sabal had finished, she stared seriously at them.

"Farewell, Knick Coltin. Keeper." To Lethan, she merely nodded. "Kada se Kada oto me nina kayo."

Lethan nodded back to her and motioned for them to follow. Shade took one last look at the starry expanse above them and the aurora-like shimmer of color. When they were out of earshot of the Kada, Knick tapped Lethan on the shoulder.

"What was that about?"

"It was a blessing," Lethan replied, "something we Krueh-jin say to one another when we must part from the whole."

"What does it mean?"

"Roughly…to go where you must and return to where you belong."

Knick took a deep breath and folded his hands behind his head. Shade peered at him and studied his expression as they walked.

"What are you thinking?"

"Hm?" He glanced back at her and shrugged. "Oh. Nothing. Just that I don't really belong anywhere. I was forced to be an angel. I was a cogwheeler out of necessity. Even you had Asgard and the Keepers. Lethan had the Krueh-jin. I don't know where I'd go at the end of all this."

"Perhaps you have not been there yet," Lethan said thoughtfully. "Perhaps Mesopotamia is your home, the place where you belong."

"Or perhaps it's right beside you," Shade said quietly. Knick stopped and stared at her in shock and hope and something else she didn't know.

"What?" he whispered.

"You said as much yourself when you interpreted your own prophecy. That the One was meant to be with the Shadows. For now, that is where you belong."

She saw the disappointment in his eyes when she justified her words with prophecy but he quickly masked it with annoyance.

"You're a tease," he muttered and continued walking.

Shade suddenly laughed. Knick glanced back at her and his expression softened. She didn't know why but she continued to laugh, some heavy burden suddenly lifted.

In the aftermath of the Angel-Keeper confrontation, the holding of Hojo was quiet. The early morning fog settled thick among the low-hanging smoke and a light rain blew in from Tarsus. Most of the fires had been put out, the only remaining ones being the contained burners eating through the last remains of scattered wood. A voice made hoarse from all the smoke was calling out in the mist.

"Vox!" Dimitri yelled. "Vox!" He followed the scorch marks on the ground to where they ended in an ash heap and angel corpses. "Vox!" He kicked smoldering boards aside and shoved fallen arch frames away, but Vox's corpse was not among the dead. Relief flooded him with the same amount of dread. Where was she? "Vox!"

Dimitri remembered Dr. Basset's words. Perhaps whatever the doctor had been concerned over had plagued her once more. She would return to Sanctuary if she wasn't fit to fight. Dimitri jogged back to the Kur, reminding himself every step of the way not to run. There was nothing to run for. He would not panic. Vox was back at Sanctuary and she was fine and their baby was healthy.

"Captain," he called when he saw Delia discussing something with a young, twitchy boy. "Your compad."

"Sir," she said and looked elsewhere. "Kallo!" Her brother turned from his business. She held out her hand and said nothing but Kallo understood. It could have meant a million things but somehow the twins always knew what the other was thinking. He brought it quickly and Delia passed it to him. "Here you are, sir."

"Thank you." Dimitri walked away from them and tapped the symbols for the corresponding compad. The busy signal did not persist long before Eros' face appeared. "Baron."

"Dimitri. What's happened?"

"We've beaten back the angel presence in Hojo, though the city itself is in disrepair."

The Baron sighed. "And the tunnel?"

"The angels interrupted the process of sealing it. Delia and Kallo are still working on it."

"I see. You should remain behind and guard them until the job is finished. Send Vox home."

"Vox." Dimitri's blood ran cold.

"Yes?"

"She hasn't returned to Sanctuary?"

"She hasn't." The Baron's expression changed. He must have been thinking of Basset's warning. "She isn't in Hojo," he surmised.

"I haven't found her but I've only searched the battlefield."

"That does not mean she is not within the city. She could have been injured or was feeling unwell and retreated to the safer parts. Find her."

"Yes, Baron. I will update you soon on our progress." He ended the call. "Captains!" He turned to Kallo and Delia. "Organize a search party. Interim Vox has gone missing."

"Yes, sir, of course," Delia said. "But sir, we've lost so many men as it is. We don't have enough to search for Vox and gather the supplies we need to blow the tunnel."

"She is here and she is safe!" Dimitri exclaimed, feeling his nerves begin to fray. At his outburst, the Kur went rigid. He had never been one to shout. Dimitri took a deep breath. "It won't take long," he said quietly, "to find her. Organize a search party."

"Yes, sir," Kallo replied solemnly.

As the twins turned to gather their men, Dimitri immediately headed off into the city. His blood was ice and his heart was racing and a nauseating knot in his stomach made him feel as though bile was trapped in his esophagus. He didn't know why he was scared. Vox was a warrior of remarkable skill. She would laugh at him when she found him so worried. But he couldn't shake the feeling that something was wrong. Something was wrong with his lover and his child. They were in danger.

The idea was a threat that nearly drove him to madness.

The thirteen delegates sat in the circulet quietly, staring beneath hoods that covered their eyes to protect their identity and impartiality when in front of those who were not the Regent, Baron, High Counselor, or Cleric. Pointless now considering the circumstances but old habits and tradition died the hardest. From what Rexis could tell, the delegates were all in good health; there was no unusual aging or rot on their hands or around their mouths. Not like the Regent. As he spoke, the decay was becoming hard to ignore. He had not looked this way the day they had left the Order. He was beginning to think the two were connected. And if they were, should he be worried? He was too young to rot.

As the Regent discussed his plans, Rexis took a deep breath and held it for as long as he could. The smell was getting stronger. He wasn't sure how the delegates sat there day after day.

"As for your missions," Muriel said, "once Malkira is found, we will need to hurry. There is something very important we have not attended to."

"The Enoch," Rexis guessed.

"Yes," Muriel whispered. "She is the key."

"She?" Donovan asked.

Muriel grinned, revealing two rows of rotting teeth. "My scouts tell me that she is no longer within Asgard walls. Eros must have smuggled her out during the attack. He and the others will be cowering within Sanctuary." His gaze turned to Rexis, the whites of his eyes now spotted gray and brown. "You couldn't have known the Enoch's true nature then, but tell me now: do you recall a small wisp of a woman with long, blonde hair being smuggled out?"

"No, Your Excellency, but that does not mean she was not there. There was so much chaos during that time. The other Interim and I headed and followed the survivors, and there were so many wounded... We wouldn't have noticed." Rexis hesitated and then added, "The Enoch is a woman?"

The Regent might've smirked but the slight lift of his lips beneath the wrinkle of skin looked more like a snarl.

"The Enoch is a child," he hissed, "and a child we desperately need if we are to rebuild the Keeper Order as it was meant to be—powerful and uncorrupted."

A side door down to the archives suddenly swung open and an old man hobbled into the room. All heads turned in his direction and silently watched him struggle to stand before the Regent. He tried to bow but collapsed onto both knees. Pain streaked across his face but the impatient scowl of the Regent forced him to overcome the anguish. Rexis pitied him.

"My Lord Regent," the scholar rasped. "We think we have found it. Malkira's location." He waited in the silence for some sort of affirmation but all he received was expectant stares. "The texts seem to indicate a site called Go'sam where sacred artifacts were stored. Many of them were poached during various times, but Malkira would have been especially protected." Another pause yielded more silence so the monk continued. "The site itself was buried within Kishar but the only access point is in Anshar on the outskirts of Monarch at Tiboili."

Finally the Regent nodded and motioned to dismiss the monk. "Well done," he said. "Assemble an excavation team and have them leave immediately." When the monk nodded and hobbled off, the Regent looked at Rexis and Donovan. "Go. Find it."

Daelus traversed the sky, a black shooting star in the twilight. The place where Shade had disappeared was in Rashrima Haan and that opening had been closed with the aerial attack. Many mine entrances had been sealed by Keepers already but the sewer entrance close to the ruins of Asgard was still open. That was his destination. So he flew, an embodiment of void, consciousness subdued to a primal level. There was no room for deep thought in the black star. It was almost a relief to his burdened mind and troubled heart. So he held onto the rumbling void that threatened to spit him out if he relaxed his grip just a little, held on to steer it to his destination—to Shade.

Then he heard it. He heard it before he saw it—the sound of men screaming both in fear and in anger, the sound of guns popping off and explosives rocking the earth. He guided his body toward the ground then relaxed his grip on the void and was ejected from the black cloud, falling out of the sky and landing in a crouch. He stood up and walked to the edge of the platform he had chosen as his perch. Beneath him was the empty water basin where his entrance to the sewers was located, and filling up the basin were cogwheelers and angels in open war. The carnage had spread beyond the basin toward Rashrima Haan and he knew that reinforcements would be coming—from both sides. The fighting would spread to the city. People would be hurt, killed.

His hand went to his sword and pulled it two inches out of its sheath before he stopped. The war had begun in spite of the Keepers' efforts to stop it. And even if they had plugged a few holes to the Mine, they couldn't get them all. If he stopped for every skirmish, he would never proceed with his mission. Daelus let his sword slide back into the sheath. He couldn't fight every battle. He couldn't pick sides—there were no sides to pick. The orders had always come down from above, guided by the wisdom of the Oracle and Enoch. Who was he to make a choice on his own? The cogwheelers were assaulting Anshar; they started this war. That seemed the logical course, but there were thousands of invisible factors that tied into the Balance. He couldn't possibly know them all.

There was one detail that he couldn't get out of his mind, however—that all of the men in the basin were killers and that the people of Rashrima Haan had seen enough death.

Daelus ran and jumped off of his vantage point, drawing his sword in midair. The bells on his wrist jingled as he brought the tip of the sword down in front of him. It struck concrete before his feet did, and a shockwave of electricity lit up the basin in a flash, thunder crackling from the discharge. When he stood up, there was silence and charred bodies surrounded him. He sheathed his sword, gently removed a corpse from the sewer passage, and climbed down into the darkness.

The problem with the Grey was that it all looked the same, all pipes and natural tunnels and caves that made up the Road, the name the Krueh-jin had given to the "highway through the Grey". Sometimes there were big pipes you could walk through and other times just long crawlspaces of hollowed out earth but it was always the same change in scenery, minus the occasional cave covered in colorful fungi. And it completely disoriented one's sense of direction. The brain automatically calculated the direction headed as north and to move in any other direction—say east—was considered the subsequent heading until it was traveled so long that the brain turned it into north again. There was up and down and, since it was impossible to tell how close to the surface or the Mine one was, it was just imagined that up meant closer to the surface and down meant closer to the Mine—and neither direction was comforting to walk.

But walk they did, following Lethan blindly far to the southeast—so he said—heading for the Na Varen. Knick glanced at Shade. Every morning, Lethan woke Shade to keep watch and left to scout ahead—always gone an hour, maybe two—and then Knick would be woken, they would have a quick breakfast, and be on their way. Only lately, Shade had taken to waking him, too. To spar. He had thought he would be receiving combat lessons but all they had practiced was simple hand-to-hand combat. That was something he could do blindfolded.

Knick wondered if there was some other untapped potential inside of him. As much as he denied being a Keeper, Shade had seen the glyph on his forehead. Did that mean he had some sort of strange power like her? Knick yawned and folded his arms behind his head. He wasn't sure if the idea freaked him out or excited him.

"Hey," he said, catching her attention. "You've said I'm the One and all, but you never told me what that means. What is the *One* exactly?"

Shade stared thoughtfully ahead of them, looking but not really seeing the gently curving tunnel. "I'm ashamed to admit it but there is little about the One that the Keepers remember. A coming legend originated so far in our histories that we know next to nothing of him, only that we are to revere and expect him…the One, the ender of all things."

"The ender of all things?" he echoed in distaste. "No offense but you guys are crazy. I wouldn't be waiting around on me to show up."

"You are not meant to be feared, Knick." She looked at him a moment then back at the Road. "You embody a change sanctioned by the Balance. Sanctioned imbalance."

"The Kada has a different view," Lethan said from over his shoulder. "For our people, the Kada-Ka was a legendary figure from our stories. We call him the Nomad. He wanders place to place, changing faces to blend in with his surroundings as he searches for the secret the world lost. Sabal says this secret is the home of the Tribes, and that Kada-Ka will guide us there so that we wander no more. She believes we are in the time of our Last Wandering, and I believe it, too."

"So in one version, I give lost people a home and, in the other, I destroy everything." He pointed to Lethan. "I'm going with his version."

"Go with whatever you like," Shade said, "they are all parts of the same whole. Refusing to see that will only incomplete you."

Knick frowned. "That's not fair."

They walked into a dead end. A stone wall completely blocked their path but about ten feet up was a large hole that led into another tunnel. Lethan sent Whiskey up before he quickly scaled it and disappeared, scouting ahead.

"Do you think I have any kind of, you know, special powers or anything?" Knick asked as they waited. Shade shrugged.

"I don't know. It's possible." She looked almost bashful when she said, "We are all a bit interested in seeing what you can do."

"We?"

"The Keep—" but she stopped herself. After a moment, she quietly said, "I am interested in seeing what you can do."

"Then why the sparring? When are you going to teach me something serious? Try to tap into my potential?"

"I will. But it is dangerous to proceed too quickly. Interim train for years before they are allowed to use the ethergy of their aegis."

"Whoa, whoa. Stop. Ethergy? Aegis?"

"Ethergy is the positive, borrowed energies of the world. Most of the Interim's powers are fueled by ethergy. Vox's flame, Dimitri's sea, Donovan's ice—they are all things apart of this world, energies borrowed to create new flames, more sea, ice shards. The aegis, our weapons, channel the ethergy, triggered by various frequencies programmed into the bells we wear. The counterpart is nethergy, the negative force that takes energy out of this world." She touched the hilt of her sword. "Like mine."

"Takes it out?" he asked. "Where does it go?"

She looked at him in surprise before answering, "To the shadows, I suppose. I don't really know."

"That's kind of creepy."

Shade stared at him for a long moment, brows creased and eyes wide. And then she laughed. "A little bit," she admitted.

Lethan reappeared above them.

"The way is open," he said and threw down a rope. "Come."

They climbed up and found themselves in a large, dark cavern. Knick couldn't see two feet in front of his face but he could sense the gaping space of the room. Their wrist-lights were swallowed by the darkness so they switched them off and pulled the goggles the Krueh-jin had given them over their eyes. When Knick looked around, he gaped at his surroundings. They were in an abandoned transit tunnel, made for the old megatrains that had stopped running a century ago. They were close to the surface, Knick realized, and beneath some kind of water source. The brick was old and moldy, and a musty smell wafted occasionally in the stale air. The tunnel went on so long that all he saw was a thick blackness in the distance.

Lethan whispered something to Whiskey. The lehn screeched and darted off into the tunnel. Once the echo subsided, the three of them quietly headed into the darkness.

Otto listened to Isis, Jilk, and Etrusca arguing outside of his door for at least a half an hour before Isis quietly walked in and smiled at him. He still couldn't get over that smile. It made his heart beat in leaps and bounds.

"Otto," she began, "we're going to have to leave now. The High Healer believes you are strong enough."

"It's okay," he assured her. "I'm practically brand new."

That was an obvious lie. He didn't look healthy by any stretch of the imagination but he definitely felt better and was more than ready to get out of his bed, though the prospect of going out into the Mine was terrifying. He had only coped with his relocation due to the fact he had been stuck in a single room without any way to prove where he really was, so his mind was convinced he was safe. That was about to change.

"Jilk reports cogwheelers gathering in the town just over from this one. He anticipates them coming here next," she explained as he pushed back the covers and swung his legs over the bed. "At worst, they will find us. At best, they will simply make it difficult to leave. So we are leaving now."

He stood up, took two steps, and stumbled when his foot connected with a shoe. Isis ran to his side to hold him up, worry splayed across her face. He laughed, trying to hide the discouragement he felt at the pain rippling up his foot.

"I'm fine. Just a shoe."

Isis stared long and hard at him, her small hands reaching out to support him. He gently, hesitantly touched her shoulder, afraid anything more would be crossing a line. She wasn't just any girl. She was his dream girl. She was the Enoch, the sacred figure of the Keepers. She was important. She existed in a realm far above him.

"The world will never know what you have done for it," she whispered.

Soon after, the Obeahani were helping him bathe, shave, and dress. He kept insisting he could manage on his own but they considered it at last chance to examine their patient before he departed from their care and wouldn't let him out of their sight until they were satisfied he was capable.

"You look very handsome, Otto," one of the sisters told him as she brushed off his shoulders. "You look a fine gentleman cleaned up."

He didn't really see anything gentlemanly about the way he was dressed. Back home, he would've worn something like this to the store—jeans, a thermal shirt under a t-shirt, and a jacket. But he supposed that compared to an old night gown and looking near-dead for weeks on end, he was practically ready for a ball.

Isis was waiting for him in the hallway outside of his room. She smiled when she saw him and he felt a little bashful. If she had been a normal girl, this might've been how he would've dressed for a first date. He would've taken her somewhere fun—maybe the Lotus market downtown where all the merchants peddled exotic goods and foods. But that dream was hundreds of miles away from reality.

Out in the lobby, Jilk, Solo, Slot, Antion and Etrusca were waiting for them. His anxiety at going outside returned in full force.

"Look at you," Jilk said. "You look brand new, kid."

Slot slapped him on the back and he stumbled forward. "Oh, sorry," she said with a smile. "Forget. Hey, you have any problems, just let us know. I could carry you on my back a ways."

Otto gaped at her. He wasn't that small and she wasn't so

big. Was she making fun of him? She looked dead serious when she said it.

"A few miles at least," she said with a shrug when he realized he was staring. Otto cleared his throat and looked at Etrusca for help.

"Be well, Otto," the High Healer told him with a slight bow of her very tall frame. "I hope to see you again someday under much better circumstances."

"Thank you," he said, bowing back.

When the door opened, he hesitated only a moment. The horror stories of his life were about to meet him head on. He took a deep breath and crossed the threshold, trying to hide any apprehension he felt from the others. Outside, the street was steaming and water droplets dripped from the cavern ceiling. Buildings made of stone and wood lined either side of the road and scattered in the background in the expected patterns of a city block. Aside from the sheet of rock over his head, the town could have been one he'd visited before. Nothing was on fire, nothing in the architecture included spikes or skulls. They were just normal buildings.

And normal people. Men and women and children dressed perhaps a slight bit dingier than anyone from Anshar walked here and there on whatever business they were about, talking to each other, nodding in passing, carrying groceries and signing for a delivery and eating lunch on a side street bench. They were not convicts or crazies or druggies—not like he had been led to believe. They were normal people living their lives.

Jilk picked a direction and they started walking, passing by more of the same kind of scenery. Otto was reminded of Tirmaline, his hometown, as he took in his surroundings. Both towns seemed on the edge of something greater, quiet and unnoticed. There was a sense of fear that filled Gehrs, disquiet behind every face and every door, but he assumed that was because of the war and the nearby cogwheelers.

He thought back to a conversation he'd had with Knick.

"What's the Mine like?" he asked. "From someone who's been both here and there, what do you think?"

"You scared?"

"Tell me not to be. You know the stories. Well, as an angel, maybe you knew the truth all along… They can't all be true. But you

know what the rest of us think."

"Helped propagate it," Knick confessed casually. "Not me. I was an agent. But the department? They're responsible for your thoughts."

"So it's all a lie?" Otto muttered. "That's hard to believe."

"It's no more a jungle than Anshar. Maybe more wild. Definitely more civilized."

"That doesn't make any sense."

"You want to know what the Mine is like?" Knick asked, leaning forward in his chair. "It's freedom, kid, about as free as any person can ever be. But it won't look like freedom, because people behave in predictable patterns, and everyone here," he pointed down, "came from everyone there," he pointed up. "Generations later, not much has changed."

"It doesn't look like freedom. You're trapped under all this rock. You can't leave."

Knick shrugged. "True, too."

"So that sounds more like a cage."

"Exactly."

"You're pissing me off," Otto mumbled.

Knick grinned. "You go outside, though, and you'll see what I mean."

And Otto did see what he meant. Nowhere in sight was there an angel eye or a White Hand Watcher. Topside, everything was structured and people fit within that structure, changed by their environment, not the other way around. But here, the world seemed malleable, as if just at the beginning of something greater. The sludge of evolution holding the promise of complexity. And everywhere people were changed by their environment, but here they didn't have to be. There were no angel eyes recording their every breath of every day.

Somehow the cavern ceiling didn't seem so threatening. It could've been a sky for how likely he was to touch it. Sky somehow represented freedom but it was as much a cage as anything else. And for those that dwelled in the sky—or for those creatures that used to, nothing survived up there anymore—they were caged in by something greater as well. The universe was an infinite cage. It was almost depressing.

Otto was pulled out of his thoughts when Jilk hissed at them to get off the road. They scrambled between some buildings and huddled together in choked apprehension. Jilk broke away from the group and peered around the corner, watching something Otto could only guess at.

"What is it?" Antion whispered.

"Cogs," Solo mumbled. After a moment, Jilk came back, brow damp with nervous sweat.

"Listen. It's just a small group. Never seem 'em before. Keep your head down. Spread out. Solo goes with Antion. Slot with Otto. Isis with me." He focused on the cogwheelers. "You know what to do if shit gets out of hand."

The siblings nodded. Solo and Antion were the first to leave the alley. After a few minutes had passed, Jilk motioned to Slot. She tugged at Otto's sleeve and jerked her head in the direction she wanted him to go. He glanced back at Isis, suddenly afraid to leave her. His dream girl waved him toward the exit so he left with the cogwheeler. They drifted across the street at a normal pace with Otto walking on Slot's left side to try to hide her from the cogwheelers chattering nearby. His stomach bundled up tightly, nerves wriggling non-stop. He couldn't help but constantly glance in their direction, heart nearly stopping when one of them noticed. The man peeked around his group of friends, narrowing his gaze on them. Otto could faintly hear their conversation.

"It'n that her? That Heavy girl?"

"Huh?"

"Who?"

"Slot. Look, look."

One of them twisted around to look, prompting all of his buddies to turn and stare. Otto felt Slot tense up beside him. He glanced down at her, saw her brows pulling into a frown and her fists clenching up. Was she going to fight them? He threw his arm around her shoulders protectively and refused to look at the cogwheelers anymore.

"No way," one of them said.

"Slot and Solo are never separated."

"That's not him?"

"No fucking way. Solo's got a head on that guy."

"Yeah, but—"

"Man, that's not even a girl."

"I don't know, looks—"

"Leave that guy's kid brother alone. Anyway, what were we saying?"

Otto tuned the rest out as they broke through the town limits and started onto a sloping path toward a rocky expanse. He didn't breathe easy until they met Solo and Antion down the road near an old set of tracks that ran straight into a wall.

Solo put his hand on Slot's head and pulled her against him. She hugged her brother. Neither said anything. When Jilk and Isis came around the bend, everyone sighed in relief.

"Let's not do that again," Jilk mumbled.

Dimitri slammed another door, skipped down the steps to the street, and started toward the next house on the block when he realized he had just visited the last one. No sign of Vox. He looked up into the sky and noted the dark clouds churning threateningly above him. For days it had seemed like rain would fall at any moment but nature had mercifully held off. How much longer until the sky broke, he could not say, but the longer the storm postured above, the angrier it became. He felt a lot like that sky.

Anxiously, Dimitri made his way back to the fallen dragon statue that Kallo and Delia had made their point of operations. He picked them out of a cluster of people rushing here and there in their rebuilding efforts and hurried to meet them just as a scout finished giving his report.

"Any news?" he exclaimed.

"No, sir. There is still no sign of her," Kallo replied.

"We have covered only a fraction of the city, my lord Interim," Delia told him. "It will take many weeks to cover all of Hojo with our few numbers. We must return our concentration to the bomb. We *must* collapse the tunnel."

"No," Dimitri immediately answered. "Ross is working fine on his own."

"He is having trouble finding supplies, sir," Kallo explained. "The Kur bring back what they can but their search is inefficient."

"Kallo—" his sister began but Dimitri cut her off.

"Inefficient?" he growled.

"I mean only in the search for supplies, sir."

He knew it was true but he could not suppress his agitation. When compared to Vox's safety, the collapse of a tunnel seemed trifle. He knew he had to take a deep breath and focus. He had always known that romantic attachments were forbidden because they interfered with a Keeper's good judgment regarding the Balance, tempting one to forsake his duty to the Balance in favor of the person he loved. He had understood that but he had loved Vox anyway. They had spent years going in and out of danger, completing their missions with perfect clarity, and yet all the while maintaining their feelings. Taking the plunge into a relationship hardly seemed to be crossing a line. They were Keepers. They could indulge their love but they would never forget their duty. The Balance was everything.

But when he had gotten her with child, everything had changed. He hadn't known to what extent but he could feel the fear begin to creep into his heart and knew the truth of their compromise. He had not expected to have fallen so far so quickly, however. Vox had been missing less than a few hours when he had ordered the search party instead of organizing the bomb effort. Even now, he found it impossible to put his feelings away and do his duty.

He would do more harm than good remaining here.

"Sir, if I may," Delia began, "if Vox remained in Hojo, would she not reveal herself to us? It is possible she is no longer here, sir."

Dimitri nodded absentmindedly, thoughts racing through all of the places she might have gone to. Delia was right; if Vox was in Hojo, she would have called to him. She had not. She had moved on. But why? His mind was too clouded to answer his questions.

A burst of black smoke fell out of the sky and landed near them. Sonia rushed out of the dissipating cloud to meet them.

"Dimitri!" she called in her exotic accent. "I'm here."

"Good."

"Where is she? Vox. Have you found her?"

"No." Dimitri shook his head, finally feeling resolved. "It is clear to us she is no longer in Hojo, but it is good you've arrived. You must take my place here. I have to go."

"Dimitri!" she exclaimed.

"Sir!" the twins shouted.

But he did not stay to listen to the protests. He folded into himself and projected his body across the sky in a ball of dark light.

A siren howled in the distance. The angels had returned.

Shade sensed something was wrong the moment their feet began sloshing through water. At first, the water was shallow, running a line down the center of the tunnel that the soles of their shoes slapped harmlessly against; but the deeper they went, the more water they encountered until they waded in murky blackness that was sometimes so deep it came up to their shins.

"We're approaching Karnak," Lethan explained, "but there is a passage that we can take that will bypass the ocean entirely."

"Sabal called our destination the Bleak Shores," Shade said. "Did she mean the battered bridges of Tarsus?"

"Yes," he replied, "city of storms."

"I know Tarsus," Knick said. "I never went but I saw the data. It's always raining—sometimes a drizzle and sometimes a hurricane, but water's always coming out of the sky."

"And from the sea," Lethan replied. He peeked over his shoulder at them, his blue eyes glowing brightly viewed through the Krueh-jin goggles. "Stories tell us Karnak was a desert long, long ago."

"Impossible," Knick snorted, shoving his hands into his jacket pockets. They pushed water around as they surged forward into the darkness.

"Maybe," the Jin said. "Time makes many things impossible and many more things possible."

"What about the tribe we're going to meet?" Knick wanted to know. "Sirens, she said."

"The Na Varen is a clan of women, the daughters of Uruk."

"Commonly called the sirens," Shade added.

"There are no men?" Knick asked.

"None."

"Then how do they—"

"When it is time for them to bear children, they are sent to the *House of Heaven* and sleep with men until they become pregnant," Lethan explained. "If a boy is conceived and the father is unwilling to care for him, he is released to the city. If a girl is born, she is dedicated to their goddess and baptized in the waters of Karnak." He suddenly stopped and pointed to a side chamber. "Here."

He and Knick heaved the wheel on the door and opened the way to a smaller, darker tunnel. Shade was the first inside. She took note of the water trickling through the cracks in the ceiling. It made her nervous. She turned to warn Lethan but he was already sealing the door behind them.

"We're close," he announced. "Another day and we will surface near Tarsus."

"So basically the *House of Heaven* is a whore house," Knick continued.

"A very expensive, very exclusive whore house," Shade told him as Lethan brushed passed them to lead the way down the new path.

"I get this deal is pretty sweet for the guy but what if he actually wants to be, you know, involved in his daughter's life?"

"Sirens do not give up their daughters," Lethan replied.

"Okay, what about—"

"They do not marry," he interrupted, "and the men don't even know they are fathers until a boy is born."

"As outsiders understand it, they serve the goddess Panghora," Shade explained, eyeing the thick mold on the rusted tunnel walls. In the light of the goggles, it glowed in bright green swirls. "Dark star. Little is known of her."

"Dark star?" Knick echoed. "Is she evil?"

"Ambiguous," Lethan corrected him. "Panghora is ambiguous, as are the sirens."

"What does that mean?" he asked as they turned down a new corridor. "What are they like?"

"I don't know," the Jin confessed. "I've never met them. I have only heard the stories."

"Didn't Sabal say something about me uniting the Tribes under the shadow of Panghora?"

"So you think Panghora was once a goddess of the Tribes?"

Knick shrugged. "No idea. I think it means the Sirens will at least be able to shed some light on it."

"Perhaps. They are very secretive."

"The old ten percent rule, huh?" Knick muttered.

"The what?" Shade asked.

"Jilk would say women are a ten percent increase, meaning the larger the group, the greater the odds of deception and manipulation. *A* woman is sweet; a group of them is deadly."

"Ten percent," Shade echoed. "Is that all?" She watched as Knick and Lethan grinned at each other, and she smiled to herself. "I met one once," she said. Knick looked at her with undivided attention. His silhouette and all of the details of his person were broken down into bright red lines. "I was on a mission in Darmstadt when our paths crossed. Her name was Coda. She was beautiful, like moonlight on water."

"What happened?"

"I saved her life. She wanted to sing me a song. I refused." Shade shrugged. "We went our separate ways."

"Anti-climatic," Knick muttered.

"To refuse a Siren's song shows great disrespect," Lethan said.

"I didn't have the time. I told her as much. The Balance is more important than any melody."

"Her song could have inspired you. Empowered you."

"It could have debilitated me. Sirens are not known for their honesty."

"You had saved her life. Did she have a reason to trick you?"

"Do they need a reason?" Shade asked. "My allegiance is to the Balance. Theirs is to Panghora."

"I under—"

Whiskey began shrieking. So loud and so sudden was it that they all jumped, startled, and Shade drew her sword. All eyes went to the bouncing lehn, now a detailed outline of red fur, waving his arms wildly. Just ahead of him was a sudden drop. Lethan inched forward and kicked a rock over the edge. They heard a splash and were suddenly very aware of the sound of running water.

"Whiskey," Lethan called and the lehn squeaked as he hopped up onto his shoulder. "Sata-sata." There was another shriek and then the creature scurried down into the chasm. "It isn't too far down. If we jump, we could make it."

"What's down there?" Shade asked.

"Water."

"And what else?"

"A good question." Lethan crouched near the ledge. "Whiskey will tell us."

As they waited, Shade inched toward the edge and looked up. They were near the ceiling, a smooth and arching surface. She peered left and right to try to gauge the size of the room but her goggles could not penetrate the distant blackness. In a moment, Whiskey was back, chirping a report only Lethan could understand.

"Wait here," he said and then hopped down into the darkness.

Shade reached up and began toying with the spectrum setting on her goggles until she found one that opened up the world to her. The ghost-light revealed all but the farthest corners of the room. Everything was washed in white light and shades of gray. They were standing before a giant storm water drainage basin. Eight large intake pipes, four on each side, lined both sides of the room near the ceiling. Water trickled out of several of the openings. Below them toward the base of the pit were eight outtake pipes. The center of the pit was filled with water that looked like black glass and Whiskey was picking his way across the room on stones that broke the waterline. Lethan waded through it as a pale silhouette cutting through shimmering, shin-high black ice toward a door on the far side.

"Wait here," she whispered, the feeling of unease growing. She shadow-stepped to the bottom of the basin and Whiskey shrieked in alarm. A moment later there was a loud splash and Knick came stomping through the water, shaking his limbs like a dog.

"Tired of being told to wait," he muttered.

"That wasn't very smart."

Knick shrugged and they joined Lethan on the far side of the room. Lethan was examining the pressure door.

"Our way through," he said and took hold of the valve.

Shade was suddenly filled with inexplicable dread. Little voices like intuition whispered warnings, shouted at her to go no further. They were the voices of the shadows. "Wait!" she cried, but it was too late. The wheel had turned. Water spewed from around the crack in the frame and the door groaned in loud protest. A bolt popped out of the metalwork. Then another and another.

"Run!" Lethan cried, and they all turned to flee, chased by the sound of metal being warped and crushed by tons of water.

There was a loud bang like a canon being fired and the door bulleted across the room, banging against the far wall. Shade lunged for Knick and attempted to shadow step, but a cascade of water flooded the chamber, sweeping them off their feet and pulling her out of the shadow realm. Shade scrambled for Knick's hand and, for a moment, their fingers linked. And then they were ripped apart, caught up in the whirlwind that carried them in loops around the room.

"Shade!" Knick cried, voice drowned by the rushing water. Shade splashed around, trying to keep her head above water, turning this way and that to find him but everywhere her vision was filled with glittering black diamond-like liquid. She saw a ghost-like figure break the surface before being pulled down again.

"Knick!" she screamed, fighting to swim against the current, but she was swept along effortlessly. Whiskey screamed, filling her with the fear he felt. She looked up and saw they were racing toward the ceiling seconds before she was sucked under, tumbling in the shifting undercurrents. Bubbles like clusters of gems filled her vision as she struggled to orient herself.

And then the floodgates in the outtake pipes gave way and the spiral of water began vacuuming out of the basin. Shade kicked wildly, breaking the surface only seconds for a gulp of air before being pulled down again. She swam as hard as she could against the current, breaking out of the drainage vortex to return to the spiral of the surface flow.

"Knick!" she screamed again, but her scan of the room found no one. She hit the wall hard and cried out, fingers scraping along the edge until she finally found a hold on the lip of one of the intake pipes. "Knick!"

A ragged gasp for air pulled her gaze and she saw him struggling to stay above water, whirling around the room in a wide loop. She turned herself around and secured her hold on the pipe. As he came around toward her, she reached out and caught him by his jacket. He latched onto her and she pulled him in with all of her might.

But the draw of water was too strong and her fingers began slipping. She shut her eyes tight and braced her muscles, bones aching under the pressure, but she could not hold on.

The vortex pulled them under and, in seconds, they were being whisked down a pipe, tumbling hard against the edges as the water rushed them along. She tried to hold onto Knick but the current was too strong. As they were ejected into a massive body of water, they were ripped away from each other.

And then Shade could see nothing but blackness all around her. A burning sensation filled her lungs as the last of her oxygen was depleted. She stopped struggling and allowed herself to be carried away, floating gently in a world made of shale and shadow. She was staring up at the ziggurat, waiting anxiously for the darkness to reach her. It rushed up to meet her, a loud whistling sound running ahead of the energy. And then that darkness became flowing strands of black hair surrounding a pale face. Soft lips touched hers, forced her mouth open, and a rush of oxygen filled her lungs.

The Mine was full of chaotic energy but Daelus was able to pick out the trace of ethergy and track it all the way to *The Bright Mermaid* in Gehrs. He kept his distance and stared thoughtfully at the structure, the small building tucked away amid a row of larger establishments. It seemed to fade into the background, a place you could walk by a thousand times and never know it was there. Daelus could feel the wards protecting the place, masking its presence—existence, even—to all eyes but those looking for it, those in need. He reached out through the energy around him and instantly sensed the absence of Keepers.

The trail was distinct, however. Daelus closed his mind and sought out the specs of lingering aegis. It was faint. There was a very noticeable smear of energy pathing away from the *Mermaid* and out toward the OT. Daelus followed the path with his eyes and counted several clusters of cogwheelers moving through the town's traffic. There was no sense of crises that differed from the usual tension of war, no high alert for signs of an intruder or scramble to find a hidden enemy. There were many possibilities that little clues gave rise to, but Daelus knew Shade very well and decided she had left the town altogether.

Tucking himself into the flow of people, Daelus made for the town's exit following the Keeper's trail.

The first OT town they came to was one of the larger settlements outside the cradle called Jaco's Bluff. It was built on the old subway system until half the town collapsed when the coal miners drilled along a fault line that ran right under the Bluff, leaving behind a 120 meter vertical drop. Since it was the main route to the outlying towns, they constructed a lift system to move people up and down the cliff to a bridge that stretched along the chasm. The rest of the town was built into the wall.

Jilk left Slot and Solo to guard the kids and went into town to see if he could find any cogwheelers or catch any rumors of their movements, but surprisingly not a single cog flag popped. It made him wary. He returned to his friends and warned them to stick close.

Jaco's Bluff was certainly one of the most colorful towns in the Mine. The homes and smaller establishments were average in build and design, constructed of stone or clay with pitched roofs, but the bigger businesses had slabs of painted wood nailed to their most visible sides and colorful roofs made of tile chips and shells. They passed by a dome of glossy, red shards with a sunset painted along the roadside face followed by a hexagonal-shaped turquoise mosaic roof over a painting of sea nymphs riding a great tidal wave. Strung up on poles were colorful strands of lights and hanging from all the buildings were lanterns covered with colored paper.

All around them the people bustled here and there, selling their wares out on the street. Carts hanging with brightly colored scarves and shawls and jewelry were always within eyesight, and the people dressed just as ostentatious. These were the Uptowners, the residents of Jaco's Bluff closest to the Cradle. They looked down—literally and figuratively—on those who lived closer to the chasm bridge, the Downtowners. The Downtowners, however, spat at the mention of the Uptowners; they thought their view of all the colorful buildings rising up the canyon wall was well worth a little extra dust in the lungs. Somehow, they all met in the middle and managed to get along well enough to not bring the city to second ruin.

Jilk glanced back and counted the five heads he was responsible for, making sure they were sticking close. Otto and Antion were gaping at the buildings in wonder. He snorted and led them to the lift, a system of endlessly rotating platforms, each with one small handrail to protect the passengers from falling into the chasm. They waited for their turn, stepped on, and were slowly lowered down the side of the canyon, passing one level after another. The lift never actually stopped but it moved slowly enough to allow anyone who wanted to get off at a certain floor plenty of time to unload.

Slot perched against the railing as casually as she would against a rock. Solo just folded his arms over his chest and looked around. Isis, Otto, and Antion all crowded together in the center of the platform as though moving might tip the thing over and send them tumbling into the chasm. Jilk resisted laughing and tapped Slot's shoulder.

"Get down from there. You're making the newbies nervous," he said. She looked at the others in bewilderment.

"Jilk," Solo whispered and nodded his head toward the rising half of the lifts. Four platforms down was a load of cogwheelers.

"Shit," he cursed. "Come on. Get off."

Jilk rushed them off at the very next stop, forcing their way through a crowd of people. Behind him he heard someone say, "Hey, wait a minute, isn't that—" but he didn't catch the rest as they lost themselves in the throng. He picked out an indigo-colored awning and pushed them inside a restaurant.

"Split up. Two tables," he said, pointing to separate corners of the room.

"Why are we running?" Isis whispered as she and Slot followed him to one corner and Solo took the boys to the other.

"You think we should fight and draw attention to ourselves?" he shot back. While that was part of it, the truth was that he still considered himself a cogwheeler and wasn't anxious to turn on his brethren, regardless of whether or not they had turned on him.

"Now what?" Isis asked when they were sitting down.

"Eat."

"What?"

"Eat. Might be your last chance for awhile." Jilk peeked around at the door. "They must be coming up from Cobbler. What shit luck." As he was turning back to his table, he noticed a fidgety kid at the central common table that he thought had been looking his way but he couldn't get a good look at his face.

They ordered food and were halfway through their meal when the front door swung open and a pack of cogwheelers walked in. He went rigid and stared at his half-eaten burger, straining to hear over the crowd. Slot tapped his hand and pointed at the bay window adjacent their table right next to where Solo and the others were sitting at. He nodded but motioned for her to wait.

"Hey!" one of the cogs called. The volume of the eatery quickly decreased to silence. "Hey! You. I'm talking to you." Footsteps came closer. Jilk's hands curled into fists and he nodded to the girls. Slot cracked her knuckles. "Yeah. You. I know you."

Jilk slid out of his seat and stood up to square off with the cogwheeler but froze when he saw the man had the fidgety kid at the common table by the scruff of his neck. He thought about ducking back into the booth but it was too late; the cogwheelers had seen him.

"Shit. Jilk, right?" the Cogger said, dropping the kid. "You're wanted big-time. Boss' got BOLO on your crew. Slot an' Solo with you, too? Come on out, chicken shitties." He grinned. "This'll be a big break. Lookin' forward to it."

Jilk counted three Gunnies with the Cogger, all positioned at the end of the common table. They lifted their guns when Solo and Slot slid out of the booths. Jilk ran his tongue over one of his canines as a variety of scenarios sped through his mind. Knowing his crew like he did, he quickly calculated exactly what would happen. He would dive away from the bay window toward the booths to draw the Gunnies' fire. Slot would rip the common table up and dump it on their heads to stall them long enough for Solo to break open the bay and start loading people out. The Cogger didn't even have his gun drawn, exuding confidence and arrogance that gave them the upper hand. He would try to draw as Slot pulled Isis out of the booth but Jilk would have his shotgun out by then. A buck shot at the table would force the Cogger into cover and allow him plenty of time to escape.

"Nighty-night," the Cogger croaked.

Chaos erupted as Jilk dove onto the table of a family of four, curling up and covering his head as bullets pelted the wall above him. There was a loud crack of wood splitting as the common table was ripped out of the floor and thrown across the room. Jilk scrambled out of the booth and blasted his sawed off, grinning satisfactorily as the Cogger was thrown back in shock, his weapon flying out of its holster and skittering across the ground. Jilk bounded across the room and followed Slot out the bay window.

"Brusco!" the Cogger screamed and a thundering series of footsteps rattled the whole level. People were pushed aside like balloons swatted in annoyance. A giant of a man with bulging muscles broke through the crowd, wildly looking around for his target. "Brusco!" the Cogger shrieked, pointing at the window. "There!"

The giant's eyes fixated on Jilk. He growled and charged toward him. They took off in a sprint down the platform, weaving through the panicked crowd, but were running out of tread quickly.

"Jilk!" Solo yelled, spying a line hooked to a small advertisement dirigible. "Rope!"

"Go!" he told him. Solo was already pushing Antion onto the line, whose body weight began anchoring the dirigible. Slot slid to a stop and headed back toward the giant. Jilk's heart jumped into his throat. "Slot, no!"

The two Heavies collided in a heap. Slot punched Brusco in the face so hard that he reeled. She ran in for a second blow but he had already recovered. Solo screamed as his sister was picked up and smashed into the wall; he tried to run to help her but Jilk stopped him.

"Get them down there! Now!"

Jilk's eyes went back to the fight. Brusco slammed Slot into the wall twice more before trying to smash her head into paste but she reached up, stopped his fist two inches from her face and, with a fierce look in her eyes, pushed him away, twisting his fingers apart. Brusco, straining against her strength, watched in horror as she began pulling them beyond their limit. He howled and released her, swinging with his free hand. Slot ducked under the blow, kicked his shin, and shoved him toward the railing.

Brusco's Gunnies and Cogger appeared, recovered and lining up to fire on Slot. Jilk blasted two warning shots in their direction, nicking one of them with ricochet. They backed off as the giant roared. He flew over the rail, catching the ledge at the last second. Slot immediately pounced him, bringing a hard-knuckled punch down on his skull. There was a loud crack but, instead of slowly the beast down, it only seemed to anger him more. He swung at her like a crazed animal and she dodged out of his ham-fisted flailing. Her foot came up and connected with his jaw. His head snapped back but he didn't budge off the railing. He just glared and began waving even more wildly. Slot backed away as he tried to climb over the railing again.

"Jilk!" Solo called, drawing his attention away from the fight. He was over the railing and about to go down. Jilk scrambled for the rope and, just as he was climbing over, saw Slot sprint toward Brusco, jump, and kick him in the chest with such momentum that the railing snapped and the giant began falling. Slot caught the edge and watched Brusco fall, flailing, and snap the next level's railing before catching himself a third down.

"Slot!" Solo warned but it was too late. She let go, dropped right onto the giant's brawny shoulders, and bounded onto the level.

"Shit, shit, shit!" Jilk cursed, climbing down the rope as fast as he could. He met Isis, Otto, and Antion below. Solo was already racing along the platform to the lifts, jumping over the debris from the smashed railing and looking over the edge every time he heard a crash. Jilk went after him, keeping an eye out for every object that got flung into the chasm, terrified one of them might be Slot.

The clatter of footsteps above told Jilk the rest of the Heavy's team was hot on their heels. Solo fired his pistol at the floor overhead until there was a loud shout and team was down by one. Jilk growled. This showdown was going to bring the cogwheelers down on them even harder and it was his fault for reacting too quickly back in the restaurant.

There was suddenly a loud snap and a body was flung from the level below them into the chasm. They all stopped and looked over as Brusco's bulky form disappeared into the darkness. Slot appeared and peered up at them. She grinned and gave them a thumb up even as blood was dripping down the side of her head and a gash across her cheek was oozing into the dust caked on her. Jilk thought she looked so damn beautiful he wanted to kiss her.

And then she stopped grinning and ducked as gunshots railed down. Solo returned fire with extreme prejudice. Slot appeared once more and motioned to the lifts. Jilk nodded and they all started running again. They piled onto a platform that a load of people were trying to escape from but Jilk grabbed two of the stragglers and forced them onto the lift with them. If they were lucky, the Cogger wouldn't order them to fire on civilians. He looked up just in time to see what was left of the team reach the lifts. The Cogger pointed and the Gunnies popped off several shots, all but one flying clear into the chasm. The last one struck the girl Jilk had grabbed as a shield and she yelped and collapsed.

"Shit!" Jilk cursed, lowering her down. Blood painted her right breast, skin paling and body trembling. He hadn't meant for anyone to get shot. He hadn't thought the Cogger would do it. "Get her off. Get her some help!" he ordered the other civilian. The person whimpered and cowered until he pointed his shotgun at him. The guy just screamed and jumped down to the next available platform, crashing into a junk cart. "Take her!" Jilk howled as the lift lowered but everyone shrank away from him. The girl began jerking as she went into shock. "Fuck!"

She was dead by the time they saw the bridge level come into view. Slot was waiting for them. She reared back like a pitcher and then chucked something toward them. It sailed right over to the lift above, knocking a Gunny right off the platform and down to the bridge level. He landed with a smack. She sprinted to cover as the Cogger emptied his clip into the rocky outcropping.

When they touched down, Jilk and the others met Slot and sprinted across the bascule bridge that closed the gap between Jaco's Bluff and the rest of the OT. Behind them, the Cogger was yelling for someone to raise the bridge. He risked a glance over his shoulder and saw two more teams of cogs gathering at the lifts. They made it to the other side before the cranks began grinding and ran through the last stretch of the town, dodging the main road as soon as they saw a cluster of cogs gathered around an unmarked building.

"There!" someone yelled and racing footsteps chased them into darkness.

And then Jilk collided with someone familiar. Reemer gaped at him, wide-eyed. The kid had been part of his crew until Jilk had defected.

"Jilk?" Reemer gasped.

"Hide us!" he hissed. Reemer glanced at the others behind him and frowned as shouts to 'find them' rallied through the alleys. "What's it gonna be, kid?"

Reemer swallowed visibly and motioned them through an iron gate into a tiny gap between the cavern wall and a building. He closed it behind them and skipped off down the alley. They were trapped.

"Can we trust him?" Otto whispered.

"We can," Jilk affirmed then added, "I hope."

"Reemer!" a gruff voice shouted from not too far away.

"Sir."

"You seen your old boss come through here?"

They held their breath.

"No, sir. Jilk's here?" Reemer asked and they silently exhaled in relief. The other guy groaned.

"Get outta my way," he growled and footsteps trailed away from their hiding spot.

Reemer did not immediately come back for them. They were left there more than an hour in cramped and terrified suspense. When he finally did return, the town seemed less riled. Reemer motioned for quiet as they slipped out of the gap, one by one.

"Thank you," Jilk whispered.

"Why'd you do it?" the kid asked him, hurt in his eyes.

"Didn't want to," Jilk replied. "Did it for Knick."

"Knick?" he echoed, confusion pulling his brows together.

"Boss always said he was meant for big things. And it's bigger than the cogs, kid. Bigger than the Mine."

Reemer nodded and pointed their way to freedom. Jilk touched his shoulder, gave it a squeeze, and led his group out of Jaco's Bluff.

Gentle hands touched his shoulders and glided down his chest. A soft whisper called his name, breath tickling his ear. These were the first sensations Knick became aware of as he regained consciousness. Still in the lull of a dream, he thought perhaps Shade was leaning over him trying to wake him…but then the hands on his chest were traveling lower on his abdomen and it dawned on him that Shade would never touch him so intimately.

He quickly awoke, eyes popping open to stare into pink irises. A girl was hovering over him, her thick tangle of curly blonde hair falling over her shoulders. She giggled. A second chirp of laughter pulled his gaze elsewhere and he soon realized he was surrounded by women. Beautiful women. Some were tall, some short, all gracefully slender and dressed in next to nothing. They were exotically gorgeous with eye and hair color variety like a rainbow and skin tones of all regions.

The girl above him shifted over his lap, calling his attention back to her. Her ass was planted on his crotch, her fingers toying with his belt buckle, and it was hard not to notice how incredibly beautiful she was. He swallowed the lump in his throat, wondering what the hell was going on.

"Get off," he said. The girls laughed but said nothing, and the blonde straddling him did not move.

Knick frowned and looked around, trying to get his bearings. He was in some kind of bedroom with blue-painted walls and ceiling. The bed was big enough for five of him and covered with a thick, turquoise comforter. The windows were covered with ivory lace and velvet drapes but he could see the storm through the curtains and heard the patter of rain. Beneath the cadence, he heard a soft melody, a faraway song without words that went in and out with the rain, so soft that he wasn't entirely sure he wasn't hearing things.

The realization hit him in full force. Sirens. He was looking for the Sirens. He stared wide-eyed at the woman on top of him, at how she watched him with curious amusement in her eyes. He tried to get up but she immediately crouched over him, caressing his cheeks and neck.

"We saved you from Karnak," the girl said, her voice a soothing melody. "You were close to death. Rest now and regain your strength." She smiled a seductive smile. "I will take care of you."

"Get off," he groaned, feeling his mind begin to cloud. She was so pretty. She smelled so nice. It was a trap. He tried to sit up again.

"If you do that, you'll only upset your recovery," she told him. She said it so kindly and so logically that he found himself believing her. He hesitated then lay back down. She smiled and stroked his brow lovingly. "I will take care of you," she said again, her voice a hypnotic lullaby. "You are safe here."

Those four words rumbled wrongly inside his mind, tossed this way and that as female hands massaged his limbs and fingers combed through his hair. They were humming and singing and the sound was so relaxing. Safe. He was safe here. The pretty girl above him tugged at his shirts, pushing them up as her hand glided across his abdomen. He felt his stomach tighten anxiously. She kissed his cheek and jaw and neck. He was safe here. He sighed contentedly, letting his eyes drift closed. He focused on the melody and the touches. He remembered the girl's words: you are safe here.

But why did that concept feel so wrong? The ex-Regent was hunting him down. He shouldn't be safe anywhere, but he was. He *was* safe—that part felt true. So why did her words ring false? He was safe, he had Shade—Knick went completely still and his eyes shot open. Shade. Without Shade, he was not safe. And she wasn't there.

Knick suddenly pushed the girl off of him and tried to sit up. A dozen hands reached out to stop him but he slapped them away.

"Shade!" he exclaimed, struggling to slide off the bed. The girls blinked in confusion and tried to coerce him back to the bed but he waved them off. They followed, still humming, still singing—the detail that shattered the illusion for him. He knew beyond all doubt that they were trying to subdue and seduce and manipulate him with their song, trying to hold him prisoner. "Where is Shade?"

"You must lie down," the blonde girl said, stepping in front of him. She was topless with a beaded thong wrapped around her hips. "You are unwell."

"Yeah, right." He shoved her off. "What kind of nurse dresses like you? Shade!"

"You *must* lie down," she said again, and this time he felt his mind bending toward her will. The chorus of voices became a blur between his ears, a soothing song coaxing him back toward the bed. "You are unwell. We will take care of you."

"No," he growled through gritted teeth, trying to shake off

the urge to obey her. "Shade!" He broke out of the room in a sprint. Where the hell was she? Was she all right? Had the Sirens saved her, too? What had they done with her? "Shade!"

He found himself in a red hallway of doors. The girls were coming after him, their pitch rising, and suddenly his head was splitting open. Knick cried out, even more determined to escape, and ran. He threw open every door he came to, shouting Shade's name over and over again. He screamed and stumbled, vision momentarily whiting out, and fell into the next door.

"Shade," he groaned, falling to the ground. Their voices were like a spike being hammered into his skull. He looked up into the room and saw her there. Shade was perched on the end of the bed, dressed in sheer, black layers like some kind of dancer, her head bowed and eyes glassy as one woman dressed her in jewelry and another brushed her long hair, singing her into a stupor. "Shade…" She twitched. "Snap out of it… Shade…"

A pulse rocked out of her. The shadows in the room leapt to her defense, taking form and attacking the sirens. The women immediately backed off, stumbling around in terror as the dark shapes pinned them in deadly restraint. Shade's violet eyes snapped into focus and she pulled her sword as she leapt to her feet. She thrust the blade at the blonde kneeling over Knick, angled it against her neck.

"Let him go or I will open your throat," she growled. The blonde stared defiantly up at her. Only when she pressed the weapon tighter into her skin did the blonde throw up her hands in surrender. The pain in his skull subsided and he slumped down in exhaustion. "Are you all right?"

"Let me get back to you on that," he muttered.

A great commotion down the hall caused them all to tense. A creature was shrieking violently, the sound growing closer, and then a door broke open and Lethan and Whiskey ran out into the hallway, the Jin half-clothed and his lehn bouncing frantically.

"Knick!" Lethan exclaimed, racing toward him.

"Found the Sirens," Knick muttered and the Jin tossed him a dirty look.

Suddenly, one of the women cried out and collapsed, holding her head with white knuckles and groaning in agony.

The blonde rushed to her friend's side and the other women nearest her collapsed to comfort her. Knick scrambled to his feet and backed away from them.

"Coda!" the blond gasped before turning a frantic eye on Shade. "Stop it! Stop hurting her!"

"No, Chorda," the one called Coda ground out through gritted teeth. She groaned again, falling into her friend's arms. "It was my fault. I touched her melody…" She lifted her terror-stricken red eyes to look at Shade. "Your shadows…they shatter…everything."

The women gasped and drew together in fear.

"Only Daedalus had such power," one of them whispered.

"Truly, their souls are tied."

"They were meant for each other."

"Without a doubt."

Knick clenched his jaw and glanced at Shade. She looked just as uncomfortable with the assessment as he did.

"Please forgive us," the blonde suddenly said, "but this has all been a misunderstanding. We had to be sure you were the ones we waited for—the Keeper and the One—so we tested you. Forgive us."

"Forgive us," the other women said at once, their voices an angelic harmony. The Sirens bowed at the waist, their fingers practically touching the floor. The blonde, who was still kneeling, bent over until her forehead touched the ground.

"What test?" Shade asked.

"The One's mind will be immune to domination and, through him, so will the Sword of Panghora."

Knick and Shade exchanged glances before she lowered her weapon and the Sirens straightened out. The blonde stood up as another woman brought her a beaded wrap she tied over her torso. There was a thin line of blood on her neck from where Shade's sword had bitten her. Her thin fingers delicately wrapped around her throat for just a moment before lowering her hand to examine the blood. She dismissed the wound and looked at them again.

"I am Chorda. This is Coda, Breva, and Lyrica." She pointed to the other women. "We pulled you from the sea."

Coda was tall and slim with porcelain skin, blood red eyes, and a black bob cut. She reminded Knick a little of Shade, but more sinister. Breva was short with dark skin, amber eyes, and yellow hair pulled into a curly bun with long ringlets framing her face. Lyrica was somewhere between the other two in height with olive skin, light brown eyes, and a head of thick, auburn red hair. They were the most exotic women he had ever seen.

"Come," said Chorda. "We must take you to the Shaman. She is waiting for you."

Eros stared at himself in the mirror. His hair was still dripping wet from the bath. He looked passively at his gnarled flesh, at the frightening display of his legacy as Baron. Thousands of scars covered his body from his neck to his wrists to his toes. Most were jagged lines crisscrossing over one another, the new overtaking the old, but some were creative twists and shapes that told of his more interesting battles. And of his failures.

To the Keepers, the Baron had been a flawless leader, but he knew otherwise. His many secrets—those he shared with the Council and ex-Regent—hid decisions made for the good of the Order and the cover-ups of mistakes, and remained hidden for the sake of the people that comprised the Order. Then there were his own sins that only Daedalus knew the truth of.

Eros ran his fingers down the rippled flesh on his chest and lamented. Not for himself, but for the time. The Order was a wounded deer hobbling through a hunter-filled forest and the beasts could smell blood. They did not have the numbers to respect the Balance. A war was inevitable. Soon, Eros knew the Keepers would have to go into hiding to rebuild and the world that survived the war would be the one they would return to equilibrium. He would be the head of the Order that toiled that new world, but could he do it? Did he deserve to?

He was old. He could feel it in his mind, though his body was no older than a man in his late thirties, aging suppressed by the energy force projected by his aegis. All Keepers were shielded to some degree from growing old, the Balance protecting the servants who would protect it. And though Eros looked into the face of a young man with a body covered in scars, he wondered if it wasn't time for him to go.

A loud scream of a wounded soldier in the main hall caused him to tremble inside. Their pain, little by little, destroyed him. They followed his orders, they looked to him to guide them and, even though he sent them to pain and probably death, they kept going, kept returning, kept going. And he would relinquish responsibility in a heartbeat if he wasn't positive that there was no one quite yet ready to step up.

Daedalus could have, once.

Eros reached for his white shirt and buttoned it all the way up to the collar, leaving no scar exposed. He finished dressing and left his bedroom. He was headed for the nagarem to check on Camilla when someone began shouting his name. He turned around and backtracked through the hallways, moving closer to the voice still calling for him. Dimitri had come back to Sanctuary. But why? What had happened? He started to run when the Sovereign appeared around the corner.

"Baron," he gasped, eyes wide in alarm.

"Come inside," Eros said, opening the door to his office. "What has happened?"

When they were alone, Dimitri began pacing, pale as a ghost, in front of his desk. Eros waited with as much patience as he could muster, fear worming a hopeless knot in the pit of his stomach.

"We should've told you," Dimitri said at long length, his once-calm voice now haggard. He stared at the floor. "We were afraid. I am afraid. Vox and I—" The words stuck in his throat as he finally looked Eros in the eyes. "We're pregnant."

Eros felt something strike him like a wrecking ball aimed at his face. He stood there gaping. He had known the two were close but not how close. He had never suspected they had gone so far. They had played their game well, almost as well as he once had. Anger began mingling with the shock, overtaking him until he was shaking with outrage. Vox was pregnant!

"She's missing," Dimitri said, fear pitching his voice. "During the battle at Hojo, she and I were separated. Afterward, I went to look for her, but she was gone. I can't find her. Something's happened—I don't know what."

The battle? Hojo? Eros felt a wave of angry nausea overtake him. So Dr. Basset knew. That was why he tried to stop him from sending her. She had lied to his face.

"Do you know what you've done?" Eros boomed. Dimitri bowed his head stiffly.

"We have forsaken the Order—"

"You have probably killed her!"

If it was possible, Dimitri's face paled even more. "What?"

"Interim children are volatile! Even with just one Interim parent, the ethergy in the child's blood is too powerful! It destroys the womb!"

"No," Dimitri protested, expression screwing up into torment.

"You should have told me!" Eros slammed his fist against the wall. "You should have told me immediately!"

Dimitri crumpled to the floor and tucked his head against his chest, clutching fistfuls of his hair so tightly that his knuckles were white. "Is it too late?" he asked, voice muffled by his knees.

"I don't know," Eros replied quietly. "We have to find her. She is in danger." He took two steps toward his Interim and stopped. "Dimitri. I do not think her body can handle this."

"No." Dimitri shook his head and looked up, eyes red. "No. I won't let that happen."

"You should've told me."

"We couldn't!"

"Why?" Eros shouted. "Because you were afraid? I love you! I love you like sons and daughters! I would never forsake you!" He stormed over to Dimitri and picked him up by the collar, sternly putting him on his feet. "You have to find her. Now."

"I will." He hesitated. "I'm sorry, Eros."

The Baron put a firm hand on the Sovereign's shoulder. "Find her."

Dimitri swept out of the office and Eros had to catch himself on his desk to keep from falling over. Vox was pregnant. She would put a precious little girl or handsome young boy into his arms, the arms of a self-appointed godfather. And all he could think was how terrible that was. She was going to die. And the child might die with her.

The sky above Tarsus was dark as night and rain poured in steady, heavy drops as the Sirens led them out of the *House of Heaven* and into the dock city. One long, thick wall ran the length of the shore for about three miles with transport holes every quarter mile notched into the base. Inside the wall, which was half-a-mile thick, were countless apartments and businesses. The rest of the city was a giant slab of wet concrete and rows upon rows of docks. Wooden shacks and other separate constructs dotted the slab in clusters here or there, such as the *House of Heaven*, but mostly it was a wide open space. The place was lit with lanterns everywhere there was a hook for one. They looked like fireflies in the distance, bobbing about in the wind and rain.

People in thick raincoats wandered around quietly, sullenly. They passed a ship come to harbor late with a bunch of rowdy sailors unloading their cargo, but eventually that noise faded into the sound of the storm. Knick, Shade, and Lethan walked hunched while Whiskey rode beneath the Jin's jacket, assaulted by the downpour, but the Sirens walked with their backs straight and heads held high. As they crossed the docks, Knick became increasingly aware of a song—the same song he had faintly heard in the *House of Heaven*—carried on the wind. His eyes kept being drawn to the black waters beyond where he thought he saw people in those raging currents, but he chalked it up to the lightning flashes reflecting off the water playing tricks on his eyes. There was no way a person could survive in waves like that.

When they had been soaked through to the bone, the Sirens finally turned onto a flooded, slippery dock and led them through two inches of swirling water that tugged at their ankles and threatened to sweep them away. A short, thin wisp of a woman with pink hair and bright, cyan-colored eyes stood at the end next to an anchored boat with a single lantern. As soon as he saw it, Knick began shaking his head.

"No way. You've got to be kidding me," he said.

"We must cross the Karnak to reach the Shaman," Coda said.

"It's a raging storm out there!" he protested. "We'll capsize as soon as we cast off! You got little more than a rowboat there."

"We will not," Breva chimed in. "These waters are our allies. You can hear the Chant on the wind. Even now, our sisters swim…"

"Then they *are* people," Lethan murmured. "I thought it was merely light-play."

So he wasn't the only one. He didn't know if he should be

relieved or alarmed. "Where the hell do you expect to go anyway? There's nothing but water out there."

"We go to the temple," Lyrica told them and motioned out across the bay. "To the garden of souls."

Knick and Shade squinted to see into the darkness through the fierce rains and bright flashes. After a moment, what he thought was just a large wave became apparent. He could see triangular shapes spearing out of the water on the bleak horizon. Portentous black pyramids were lurking in the never-ending storm. Lethan murmured something in the Jin language and Knick felt compelled to agree with him even though he had no idea what he had said. Something about those pyramids screamed dangerous. Not evil, but definitely not safe or welcoming.

"Come," the pink-haired girl said with a disarming smile. "The Shaman awaits."

Lyrica, Coda, and Chorda climbed in and offered their hands to help. Lethan, Shade, and Knick exchanged wary glances.

"Trust me," the pink-haired girl said. "I promise, no harm will come to you."

It was as though she had compelled them. One after another, Lethan, Shade, and then Knick climbed into the boat. Breva and the pink-haired girl followed them. Breva cast them off and their boat went tumbling purposely through the waves. Lyrica and Chorda rowed gently. The Sirens periodically began singing, joining the song on the wind. Occasionally, Knick thought he saw a woman's head emerge from the waters to watch them.

"You are the One," the pink-haired girl said as she moved to sit next to him. He glanced around and suddenly felt very far away from everyone else on the boat.

"That's the rumor."

"I am Tikal."

"Knick Coltin."

"Yes." She tilted her head to the side, eyes wide with curiosity. "We have waited for you for so long."

"That's what they keep telling me," he muttered, wrapping his arms around himself as if he could somehow keep warm. He wasn't prone to seasickness, but the rolling of the boat made him feel queasy. Tikal, he noticed, seemed perfectly at home in the turbulence.

"Are you sick?"

"No," he lied. "But I've had enough of being tossed around in this storm."

"You mean how you almost drowned," she said and he nodded. "The Shaman warned us you were in danger. Lyrica and the others were picked to save you. I wanted to go but they wouldn't let me."

"Why?"

"Hmm," she hummed thoughtfully, and then smiled. "Because I am...their 'precious, little sister.'" Then she laughed, and it was so bright and free and contagious that Knick chuckled, too. "They are very protective, these sisters of mine."

Tikal was small in height and body mass and, because of it, perhaps almost childlike, but she was definitely a woman. He could see from the wrapped linens she barely wore that her body was mature. And her young face held a wisdom he could barely fathom. Her smile was genuine and her laughter devoid of the weight of the world—that, he decided, was what made her seem so young.

"Overprotective," he muttered as he cleared his throat. "Were you in any danger?"

"No," she said as a matter of fact. "I am the safest I have ever been...now that you are here."

He frowned at her. "What does that mean?"

"It means I trust you completely."

Knick flicked his eyes to Shade and then swept his gaze out to sea. "Because I'm the One?" he growled agitatedly.

"This does not please you, being the One."

"Why should it?" he spat, water spewing from his lips. "Everyone knows who I am, but they don't know me. They know who they want me to be. I had a life before this. Maybe it wasn't great but it was mine."

"You want people to embrace you as Knick, not as the One."

"Is that too much to ask? Do you know what they say about the One?" He snapped his head to look at her. She waited patiently for him to tell her. "The 'ender of all things', that's what they say. How am I supposed to feel about that?"

"They," Tikal echoed. "You mean the Keepers."

"Yeah."

He glanced over at Shade further down the length of the boat talking to Coda. She was just a few rungs away but it felt like a chasm lay between them. Tikal turned to look at Shade and he realized she was following his gaze so he quickly looked at the watery bottom of the vessel. He wanted to smoke but he'd lost his pack in the near-death-by-drowning experience. Even if he'd had a cigarette on him, it would've been waterlogged by the rain.

"And what of the Krueh-jin?" Tikal asked. "Do they call you 'ender of all things', too?"

"No," he mumbled. "To them I'm some kind of wandering nomad who will lead them to their long lost home."

"That's not so awful," she said as thunder rumbled loudly. "Don't you think?"

"Can't help being skeptical."

"Then I shall tell you how Na Varen know of you. The legend is not so different from the Krueh-jin's." She smiled excitedly and inched closer. He tightened his arms around himself, feeling uncomfortable with her so close. She was a very pretty girl. "To Na Varen, the One is Inanna's Chosen, the only man allowed to rule her. When he arrives, the floodgates will open and the sea will flow back into the shadow of Panghora, and Na Varen will be brought back from exile and returned to their holy places."

Knick stared at her as they cleaved left and right between overbearing waves. Tikal stared back, her cyan eyes almost glowing in the storm. Neither said a word. The other Sirens on the boat raised their voices to join the song on the wind, and suddenly a thousand voices in the water began to sing. It was as though the storm and sea were singing. It surrounded him, flowed into him, a forlorn melody. There were no words that he recognized, just music, melodic music.

As they sang, a series of feelings settled into his bones. He forgot his questions about Inanna and the Na Varen's exile. He even forgot his nausea. Instead, he went through tumbling emotions as turbulent as the sea they crossed. Sadness, hope, despair, awe—all accompanied with a sense of intimacy. He looked at Shade and saw she, too, was affected by the song. He thought to look over his shoulder at Lethan but something about the music paralyzed him.

"They sing of Inanna, our divine mother," Tikal whispered. "They sing of our exile, of our malformation, of the pilgrimage and sojourn that lasted through the ages. Of the days we were many," she paused to hum several bars of the song, "of the days we were few." There were suddenly tears in her eyes, as though she felt all of the pain of her ancestors. Something about it compelled Knick's emotions and suddenly there were tears stinging his own eyes. "They sing of how our suffering is at an end. They sing of the new dawn. They sing of you."

She lifted her hand and he hesitantly reached out and touched it, palm to palm. He was suddenly filled with warmth, his insides humming like a song. A faint, pastel light appeared between their touching fingers. Tikal smiled, closed her eyes, focused like she was listening to something, absorbing something. When she opened her eyes, they really were glowing. Then her hand slid from his and the glowing stopped.

"Tikal," he whispered. He wanted to ask her what the hell just happened but another question popped out instead. "Who is Panghora?"

"Not who. What." Tikal tilted her head again and a bright streak of lightning suddenly split the sky. "Panghora was the great temple and throne of the King of Light, and everything the shadow of Panghora touched belonged to him."

"Malikiel," Knick mumbled.

Tikal lowered her head sadly. "Our records are lost. The pyramids hold fragments of our history, but much has been weathered away with time. The only song retained from those days is the Chant. We have never let go of it, for it was our duty to sing it always. And we do, even now, though we do not know why."

"That's strange."

"Is it?" She smiled at him again and he felt a sense of peace flow into him. He thought he understood why the other Sirens protected this girl. "You do not have to pick between being Knick Coltin and the One. They are the same. When you embrace that, you will see that everyone else has as well." Suddenly Tikal looked out to the black pyramids. "We are here."

All at once, the music stopped. All that remained was the

rush of the storm. The pyramid thrusting out of the water loomed over them, its four, once-blocky faces eroded away into mostly smooth surfaces. It looked black under the dark sky and raging rain. Even with the great size of it, he knew it was the tip of the iceberg. This close, Knick could see dozens of pyramids scattered in the sea, some just small peaks and others rising monuments. But none were as large as the one they were about to board.

"Why do you call it the garden of souls?" he whispered as their boat approached the dock. There was a lantern calling to them as it swayed in the wind. The Sirens all stood so Knick and the others followed suit. There was a hooded figure waiting at the end of the dock, robes fiercely tugged this way and that.

"These pyramids were the last resting place of the Tribes before they scattered. Meager homes for the fallen compared to what had once sheltered them." She bowed her head respectfully. "Their bones fill the rooms in desperate hope, now ashes, now nothing."

As the boat drifted closer to the dock, Knick could see a sea of faces in the water. Women were clinging to the pyramid and dock, some scattered in the nearby waves, all staring with feline-like eyes glowing in the dark, watching with expressionless curiosity.

"Now we sing the final verse of the Chant," Tikal whispered, "for the first time since the breaking, for the last time in eternity."

As the boat rocked against the dock and Breva hopped up to tie it off, they could see the cloaked figure was an old woman, weighed down with wrinkles. Her dark, leathery skin was patterned with pale tattoos that covered every visible part of her skin, face included. Beads, coins, bones, and various trinkets clung to her tattered layers of clothes. She gave Knick the creeps for one reason only. Her eyes. The irises were white; not white with disease or age, but an unnatural luminescent white.

The Sirens climbed out of the boat and helped their passengers onto the dock. Shade reached back for Knick and, when he took her hand, he refused to let go. Tikal went to the Shaman's side, standing two steps behind her like an acolyte to her senior. Her cyan eyes zeroed in on Knick and Shade's clasped hands and then she smiled.

"Welcome to the garden of souls," the Shaman said. Her bony hand covered with jewelry dropped something to the ground. Hand-carved dice clattered along the planks and stopped, weighted down like stones in the currents rushing around their feet. She knelt down and stared at the tiny scrawls on the upturned faces. "Come closer." After a moment's hesitation, Knick knelt down followed by Shade. Without looking up, she added, "All of you."

Lethan lowered himself down with Whiskey still bundled in his jacket. He looked uneasily at the Shaman, brow creased in deep concern. Knick wondered what he was so tense about; he didn't think the Shaman was that much scarier than Sabal.

Suddenly a long, skeletal finger was pointed at Lethan. A rusted silver serpent wrapped her knuckle to base, and the long, curved fingernail was pierced with three small rings.

"Guide," she said, turning her white gaze upon the Jin. "To the edges of the quarry, in the near deep, must you take your master. To the ruins for a beast, the way opened by children, call for Molly. She will be waiting. The ghost of Babylon. Ataashvatan." Then the Shaman turned her finger to Knick and those white eyes captured his. He could not blink, could not look away. "The last of your vassals will be a harbinger of death, wailing of the flame to be extinguished. The King will offer himself. Accept no other but the harbinger." Finally she released him and he felt some invisible tension flow out of him. The gaze had shifted to Shade. "Power to affect and effect roils within you. It is yours to command. A pact of shadow. A balance delicate. Form mirrored, essence halved. Restored at the close. But careless in your haste to save him, and you will become a shadow forever."

The Shaman lowered her hand to scoop up her dice then folded her fingers together. She stood up and waited for Knick and his companions to do the same. Knick's uneasy feeling grew tenfold. What did she mean by that? That Shade could become a shadow forever?

"It is time," the Shaman declared and turned to walk into the pyramid. Tikal smiled at them and followed her. The rest of the Sirens urged them into the bowels of the great beast.

The dusty, square-shaped corridor went on for a long time with confusing lefts and rights and steep steps down like they were back in the Grey. Torches were bolted onto the walls, illuminating faded hieroglyphs. In the rooms that branched off the main corridor, they could see more broken images.

"We should have brought the scholar," Lethan mused quietly, his voice echoing down the corridor.

"Antion," Shade agreed.

"Think he could've made something out of these?" Knick asked, motioning to where one of the images had degraded so poorly that it was a mere splotch of washed out white on the wall.

"In decades, perhaps," Shade replied with a faint smile. "The collective never abandon their pursuit of knowledge."

"Lucky them."

The rest of the journey to the heart of the pyramid was made in silence. The room they sought was a magnificent central chamber. Ancient stone giants lined the walls, arms crossed over their chests and hands gripping strange scepters and obsolete weapons. Four massive braziers blazed with bonfires, one in each corner. There was a shaft in the ceiling that directly connected with the surface of the pyramid, bringing in a wash of fresh, cold air to dilute the stale environment. The light sneaking in from the shaft beamed directly upon a circular altar in the center of the room, raised up on a dais surrounded by steps. And all around them, Sirens were gathered, silently looking on.

"We Na Varen have a gift for you, Knick Coltin," the Shaman said, motioning to the girl with pink hair. "Tikal, Inanna's Dirge, your soul shield, death eater."

"I, uh," Knick stammered as he stared at Tikal in disbelief. Heavy titles for someone so innocent-looking. "I don't know what that means."

"She is your protector," the Shaman explained. "She will go with you to the end."

"I have a protector," Knick told them, tipping his head in Shade's direction.

"And she will protect you," Tikal said, "but there will be battles fought on many fronts. She cannot fight them all. You will forget me but I will be there. Nothing can harm you as long as I am with you."

"Look, I have enough help as it is. I don't need anymore."

"You will," Tikal replied calmly. "You just don't know it

yet."

"Why? Because some prophecy told you that? I'm tired of that shit. I don't need anyone else."

"You mean as long as you have her," Tikal said and motioned to Shade. Knick choked for a minute, shocked that she had read his feelings so completely. She giggled—a light and sweet sound. "You are already beyond that truth you cling to."

Knick felt angry. "Aren't you a little young for this?"

"I was born to do this. I told you my sisters were protective. This is why. They have been shielding me for this moment."

"Yeah? Well do they know what's out there? Do *you*? There's a growing list of assholes aiming to take my head. You come with me? You're putting yourself in the line of fire."

"I told you that nothing can harm you as long as I am with you. Just so, nothing can harm me as long as I am with you."

"This is the will of the Tribes," the Shaman told him. "Our best we send with the One. It was written, and we obey."

Knick fought the urge to roll his eyes and looked pointedly at Tikal. "I can't afford to keep eyes on you," he confessed.

"Don't worry," she promised, "you won't have to."

Knick frowned but said nothing, once again beaten by Tikal's kind eyes and smile. He didn't really know what she meant by 'you won't have to' but decided arguing was worthless. He shoved his hands in his jacket pockets in frustration.

"The ritual must begin. Proceed with the tuning," the Shaman declared. "Remove your clothes, Knick Coltin."

Knick felt as though he had been slapped in the face. He gaped at the Shaman and opened his mouth to protest.

"What?" Shade blurted before he could say anything and Knick snapped his gaze on her. Part of him wanted to smile but he was too shocked by her reaction.

"Tikal must tune herself to the melody of the One," the Shaman explained. "She must know him entirely, every note of his core. An act of intimacy is the only way to achieve such harmony."

He was tired of running. They were all tired of

running. Not mentally tired. Not in the way that one lost hope or the drive to keep going. It was worse. They were physically exhausted, lungs burning and legs aching. Any reprieve was short-lived, hiding spots quickly ferreted out, and then they were on the run again, from Jaco's Bluff to Britz. Any minute now, Jilk was afraid they would be incapable of going on, especially with them taking turns carrying Otto on their back. "We have to stop," Isis would say, but Jilk would just ignore her. The cogwheelers had kept up the chase, and Jilk could only guess at why. They were going to war with the angels; why waste manpower on a handful of deserters? It bothered him.

As they approached the town limits of Britz, anxiety overwhelmed him. After Britz, there would be almost nowhere left to go. Beyond this were a few small settlements and the quarry mazes then the dangerous nothingness of black caves. People didn't go to the caves. Creatures they didn't understand lurked in those caves. It would be suicide. The only place left would be the coal mines below, but that was just as much a bad idea as the caves.

They would have to stand and fight, and probably die.

Shouts from cogwheelers closing in chased them into the town. Jilk slowed down and pushed Isis and Antion ahead. Solo carried Otto on his back, huffing and puffing with Slot jogging steady at his side. Jilk motioned for her to match pace so she fell back to join him.

"We have to defend," he told her and she nodded. "We set up around the *Toxic Ox*, hide the Keepers, make them think we got no one with us but us."

As the bar came into view, Jilk was slammed with a memory. The Keeper attack that had gotten Knick caught up in all this nonsense happened right here. Knick. Jilk wanted to smack himself as it hit him. The cogwheelers were looking for Knick. He had inside information on MAAR. That kind of information was priceless to them. Of course they wouldn't skimp on resources to find him.

"Shit," he muttered. "I think we're in trouble."

"They're lookin' for Knick," Slot muttered grimly and Jilk nodded. "I won't talk, Jilk, and I won't let them take me. You put a bullet in my head if they pass us." She bashfully looked at the ground. "I don't think Solo could do it."

Jilk frowned, nausea rising from the pit of his stomach at the very idea. "It won't come to that," he lied and she shot him a reprimanding look. "It might come to that," he conceded, "but not before we kill as many of them as we can."

They swung inside the *Toxic Ox* and hailed Duke before rushing the few scattered patrons out the door, all but the drunk at the end of the bar. They ripped up benches and borrowed boxes from nearby establishments to make a small barricade around the door. Time was short so they threw scrap metal over the windows and laid out their ammunition.

"The hell is going on?" Duke asked.

"Cogs are comin'," Jilk replied tightly. "Long story. Tell you if I live through the next few hours." He walked over to Antion and pressed a pistol into his palm. "Take those two," he motioned to Otto and Isis, "upstairs and if they get through us…well, you know what I mean."

"You mean 'when'?" Antion asked, his face gaunt.

"Give us a little credit," Jilk scolded. "You know how to use that thing?"

"No, sir," he replied numbly.

"Aim for a big target, not the head—that's just gonna be a waste of ammo. Go for the gut. There're a lot of vital organs you can snag without trying. Squeeze the trigger—don't pull it. Try not to panic. You got a limited number of bullets, kid, so you want to make every shot count."

Antion nodded and went upstairs like he was wading through mud, Otto limping under his arm. Isis stared hard at him. He felt the urge to bark, "What?" but resisted. He turned away and eyed Duke coming from the back of the shop with a pump-action rifle. He pumped it once and settled into a nook next to a window, carefully placing the barrel through a crack.

"You sure about that?" Jilk asked. "If you just stay back there, the cogs won't involve you."

"Roll over and let them tear up my bar?" Duke scoffed. "Fat chance."

"Lotta good you'll do with that thing," the drunk at the bar grumbled.

"Shut up, Cakes," Duke growled. The drunk shrugged and ducked behind the bar with a bottle of whiskey.

Jilk nestled into the barricade with Slot and Solo, broke his shotgun open, and shoved shells into the chamber.

"Feels wrong," Slot said.

"What?" Jilk muttered.

"Killing our brothers."

"Yeah," he said, snapping his weapon back together. "Well there are no brothers when you're backed in a corner. No friends, no family, just enemies. So kill them quick, because they'll do the same to you."

Slot nodded and cast her eyes downward regretfully. Solo reached over and put his hand on top of her head. Jilk envied that measure of comfort, to be able to give it and receive it. Then came the sound of footsteps pouring across the town limits and they lined up their shots. The cogwheelers came into view.

Ten minutes of gunfire felt like an eternity. They managed to take down half-a-dozen in the surprise attack but after that it was a series of misses. It didn't take long to burn through their small ammunition stock and it was anyone's guess how much the cogs had brought with them.

Slot reached up and gripped the barricade, glaring over the top. Jilk shook his head but she didn't seem in the mood to listen to his orders. Solo popped a few rounds over the top and ducked back down.

"Don't you dare," he growled when he saw the look on his sister's face. "Slot—"

Slot screamed and, using the overturned table as a shield, broke away from the barricade and rushed across the dusty yard. Bullets tore into it, chipping off wooden chunks from the legs and ends as she whizzed by. Jilk and Solo returned fire immediately, giving her as clear a path to the other side as they could. She crashed into the median the cogs had hidden behind and flipped the table onto their heads. The cogwheelers tumbled back as splinters of wood flew everywhere.

Solo scrambled across the yard and jerked up a scoped rifle one of the earlier kills had dropped. Bullets pinged off the ground near him but he managed to dive back into cover without getting hit. He recovered, took aim and, after just a few measured breaths, squeezed out a single bullet. It struck a cog in the head just as he was moving between cover. He picked another target and put a bullet in his head. Three more clean headshots had cleared the field of the cogs that were crossing the clearing toward Slot.

Jilk kept the gunnies ducked with suppressing fire while Solo took his time lining up his next shot. Slot, meanwhile, rampaged the group she had crashed into, trading punches and cracking jaws. One guy bear-hugged her from behind but she just used the leverage to kick another cog in the chest before planting her boot in the bear's kneecap.

For a moment, he thought they were doing really well. They were actually going to come out of this okay. And then the reinforcements caught up to them. Jilk went five shades pale as a cluster of spare cogs rolled into view. Solo yelled for Slot as she went up in the sightlines of the reinforcements. Jilk watched helplessly as she threw her hands over her head, waiting for the cascade of bullets.

Columns of electricity shot up out of the ground, ripping through the reinforcements. The survivors scrambled away from the spot, gaping in horror at the crispy remains of their comrades. Slot peeked through her arms. A black ball of smoke dropped out of the darkness and landed between the bar and the cogs. He wore a trench coat, wielded a sword, and had a stance like Shade's, immediately convincing Jilk this man was a Keeper.

The man motioned to Slot so she ran back to the barricade and right into Solo's arms. Her brother squeezed her tight, eyes red-rimmed and raw with fear.

"You will leave," the man told the cogwheelers. "You will not come back. Or I will kill you."

The cogs stared at him, debating their chances of survival if they didn't listen. It didn't take long for them to make the right choice; all it took was once glance at the charred lumps of what used to be their friends before they all started running.

The man turned to them and sheathed his sword. At that sign of peace, Jilk, Solo, and Slot came out from around their battered barricade, quickly joined by Duke.

"My name is Daelus," he told them, searching for something beyond them, inside the bar. "I'm looking for Shade but she isn't with you."

"We split ways at Gehrs," Jilk admitted, thinking that little bit of truth couldn't hurt.

"With Knick," Daelus surmised, nodding to himself. "But she will come find you, won't she?" he asked, but no one said a word or offered the slightest of nods. "I'll wait for her. And while I wait, no harm will come to you."

Jilk thought it over. The guy was a Keeper and capable of killing them all with a flick of that special little sword he carried. He probably wasn't Shade's enemy and he was their only line of defense against the cogs. At the very worst, they had just delayed their death a little longer. Weighed like that—to die now or die later—it wasn't a hard decision to make. So Jilk nodded.

"You," a voice said from behind them. Isis walked out of the bar, her green gaze locked on Daelus. "You have come for her."

"Who are you?" Daelus asked, frowning.

"I am your Enoch."

"Enoch," he whispered, expression going slack. "It's not possible…"

"You never knew me," she said, walking closer to him, "but I knew you. When she was just a tiny child, I showed you her face, the woman, so that you would one day save her life."

Daelus seemed to crumble under the weight of those words. Jilk gaped as the Keeper fell to his knees before her. To him, Isis had been, on her best days, annoying. Antion's reaction to her identity had been bizarre but hardly inspiring. Seeing someone as powerful as Daelus fall to the ground, however…that was something impressive enough to make him think he had possibly misjudged the small, blond girl.

"Please don't," Isis said as she gently touched his head, her thin, pale fingers disappearing in his dark brown hair. "Stand up. You are welcome here."

Daelus looked up at her and Isis smiled at him. A loud thunk caused Jilk, Slot, and Solo to jump and everyone turned around. Antion, who was leaning on the swinging door, had dropped the gun Jilk had given him. He sighed in relief.

An act of intimacy is the only way to achieve such harmony. The words echoed between Knick's ears.

"You want me to—" he started, and then another realization struck him, "—right here, in front of everyone?" He looked at the faces staring back at him. Nothing in their expressions led him to believe they saw anything wrong with their request. "Sorry, sweetheart, but," Knick looked at Tikal, "you're not really my type."

An upset murmur shuddered through the Sirens. Tikal giggled, bringing her hand up to stifle the noise. The Shaman glared at him.

"The tuning is vital to the metamorphoses!" the old woman exclaimed.

"Too bad," Knick said with a shrug. "I'm not doing it."

"You must!"

"It's okay, Shaman," Tikal said, silencing everyone in the room. "I already know everything I need to know."

"But Tikal—" Chorda began.

"It's okay," she insisted. "I can hear his sound like I can hear the storm. It overtakes everything, rushes into the depths of me, past every barrier. It soaks into my skin, into my soul. Already, my sound is syncing with his." She wrapped her arms around herself and looked up into the pale light, smiling. "When it harmonizes completely, the song will burst out of me."

"How is that possible?" Breva whispered.

"Prepare the ritual," the Shaman said. "Daughters of Inanna, the Chant of Panghora."

The Sirens began to sing as one, all but the Shaman and Tikal. The Shaman scattered leaf and bone and feather around Tikal's feet before flicking a strange powder at her shins. Knick thought she looked like an old woman brewing a suspicious potion. But then something strange happened. A soft blue light began to haze around Tikal, her form softening in the glow. No, wait. It wasn't around her. It *was* her. What was happening to her? What the hell was this ritual, anyway?

The Shaman then drew a sinister weapon that looked suspiciously ceremonial. Knick lunged forward.

"What the hell are you doing?" he exclaimed. The Sirens did not stop singing but all eyes turned to him. "You're going to kill her?"

"This is the way it must be," the Shaman told him.

"No," he shouted. "No fucking way!"

"Let me do this, Knick," Tikal whispered, her voice ethereal.

"No! I caved when you said you wanted to come with me but this is *not* what I meant!"

"This is the way I was meant to go with you."

"No! No fucking way! Are you crazy? Are you all fucking

crazy?"

"I was born for this. I have been waiting for this moment my whole life. I am not afraid."

"You don't have to do this! I don't want you to do this! This is insane!" Knick stormed up to the altar but Breva, Coda, Lyrica, and Chorda intercepted him, holding him back while their voices continued to harmonize with the others. "You said you were safe with me! You said you were *safe*—" His voice cracked. "You brought me here so they'd kill you!"

"It is not dying," the Shaman said, "what our Tikal goes to do. It is rebirth. The purest form Na Varen can take. A soul song."

"I don't know you," Knick begged the girl. "Don't die for me. Don't do this. I'm not worth it. Please." He looked at the Sirens holding him back. "Stop her. You have to stop her. She's going to kill her! Doesn't that mean anything to you?"

"You are worth it," Tikal said, her form a mere suggestion in the blue shimmer of light. He saw her bright smile in the haze, her cyan eyes glowing as they gazed upon him with that same look that compelled him. "Let me do this, Knick. Let me protect you."

"No!" he yelled as the song reached its crescendo.

Tikal's legs gave out from under her. Before her knees ever touched the altar, the Shaman plunged the dagger into her chest. Light ripped out of the wound, tearing a glowing hold in the center of her, splintering into a dozen, light-filled lines that reached to the very tips of her body. Her mouth opened and a song burst forth, paralyzing everyone with its sound. It was the most beautiful and powerful thing he had ever heard. And as she sang, she dissolved into it, into the light that glowed around the vibrations of her sound. It speared him like a blade, flowed into his chest and burned into his skin.

The Sirens lowered him to the ground and backed away. Where she had stood was now an empty space. The light was gone, her voice was gone. He touched his chest. Through his clothes, he felt the ridges of a scar that was all that remained of the girl called Tikal.

Dr. Basset had heard the rumors of a pregnant Keeper and knew instantly that Vox's secret was out. And when he was summoned to the Baron's office, the long, shadowed expression Eros wore confirmed it. He sat hunched over in a chair, his elbows on his knees and the bridge of his nose caught between his fingertips. Neither man said anything for a long time, reigning in their scattered thoughts. They just acclimated to one another's presence, with coughs and worried sighs and deep breaths, with a sense of naturalness and familiarity, like an old house settling.

"You knew," the Baron finally said.

"I did."

"Why didn't you tell me?"

"They begged me not to. I didn't know you when I gave them my word, but later I encouraged her to confide in you. Something was…" he hesitated and tiredly rubbed his face, "was wrong."

Eros nodded. He took a deep breath and exhaled slowly, like a man on the verge of losing control. He kept his gaze pinned to the ground. They simmered in that understanding for awhile.

"Something has happened," Basset said, "hasn't it?"

"Yes."

A lump formed in his throat. "Tell me."

"Vox has gone missing. Not even Dimitri knows where she has gone." He looked up and Basset was shocked by the dark lines in this man's once-youthful face. He looked so tired, so haggard, as though he had aged ten years in just a few nights. He drew in a lungful of air and paused, almost like he was afraid of the words he had to speak. "Vox will die. If they had come to me before, I might've…" He looked at his hands. "I might've helped her. Helped the child. They're both at risk."

"I didn't know," Basset choked. "I'm sorry. I didn't know."

"You couldn't have known. Not even the Interim know. There are rules for a reason but those reasons are not always what we think they are. Love interferes with one's devotion to the Balance, but that is not the only reason it is forbidden. The human body can only withstand so much; it is not built to hold more energy than it creates on its own. The Interim harbor a foreign energy within their bodies, channel it, enhance it, but always expend it until all that's left is a passive kernel at their core, the potential to be, but nothing more than their body can hold. To contain it for so long, let it grow…"

"This has happened before," Basset murmured in realization. Eros nodded. The longer he studied him, the more he realized how personal this was. "This happened to you."

Eros looked at him for a long time and nodded again. Basset grabbed a chair and sat down. The Baron looked down at his own hands again, studied them, saw something there that Basset could only guess at. He waited for an explanation, for a story, for a rebuff, for an order, for any word at all.

"I loved a woman once, a long time ago...when I was a much younger man. I was already Baron, deeply devoted to the Balance. We had fewer Interim back then, so I worked as often in the field as they did. That's when I met her. She was beautiful, the first and only person I ever desired, and I indulged in her...but I never let her come between my devotion to the Balance. And then she became pregnant.

"I knew I had to end it. I could never have a family. She could never be brought into the Order. I was going to send her away, help her start over somewhere new. She was carrying a child, but it never truly sank in that it was mine."

"What happened?" Basset asked quietly.

"Her pregnancy became complicated. She started having pains. Her health diminished. And one day this beautiful, vibrant woman was like a sick child on the verge of death. Her womb could not handle it. The labor was...agony. She died giving birth." Eros looked at Basset. "This woman was not a Keeper. She carried the seed of my energy, the energy that became a new Keeper. And it destroyed her." He shook his head. "Vox now carries the energy of *three*."

Basset closed his eyes regretfully, jaw tightening up with stress. "Maybe her energy will protect her," he mumbled when he was once again capable of speech.

"Maybe," Eros said, but nothing in his tone suggested he believed it for even a second. The unspoken danger reverberated between them, that Vox and the infant would be destroyed.

"And your child?" he asked, drawing the Baron's gaze. "What happened to your child?"

"My child," Eros whispered, staring at his hands again. "The moment I laid eyes on that child...*my* child...I fell in love. For the first time in my whole life, I knew what it meant to love someone."

"And the child," he urged, "did the child survive?"

Eros closed his hands into fists, face pulled tight like he might laugh and cry at the same time. He gave a single, solemn nod. "Yes."

Tiboili was a small settlement on the edge of Monarch, Anshar's equivalent of the Cradle. It was mostly a deserted mining town, save for a few settlers that refused to leave when the dig site dried up. The workers the Priori had rounded up were sent in under the direction of two scholars and the protection of a single unit of Priori. Rexis and Donovan were acting supervisors.

As they dug through the first layer of rubble to clear the shaft down to Go'sam, the two Interim relaxed away from the cloud of debris that sifted in the stale air.

"It's remote enough," Donovan muttered.

"Perfect for a hiding spot," Rexis agreed.

"Still, you really think we'll find anything here? If the miners struck Go'sam, it's likely they plundered whatever they found."

"Before our time," Rexis reminded him. "I doubt the Regent would've let that happen. The place is shut down now. You going to tell me you don't think we had anything to do with it, ay?"

"Fair point." He looked at the workers shuffling stones this way and that. "This is taking too long."

"Give them time. We just got here."

"We don't have time," Donovan muttered, pushing off the wall he had been leaning on.

"Don't."

"Just a quick blast," he called over his shoulder and then yelled, "Out of the way!"

Workers scattered as the Interim drew his icy fang and the bells jingled on his wrist. A wave of energy struck the sealed tunnel entrance and encased it in ice. A second blast followed and the rubble exploded into a thousand shards. Some of the workers were struck and fell over in pain, screaming and rolling on the ground. Donovan grinned and peered down into the tunnel, at the icy glaze that reinforced it all the way down.

He looked back at Rexis. "After you."

Part Four

"A blind man sees with his cane, like all the rest of us."
Marty Rubin

When his feet hit the gangplank that zigzagged up to his house on the cliff, Roskolniv immediately noticed the black dog perched quietly outside the front door. That could only mean one thing. He ran the rest of the way and threw open the screen door.

"Red!" Roskolniv shouted, wildly looking around. "Red!"

He found her stuffing her clothes—the ones she kept at his place, her favorites she called them—into a small leather sack. She nodded when she saw him and continued packing. He stared dumbfounded.

"What are you doing?" he blurted, the only of many words buzzing around his head that actually made it to his vocal chords.

"Packing," she replied, annoyed. Red didn't like it when people asked stupid questions.

"Why?"

She glared at him. "Why do people pack their bags, Rosk?"

"Why are you leaving?" he snapped, frustrated and feeling panic start to crawl into his mind.

"Got to. It's time."

"Time?" he echoed numbly. "Are you leaving me? It is us? Did I do something?"

She looked pointedly at him. "I'm going on a trip." She folded her arms across her chest. "Why do you try to find meaning in things that aren't there?"

Because he was an insecure bastard, because he didn't deserve her, because he loved her more than she loved him, and because he was terrified that at any moment she would realize it and he would never see her again. He nodded, took a deep breath, tried to calm down. She had gone on trips before.

"You're right." He watched her return to packing. "How long this time?"

"Don't know. A few months, at least. Half a year, could be."

He cringed inside but kept the emotion from showing on his face. "You are coming back, right?" He said it like it was a joke but there was nothing funny about the question.

"Probably."

He frowned. He didn't like that answer. Was she joking? He couldn't tell. Why did he ask in the first place? Idiot. He ran his hand through his wavy hair as she closed the sack and fastened the buckles. He couldn't stand this silence.

"Where you going?"

"Home."

"What?" He forced out a laugh. "Like to that shithole out the OT way?"

"No. My real home. First home."

"Stop being cryptic, Red," he warned, shoving his hands in his pants pockets. "Just spit it out."

She grinned at him like she was amused by his confusion and agitation. "I'm not from here, Rosk," she told him. "And neither are they. This is something I have to do. For the Vatan, for Typhi."

He didn't know what she was saying but he could tell she was serious. He had no clue what Typhi was but the Vatan was that weird crew of hers she was always sailing off with. He didn't know what they did, just that they went away. He didn't care, not if answers meant losing her.

He rubbed the stubble on his jaw, thoughts racing too fast to think logically. "I just closed my major cases. Let me go with you."

"No. It's not a place you can go, Rosk."

"Why the hell not?"

"Because it's not your home."

He hated that. He hated when she talked like they somehow belonged to separate worlds. He hated that no matter how intimate they were, they weren't equals. She existed in a world he couldn't fathom and he wanted to hate her for it, but instead he just wound up hating himself.

She walked over to him, leaned up, kissed him. "Let's get dinner," she said then started to walk away. He pulled her back and kissed her, wrapped his arms around her, instantly lost himself in the feeling of her.

They made love and then ordered in. They lounged naked wrapped in blankets by a fire, eating straight out of the cartons. They laughed, stole bites of each other's food, talked like the things they had to say would still be relevant come morning. He smiled for her, smiled because he couldn't help it when he looked at her. Her stone gray eyes flecked with red and that blood-red hair made orange by the firelight—she was so beautiful. But the happiness he felt was shadowed by the knowledge that in a few hours she would be gone.

When the fire died down to glowing embers, they made love again and slept the last few hours to morning. He woke up when he heard the shower running, tried to get dressed, pulled on his pants then gave up and slumped numbly onto the bed. It was time. How had the hours flown by so quickly? He wasn't ready for this at all.

He sat there like a statue and stared straight ahead, not seeing anything. He listened to the sound of her towel off and put her clothes on, to the snap of laces as she tied her feet into her boots, the crinkle of leather and clanking of buckles as she slipped into her jacket.

Suddenly she was next to him, her presence a wall of warmth. He could smell the shampoo in her wet hair, feel the cold droplets drip onto his arms. She leaned down and pressed her lips against his. He kissed her back, lovingly and desperately. And in a second, it was over.

"Bye, Rosk."

And then she was gone. Bye. Bye? No, that wasn't right at all. "Seein' ya." That's what she always said. Not bye, bye like it was forever. She had left before but something about this time felt different, felt permanent. Maybe it was the way she said "bye". Maybe it was because he was terrified.

He jumped up and threw himself through the front door. The dog started barking. He ran down the gangplank and jumped the last railing, cursing as his bare foot landed on a rock, and hobbled to catch up to her, to his woman.

"Don't do this."

"I have to," she said calmly. "It's done, Rosk. Deal with it."

"I won't fucking deal with it!" he yelled over the barking. "You belong here! You belong here with me! Baby, listen to me—" The stupid mutt just wouldn't stop. "Stay with me. Move in. I don't want there to be anymore reasons why we're not together." The dog kept barking, an insistent rhythm. "Shut up!" he yelled and finally there was silence, except for the water crashing against the bottom of the cliff. "What do you think?"

"Sorry, Rosk, but this is more important than you."

He grabbed her as she tried to leave, unraveling right there in front of her. She hated weakness the most. She would hate him after this, he knew. But he couldn't stop. He wasn't in control. He was desperate.

"Please don't do this. Red, please," he begged. How much lower could she bring him? "Don't leave. I don't want to lose you. Please. Stay with me, please. I love you."

"I know." She smiled one last time and tried to leave again. He caught her, turned her back to him.

"Do you love me at all?" he finally asked. She just looked at him. And then she whistled and the dog was at her side instantly, soft, black coat bouncing as it trotted alongside her. She turned and left, and he was too numb to stop her again.

Red didn't even turn around when she lifted her hand in goodbye.

Knick sat on a bed in the *House of Heaven* hunched over with his head in his hands. He stared at the eight-pointed star scarred onto his chest, his mind locked in an endless loop of Tikal's smile and her death. The glowing light, the dagger that plunged into her chest, the wound ripping down her body. He had only known her for an hour, nothing more, and yet she had sacrificed herself on some stupid, twisted notion that her death could save him. Soul songs and death eaters and Typhi magic—he was sick of it. Sick of prophecies, sick of sacrifice, sick of all of it. Just when he had found the resolve to be the One—whatever that meant—and to see this through, another stupid stranger had to go and die in his name. Tikal was too young. Too innocent. Born for this? Brainwashed for this.

His fingers curled into his hair and took angry fistfuls. When he had broken with the Hive Mind and fled into the Mine, all he had wanted was to disappear. He was tired of bearing the responsibility of other people's misery. Sure, the cogwheelers were thugs, but they were human. That counted for something. And then someone wants to drop into his life and screw everything up, put him on a global stage of change, throw the responsibility of the world's future on his shoulders. That was ten kinds of fucked up. Why had he ever thought he could be okay with it?

"Damn it," he cursed under his breath. His head hurt. His chest hurt. The rest of him felt numb. "Damn you."

A person quietly entered the room on bare feet and placed a pack of cigarettes on the ground in front of him. He looked up and saw Coda staring with her sharp, red eyes. He didn't know why she ever reminded him of Shade. She couldn't compare at all. In just an hour, the Sirens who were once incomparably beautiful to him had become the opposite—an ugly kind of beauty, traps of deceit and death. They would never snare him, not after what they had done to Tikal.

"They are ready for you, Chosen One," she said. He bit his tongue to not respond. "The fastest way back to the Mine is through Hojo, a quick ride across the river."

He managed a curt nod. As Coda's image fell away from the door, Shade's filled it—the imposter replaced with the real thing. He was conflicted at the sight of her.

"Knick," she said like a parent calling to a willful child. "It's time."

He just stared at her until her violet eyes were too much to look at then hung his head again, exhausted. She waited for him to move, to speak. He tried to get up but his body wouldn't budge. The numbness ebbed, overcome by a sudden surge of anger. There was just one question he needed answering. He picked up the packet of cigarettes and drew one out, lit up, took a drag.

"Why?" he rasped on gray smoke. "Why didn't you help me?"

Lethan had been paralyzed by the song, but Shade hadn't. She had been free to move, to fight them, to save Tikal, but she had done nothing. Why? He needed to know.

"Because I heard a voice in my head…telling me it would be all right." She waited to continue until he looked at her. "I pulled my sword," she told him. "I went to you. But Tikal spoke to me. She asked me not to interfere. That the choice was hers as much as it had once been mine."

"I never asked for either of you to make that choice!" he yelled, jumping to his feet. "I didn't ask for any of this!"

"These are not things you ask for. They are choices we make for ourselves based upon who we know you to be."

"Choice? That's rich. You made me your 'One' but I didn't

have a *choice*—"

"I made you nothing—"

"—I don't have a say, my opinion means shit! You can't claim to do things for me, in my name, when I all but beg you do the opposite!"

"You can run from this if you want," she said calmly. "I do not think you will like the results any better."

"Fuck!" he screamed. "Why the hell did you do this to me? Why the hell did you put me in this position?"

"I did nothing but follow orders that led me to you." She frowned. "You…changed everything," she continued slowly, hesitantly, before it all poured out of her. "After I met you, I was betrayed. My brothers and sisters were slaughtered. My home was destroyed. I became an exile."

"Shade," he began, feeling as though cold water had been dumped on him. He tried to say something but nothing came to mind.

"We can run from this if we want," she said quietly. "Things beyond our control will happen regardless."

Knick started to lift the rette to his lips when her gaze dropped to his chest, to the scar left behind by Tikal. She gently reached up and placed her hand over it, and he forgot about his smoke. His heart started hammering so hard that she could probably feel it. He grabbed her fingers and held them tightly, bringing her eyes up to meet his again.

"When I first met you, you know what I thought?" he asked. "She's trouble." There was a ghost of a grin on Shade's lips. "The kind of trouble I could get into…" He looked at their hands on his chest for a long moment before continuing. "Some people teach themselves how to not feel. I never made that choice; Operations made it for me. So when I disconnected, I started feeling everything, all at once. These people I don't know…making these sacrifices for me…it's hard not to feel something. I don't want any more people dying. "

"Knick… I don't think it will get any easier from here on," she told him quietly.

Knick smirked but there was no mirth in his eyes. "Never crossed my mind to think otherwise."

"Do you want to stop? To disappear somewhere and wait until it's over?"

"I want to go wherever you're going," he said. "And

you're going to Britz, aren't you?" Shade nodded. "Then I guess I'm going to Britz."

If Knick was a dog, Shade would be his master. He would follow her for no other reason but that she was. There would be no leash, no whistle or summons; just the sight of her back moving away from him would be all that was needed to call him to her shadow. He couldn't fully explain it. She had spurned his advances, saw him as no more than a chess piece in a great prophecy—except, of course, when she was doped up on painkillers. He probably had less-than-zero chance with her and yet he continued to follow her. Because all he wanted was to be with her.

Shade's hand slid down his chest, fingers lightly brushing his abdomen, before she turned and walked away. Knick jerked his shirts from off the bed, pulled them on, and slipped into his jacket. He pocketed the smokes as he followed her out, lifting his remembered cigarette to his lips for a drag.

Daelus had been true to his word; the cogwheelers had been kept at bay, giving them time to recover. While Duke patched Slot up, Jilk and Solo cleared the streets of the bodies and gathered the scattered ammunition and guns. When it was done, they admired their collection on one of the remaining tables still intact. Jilk, Solo, and Duke stood around it while Slot perched on the bar top, eyeing the selection with mild interest.

"I gotta admit," the drunk said, lounging back on the bar, his butt half off his seat, "you guys lasted a lot longer than I thought you would."

"Shut up, Cakes," Duke growled.

"I'm just saying."

"Is he still here?" Jilk asked.

"Still? The man never leaves." Duke went back to looking at the gear. "Pretty heavy equipment," he observed. "Is that a six-pack of grenades?"

"Yeah," Jilk mused in wonder. "Wonder why they held off throwing these puppies?" He hoisted them up and saw the red skulls spray-painted on their sides. "Oh. Guess they just wanted to kill us, not everything in a quarter mile." He looked at Slot. "Remind me to put these somewhere safe, like the bottom of hell or something."

Slot saluted him.

"Pistol. Pistol. Shotgun. Shotgun." Solo picked through the selection, each piece offering a heavy thunk as it was moved aside. "Oh, SMG."

"I always liked an Uzi," Slot confessed.

"Eh." Solo shrugged with a pained expression as he finished sifting through what they'd gathered. "I'm not feeling so good about this. If we're fending off cogs, I'm going to need something serious. I want a security blanket—a .50 caliber magnum, maybe a HK 416 or M4, three round burst or full auto. I'm not picky."

Duke cleared his throat and motioned toward his storeroom. "I may have an AR-15 in the back."

"Bless you, Father."

"Not a priest. Just a bartender."

"Amen," Solo agreed and went to go check.

Slot watched her brother go then looked back at the men at the table. Duke was staring intently at Jilk, who seemed to be doing all he could to avoid looking back. He picked through weapons and ammo stores, but his gaze was fixed on one spot, not really seeing anything.

"Jilk," Duke said in that tell-tale way. "What're you doing here, Jilk?"

"Business as usual, man."

"Fighting cogs? That's not business as usual for a cog himself. I've known you a long time, Jilk." The bartender rubbed the stubble under his chin as her boss began slipping bullets into a fresh clip. "You're usually a better bluff."

"Cogs're going to war, Duke. Something bigger happening, though."

"Deserters?"

Jilk slammed a pistol on the table in agitation. "Not because we wanted to be. Necessity." He jammed the new clip in the gun. "Don't tell me you think war with Anshar's a good idea, Duke."

"Not even a little bit. But that doesn't answer the question, Jilk."

"What question's that?"

"Why are you here?"

"Had to get outta cog territory. Waiting on Coltin and then we'll be out of your bar. Not looking to trash it."

"Fuck the bar. It can be patched." Duke scratched his jaw. "Coltin. Knick Coltin? So he's your boy, huh?"

"That's right."

"I knew I liked him for a reason." He firmly took hold of Jilk's shoulder. "If you need a place, the *Toxic Ox* is all yours, old friend."

Jilk looked at him seriously. "I'm not looking to get you in trouble with the cogs either, Duke."

"Fuck the cogs, too," the bartender said with a grin. Jilk smirked and grabbed his shoulder.

"Jilk!" Solo hollered as he reappeared. "You're not going to believe this, but this sonuva bitch has a Liberty." He held up the roller-delayed blowback-operated semi-automatic rifle, beaming like it was Christmas morning. Slot's jaw dropped. Jilk eyed his friend.

"*Are* you a bartender," he asked, "or a priest?"

Duke laughed. "About fifteen years ago, this guy Ward comes to me and says, 'Guy named Reinhardt is putting together a group of freedom fighters and we need places to stockpile munitions for the big liberation day. You in?' Back then, there was a cogger cell hassling people in the OT, had trashed my bar a couple times, so I was all in. Few days later, some guys show up to install a secret vault in my storeroom and load it up. Ward gives me a key and leaves. Rumor has it, he was killed a year later in one of Reinhardt's early tussles. Never saw any of that band since." He motioned to the Liberty. "But they had good taste."

Slot laughed. Jilk looked back at her and smiled. Her brother sidled up next to her as the others went back to chatting.

"You doing okay?" he asked. She showed him her bandages and grinned. "Glad to see you're in good spirits."

"Solo," she began, drawing her knees up to her chest and wrapping her arms around her shins. "You sniped those stragglers."

He shrugged. "One or two."

"More than that. You're always looking out for me when I do something stupid."

"You were trying to help," he said as if to remind her.

Slot laughed. "I'm so lucky."

"Why is that?"

"I got the two of you carin' about me so much."

Solo snorted. "We're family," he said then started examining the Liberty.

He didn't know she knew, but she did. Slot wasn't stupid. Solo had given up his life for her. Family, he had said. But Slot knew for a fact that family didn't mean a lot in the Mine; it hadn't meant anything to hers. Sure, she was his sister, but Slot had seen a lot of brothers sell their sisters for some rials and a false sense of security. She had seen a lot of brothers ditch their sisters when they couldn't keep up. She'd especially seen sisters left to fend when the brother started drooling over some other girl.

Not Solo. He had built strengths to compensate for her weaknesses, fought with blood to protect her, and abandoned any potential romances the moment those interactions demanded he let her out of his sight. He had lived a stressed and anxiety-filled life, and no matter how strong she got, he just couldn't seem to breathe easy. She wanted to do something for him, to help him like he helped her.

When those cogwheelers had been closing in on them, all she could think was that they'd take Solo and she had to stop them. She *had* to. She didn't have to worry about forgiving or not forgiving anyone who hurt him because she would stop anyone who tried long before they could ever make their move. And blinded by that, she had done something stupid again. Charged in recklessly, nearly got them all killed by abandoning the barricade and forcing her friends on the offensive. Thinking about it made her want to crawl into a mine shaft and disappear.

One day, she vowed, she would return the favor. She would give him peace of mind. If nothing else, she would give him his life back.

"Hey, Solo," she said to get his attention and then hugged him tight. He bopped her on the head with his fist then casually draped his arm across her back.

"Love you, too, sis," he said.

The sound of deep, steadied breaths filled up Sonia's ears, drowning out the noise of the battle that raged around her. She could see Kur locked in combat with angels, individuals fighting against whole groups. The twins would flash into her peripherals and then disappear, but even they were flagging. The angels would not abandon Hojo and the Keepers were losing the ability to hold them at bay. Soon, it wouldn't matter. The bomb was almost ready. The tunnel would be sealed within the hour.

As a group of white suits closed in on her, Sonia shuffled and side-stepped, luring them into her trap. They surrounded her like all of the tactical fools she had met. The bracelet on her wrist jingled and she stabbed her sword into the ground. Five giant spikes burst out of the street and stabbed through each angel. Their bodies hung like warnings from those spikes, their legs still kicking in the throes of death. Sonia stepped between the shafts and back into the battle.

Other Interim kills were clean, but not hers. Not the Sovereign of Thorns. She left tattered corpses and pools of blood behind, bodies strung up on thorny vines or hanging limp from giant spikes. She left the battleground littered with razor-sharp barbs and clusters of sharp spines. She was an Exotic, from the far west and the island of Razhada. Her people were a beautiful, golden-skinned clan of hunters and warriors, bound by a fragile alliance with MAAR but a wish for total neutrality. Their borders were closed off minus the trade ships, and those non-merchant folk that ventured too close were killed and sent back holding their own heads.

She spoke with an accent and her features carried the fear of the Exotics—the slant of her eyes, the color of her skin, the texture of her hair. But the Keepers had seen her merely as the one chosen to wield the Sword of Thorns. They had shown no fear when they brought her into the fold, only welcome. It had surprised her and troubled her. Even her weapon was like her, the bloody and gruesome sword of Thorns, demonstrating her Exotic legacy. How could they not fear her?

And then came the day she realized that the Keepers feared nothing, that she had been foolish to think her heritage would give them pause. It was the day she had tasted fear for the first time in her entire life.

Since that day, she had ceased being a Raszheemi—an Exotic—and had become a true Keeper. She was Siri sa Sonia Momora Liera da Rakim no longer. She was only Sonia, Sovereign of the Sword of Thorns, Keeper of the Balance, and Interim of the Order. She had been chosen not because of her heritage but because she was meant to wield the sword.

Bullets whizzed by her. A shield of thorns immediately erected to protect her, absorbing the hot metal chunks aimed for her back. She whirled around and threw up her blade as another bullet glanced off of it. Roots crashed out of the earth and strangled two angels trying to snipe her, thorns puncturing their throats and chest, digging deep into the lungs. The other offenders she engaged with her blade, its teeth ripping through their battle armor to rake the meat beneath. They screamed as they died.

Sonia's honey-brown hair was caught up in a sudden breeze and she focused her emerald gaze to the source, beyond the bodies tangled in her vines, punctured by her thorns, beyond the carnage wrought from battle after battle—the burnt corpses, the charred buildings, the stagnant water sprinkled with ashes, bullet holes and shell casings and grenade caves. Far in the distance, she felt the presence of another Keeper. She recognized it immediately.

Sonia disengaged herself from the battle, eliminating only what was in her way as she ran to meet her, her long lost sister. The crumbling buildings passed her in a blur, feet gliding over the scorched streets at top speed. Finally she reached the clearing where a stream of black hair was blowing in the breeze. Shade's violet eyes turned on her, Sword of Shadows rising to stop her dead in her tracks. Sonia stared down the silver length of the weapon and into the pale woman's sharp gaze.

"Shade," Sonia gasped, remembering that expression her sister wore from days long gone. It had been this expression that had frightened her for the first time in her whole life, the expression Shade wore when she sucked life out of the world with her dark and mysterious Sword of Shadows. That had been Sonia's awakening, that the Exotics should fear the Keepers, not the other way around. For Sonia had been certain that Shade feared nothing, and so too should she fear nothing.

"Don't make me," the Interim growled. Sonia frowned. Why the hostility? Why would she treat her as another enemy? Only then did she notice the other two with her—the mocha-skinned man with a lehn perched on his shoulder and the black-haired man with gray eyes. There was something about the way Shade moved to protect him.

"That is him, isn't it?" Sonia whispered. "He is the One."

"Don't," Shade hissed, her foot sliding out in front of her, sword thrusting closer to Sonia's face. The Exotic held up her hands in surrender. "I don't want to hurt you."

"Shade…" she gaped. Hurt her? "Why?"

"Do you think I do not know what I have done?" she asked. "But there is much I have to do before I let the Keepers take me for it."

"What Keepers?" Sonia whispered. "We are dust already, remnants of what we once were."

Shade hesitated before she asked, "Did so few survive?"

Sonia nodded. "And more are lost every day. We cannot stop this war, only stall it. The Balance will shift. It is inevitable. There is nothing left to us but change." She looked beyond Shade to where the black-haired man stood. He was handsome, alluring, something about him powerful and reserved and unknown—like looking at a strange animal backed into a corner with no idea as to what it was capable of. "And to answer it, more change must be brought about. Shade," Sonia took a step toward the tip of the sword angled at her throat, "I harbor you no ill will. Believe me."

"Then why are you here?"

"Eros ordered us to seal the portals to the Mine but we have been unable to secure Hojo." She looked around at the dead angels that Shade had dispatched. "They keep coming. We don't know why."

"Is the tunnel still open?"

"It is." Sonia studied her comrade. "But not for long."

Shade looked back at the two men that traveled with her then back to Sonia. "You say you harbor me no ill will, then help me."

"Done."

"We need to get to the Mine."

"Will you not return to Sanctuary with me?" Sonia asked, disappointment bruising the happiness she had felt at their reunion. "We need you."

"I cannot. Our path is set."

"Then come. I will take you there."

Sonia watched Shade hesitantly lower her sword and then they were off, racing through the streets and alleyways. Angels crashed in on them and they fought in unison as they had long ago, before the world had turned upside down and friends had become enemies. When they reached the forum where the great dragon statue was broken open, the battle fell upon their ears in thunderous pops and shrill clanks. Sonia called for the twins as she led Shade and her company to the opened belly of the dragon where Ross was assembling the last of the explosives.

"You must go quickly," Sonia explained as the twins joined them. "We will give you all the time we can and then we must blow the tunnel. We can no longer hold the city."

Shade looked around at the carnage, at the muzzle flashes and the bleeding Kur. She looked torn, muscles tense, fist clenched tightly around the hilt of her sword. Sonia shook her head.

"Go," the Exotic told her. "Don't waste time on a dying city. The angels will abandon Hojo when we do."

"Why do they want it?" Shade asked.

"Who can say? We need only know that the tunnel must be collapsed. Balance will be held a heartbeat longer than before."

"Ross," Kallo called to the Miner. "Go with the Lady Interim. Guide her back to the Mine."

"But—" he started to protest.

"Go home, Ross," Delia said gently. "You have done your part. Thank you."

Kallo held out his hand and Ross hesitantly handed him the detonator. The boy gave them all one last, long look and then headed into the black of the tunnel. The mocha-skinned man went with him. The One started to go but stopped.

"Shade," he called to her.

"Goodbye, Sonia," Shade said quietly and turned to go. Sonia suddenly reached out and grabbed her arm.

"Daelus was sent after you," she told her. "I do not know why. But by Eros' order, he will find you. Be careful."

Shade nodded. Sonia embraced her tightly, suddenly wondering if she would ever see her again, and then the Sovereign disappeared into the blackness. She turned her eyes to the One.

"She won't admit it," he said, "but that was important to her. Thanks."

"Thank me?" she asked, baffled. "No. You are the One. I

believe that now." Sonia hesitated and then reached out to him. "May I?" He frowned and shrugged. She placed her hand on his chest, felt the beat of his heart beneath his skin. "The Keepers were meant to serve the One, to protect the Balance until he came to us. When you call," she promised, "we will come."

He nodded and followed after Shade. Sonia turned back to the battle and rushed into the fray, shouting for the Kur to disperse. The remaining Keepers pushed through the angel assault, creating a perimeter around the fallen dragon. Sonia counted the minutes in her head until finally they couldn't hold the line any longer. She found Kallo's amber eyes and nodded once.

The whole city shook with the explosion.

Jilk's eyes opened to the darkness of his bedroom and he listened to the silence of the bar. Since the cogwheeler attack, the town had shied away from the *Toxic Ox*. He couldn't blame them. Getting caught up in cogwheeler business would only get innocent people killed. He checked his pocket watch and groaned. He wasn't scheduled to be up for at least another hour. He rolled over and closed his eyes, hoping to snatch a little more sleep, but his thoughts kept cycling endlessly.

Near a week at the *Toxic Ox* and everyone was restless. Daelus disappeared almost every night but was always back by morning. Jilk, Slot, and Solo took watch shifts but there hadn't been anymore cogwheeler attacks. Jilk couldn't help but wonder if Daelus was responsible for that or if the cogs were just regrouping somewhere else, planning their big move. Maybe, just maybe, they had given up, but as soon as Jilk found himself thinking it, he kicked himself in the head. Knick was too valuable to Black Tuesday for them to let a few setbacks stop them.

Jilk rolled over again, realizing his mind was too awake for any chance of additional sleep. He climbed out of bed, stuffed his feet into his boots, and stumbled into the bathroom. He unzipped his jeans to take a piss and glimpsed his face in the mirror. Before he'd gotten shot with the back-blast of his own weapon, his face had been full of metal. Now, he wondered why he had ever bothered. Jilk couldn't say he was a handsome guy, but he wasn't all bad. He turned his chin this way and that, trying to find a good angle. He wondered if Slot liked him better like this or if she missed the piercings. Maybe he should ask her.

"Yeah," he muttered as he zipped up and headed into the hall. "Exactly how do you plan to do that, huh, Jilk?"

A sliver of light cut the hallway in half, emanating from a crack in Otto's door. He stopped outside to listen.

"No," Isis said. "There is nothing more I can remember."

"Nothing, my lady?" Antion asked.

"Nothing. I'm sorry, Antion. Self-aware, I cannot access the Weave, past or present."

"Then I go back to Asgard," Antion declared. "I have to try."

"It's too dangerous," Otto argued. "You don't even know the way."

"What am I to do? There is no knowledge here."

"Nor in Asgard!" Isis reminded him. "You saw the shelves. They were broken, burned, shattered. The knowledge in Asgard is lost to us."

"Not everything," he said desperately. "Not every book and scroll could be destroyed. There could be something there—"

"Anything of use to us is probably already in angel hands," Otto said. "The tower blowing itself up gave us a few days of peace, but by now they've sent their ISI teams in and bagged everything."

"Then," Antion began, but a long silence followed as he struggled to come up with a Plan B. "Then…"

Jilk pushed open the door, causing everyone to jump in surprise, and walked in. "Then nothing," he said. "You're staying put just like they told us to."

"How long have you been there?" Antion asked.

"Long enough." Jilk kicked a chair over to the bed where they were gathered and sat backwards on it. "You won't survive two minutes out there on your own. Sit tight and wait for Knick."

"My lady Interim bid me find answers," Antion told him, "and so I must!"

"Have you tried the Wired?"

"The Wired," the scholar repeated. "I don't understand."

"You know, digital information highway?"

"If we need to know something, we read a book," Antion explained. "My lady Interim knows this and will be expecting this result."

"Why do you call her that?" Jilk wanted to know. "My lady Interim. Like she's royalty or something."

Antion looked down at his hands for a long moment. "The Interim are the most noble of Keepers," he said quietly. "Not just anyone can be an Interim. They must be chosen by the Balance."

"Aren't all of you chosen?" Otto asked.

"Well, yes. But not like they are. There were hundreds of scholars, but only ever a handful of Interim. The physical, emotional, and spiritual hardship of the inheritance is something only the rarest of individuals are capable of enduring. They are the sacred guardians of the Order. They deserve my upmost respect."

Jilk looked at Isis. Her clear, green eyes sparkled. He waited for her to say something but she only looked at him, as if waiting for his next words, waiting like she knew what he was thinking.

"But they couldn't save you," Jilk said. "The Order fell."

"The Order is alive," Antion corrected him. "Asgard was lost because we were betrayed. They saved us. One of them died to do that." He closed his eyes in mourning, making Jilk squirm uncomfortably. When Antion opened his eyes again, he had a serious expression on his face. "That is why I must do all I can to help her." Suddenly his face lit up. "Lake Hern. The Keeper outpost at Hern—that's where we can go!"

"There's nothing at Lake Hern," Jilk said, "but water and a small village on the shore."

"The outpost is under the lake," Antion told him. "A Keeper could get inside. It was one of many abandoned refuges. It was once a great base of operation so there is an archive there. If I could get inside, I could find answers for my lady Interim."

"I don't think that's a good idea."

"Jilk," Isis said soothingly. "What good are we waiting around here? If there is something we can do to help Knick and Shade, should we not try?"

Jilk gnawed on his lower lip. Lake Hern wasn't too far

from Britz, south side of Kettle Kot for about ten miles of winding tunnel. There would be no reason for cogwheelers to be that far from the Cradle. Lake Hern was about as far in the OT as one could go before they hit the caves. And if the outpost really was abandoned, they would be safer there than anywhere else.

"We wait for Knick and Shade," Jilk insisted as he stood up. "This is the meeting spot and I'm not going to risk missing them on a hunch." He tapped Antion's shoulder. "I'll get you a deck, show you how to jack in. You can find anything there."

"Maybe, maybe not," the scholar muttered.

"Hey, it's better than doing nothing, right?" Jilk snapped.

He didn't wait around to hear any arguments or agreements. He went straight downstairs and outside to have a smoke, ignoring Cakes snoring at the end of the bar, arm tucked around a bottle of whiskey. It was the early morning hours, when people were just waking up to get ready for work; he could tell by the dim lighting over the tunnel. A man down the street had already set up his food cart and was cooking the first batch of whatever it was he sold. Slot was standing in front of it with some stranger. Jilk lit up his cigarette and side-glanced at Daelus leaning on the side of the building.

"Guess I should thank you," he said.

"For what?" Daelus asked.

"Keeping the cogs at bay." He exhaled a cloud of smoke. "That is you, isn't it?" The other man only smiled. He took several drags on his rette before changing the subject. "What do you want with her anyway?"

"Why are you asking me that?"

"Because she's kind of the love of my best friend's life. So I need to know: do you plan to kill her?"

Daelus frowned. "Never. Why would you think that?"

"Because she thinks that." Suddenly he had the man's full attention. Daelus' eyes were wide with shock. "She says that war up top was her doing and the Keepers will be out for blood. That wrong?"

"It's wrong," he said immediately. "Shade is at the heart of this matter and the only one who seems to know what is happening. I'm here for guidance, not blood."

Jilk nodded, watching the end of his cigarette burn bright red. He held it away from him and let the diaphanous smoke seep from his mouth like a gray flame.

"Good," he finally said. "'Cause I think she can take you."

Daelus slightly smirked. Jilk looked at Slot across the way at the food cart, saw her turn excitedly and run toward him. The merchant began shouting after her to "pay for that".

"Jilk!" she exclaimed as she slid to a stop in front of him. She held up an unidentifiable bun wrapped with crinkly paper. "Hey, buy this!"

"Why?" he asked. "How does it taste?"

"I don't know," she replied, "but some guy over there just bought four."

Jilk laughed, grabbed her hand to steady it, leaned in, and took a bite. Slot's eyes lit up as she waited for a verdict. He nodded and passed her some bills and coins.

"Double that order."

Casey's head snapped up from the bandage she was changing as the door banged open and Keepers returned to Sanctuary. Sonia, the twins, and a handful of battered Kur stumbled inside, worse for wear. The Interim was the least injured but Casey found several blood stains between her armor chinks that looked fresh. Her father rushed to meet them with several naga in tow but Sonia refused assistance, insisting he see to the Kur first. One man collapsed as if on cue. The patient was carefully loaded onto a nearby bedroll and the others were ushered to their place.

Casey picked up the fresh padding and gauze, rolling it over the healing scar on her patient's arm as she strained to listen to what the Interim was saying.

"I'm fine, I am," Sonia was insisting. The Twins, she noticed when she flicked her gaze at them, were refusing help as well. They were trying to leave the room, urgent in the way they brushed the naga off.

"Sonia!" the Baron exclaimed from somewhere behind Casey. Her fingers began working more quickly to tie off the bandage. "What of Hojo?"

"It is done," the Interim replied. "There were many casualties. We lost sixteen men and the city is in utter ruin."

They began moving down the hall. Casey smiled at her patient as she finished her work then bounced up to follow the Baron. She grabbed a basket full of old rags to take down to the washroom, her buffer against suspicion that she was following them.

"Dimitri?" Sonia asked.

"Both he and Vox are still missing," the Baron told her.

"Where is Balthazar? He will want to hear this."

"Kibri, assisting General Gorric."

"Then it can't be helped. Eros, we saw Shade at Hojo," the Exotic told him. Eros stopped dead in his tracks and turned to her. That's when the twins noticed Casey and everyone stopped talking, shuffling to either side of the hall to let her pass. She forced a smile and slipped by, desperately looking for a room to duck into or an alcove to hide around. "She was well," Sonia continued. "And she was with *him*. The One. They were coming from Tarsus but I don't know why."

The group started moving again and so Casey picked up her pace.

"Where were they headed?" the Baron asked as they swung into his office.

"The Mine. That's all she said," Sonia explained. Casey peeked over her shoulder and watched as they all disappeared into the room. "We helped her along her way and then blew the tunnel."

"And Daelus?"

Casey put her back to the wall and strained to hear.

"No, he was not with her," Sonia admitted.

"I am sure he will find her in the Mine," the male twin said as the door closed. Casey pressed her ear against the wood but she couldn't hear anything through that thick slab.

She sighed and went down to the washroom, replaying the conversation over in her head and trying to figure out what it all meant. The Keepers had once again taken heavy losses, their forces spread thin. What was going on? Who was Shade? And why was it so important for Daelus to find her? She wanted to trust in his words, that the Keepers would protect her and her family. But she was afraid. Her gut told her something bad was coming and Sanctuary was nothing more than a trap.

As she rounded the corner, she collided with her mother. The sudden shock unraveled her, brought tears to her eyes. Her mother laughed as she reached out to steady them, noticed her daughter's tears, and frowned.

"Casey, what's wrong?" she gasped. "Did I startle you?" Casey shook her head. "Did I hurt you?" She kept shaking her head. "No? Then what's wrong, sweetie?"

For a moment, she didn't have any words. She was too busy trying to stifle her emotions, keep the tears at bay. If she opened her mouth, she wouldn't be able to stop it. Her mother reached out and pushed her hair from her face, took the basket out of her arms and set it on the floor, then pulled her into a hug. As she struggled to calm down, her mother swayed side to side, rocking her in a soothing embrace.

"What's the matter, Casey?" she asked again when she pulled back.

"I'm scared," she replied between gulps of air.

"Of what?"

"This place." She took more deep breaths to try to calm herself. "It's a trap. There's one way in, one way out; if something comes through that door that isn't a friend, we're in trouble." The more she talked about it, the angrier she got, which effectively redirected her from the verge of tears to furious. "They brought us here, trapped us here. We're going to die if we stay here—you, me, Dad, Clara—all of us. And it's them, it's their fault. They say they'll protect us but they can barely protect themselves."

Her mother nodded and again brushed Casey's stray hair from her face. "I want you to think about something, sweetie," she began. "The Keepers are the only reason we're still alive. The day that man showed up at our door, angels were lined up to attack. Not him. Us. He saved us. That same day, your father was also attacked. The pregnant woman saved him. The angels wanted to get rid of your father because of what he knew, and they wanted to get rid of us because of your father. Without them, we would already be dead."

"So they save us to prolong our death sentence?" Casey asked, unconvinced.

"Maybe," her mother conceded. "Maybe not. I do know that without them our family would be gone, so it's only right that we do everything we can to save their family in return. And I would rather die helping these people that protected my most important treasures," she touched her daughter's cheek, "than to die sitting on my ass drinking tea while my husband and little girls are murdered."

"Mom," Casey mumbled somberly as her mother swiped at her own tears. "I don't want us to die here…"

"I don't either. But if I die here, I'll still be grateful that I was given more time with you, with Clara, with your father. To see how well this family can pull together in such tough times. To see my little angels working so hard to help their father, to help these strangers. I'm so proud of you, Casey."

Her mother embraced her again and Casey buried her face in her mom's neck. This time, she didn't fight the tears.

Rexis sat under the command tent and stared through the dark gloom of the cavern, at the torches burning in the haze of the dust. It was so thick in some places that the light could only bounce off of the microscopic particles, illuminating great clouds of excavated earth and nothing more. He hated it. He couldn't breathe properly. Even though he wore a filtration mask buckled to his mouth, the air felt stagnant, recycled, old, thin. He needed fresh air. He needed to get out of this haze.

Rexis touched the hilt of his sword and idly wondered how much metal lay between him and the surface, then dismissed the idea before it could form. There wouldn't be near enough to travel through; he would be wasting precious energy trying. He reached out to touch the rock wall he leaned against. Balthazar could do it. The Sovereign of the Sword of Stone would easily be able to move through this heap of rock looming over them — well, if he was capable of such a feat. Aside from him and Shade, the Interim had not unlocked anymore of their power. Not even Donovan, who floundered impatiently for the relic of Malkira to be discovered so that he might be granted awesome power.

He heard a commotion deeper in the site but did not stir. The last several commotions had turned into disappointing dead ends or false discoveries. Soon, as expected, the roar of excitement died down. He waited for Donovan to appear in the dust cloud, shaking his head and cursing behind his mask.

"Dead end?" Rexis asked as the other man entered the tent. "Or another useless token?"

"The latter," Donovan spat. "How long will this take? We've been down here too long already."

"Half a month, ay," Rexis reminded him. "Sit down and shut up. When they find it, they'll find it."

"I'd rather motivate the useless sows."

"More of your torture?"

Donovan shrugged. "I'm bored."

Rexis glared at him. "You've fallen too far."

Donovan's eyes crinkled and Rexis imagined his sinister grin behind that mask. Without seeing the fanged smile, Donovan's amusement was evident in his cold, ice blue eyes. Rexis watched him go and wondered how the Sovereign could have become so twisted. He hadn't always been this dark. To think of the Donovan of old and the one walking away from him now—they were like two different people. He had always been aggressive and competitive, but he had also been fair. He had respected the Balance and never used his power to excess. But the only word that came to his mind to describe the new Donovan was "evil".

The world was made of shale and shadow. A bottomless chasm divided the land behind her, and before her was the black gate and endless wall. The eyeless golems stared at her, waiting. Waiting for her to move. They were all waiting, eyeless gazes fixed on her. The city, the golems, the gate and the wall, and everything beyond.

Living shadow clung to her like the folds of a dress, trailing behind her as she walked, smoky vapors misting from the dark garment and excess shadow sloughing off. A grinding noise echoed around her and the gate opened. A city from another age stretched out before her. Flat-topped buildings clustered as far as the eye could see, their windows black and the streets between them empty. There wasn't a single sign of life but she could feel the eyes on her, thousands of eyes all focused on her from every direction.

She walked the city until she found herself on the road that ran straight to the ziggurat standing on a hilltop at the heart of the city, towering over everything. She stopped to stare at it, knowing it was the reason she had come to this place. Suddenly, a pulse rocketed through the earth and shook her to the core. Her shadowy dress shifted to became a set of armor. She focused on the black opening of the ziggurat, felt the dark thing inside stirring. She could not see it but she could feel it, feel it seeping out of the temple and slithering down the steps. A loud whistling sound came from far away and quickly grew louder, as though racing toward her.

Shade's heart began pounding. The whistle, she realized, was a scream. She drew her sword and prepared to meet whatever was coming at her.

"Don't!" a voice whispered in alarm. She felt someone reaching out to her. "Run!"

But Shade was not going to run. She braced herself in the dirt and twisted at the shoulders, blade held behind her. As the darkness came, she swung, waiting for the impact. But the blackness broke around her, splashing into the ground and disappearing. Shade waited, frozen to the spot, for some sign of attack. Everything was still. She tilted her head to the left and then turned her whole body to the right, alert.

"Shade?"

She whirled around and saw Knick standing there. Her heart nearly hammered out of her chest. Fear bloomed inside of her. She was afraid, so deeply afraid.

"No!" she screamed and lunged for him.

"Whoa!" Knick exclaimed, catching her as she lurched off of her blanket. "Happy to see me?"

"Knick?" she whispered, clinging to his jacket sleeves.

"No, Lethan," he joked. Something struck him in the head and he made a face, rubbing the back of his head as he glanced over his shoulder. "Ow," he muttered. She followed his gaze and saw Whiskey perched by Lethan's empty space, idly chewing a nut. He looked over at Ross, who paled and pointed to the lehn. Knick glared at the creature. "Why you—"

Shade tried to pull out of his grasp, feeling awkward with him so close after her dream.

"Hey, hold on," he said, forgetting the lehn and reaffirming his grip on her arms. She avoided looking at him. "You okay?"

"I'm fine."

"So why are you having nightmares?" he wanted to know. "You were tossing and turning all night."

"You watch me sleep?"

"I—okay, that's not what I meant."

"Then how do you know?"

"C'mon, I have shifts, too."

"When you should be watching for enemies, but instead you watch me sleep."

"That's a trap and, no, I don't. Well I do, but not how it sounds. That's not the point. You're distracting me."

"Then just leave it."

He sighed in agitation and released her. "You don't want to tell me, fine. Was just trying to help." He got up to go.

"Death marks you, Knick," she told him. "The worse the death, the deeper the mark. The loss is replayed by your subconscious. And even things that have not happened yet," she looked up at him, "loved ones not yet lost…just the idea of it can be frightening."

Shade was never good at saying what she meant, not when it came to her feelings. And until she met Knick, she had never really had to. She didn't know the meaning behind her dreams—if they were a product of her subconscious or something else—but part of her explanation had been true. She wondered if he understood as he stared down at her with that passive face.

"Yeah," he began quietly, "I know what you mean. But don't worry." He suddenly grinned. "I'm not going anywhere."

Shade glared at him as he walked off. When he was far enough away that he wouldn't be able to see her face, she smiled to herself.

When Lethan returned, Shade was in the middle of modifying Knick's combat style, working more fluid Keeper techniques into the sturdy angel stance while Ross watched from the corner of their cave. He was making progress, fighting style morphing more and more every day into something more powerful than it had been. She couldn't deny she was curious to know what kind of ethergy was running in the One's veins but she was afraid to try to find out. Training Interim was the Baron's realm of work, not hers. She did not want to hurt him in her ignorance.

"The way is clear," Lethan said. "Cogwheelers crowd the cities, however, so we will continue through the Grey."

"I can't believe you can see in the dark," Ross muttered, one of the few things he had said since joining them. Shade watched how the boy tapped the stone with his middle finger subconsciously. "You don't need me at all. They sent me away for no reason."

"They sent you away to save your life," Lethan told him

as he rolled up the blankets and buckled them to his pack. "What is your skill?"

"I can, you know, I guess feel things out. Tap out the terrain."

Lethan was surprised. "A mapper. You descended from Krueh-jin."

"Naw."

"You did. It was not common, even then. Before the Kada-Ma shined their eyes, the Krueh-jin wandered through the Grey using the mappers, who could feel the world around them from tapping the stone." Lethan smiled. "It is a rare gift you have."

Ross shrugged, still wearing the half-terrified expression he'd had on since the tunnel had blown. They headed out shortly after and walked in silence for many miles until Knick finally cleared his throat.

"So I have a question," he said, and Shade felt relieved. On their journey to see the Sirens, he had been very inquisitive. But after Tikal, he had been too quiet. She took his question as a sign he was getting back to normal. "You used to turn into this black ball of energy and sort of…shoot off into the distance. What the hell was that and why don't you do it anymore?"

"Do you think you could keep up?" Shade asked with a hint of a smile.

"Point," he agreed.

"The voidstar," she began, "is ancient Keeper technology. It allows the Interim to concentrate our ethergy, to compress it, change form. We find the void, cling to it but never enter it, and—" She stopped when she saw the confused look on his face. "It's not easy to explain. It's a feeling."

"Can you show me?"

"No," she replied instantly. "It's something only an Interim can do."

"But you took me through the shadows," he protested, "at Heaven. We went through the shadows and came out in Asgard. I remember."

"That was…" She had no idea what that was. "That was different. I—" Her words trailed off when her eyes fell on a dull glyph scrawled on the tunnel wall.

"What?" he asked as she walked over to it. "What is it?"

He came up beside her and reached up to brush the curves of the symbols. "What do you think it means?"

"It's a Guide," she replied in awe. "A marker to lead Keepers to a safe haven, but it has been out of use for generations. We must have once had an outpost nearby —" She suddenly stopped and stared at his hand touching the marking. He had gone right to it without any guidance. "You can see it."

"Yeah."

"You can see Keeper glyphs."

"Oh." Knick sighed and ran his hands through his hair, grimacing guiltily. "Yeah."

"Why didn't you tell me?"

"I don't know. Maybe I didn't want to know what that would mean. Maybe I didn't want to make it true by mentioning it. I thought that it would go away. But now I see them everywhere, sometimes glowing and sometimes like this." He tapped his knuckle against the dull sigil. "I can't figure that out, why some glow and some don't."

"Everywhere?" she echoed, gazing up at his forehead. She still couldn't see his glyph at will. "Even mine?"

Knick nodded slowly. "Yeah. I see yours." He reached up and traced a few of the lines on her forehead. "All the time."

"When?" she whispered.

"You remember the day we met?" he asked. "In the alley, there was this weird reaction with your glyph to mine. That's when I saw it. Started seeing all of them, in fact. I guess you didn't just find me. You *found* me."

Ralph Gobol's words reverberated between her ears. *The child born under the third sign...will pave the way for the One, whom this child will find.* Knick grinned at her, shrugged, and started walking away. Shade had lost all interest in the old glyph on the wall. All she could do was look at this man who had changed the rules of her universe.

"Sorry I didn't tell you before," he threw over his shoulder.

Shade stared at his back and felt far away from him. She knew nothing of the One, knew nothing of Knick's capabilities, and now she realized she knew nothing about him. Their relationship had been a series of chases. She had chased after him to kill him, to save him, to help him, to protect him. She was constantly running after this man, an attack dog at her master's heels, ready to rip out the throat of anyone that came near him. And if that was all that she could do to help him, she would do it gladly. He had taken her allegiance to the Keepers for himself.

And even though they walked side by side, he felt far away from her.

She thought of Tikal, of how she said she was going to protect him, how no harm would come to him as long as she was with him. She died for him, morphed her essence into a soul song and merged with him. They were one now. The Shaman had said they needed to be intimate so that Tikal could achieve ultimate understanding of him. Tikal had said she already knew. And yet Shade barely knew anything. She couldn't decide what bothered her more—someone else knowing him better than she did or the idea that Knick was meant for another. She had no idea what other companions awaited him at the end of every Typhi trail. They were as much a part of his destiny as she was.

She had been foolish to twist a prophecy into meaning what she wanted it to mean: that they were meant to be together. Knick was meant to be with many people, to walk an unknown road, to change the world. She was one of many witnesses, one of apparently many protectors. There was nothing special about her role in his life.

It was unsettling just how much this revelation caused her chest to hurt.

Isis gasped and opened her green eyes in the dark, heart pounding. The world of shale and shadow was still fresh in her mind, and so was the fear. Her chest tightened, pain spiking through her uncontrollably. She twisted in her bed, hugged her knees to her chest, and sobbed. She had once been True Sight, omniscient, untouchable, unfeeling. Now, she suffered under the tension of mortality. Her legs had ached as they ran from the cogwheelers, lungs had burned in desperate need for a rest. She felt fragile and weak. And these emotions, they plagued her. It was all she could do not to crumble in front of the others. She was the Enoch. She had to remain strong, resolute. But there were tears, inexplicable tears, fear and anger and confusion—she was a bundle of raw nerves.

And worst of all, she was blind.

True Sight was gone, replaced with human eyes, limited and weak. Her mind felt dull. For an entity who had spent her whole life—an eternity for all she had known—following the billions of threads of the great Weave, to be forced to live one fate, unknown, to actually walk it. It was unbearable at times. She despised it, being human.

Isis swiped her cheeks when the crying spell had passed and sniffled. It wasn't forever, she reminded herself. It was necessary. She had to learn to cope until she could be taken there—to Mesopotamia—to be reconnected to the Oracle. To become her true self once more. To become Sight as she was meant to be.

She looked down at her small hands, at her thin fingers, and used her nail to prick the tip of her middle finger. She watched the blood pool into a red pearl and then drip onto the sheets.

"Kalha," she whispered to the blood. "The rules have all been broken."

Lethan shook his head as he slipped through the crack in the old pipeline and looked at Knick and Shade.

"Cogwheelers," he said, "are thick in Jaco's Bluff. It's as if they are mobilized."

"Shit," Knick cursed, running his hand over his face. They all stood there in silence, contemplating their limited options. "Disguise?"

"They're checking everyone who comes in and goes out. I watched them. They are looking for someone."

"Yeah," Knick agreed. "Me."

"They need their ex-angel," Shade surmised and he nodded. "What about the tunnels?"

"The webworks?" Lethan asked. "I do not know the works this far out into the OT. We Jin traverse the Grey, but the works is something else. If we go in there, it could be very long before we come out again. I can see well enough to guide us but I do not know the way."

Ross stepped up, raising his hand timidly. "Well, I could do it. I used to map the quarries." He looked at all of their faces and added, "For fun."

"You can take us through there?" Knick asked, crossing

the pipe back into the blowout corridor of the Road, and pointed at the dark tunnel branching away. "You can actually guide us through this maze?"

"S-sure," he said, all but inspiring confidence. "No problem."

"All right then," Knick began, "what are we waiting for?"

"R-right," Ross stammered. The young man nervously crossed to the black tunnel, cleared his throat, took a deep breath, closed his eyes, and walked in. Lethan and Whiskey followed them.

"Keep close," the Jin whispered. Knick reached back and took hold of Shade's hand, who eyed their linked fingers suspiciously.

"So we don't get separated," he explained.

Shade tightened her grip. They crossed into the darkness together. The blackness was so penetrating that she had to put her free hand against the wall to feel her way. She missed the goggles the Krueh-jin had given her; she and Knick had both lost their pair in the reservoir that had nearly drowned them. Lethan guided them, turning back every so often to instruct their next steps or to ease them into a different passage. No one said anything more than necessary.

When Lethan called a stop so that Ross could tap a safer way around a collapsed bridge, Shade stepped closer to Knick. Both of their hands were sweaty linked together but neither made a move to release the other. All she could think about was the moment they had seen the dull glyph and how it had changed her perception of their relationship. *No*, she realized with a pang of shame, *it happened before that, in the garden of souls*. Even holding hands, she felt far away from him. So she moved closer until she was against his arm, close enough to whisper in his ear.

"The glyph," she began, "was not glowing because it was dead."

"What?" he asked, turning his head toward her. His nose brushed her cheek and she could feel his breath on her mouth.

"You wanted to know why some glyphs glow and some don't. Only living glyphs glow and shimmer; the dead ones do not."

"Living," he repeated. "What about the ones on doors and things? You're not going to tell me the door is alive."

"No, but the glyph is. It is infused with energy. When the energy is gone, the glyph remains just a marker of what it once was. On objects...and on people." She thought of the dull marking on Bartimeaus' forehead and felt sad. "Everything is full of energy, Knick. And when the energy goes, so does the life."

She felt him stir and then suddenly he was touching her cheek. She swallowed the fast-forming lump in her throat, wondering what she should say next. She heard Knick open his mouth to speak and then Lethan appeared, his and Whiskey's blue eyes glowing in the dark.

"He has found it. This way."

Shade immediately stepped out of Knick's touch, relieved from the awkwardness but anxious over the meaning behind it. Knick said nothing. She was grateful for that even though some tiny part of her hoped he would say something, even if it was nothing more than one of his meaningless flirtatious quips. Perhaps he was agitated at her for backing out of the situation. Perhaps he had already given up. Regardless, their hands remained linked in a tight grip.

"Shade," he began hesitantly after a few minutes. "I want to ask you something."

She waited for his question but it didn't immediately come. "Yes?" she prompted.

"About what the Shaman said. About you becoming a shadow forever."

Shade's heart fluttered nervously. She knew what he was asking but she didn't have an answer for him. She had no idea what the woman had meant. If she wasn't careful, in her haste to save him, she could become a shadow forever. The 'him' referred to Knick, no doubt, as she had only ever used the power on his behalf, but she could not say with certainty. And what was the threshold? At what point would using it too often or too much be her doom? The Shaman had said "in your haste to save him" as though referencing a specific event but, again, Shade couldn't be certain. And to be a shadow forever? What did that mean? Would she die or was the meaning literal? There were too many questions. She had no idea what to tell him.

"I fail to see a question in that," she muttered.

"What do you think it means?" he snapped agitatedly.

"That I should be careful."

"Careful," he echoed. "Careful with what? Using your power?"

"Yes," she replied but immediately added, "No. It's complicated."

"How?"

"When I went to Heaven, I didn't have my bells. I shouldn't have been able to use the sword," she confessed. "But I did. Something happened. I heard the shadows calling to me. For a moment, there were no borders between us—me and the shadows. Maybe I was a shadow, too. They followed my orders. They killed for me. They helped me save you."

"Wait a minute, you what?" he blurted as he stepped in front of her. His hands clumsily went to her shoulders to stop her but in the darkness they just collided. Before Shade could back up, Knick tightened his grip on her, fingers branching out to her shoulder blades, and held her.

"We'll lose Lethan—" she began quietly but he interrupted her.

"The superscience employed by your sword is one thing, Shade. This…this is something else. It's dangerous."

Shade closed her eyes and, ever so slightly, leaned into him. There was a hazy kind of mental clarity this close, with the heat from his skin rushing up to meet her, the vein in his neck throbbing next to her cheek. She had misinterpreted the prophecy once, but now it seemed to make sense to her. The shadows did not simply refer to her power, but rather her potential. Perhaps she was meant to be a shadow.

"Maybe not," she whispered. His chin brushed the side of her face as he angled his head to put his lips to her ear.

"What do you mean?"

"Shadows are markers that things exist in this world. There is nothing without a shadow—they are everywhere. Knick, listen to me. If I became a shadow, there isn't a thing in this world I could not touch, a place I could not go." She took a deep breath, terrified yet optimistic. "I would always be able to protect you."

"No," he growled. "No way. I need you."

"Think about—"

"Not a chance. I need you—like this, not some shadow."

"Maybe you only think you do," she murmured.

"What's that supposed to mean?"

"You have a destiny, Knick. There are many people who are part of that destiny. You thought I was your only protector, but I'm not. Tikal gave her life to bond with you to protect you. Who knows what other gifts the remaining Tribes have waiting for you." Shade turned her face away from his, grateful for the darkness. She wouldn't have had the courage to say it otherwise. "Tikal was meant to know you intimately. There may be another meant for you—"

"Shut up," he snapped. "Whatever Tikal was meant to do doesn't matter. I didn't sleep with her. I'll tell anyone else like I told her: I'm not interested."

"You can't know th—"

"I know," he said seriously, bringing one hand up to rest on her neck. "God, I feel pretty useless. Maybe I'm the One, but no one listens to a word I say. I'm just as much a victim in this as everyone else—and maybe that's the big secret: the One is just a tool. That's fine. I'll be your tool. But while people are still bowing to me and shit, listen. Shade, I trust you with my life. Can't you trust me a little bit? Can't what I think matter at all?" He waited for her to react so she nodded, unable to speak. "Then trust me and don't think about becoming a shadow anymore. I want you to stay like you are…"

"Okay," she replied after a moment. When Knick didn't step back, she peeled out of his grasp.

"This way," Lethan said quietly from further down the corridor. Shade wondered how long he had been standing there. "This is not a nice place to be lost."

After hours of walking, Ross finally declared they were close. It was less than an hour before the network let out into a service tunnel about a mile away from Britz. Everyone but Lethan, who was used to walking in caves and under low ceilings, stretched as they hurried on. The town came into view, quiet and unassuming, but there was something within it, a presence she recognized.

"I was kind of worried," Knick muttered just as Shade stopped dead in her tracks, "that we'd find cogwheelers crawling all over. I'm kind of relieved. Hey," he turned to look at her, "you okay?"

Shade was staring at the town, eyes wide and brows furrowed. The presence screamed at her, the presence of another Interim. She drew her sword. If she felt him, he felt her. He would know she had come. A confrontation was inevitable. It was only a matter of time. It made her sick to her stomach that this inherit power to sense other Keepers nearby was now no more than a warning system to alert her of enemies instead of the beacon to her allies that it once had been.

"Knick, I need those bells I gave you."

"What? What's wrong?" Knick asked.

"Just give them to me!"

"Like hell! You tell me what's in there! Cogwheelers? Priori?"

"Cogs?" Ross whispered, alarmed.

"An Interim," she replied, shoving her hand into his jacket pocket and fishing them out. He tried to wrestle them back but she was too quick. "You want me to be careful, right? Then stop arguing."

Shade slipped the bell bracelet around her knuckles and gripped her sword, twisting her wrist to sound the jingle she hadn't heard in so long. And then she shadow stepped, from shadow to shadow until she was within the town limits, climbing higher into the cavern until she found her vantage point. She allowed herself to fall through one shadow, stepping through it to another, until she was flying down at her opponent. She brought her aegis up to clash with the Sword of Storms.

"Shade!" Daelus exclaimed, startled by her attack. Her blade was a hair's breadth from his face. He had barely pulled his weapon in time. "How did you—?"

"Shade's powers are growing," Isis said, rushing out of the bar at the sound of the commotion. Antion, Otto, and the cogwheelers spilled through the swinging doors after her. "She is now as powerful as Daedalus was."

"What are you doing here?" Shade growled. "What do you want with me?"

"To help," he confessed, releasing his weapon and dropping to his knees, arms raised as her blade angled at his throat. "I wanted to talk to you, help you if I could—nothing more."

"Does Eros know you're here?"

"He knows I went to look for you," he replied carefully,

eyes shifting to look behind her. She could hear Knick and the others running toward them. "He was the one who told me to find you, to seek answers. But he does not know where I am."

Shade studied him for a long moment, trying to discern the truth. She had been betrayed before and the shock of Donovan's attack was not something she had forgotten. Daelus had always been a good Interim, strong and loyal and effective, but he was too close to Eros for her to trust him completely. Not now, not when there was so much at stake. She could not hope that Sonia's feelings reflected those of the Order, not after what she had done.

"I would never hurt you, Shade," Daelus whispered. "Eros would never hurt you."

"He protected us," Jilk hollered, observing the stand-still, "for what it's worth."

Shade finally withdrew her sword. "Go home," she snapped, sheathing her weapon as she turned to meet Knick. He jumped to his feet.

"Shade—"

"I said go home."

"We're in the dark, Shade. We need answers. You are still a Keeper—"

"I swore my sword to the One," she declared, spinning around to face him. "I cannot go back to being a Keeper now, not yet. Go *home*, Daelus."

"Let me help you—" he started, but she turned away from him. "Wait!"

Daelus' shoulders slumped in defeat. She had always been strong-willed but this stubbornness was new. She had reason to be wary but her trust was unraveling too quickly. He was losing her. She was slipping away from him and he didn't know how to stop it.

Isis took a step toward him. "Perhaps the time has come when we no longer need Daelus," she said quietly.

Yes, he agreed. Daelus was no longer needed. He nodded and lowered his head to stare at the dust under his boots. Filled with both fear and relief, he sought the box he had buried deep inside himself. It was time to stop running, to stop hiding, to resume the life he had been forced to freeze in time. It was Daelus' turn to die. So he opened the box.

When he looked up again, Daelus was gone.

"Shade," he snapped, causing her to stop in her tracks. "You will not walk away and you *will* hear me out. If you want to fight first, so be it. I am ready." He kicked up his sword as she looked at him with shock in her eyes. When she did not lift her blade, he took it as a sign to continue. "You are a Keeper, Eros the Baron, and I am your ally. There is an inevitable war about to break on Lotus Maze and we are doing all we can to delay that. There is something at the heart of this, something more than just cogwheelers and angels." He pointed at Knick. "If you believe that man is the One, then I believe it, too. And if he is the One, then only the threads surrounding his path matter in this chaos. If he is the One, then all Keepers must answer his call. You are powerful, Shade, but you aren't all-powerful. Don't delude yourself into thinking you don't need help and don't burn bridges before they're torn."

"What's gotten into you?" Shade asked.

"I don't have to hide anymore," he replied quietly. "The reasons I had to die, assuming his identity…they don't matter anymore."

"You can't be—"

"I am." He gave her a sympathetic smile and walked closer. "Eros and I conspired together but the Regent is gone and Asgard has fallen. The One is found and the child born under the third sign is revealed. There's no need for me to be Daelus anymore." He gently took her hand and placed in her palm the bell bracelet Eros had given him to return to her. "I am here to help you."

Isis smiled and bowed her head. "Welcome back, Daedalus."

Frigid shards speared through the dense dust clouds and a thick layer of ice coated the excavation site in several places, the aftermath of Donovan's anger. A few bodies were piled up in the far corner, frosted to prevent rot. Even now, Rexis could hear the man screaming and spitting in rage.

"Find it!" he shouted. "Find it now!"

Rexis rolled his eyes as the Sovereign of Ice angrily tossed the tent flap aside and strode into the lantern-lit space, muttering to himself. His eyes were rimmed with dark circles and his pupils were wide. His obsession with the gauntlet of

Malkira was driving him to new heights of cruelty and darkness. Rexis wondered if he could get away with killing him now. Surely the scholars wouldn't care; they were the victims of his brutality. But the Priori...

He risked a glance outside the tent and counted Muriel's elite. *Patience*, he reminded himself. *The moment is coming. Nothing else matters. Just wait a little longer.* He would allow his enemies to eliminate each other before he struck the final blow.

"What are you looking at?" Donovan growled angrily. Rexis snorted.

"Nothing," he replied. And he meant it.

Rexis watched Donovan leave then tilted his head back and closed his eyes. He sought the recesses of his memory banks and walked the lanes of his first days as a Keeper. He had been eight when his glyph emerged in the Weave and the Baron came to collect him. He was gutter trash begging on the streets of Saigon. The enforcers were closing in on him to get a filthy beggar child off the pristine streets and out of people's eyesight. The Keepers showed up when he was cornered— Daelus and Bartimaeus and a handful of Kur. As an adult, Rexis knew the enforcers had been disarmed and incapacitated, but a frightened child with his head tucked between his knees remembered the bad men being killed, lying in pools of their own blood while the Keepers stood around him like tall shadows. Then the ranks parted to let the Baron through, bright light shining at his back. Eros had seemed as tall as a mountain, his face stern but safe, and in his eyes swam infinite wisdom. He had knelt before the shivering eight-year-old and lightly touched his forehead. "The Balance has chosen you to be greater than you are. If you come with me, you will be forever bound by the vows you swear to the Order and you will never go without. You will make a great sacrifice and, in turn, be given a great honor. You must make this choice."

He hadn't even needed to consider it. "Yes," was his instant reply. And he did not regret it. He had wholeheartedly believed in the Keeper mission, and he still did. That was why he had to do what he had done, what remained to be done. The Keepers were compromised. The Regent and delegates, the Primordials—they were all corrupt. It hurt him more than he could stand to watch the innocent ones die. Bartimaeus had been one of the Keepers that had rescued him. He loathed knowing he was dead.

And Eros... Eros had been his savior. He had respected him, admired him for all of his life. To know he was involved in the corruption was a betrayal, and the only reason he had been capable of betraying him in kind. It had been hard to see Eros' disappointment—hard to see all of their faces, confused and angry and hurt—but he had been resolved. The Keeper Order had to be returned to the way it was, pure and resolute and incorruptible. Once the poison was purged, Shade would start the Order anew. She was the only one who could.

He remembered the first time they had met. She was just a year younger than he was but she seemed so much older. She carried herself like Eros, like a mountain that refused to be moved. And she was graceful as she danced a swordsman's waltz, mesmerizing, deadly. "Are you afraid?" she asked him and he nodded. Was he really destined to be like this girl in front of him? He didn't think he could. "Do not be," she said. "The Balance does not choose the weak, only that which may appear weak." As she turned back to continue her training, something desperate in him released and he found himself frantically calling out to her. "What if it was wrong? What if it made a mistake?" She looked back at him with the same cool resolution she had when wielding her weapon. "The Balance does not determine what you are, only reveals what you could be. And it has chosen you. Here, you are given purpose. Out there, purpose is like a tide, coming and going, changing with the passage of time. You do not question the Balance; you question yourself. *You* are responsible for choosing your fate, your purpose. You are a Keeper or you are not. The Balance does not decide that. You do."

Rexis had been stunned. And as she had turned back to her training once more, he had yelled out, "I am a Keeper!" He had yelled it so loudly, others had looked his way, but he did not feel embarrassed. Shade had smiled a small but knowing smile and nodded in approval and acceptance.

Through it all, she had been his friend, his inspiration, his role model. In some way, perhaps, she had become the Order. He had loved them, all of them. But she was Balance. And that is why Knick Coltin would have to die.

Rexis slowly released his held breath, imagined he was somewhere else, somewhere with Shade. He imagined the bright future he was so carefully crafting, the one where she sat crowned as Regent and he knelt at her feet in service to the true Order of the Keepers.

The clock on the wall read midnight-thirty and the *Toxic Ox* wasn't exactly full but many brave souls had ventured out of their homes and stumbled into the bar, too dry to be scared of cogwheeler trouble. Knick and his friends—companions, acquaintances, partners, he didn't know what to call them—had taken up almost half the place. Everyone but Isis, who had slipped back upstairs without anyone noticing. Antion had talked for awhile with his Keeper buddies until bowing out of the conversation—for reasons Knick wish he knew—to sit with his cogwheeler friends just a few stools down. Otto was next to Knick nursing a beer, filling him in on the eventful details of their adventure from Gehrs to Britz. It's not that Knick wasn't listening; his attention was just severely divided.

He stared over his shoulder at Shade and Daedalus in a corner talking quietly, unable to get the shocked looked on Shade's face out of his mind. When that man had been revealed as Daedalus, she had almost been embarrassed. But why? What was he to her? One minute she was cold and callous, the next she was humble and respectful. Now, they were talking like equals.

Only Daedalus had such power, the Sirens had said when describing Shade's melody. *Truly, their souls are tied,* one had announced. *They were meant for each other,* another had agreed. *Without a doubt,* the last had said. Shade and Daedalus were meant for each other? He tipped his shot back and slammed the glass on the bar.

"Are you all right?" Otto asked, and Knick didn't know if he had finished his story or not.

"Huh? Yeah." He tapped the counter with his knuckles. "Otto, let me ask you something."

"Okay," he agreed hesitantly, as if he could somehow regret it.

"Isis told me how you got involved in all of this but…what are you doing here, man?"

"What am I doing here?"

"Yeah. You don't have to stay here. You did your part.

Don't you want to go home?"

Otto looked at his half-drunk glass of beer and pushed his thumb through the condensation beads along the bottom. He shrugged a couple of times as he formulated an answer.

"I should, shouldn't I?" he asked. "I should want to go home. Better home than here. But it just didn't enter my mind. Isis told me she would need my help again, but even if she didn't, I still want to be here, to help you. I know it sounds crazy, but so did a woman in my dreams who needed me to save her...and she turned out to be real. If she says this is important, then I believe it is. Besides, I don't think the angels will let me just go back to being a garbage guy."

Knick snorted, both inspired and intimidated by him. "Wish I could be so resolved."

"You're the chosen one," Otto reminded him and grinned. "It's stressful."

"You're still a better class of man than me."

Otto laughed and chugged the rest of his beer. He clapped Knick's shoulder as he slid off of the bar stool. "Somehow I don't think you'd change that. She hasn't looked at me twice since you guys got here." Otto pointed across the room and Knick followed the motion until his eyes landed on Shade. "But you," he slapped his shoulder again, "she checks you like a clock."

"You're a punk," Knick muttered and Otto laughed.

He watched Otto go and was forced to revisit his mental solitude. The steady hum of conversation and laughter created an ambience that Knick wanted to drown in. Jilk, Slot, and Solo were joking together no more than one barstool down from him but he couldn't find it in him to celebrate with them. Duke refilled his shot glass and chuckled as he immediately tipped it back and glanced over his shoulder at Shade.

"Girl trouble, kid?" the bar tender asked.

"No," he replied defensively, spinning the empty glass in circles. "Just a girl. No trouble."

"Is that right?"

"That's right." Knick flicked the glass over to Duke and watched him refill it. "Not interested, not interested, and then when she found out I had to sleep with some other girl, she goes and gets upset."

"Upset?" Duke raised his eyebrows. "Define upset, 'cause

the last time that girl got upset she killed four people."

Knick remembered their first meeting and how she had taken out several cogwheelers to catch him. "Not that upset."

"No?"

"No."

Duke chuckled, wiping down the counter. "Man, you really don't know anything, do you, kid?"

"What's that supposed to mean?"

"About people. Their feelings. About your own. You really don't see it."

Knick was silent for a moment, thinking about denying it but knew there was no use. He had had too many shots to bother saving face. He pushed the glass around the bar as he spoke. "You really want to know?"

"Shoot."

"I was born an angel, Duke, before I came here. That surprise you?"

Duke chuckled, eyes sparkling in amusement. "Hell, nothing surprises me anymore, kid."

"My whole life was feelingless perceptions, people and their actions boiled down to numbers. So, no, I don't know anything. When I broke from the Hive Mind and came here, I did what I'd always done: listened. Watched. Pieced together a personality, and here I am. But when it comes to feelings, reading people—no, I don't know. Angels don't know what feelings look like, just facial tics that correlate with the proscribed levels of hostility or fear, 'cause that's all you get when you're Heaven's messenger."

Duke nodded seriously, thick gray brows pulled together. "So basically what you're saying is...you're a virgin." Knick just glared at him. Duke shook with laughter. "You're telling me you break free of Heaven and the first thing you do *isn't* get laid?"

"Survival comes to mind."

"Yeah, I guess." Duke poured him a shot as if to salute him. "So why her, kid? What's so special about that one?"

"If I knew that, I might not be in so much trouble." He started spinning the shot again, watching as tiny drops of green liquor splashed onto his fingertips. "I don't know...when I look at her, I can see the whole world fall away...and I don't give a shit, just so long as she's there." He grabbed a frustrated fistful of his hair. "But she blocks me out every time."

"She's a Keeper, kid. You think she knows any better than you what it means to have feelings for someone?" Duke leaned on the counter and pointed to Shade's table. "You see that guy she's with right now?"

"Daedalus?"

"Yeah. Him. I'll bet you a thousand rials that she has no clue he's madly in love with her."

Knick suddenly sat up and swiveled around to look at them, feeling his heart start thudding hard in his chest. "He is?" he asked, anxiousness creeping into his gut.

"He's so far gone, all you can do is wave, kid."

Knick eyed the bartender. "How can you tell?"

"Written all over his face, kid. He looks at her the same way you look at her. Like the world just fell away and you don't even know it." He knocked on the counter. "But I'll bet you ten thousand rials that he knows right now without a doubt that she doesn't love him back."

Knick turned all the way around to give Duke his undivided attention, suddenly interested in this newly discovered power he seemed to have. "You can tell all that by just looking at her?"

"Sure, kid."

"Well...how does she look when she's with me?"

"Why don't you ask her yourself?"

"It's not that easy."

"Yeah, it is. Look at it this way, if you still don't get it: she's with *you*, not her Keeper pals."

Knick sighed, slumping onto the bar. "She's only here because of some prophecy."

"Yeah?" Duke snorted. "And what was *your* lame excuse to follow her around?" Knick felt his face burn with embarrassment. Duke laughed again and stood up straight, flipping his rag over his shoulder. "That's what I thought. Look, she may be a Keeper, kid, but some part of her is woman. You can tell by the way she dresses."

Knick picked up his shot and glanced back over his shoulder at Shade, still wearing the remnants of their visit with the Sirens. He felt a grin forming on his lips. "It's an attention-getter," he muttered and flipped the glass back, "that's for sure."

Isis stood in the dark of her room looking out the hazy window at the white street lamp flickering in the distance and pretended it was the moon. The noise from downstairs drifted up through the wooden floorboards as a distant ambience that she tried very hard to block out. Their revelry meant nothing to her outside of the coming together of forces walking their preordained paths to trigger events threaded long ago. But the Weave was vast and complex. What had changed since she had last looked upon it? How many hundreds of thousands of butterflies had flapped their wings over that delicate sea, stirring up calamities about to crash down upon them?

It made her nervous. How did humans live in these frail, sightless skins? Perhaps because they did not know—had never known—and could walk through life taking its simple pleasures, harsh lessons, and great tragedies as easily as they would take a breath. But not Isis. She could never be human, not truly, not forever. She had seen the Weave, the great fractal web, and she knew how greatly altered one's path could become over millions of small choices and chances. It was almost maddening to not know.

But she had promised the Oracle. Walking blindly in the world was as much a part of her path as being the Enoch was. She had to trust in the unknown.

Isis leaned forward and exhaled on the shoddy glass then gently drew the number 11 in the breath-marked splotch.

"The eleven mysteries," she whispered, "are coming to light. Six have been revealed. The three traitors, Gemini, and two of the Typhi Kings. We hunt the remaining three, the Mute Advocate, and the Father. When the eleven mysteries are known, the path to Mesopotamia will bear three caravans to the ancient gates. Tiamat must not be allowed to wake."

There was a soft knock on the door before it creaked open but she did not turn to look. She knew who entered. She recognized the soft shuffle of his feet, the tentative and hesitant steps of a boy who worshiped her not as an omniscient icon of the Order but as a woman.

"Isis?" Otto prompted.

"Yes."

"Are you all right?" He hesitated. "You're standing in the dark."

"I am fine," she replied gently. "I'm thinking. There is much to think about, much to organize in this limited mind."

"I've, uh…I've been wondering something." He shifted uncomfortably. "Why are we going to Mesopotamia? And, if it's just a long, lost Keeper homeland, why does it take the 'ender of all things' to get us there?"

Isis looked back at him. "In the heart of Mesopotamia sleeps a dark and great power, a power to rule the world, to shape it, change it, corrupt it, and destroy it. A power only one can wield. *The* One. But in doing so, he will also be wielded by the power, corrupted by its darkness and bound to its fate."

"You didn't want to tell him that?" Otto balked. "He deserves to know."

"If I did, he would not go."

"Can you blame him?"

"If he does not reach Mesopotamia before the Sleeper wakens, the power will be uncontained. We will lose all chance of binding it again. The destruction…will be unparalleled."

Otto's face fell as his body slumped against the door. "It feels like the world is ending, what with the war and now this."

"If we do not go to Mesopotamia, the world *will* end." Isis narrowed her gaze on him. "He cannot know, Otto. He must not lose heart or courage. He must love and laugh and walk bravely and hopefully to his fate."

"To die?" he exclaimed, tone twisting with emotion.

"Perhaps. It is uncertain."

"Why? To fulfill a prophecy?" he choked out. He was upset, but at her or her words she didn't know. "That's cruel."

"It is the will of the Balance."

"But why? Why is all of this happening? Because the Regent betrayed the Keepers?"

"The Regent betrayed the Keepers because we were meant to be here. This moment was inevitable, all variables leading up to it. Nothing was random, nothing was chance."

"You mean I didn't choose to save you?" He looked inexplicably hurt. "I did it because I was meant to?"

"You *chose* to save me because you were *meant to*. Our actions are not dictated without thought. There is no puppetmaster. There is only the Theatre, only the Weave. The future is a cascade, a chain reaction, and the past is just the evidence of that, the tool to see the future. The possibilities would be endless except that only one history can be written, so all of those possibilities faded to nothingness. There is one future. The choices we make guide us to that one possible future, and our choices are guided by others, all recorded in the Weave, the choices made and the ones yet to be made."

"So is it fate or do our actions mean something?"

"Fate, yes. It's fate, fate because of our actions...not in spite of them. There is no magic or mysticism, only logic."

Otto shook his head. "I don't understand."

"It's okay." She smiled to comfort him but he remained forlornly slumped against the door. Her smile faded. "In almost all the certain futures, Knick will die. But in doing so, the world will survive. He cannot know until the very end, until the moment he must die. In almost every future that Knick survived, so did Tiamat...and the world ended."

"I wish you hadn't told me..."

Isis looked out the window again, past the number 11, to the flickering light that was her imaginary moon. "I couldn't bear it alone, the burden of knowing," she whispered. "I am sorry."

After a moment, Otto slowly walked over and stood beside her, his hands shoved into his pockets. He nodded. "Okay," he murmured sadly. "Then I'll bear it with you."

Daedalus listened as Shade explained all that she knew about the One, Mesopotamia, and the Tribes, but he felt more in the dark than ever. The ease with which she spoke to him, however, made it hard to care about anything other than the moment. Daelus had had a weak personality and, though she acknowledged him, he had never felt useful to her. She had flat out told him she didn't trust him. He knew she didn't respect him.

But now, she spoke to him as an equal.

"We know little else," she explained. "Tomorrow, Lethan will take us out to the quarry. That is where the old Shaman told us to go. We have found no real truth, however, but this uncertain path seems to be part of the King's Way."

"And the King's Way is some rite of passage."

"I don't know what it is." She thought for a moment. "Does Ataashvatan mean anything to you?"

"Nothing." He shook his head. "Shade, just before Asgard fell, the High Counselor saw the mark you burned into the wall and became hysterical. He kept saying he had made a mistake and that it was too late. I think he knew this was coming. This war is a diversion from the real fight."

"Mesopotamia."

"Yes," he agreed. "If Muriel was so afraid of you and Coltin, it can only be because his intention was to find Mesopotamia all along. But what's down there? What's so important?"

"Something meant for the One," Shade replied. "Something powerful."

"For the ender of all things?" he asked, frowning.

"The whole world is about to change."

"It is already changing." Daedalus remembered Eros' words the day Asgard was attacked. *Times are dark. You best make sure you have no regrets.* He nodded, resolute. "All that we can do now, what remains of the Keepers, is to meet this destiny."

"Knick doesn't believe in destiny," Shade said quietly.

"And you?" he asked. "Have you stopped believing in destiny as well?"

Shade stared at the table for a long time, brow creased in thought. He took the silence as an opportunity to look at her, to take her in. She was a very different woman from the vision he had seen two and a half decades ago. The Shade the Enoch had shown him was smiling brightly. He had never seen Shade smile in that way, but never before had she seemed so serious. The woman she had become since meeting Knick Coltin was a willful woman, stronger than before, tenacious and steadfast, and somehow more beautiful.

"Dael—no, Daedalus. I'm sorry."

"For what?" he asked, chest aching at the sound of his name, his real name.

"That you had to die for so long to save me." Her violet eyes met his, scorching him under their intense gaze. She remembered the story he had told her. Did she also remember his reasons for saving her? Suddenly she bowed. "Thank you."

"You don't have to thank me," he murmured. "I wanted

to do it. It was my idea. And I never once thought you would ever know the truth."

She frowned, looked long and hard at him, trapped between some thought and the will to voice it. She sipped her drink and so he took a gulp of his. They sat in silence bordering awkward—at least for him—until she finally spoke.

"Why?" It was almost a whisper.

"Why?" he echoed.

"Why did you save me?" she asked. For a moment, he just stared at her and hoped his expression wasn't as horrified as he felt. Would he really have to repeat the reason? But then she continued and saved him from blurting out his feelings. "Daedalus died when I was just a child. I have no memory of you. Why? Why would you die for me? I was just a baby. You could not have—" But she stopped herself. Daedalus smiled softly.

"Could not have loved you?" he finished for her, raising one of his eyebrows. She looked embarrassed as she nodded in affirmation. "You're right, you were only two. A naga brought you down to the Arena—I don't even know why—and Eros dropped everything to see you. I guess I must've felt resentful. I watched him take you, hold you, smile. And then suddenly I had a vision. You were not a babe in his arms but a grown woman at his side. You were then as you are now, but you were smiling." He almost smiled at the memory. "You were smiling at me so freely in my vision." He made sure he had her undivided attention for what he was going to say next. "I fell in love with you from the moment I saw you. And that hasn't changed."

Shade visibly swallowed and looked away. He understood her discomfort, had anticipated it. He knew on the day he had told her Knick Coltin's prophecy and watched her race out of Asgard that he had let go of any chance he might've had to open her heart to him. And even while nursing the hope that maybe, just maybe, because he had Eros' blessing...deep down inside, he knew he would have to let her go. But he wanted to tell her with his own voice, as his true self, that he loved her.

"A year later, the prophecy was uttered—your prophecy, as it turned out to be. Eros knew you were going to become a target."

"Did he ask you to do what you did?" she asked quietly.

"No. No, that was my idea. I was his most gifted student and high-ranking lieutenant, so Eros called me in to tell me what was about to happen to you. He named me his successor and explained how he planned to leave the Order and take you into hiding. I knew the Regent would hunt him to the end of days, would hunt *you* under the pretext that you were a danger and Eros a traitor—and who would believe otherwise if he had fled? It is no way for a child to grow up—on the run. So I told him I would take your place. We devised a plan to stage my death and, if it worked and you were safe, then Eros would bring me back into the Order under my deceased brother's identity. If it did not, I would smuggle you out and hide you in the borderlands.

"Shade." He frowned, remembering how she once asked him if he felt obligated to her. "I'm not telling you this so you will feel guilty or obligated to me. I made my choices for my own reasons. You were an innocent child. You are still innocent. And I was…relieved to be Daelus, to have the chance to watch you grow, to one day see your smile again. Though you have never smiled for me, not like in my vision."

She looked at him with sad eyes but said nothing. *Daelus was not someone who could earn your smiles,* he thought, *or your respect.* He couldn't be, not if he was going to maintain the illusion. But Daedalus, he hoped, was a person like that. Someone that she could trust. And maybe, just maybe, one day she would smile at him, too.

"Shade," he said, steering the conversation away from things buried in the past. "I'm here to help you and the One. That's all. Eros, Balthazar, Sonia, Dimitri, Vox," he decided not to tell her about Rexis until he had earned her trust, "they still support you. You are not alone." He nodded in Knick's direction. "And neither is he."

For a moment she just sat there quietly, studying him with an expression he could not read. And then the corners of her mouth lifted in a faint smile that was gone as soon as he blinked.

"Was nothing as it seemed?" she mused, mostly to herself. Shade had been ignorant to the deceptions of the Order, as most had been. It must be painful to realize, he thought. Just before he could open his mouth to try to comfort her, she spoke. "After seeing Asgard in ruins, Bartimaeus and Nico and the others dead, and feeling exiled from my people...it is a relief to know that not everything was a lie. To know the bond between Interim still exists. To know that I was wrong...about the Order, and about you." He smiled and held out his arm. She grasped it tightly. "I am glad you are here, Daedalus."

His heart skipped a beat as she released his arm, stood up, and walked away. He knew her words did not mean what he wanted them to mean, but they meant more to him than anyone could fathom. He watched her walk away and then turned his gaze to Coltin, who waited two heartbeats before he went after her. The cogwheelers by the bar started laughing and pointing to the dark stairwell they had disappeared into. *She's kind of the love of my best friend's life,* Jilk had said to him. *And you are the love of hers,* Daedalus thought as his smile faded. Whether either of them realized it yet or not, he knew beyond a shadow-of-doubt that Knick Coltin was the man Shade would smile for.

Daedalus got up and went outside for some fresh air.

Knick was not drunk. He had only had a few shots. He didn't sway when he walked, took the stairs without tripping, and hadn't slurred a single word. Or thought. But then again, he would have to be drunk to follow her up here with nothing to say and his heart pounding.

She was walking down the hallway, dipping in and out of the parallelograms of faint, pale streetlight streaming in from the windows in these empty rooms. She sensed him coming and stopped, turned around, stared expectantly.

"Shade," he began, clear as a bell. But he had to be drunk to say what he was about to say. "You kissed me. At the healing house." She tried to walk away again. "It's true." She stopped. There was an awkward silence. "So," he cleared his throat, "who is that guy?"

"Daedalus is an Interim," she replied, narrowing her gaze on him. "I ki—" She stopped herself, took a moment to recover. "I kissed you?"

"Yeah," he replied, casually walking closer to her. "So he just shows up out of the blue like that? Weird."

"What do you mean I kissed you?"

"What did he want?"

"Knick, what do you mean I kissed you?"

"What's his story, anyway? Don't think I've heard the name Daedalus thrown around yet."

"Knick!"

"Kissed, yeah," he said, stopping an inch away from her. "You know. Your mouth on mine. Healing house. I'm sure it was the drugs talking but, hey, you're the one who kissed me the moment your inhibitions were down."

For a moment, he had her locked in his gaze. He tracked all of the tiny flickers of shock and embarrassment and fear, but he still didn't know what it meant. Duke would know, would be able to explain it. Did she know how crazy he was about her or was she just as oblivious as he was? And then she averted her eyes, shut him out.

"Daedalus saved my life when I was just a small child," she explained as she put some distance between them.

"He's completely in love you."

Shade looked at him with wide, surprised eyes. "How did you know?"

He snorted. "It's written all over his face. What, you didn't notice?"

She shook her head somberly. "No, I...I never knew."

As relieved as he was to hear her say it—mostly because it gave him hope that Duke was right about her feelings—he was nervous at how sad she seemed by the fact that she hadn't been aware of Daedalus' feelings. Why? Why would that bother her? It was almost like regret.

"When he was just 'Daelus'," she explained, "he told me the story of Daedalus, his brother, and how he sacrificed his life for mine because he loved me." She shook her head, walking in slow circles. "It never occurred to me that he was Daedalus. The possibility never even entered my mind. I didn't question his story even a little. He was trying to tell me who he was and I didn't see. I thought he resented me for the loss of his brother, that he felt obligated to honor his brother's sacrifice. I should have wondered how a man I had never known had been in love with me." Her back slumped against the wall in defeat. "I should have known then...but I didn't. I feel foolish."

"Why?"

"Why?" she echoed. "I didn't see what was right in front

of me."

"How would you have known? You said yourself, you were a child. I can't even put the mechanics together. He doesn't even approach old enough for that story to make sense."

"Daedalus is twice my age. The Balance protects its guardians through their aegis."

His brows shot up in surprise. "Noted." He cleared his throat again. "So he fell in love with a child?" Knick frowned. "That doesn't seem creepy to you?"

"He had a vision," she mumbled, "of me. Grown. Smiling. At him." She looked elsewhere, expression warped by some sense of distress. "But I have never smiled for him, he said."

"Does it matter?"

"What?"

"His feelings. Do they matter?"

"Of course they matter," she growled. "He sacrificed—"

"To you," Knick interrupted her. "Do they matter to you?"

Shade frowned. "Meaning what? What are you asking me, Knick?"

"Why did you go to Heaven to save me?"

She searched his face, caught off guard by the question. He wished he knew what that conflicted expression meant.

"It was the right thing to do," she replied without looking at him. She tried to walk away.

"Say it to my face," he insisted, following her. She glared at him like a trapped animal. "You can't?"

"It was the right thing to do," she said flatly. He shook his head and laughed without mirth.

"Maybe that's part of it, but that's not the real reason, is it?" he snapped. "Not because I'm Knick, huh?" He pushed himself into her space and pointed at his glyph. "Is this why? Did you go to Heaven because of this? To bring back the One, not the man?"

"You're drunk."

"Bullshit, I'm angry!"

"You *are* the One!" she snapped. "You can't change that. You can question the reason behind the action but all you'll do is make yourself miserable! My march on Heaven, Lethan putting himself at your mercy, Tikal's sacrifice, and every other life that ended because of fear or hope that the One has finally come—for you as a man or you as a legend? Why does it matter? They are the same!"

"Because it does matter! Because I'm selfish!" He wasn't drunk but his head was fuzzy and yet he his mind had never felt so focused, his thoughts so clear. "I don't want to be the One to you. I want to be me, the man, Knick Coltin. Look, I know you probably think I'm like this with everyone, but it's not true. You know how soulless the angels are. All I wanted to do was survive. Until I met you. You think you're a Keeper to me? An Interim?" His laughter was bitter. "You are, yeah, because I can't make you into anything else. Because no matter what I say or do, I feel so far away from you. The Keepers, the mission—all of it, everything is something between us. And I'm the One, you swore your sword to me, I'm so fucking important—I don't feel any of it. Because I try to get close to you and you push me out." He stepped toward her and she looked away, tried to back up, frustration building up in her expression. "And maybe that's because I'm a burden and you don't feel anything for me, because I showed up and your whole life got screwed up—"

"Stop it—"

"Because it's true? If you don't want to hear this from me, *say it*," he growled. She kept her eyes turned away from him as she inched down the hall. She was trying to escape, physically and mentally. He felt a bloom of anger inside of him. "Maybe you'd rather hear it from him?" he asked as she suddenly went very still. "From Daedalus? You'd rather him tell you he sees you as a woman, not a Keeper?"

"No," she immediately protested but she blushed and he felt the sharp sting of jealousy and hopelessness.

"You'd rather him tell you how he just wants to be close to you? How he sacrificed himself to save you?"

"I said no!" she shouted, rage flying out of her as she invaded his space and forced him to step back. "Don't assume you know my mind. You have no idea how I feel!"

"So enlighten me!"

"I had one mission, Knick. One! Protect the Balance! The Order was my whole life, like the angels yours, until I met you! And you—" She stopped herself, wildly looking from one eye to the next. He waited, afraid speaking would stop her from continuing. Shade's gaze dropped to his mouth and then lifted to his eyes. "You changed everything—the world and my place in it, everything. I thought it was meant to be. Because of the prophecy, I thought I had time. But then Tikal—and the shaman, what she said, the tuning—and I was afraid. I had twisted the prophecy to suit my desires, not seen the true meaning. You are so far away from me. Because you *are* the One, Knick, and I am your shield and your sword. I am your shadow. That's what the prophecy meant—"

"Bullshit!" he yelled. He thought he was getting somewhere but was losing her again. "Tell me something real!"

"That is real!"

"Not to me! Tell me something I can understand! Why did you go to Heaven?" He started toward her, inched her back. She said nothing, locked up tight but barely contained. "Do you know why *I* went to Heaven?"

"Why?" she exclaimed, struggling to restrain her volume.

"It sure as hell wasn't because it was the right thing to do," he exclaimed, annoyed. There was fury in her eyes and fire in his veins. "You want to know why? I went for you! I'm crazy about you! That's why I went to Heaven! I'm so fucking crazy about you and you do everything in your power not to notice!"

"That's not true!"

"Bullshit!"

"I was scared!"

"Why?" He waited but she said nothing and his patience ran out. Without touching her, he trapped her against the wall. Their eyes remained deadlocked. He had to hold her gaze. If she looked away, the moment would shatter. "Tell me why!"

Shade half-glared, half-gaped at him. There was something desperate and angry about her expression, something bubbling up, threatening to burst. Some great need for understanding or vengeance or rejection or—the hell if he knew. And then her face softened just a little.

"I have always believed in one thing, Knick, and that is the Balance," she whispered. "I went to Asgard to die for you because of this," her fingers lifted to touch his forehead where the glyph had appeared, "because you were a part of the Balance. But I went to Heaven, because...now, to me...you *are* the Balance."

Silence hung thick in the air and Knick's pulse was thumping so loudly in his ears that he couldn't even hear the noise drifting up from downstairs. He just stared at her, took heavy breaths, and desperately hoped he hadn't heard wrong, hadn't misunderstood her again. He was the Balance? The Balance that was the center of every Keeper's life, more important than anything else in the universe? Him? He was?

Knick suddenly kissed her, hard and quick. He withdrew for just a moment to see her wide-eyed stare, shock and confusion playing in the lines of her brow. Even in the dark, he could see her pale face flushing pink in embarrassment. It was the proverbial green light.

Knick kissed her without reservation, inhaling sharply at the feeling. She made a muffled noise of surprise, her fingers curling into the folds of his leather jacket. She tried to shove him away but he kissed her anyway, trapped her against the wall, pushed back when she pushed him; the feeling he was filled with was all-consuming, possessive, new, uncontainable. Their verbal sparring became physical, each one battling back and forth for a claim on the other's soul. He had never kissed a woman before, never held one, never lusted after one—and now he was drowning in it, the feeling of kissing her, of holding her, and the anticipation of more. He gave himself willingly to this brand of death and never in his life had he felt more alive. His nerves were electric, the blood in his veins liquid fire, synapses firing, and his heart—both the physical and metaphorical—was pounding hard like thunder, opening up his every pore.

Shade finally shoved him away, bringing her arms up defensively. Knick threw his head back, turned away from her, tried to catch his breath, struggled to hold on to a thought that wasn't the taste of her. He covered his mouth, rubbed his chin and jaw. He *was* drunk, he realized. He was drunk and he had let his guard down, attacked her—surprised the hell out of her—and, even if she wasn't completely unopposed, he was the only one all-in. He had to fix it. He was going to lose her if he didn't fix it. So he started laughing, forced himself to turn and smile at her. She looked even more confused than before.

"What?" he teased. "You kissed me when I wasn't looking. It's only fair."

For a moment, Shade looked like she might throw him out

of the nearest window, but then she looked away, took a moment to collect herself, and shoved his shoulder as she put some distance between them.

"You're an idiot," she mumbled. He nodded in agreement. He *was* an idiot. He was a huge idiot.

"I know," he replied, still trying to catch his breath. "But I'm your idiot."

She shot a warning look over her shoulder before disappearing into her room. When the door closed, he punched the wall, ran his hands through his hair, and trapped his frustrated scream behind his teeth.

Balthazar had to duck when he walked through the secret tunnels to Sanctuary as most of the ceilings were about five inches too short to accommodate his seven feet. He was one of the giants of the Gorlotox Plains, black-skinned and brown-eyed. There were tattoos on his arms and chest and face, thin, black lines, swirls, waves, and dots that rippled across his skin. He had been given them as a child and could barely remember their significance. He was taken by the Keepers at a young age. Most of the other Gorlox giants were covered head to toe in interconnecting patterns, all signifying rank and status, successes and achievements, failures and shames, but he had lost the right to earn tattoos the moment his clanship had changed from giant to Keeper. He did not regret it. His former clansmen would call him incomplete if they saw him like this, but Balthazar was whole. He wasn't just a part of something, he *was* something. He was the Sovereign of the Sword of Stone, Interim of the Order, and Keeper of the Balance. His glyph meant more than any black tattoo.

Balthazar ducked even lower as he passed under an arch. His traveling was slow-going so he had let General Gorric and the survivors of the unit walk ahead of him. They had very few wounded; most had died during the battle or immediately after it. The force they brought back from Kibri was less than half the original size of Balthazar's and Gorric's teams put together, but at least they were mostly whole.

When he ducked into the underground Keeper complex, Balthazar took a look around at all of the wounded resting in the foyer and felt, for the hundredth time, a knife of anger slice through him. Dr. Basset had worked miracles for them and many of the Kur had been returned to the field. It was the hopeless cases waiting to die that caused his blood to boil. The Regent's betrayal had cut deep, but Donovan and Rexis—they had been his brothers. To be an Interim was to know a world separate from the others, to know a wider version of truth than the narrow perspective of the rest of the Order. And yet they had betrayed them. They should have known better. So much death and suffering belonged to them, a thorny cloak to pin around their throats.

Balthazar drifted slowly through the hallways, passing by rooms in search of his companions—what was left of them. Two traitors, one dead, and another missing. Shade. He wanted to know where she was, what she was doing. He wanted to know why she had to leave, what her mission was, and how he could help. He wanted her to come home. *Home*, he thought sadly. He wanted to go home as well. He was a third generation Interim. He had haunted those stone walls for many and long years. Now Asgard was no more than a ruin they would never get back. It was a bruise on his heart. He knew the history, how the Keepers had gone through many changes over the thousands of years, had many homes— sometimes humble hovels and other times magnificent palaces—but Asgard had been a longstanding monument to the Balance. It had been the home of the Keepers for hundreds of years. Now they were homeless, and Balthazar felt lost.

"Did you hear?" someone exclaimed. "The cogwheelers broke through to Anshar. They've engaged angels in three cities."

"More reports are coming in," another said as he crashed into the room. "Two more cities are at war."

The ensuing verbal chaos was like a hammer to his heart. *What have we been fighting for?* he wondered. *What have we been dying for?* To delay a war that would come no matter what. He was an Interim. He was supposed to strengthen morale, but he felt more hopeless than ever. Their numbers were gutted with the Asgard attack and dwindled down further with every stall tactic they had chased. The Order was on the verge of extinction.

As Balthazar came upon the room the Interim had taken to gathering, he found only Sonia sitting quietly alone. She looked up when she saw him, hope brightening her exotic features. He ducked under the threshold and closed the door.

"Welcome home," she said, and he cringed. Sanctuary could never be home. "How did things go in Kibri?"

"It is resolved," he replied, his voice a deep bass next to her soft accent. "But it does not matter. Have you heard?"

"Yes," she murmured sadly. "We have kept the fighting at bay for as long as we could."

"Where are the others?"

"Gone." Sonia visibly swallowed, worried lines appearing in her brow. "We could have used you in Hojo."

"What happened in Hojo? Vox and Dimitri left to secure it long before I was given new assignment."

"It took time to organize the effort needed to seal the tunnel. Your influence over the earth could've prevented much bloodshed."

He nodded gravely. Once, they would have known. Once, they would have been able to send each Interim to where he or she was needed most. Now, it was all blind guesses. "Vox and Dimitri?"

"You haven't been told."

"I was told Vox disappeared but nothing more. Has she not come home?"

Sonia shook her head, honey-colored waves of hair bouncing around her caramel shoulders. "Dimitri went looking for her but no one has heard from him since. Vox is...pregnant," she said quietly. Balthazar went rigid. "Dimitri is the father."

"Does Eros—"

"Eros is tormented—you can see it in his eyes. Her womb is unstable. She could be in danger. Interim were not meant to bear children."

Balthazar flexed his fists, resisting the urge to release his directionless rage. He watched as Sonia stood up and came around the table to stand in front of him. She placed her hand on his forearm, five golden fingers against his skin the color of dark chocolate.

"We can't lose hope," she whispered. "Dimitri will find her and bring her home. Daelus will return with Shade. And, in spite of our losses, we will be together again."

The unspoken thought was that there were three of them who would never come home again. Bartimaeus was dead.

Donovan and Rexis were traitors, stricken from the family tree. They had removed their branches but they still suffered from the loss, lopsided, incomplete. It was an ugly scar they wore, painful and raw.

"We cannot lose hope," Sonia said again. "I've seen Shade, Balthazar. She was with the One." He looked into her dark, emerald eyes, hope surging through him. "Our time fretting in the uncertainty will soon be at an end."

Knick, Shade, and Lethan with Whiskey on his shoulder arrived in Kettle Kot mid-afternoon. The waking had been hard after all the drinking the night before, made harder by the awkwardness of the kiss. Breakfast was a headache for more reasons than hangovers. Everyone wanted to go to the quarry but Shade refused to be a traveling caravan, prompting an argument that sounded more serious than it was with so many voices speaking all at once, made louder by the drunkard Cakes jumping in and instigating points, riling people up, and demanding to be taken along, too. When everyone realized what was happening, Shade slammed her fist on the table, spit three names, and said the discussion was over.

They followed the old transit system out of Britz where Knick had once followed in his effort to escape Shade. It brought back a slew of memories to plague his thoughts, some not-so-distant. It bothered him that Shade was acting completely normal. She didn't glare at him or avoid eye contact. She certainly wasn't more receptive than usual. She was just...Shade—no-nonsense, all business, I'm-on-a-mission Shade. If he had at least some kind of reaction, that would mean something. But nothing? What did that mean? Nothing couldn't mean nothing, could it? Knick sighed. He would have to talk to Duke again.

They walked for over two hours through dark tunnels and poorly lit ruins of station platforms with crumbling staircases. Lethan told them that some of them led to small towns built into the ruined upper levels of the old subway but most of them had collapsed. The last hour of their journey brought them to the blow-out pockets where the tunnel widened significantly, absorbing other branching tunnels into one large path; side-paths had been dug out of the earth and sloped down into smaller towns where the coal miners had lived a long time ago. The track pit was still there, though, dividing one side of the land from the other.

Knick watched a pulse of electricity race down the track as they crossed the wooden bridge Lethan called South Crossing and headed for a village named Kettle Kot. Before they descended the muddy slope, the Krueh-jin turned them away from the town and followed the slate ridges into the quarry. Mounds of old brick and rock chips sloped in stony dunes across a ruinous pit that spanned for several caverns.

"Molly's here?" Knick asked, scanning what he could see of the quarry. "Looks a little sharp for home-sweet-home."

"The Shaman told me to take you to the quarry," Lethan said, "to call for Molly. If we were meant to look elsewhere, she would have said."

"Then she is here somewhere," Shade agreed.

"The locals might know something," Knick offered. "A Molly lurking around the quarry—that's got to ring bells."

"Whaddaya want with her?" a child's voice asked. The trio turned around to see two dirty kids looking up at them.

"You know something, kid?" Knick asked.

"Tad," he said, palm to chest. He swung his hand out and put his knuckles to his friend's shoulder. "Bit. Now whaddaya want with her?"

"We just need to talk to her. That's all." The boys looked at him like they were crazy. "So where is she?"

"Can't say," Tad replied and looked at Bit.

"Nope," he said and shook his head.

"You're kidding me," Knick muttered.

"Whaddaya really want her for?" Tad asked.

"Didn't I already say?"

"You on drugs, man?" Bit began. "She don' talk."

"Listen—"

Shade stepped between them. "Do you know what I am?" she asked quietly. The boys just stared at her. "I am a Keeper. Tell us what we want to know."

The boys exchanged glances, nervousness flickering between their faces. This was an emotion Knick recognized well. It was fear. Finally, Tad pointed across the quarry to a sloping ridge on the far side that led to a black tunnel.

"In'ere," he said quietly. "By the ruins. Don' hurt her."

"She didn' do nothin' to nobody," Bit added. "Leav'r lone."

"We won't hurt her," Knick promised. "Thanks."

The boys stood their ground, arms folded across their chests. Lethan picked a safe path down the quarry as Whiskey scampered ahead and waited patiently at the mouth of the tunnel. When they reached it, Knick looked back and saw the boys still standing there, waiting. Waiting to make sure their friend would be okay. Hoping they had done the right thing.

"So you threaten kids, too?" Knick asked Shade as Lethan led them into the black tunnel.

"It was a fact," she replied, "not a threat."

"Uh-huh."

"There are no children in the Mine," Lethan told him. "Not anymore."

It was a short walk in the darkness before they reached an eerily and dimly lit cavern housing ruins. Crumbling buildings stretched far back into the darkness and rotting cloth drapes, some sheer and some thick, hung strangely from the ceiling and down the sides of ruined structures. Piles of rusting junk were half-buried in the dust, all valuables lost to looters or earth. There were no skeletons they could see but the ground was all white and gray dust and it would be hard to tell a bone from a rock without close examination.

"This is cheery," Knick said as they moved further into the ruins. "Could be needler infested. They thrive in holes like this."

All of a sudden, he noticed the black, furry lump on the ground wasn't just a junk pile, but an animal. And it was alive. It lifted his head and looked at them expectantly.

"I guess that answers our question about needlers," Shade remarked.

"That's unusual," Lethan said.

"What is?" she asked.

"A stray would be skittish, but this animal looks as though it was…waiting for us."

"Molly!" Knick called at the ruins. The dog jumped up, tail wagging and tongue hanging out. Knick gaped at the animal. "Molly?" The dog barked and shook white specks of dust out of her shaggy black fur. Knick squatted down as the dog trotted over, a collar around her neck jingling. He checked the tag. "Molly," he read aloud. "You're a dog."

"Well what did you expect?" another voice said. "A human?"

They all tensed and looked up to see a figure moving out of the shadows of one of the buildings. An old man appeared, his limbs thin and frail, back hunched, hair and beard long and white, and eyes a pale gray. He shuffled toward them, his brown layers stained white from the chalky ruins.

"Red never did like people too well," the old man continued. "Always said a man was half the person a dog was." He chuckled at that and looked into the darkness with a blank stare as if looking into the past. "'Pray you can be half as noble as a dog. To be grateful of what you're given, to love unconditionally, to be unquestionably loyal to those deserving of it, to faithfully guard your loved ones and, should the need arise, to—without hesitation—leap into the flames for the sake of someone else. If there comes a day when any of you can be so noble as a dog, then I will call you a man.'"

Knick stood up as the old man hobbled closer and scratched the dog behind the ears.

"The name's Gru," he said. "I see you've already met Mol, here." He smiled as the dog affectionately licked the dirt from his hand. "Red's closest friend. And we've been waiting a long time for you, haven't we?" He finally looked Knick in the eyes. "The One."

"Wait a minute," Knick said. "If Molly's just a dog, then who am I here to meet? I was sent here to find the next tribe."

"The Ataashvatan," Lethan said, remembering the Shaman's words.

"The Ataashvatan was the true name of the children of Babylon," Gru replied, "and they're all dead." He rubbed Molly's head and the dog whined. "Every single one of them. Sorry, but all that's left in this tomb are ghosts."

The loud noise that startled Donovan and woke Rexis was an excited shout different than the other exclamations that had momentarily roused the camp. It was a resounding cheer full of unbridled joy, not an ounce of uncertainty. The two Interim exchanged wide-eyed glances and an anxious knot began to form in Rexis' stomach. Donovan jumped out of his chair and bolted from the tent as Rexis scrambled out of bed and stumbled after him. He pushed the tent flap away and saw a thick crowd of people emerging from the catacombs. Donovan was already shoving diggers out of the way to get to the heart of the matter. The crowd reformed as he passed, making it impossible to see. Rexis stood outside the throng, waiting.

Donovan reemerged grinning wickedly. In his arms he held an old, pillowed tray. The gauntlet was unassuming, worn leather with straps and buckles to bind it to the arm. It was the most modest of relics Rexis had ever seen but there was a strange energy to it, something dark and dangerous. It made him pause, made him want to turn away, made him want nothing to do with this thing called Malkira. But he just stood there, stunned.

"We found it," Donovan hissed, showing his fangs as he grinned.

When the Ice Sovereign touched it, the energy amplified. The gauntlet seemed to change, dark spikes growing out of the leather. He pulled his hand back in shock and the energy retreated, form returning to that of the unassuming gantlet. The two Interim looked at each other for a long beat, unspoken words flying between them. Questions, guesses, caution.

And then Donovan slipped his right arm into the gauntlet and belted it on. It reacted immediately, transforming into a glove of sinister ice encasing his forearm, shards sprouting knuckle to elbow. Donovan turned his gaze on Rexis, his pupils mere pinpricks. His eyes were such a pale shade of blue, they looked white. He began chuckling. He drew his sword, turned toward the throng behind him, and slashed at the air.

The ground split open and ice sprang up, causing the whole cavern to shake. The ice spread across the ceiling to stop it from collapsing as spikes shot out of the ground and speared workers, trapped them inside frozen prisons. The chasm swallowed many of the men and they disappeared into the icy blackness. Within seconds, the ruins had been transformed into a glittering display of torment.

Donovan could not stop laughing. Rexis could only stare

in mortified awe.

Part Five

"Take time to deliberate, but when the time for action
arrives, stop thinking and go in."
Napoleon Bonaparte

The Inscriptor waved the last customer out the door and closed the shop. The dark curtains were pulled across the windows, throwing the small space into near-total darkness; the thick drapes blocking out the light gave off a faint, eggplant-colored light, unable to fully block the penetrating rays, but it was not enough to see by. The Inscriptor did not need to see, however, to maneuver the shop. In blackness, the precious tools of the trade were gathered and assembled. The center carpet was rolled away. A switch was thrown and the secret compartment beneath the rug was revealed. The hard, damp dirt pit that was revealed had only three things: a beaded mat to sit on, a stump of wood with a smooth, flat surface, and a small pool of water.

The Inscriptor sat on the mat and laid the tools on the stump. There were several inkwells and pens of various-sized tips and a leaf of parchment. There was a mortar and pestle, a handful of various herbs, a glass measuring flask, stirring stems, a stone slab, and a hammer and chisel. The final tool was incense. The Inscriptor lit the fragrant stick, placed it in its holder, and waited for the scent to fill the air. Taking deep breaths, the Inscriptor was filled with the smoke. It penetrated every ounce of being, soaked into each lung, was absorbed into the brain.

And the Inscriptor's mind lit up like fire, every synapse firing at once. The world took on a different hue, as though everything was awash in darklight—light that came directly from the eye, not the world. Objects glowed in the blackness when they were looked upon and dimmed when not being viewed. The pool of water, however, was a constant, churning vat of white light. The enhanced sight was just a side effect of the real enhancement—the trance. In the trance, the Inscriptor could find the replenishing energies of the world, draw upon them, shape them, trap them, fuse them, repurpose them, and install them.

For hours, the Inscriptor was lost in the trance. The hammer plinked and chimed as it struck the chisel that hacked and chipped at the stone slab. The glyph was well-known by these hands. It was a symbol of healing, to make the sick healthy again, to cure the incurable. Many thought the Inscriptor's work a sham, but those who were crazy enough to believe and rich enough to afford, the service provided was so successful, some might call it magic. When the symbol was finished, the Inscriptor's rough and knotted fingers lowered the slab into the water and watched it turn from white to sea-foam green.

The next phase of the trance involved grinding the appropriate blend of herbs into fine inking powder. Several inks had to be made for this particular symbol and special care had to be taken not to mix any of the powders; an impure ink could entirely negate the effectiveness of the glyph. By the time the grinding was done, the Inscriptor's energy was flagging, arms aching and hands bleeding. No matter how many times the Inscriptor sat before these tools and completed this process, the body always came away tired, the hands always bleeding. It was the price of inscription.

When each inkwell was filled with a unique powder, the Inscriptor filled the flask with water from the pool and poured a prescribed amount of the glowing liquid into each. Then, with a separate stem for each, stirred the mixtures into inks. The parchment was laid flat on the stump, a deep breath was drawn, and the first pen was dipped into red ink. The glyph was drawn in that color that represented a healthy body. Then again in the diseased color of mud green, then again in aquamarine, then thrice in sea-foam green. Each stroke had to be precise, layering perfectly. If one stroke was wrong, the energy would never seal. It would be nothing more than a symbol drawn onto a piece of paper.

But the Inscriptor had been writing power words for an innumerable amount of time. When that final stroke was completed, the whole symbol shimmered, burning itself into the paper. The Inscriptor folded it into a delicate shape, small enough to swallow, and then collapsed.

The work was complete.

"Each of the Tribes," Gru explained, sitting in the middle of the ruins, "found their niche in society and spent generations merging and withdrawing, growing and expanding, receding and diminishing. They were always separate though. Not 'tribes' but 'tribe', you get my meaning? Until Red, that is. I'm sure you've heard that name before."

"A few times," Knick admitted as he plopped down on the edge of a chunk of stone. Shade lingered nearby while Lethan tended the lowlight fire that Gru had built. Whiskey pet Molly, occasionally sharing a nut with her.

"Red was the leader of the Ataashvatan and head of all the Tribes. She spent years hunting down the others, making connections, preparing them for the coming of the One. Each Tribe had always had their legends and duties, but none had ever been visited by another tribemate. Our first instinct was to push her out. But Red... She had a way." Gru shook his head, idly scratching behind one of Molly's floppy ears. "The day was coming, she said, so each Tribe sent with her one of their most trusted to help complete her work. I was once a Krueh-jin," he told them, "brother to Sabal, the head of my Tribe." He smiled at Lethan. "I remember when you were born, those electric blue eyes."

"You were Jin?" Lethan gasped in shock. "Sabal's... brother? She never spoke of you."

"You know as good as I do that leaving the Kada is to *leave* the Kada. When Red called and Sabal sent me, I wasn't on an expedition for the Kada. I was serving a greater purpose, but a purpose outside of the Kada's survival. The clan wouldn't understand—couldn't understand. It was a sacrifice I would have to make, Sabal said. I resented it at first... I was Krueh-jin, not Ataashvatan. Red led a band of pirates, mercs, bounty hunters. She had her feet on deck more than dirt. But that bitterness did not last long. I was not treated like an outsider. I was treated as one of the Tribe. Not *her* Tribe, but *the* Tribe— the Tribes of Typhi. We were once one people. Everyone had forgotten that. Everyone but her. To her, we were still one people. I decided then that I would follow her, do whatever she asked of me."

"And what was that?"

"They don't matter now, none save for the last thing. The last time I ever saw her, she told me if anything happened to her and the children of Babylon that I would have to represent the Vatan. She gave me a box. Told me to hide it and, if something happened to her, to wait twenty-five years to the day of her death then find a Bloodsworn and send that box.

Two words were all she gave me. Moscow. Roskolniv."

"It was you," Knick muttered, mind flashing back to the days he had traveled with Hezara, met Rosk, and discovered the statue. "Red gave it to you and you—shit. It really all does come back to her."

Gru nodded. "I sent it off like I promised, like I swore. And then I came here to wait like she told me to. To wait for you to show up. You would come. You would come looking for Red. You would have to because she was the key but you wouldn't find her because she's dead. You needed to know."

"Know what?"

"The next step. I don't know what it matters now, but she told me to tell you and to give you her gift."

Gru's lower lip twisted, lifted, mashed against his upper lip as he struggled to contain his emotion. His eyes were foggy with age, moist with sickness or sadness—Knick couldn't tell which. What was obvious was that this man still mourned her even after all this time. He thought back to Rosk, how the man had deteriorated into nothing when this woman called Red had died. After twenty-five years, he still loved her. And so did this man called Gru. Knick couldn't help but wonder what kind of person could inspire such loyalty.

"Tell me about her," Knick prompted. Gru rubbed his old, wrinkled face before staring numbly into the bouncing purple-blue flames. It took a long moment before he was able to speak again.

"She was fearless," he finally said. "Not in the way you think—afraid of pain or death—but truly fearless. Every person she spoke to, she did it with absolute confidence. She treated those around her with an equality most people spend decades earning, with respect others spend a lifetime cultivating. She had expectations of every human being in this world—high expectations. And she didn't give you a chance to find out what they were. You lived up to them or you disappointed her. And you didn't want that. More than anything, you didn't want that. Because to feel a part of her strength made you strong, made you brave, made you fearless." He looked up at them and his eyes were alarmingly desperate. "She didn't ask you if you were brave enough to face oblivion. She assumed you were. And that made you want to be. The cowards fell away, became nameless nothings, and shadows swallowed them until they were lost to memory before they had even lost their lives. But the brave who stood beside her were men, we had names, we were Babylon's immortals." He looked at Knick, grabbed his gaze with a frenzy Knick found impossible to look away from. "She was the key. She was everything. And now she's gone."

"What do you mean 'the key'?" Shade asked.

Gru's eyes twitched over at Shade then to Lethan, to Molly, and back to Knick. He shut his eyes tight, squeezed the bridge of his nose, and took several deep breaths. When he was calm again, he explained.

"To Mesopotamia. She was the only living soul who knew the way. It's a long and dangerous road. There's only one safe path. Red knew that path, had been taught by her predecessor, who had been taught by his, for countless generations until the city first disappeared beneath the sands. The last time she left was to retrace her steps, walk the road to Mesopotamia. She did it every few years, to keep the path fresh. The day she came home, she was murdered. They all were. Every last woman and child. You're looking at the last surviving member of the Vatan right here." He patted the dog's head and the animal whined. "Molly."

Knick sighed and hung his head. "So I came here to find the only one who could take me to Mesopotamia...and all that's left is a dog?"

"Not just a dog. Red's best friend." Gru smiled lovingly at Molly. "And her gift to you."

Knick frowned. "So I have a pet now," he muttered. He could try to turn down the "gift", but it hadn't worked with Lethan or Tikal. What was the point?

"Molly's not a pet," Gru told him. "She's a friend. You best treat her as such. She's smarter than you. Don't forget it."

Knick looked into the dog's pale blue eyes and was surprised to find her looking back at him with the same level of intensity. She was studying him, measuring him. She tossed her head as though she were nodding. Knick returned the gesture.

"Okay," he said, and Molly's tail began to flop back and forth, scattering dust. He lifted his gaze to Gru's. "So you've been waiting here all this time just to tell me that?"

"No." Gru cleared his throat. "I have one more message

for you. Have you heard of a place called Fiddler's City?"

"Sure," Knick replied. "It's on the other side of the Cradle, few hours out from Thebes."

"There's a small town tucked away in the mud slopes called Kresht."

"I know it," Shade said, and something about her tone told Knick the place was trouble.

"There you will find the next tribe, the Skahradahn of Nineveh."

"Sorcerers," Lethan muttered with distaste. "Dishonest, difficult people."

"Sorcerers?" Knick echoed. "I haven't heard anything like that in cog-chatter."

"There is only one," Shade said.

"Two," Lethan corrected her, "and who knows how many others they hide."

"The clan heads inherit the power, no other. We made sure of it. The Rope Woman is powerful, but not in the way she once was. The only problem is Serena."

"I know her in name only," Lethan admitted, "her and her Dirt Men."

"Dirt Men?" Knick exclaimed. "Now I *have* heard of them. They lead raids on Fiddler's and other nearby cities. Mud giants, some say. Can't be defeated. Cogs went up against them a few times but they stalemated."

"The Dirt Men don't want a war," Shade explained, "only supplies."

Knick looked back at Gru who was waiting patiently for them to finish, idly petting Molly and staring into the fire.

"What's the point?" Knick asked and the old man looked up at him. "Red's gone. Everything she knew is lost. What's the point?"

Gru stared thoughtfully into the distance, nodded once then twice. "The way isn't lost," he finally said, as though just discovering the truth himself. "It's still there. You just have to find it." With a satisfied smile, he stood up, dusted his pants off, and turned to leave.

"Where are you going?" Knick wanted to know.

"Home," Gru replied, "to see my sister's face one more time before the end. I've lived too long without either family, the Vatan and the Jin. I'll go home to just a little peace…and

I'm sure I'll pass right into the next dream, to the place where Red walks." He smiled so happily that it made Knick's heart hurt.

"Look for them near Tsukino," Lethan said quietly and Gru nodded before looking at Knick.

"Goodbye, Vaas," he said. "Go and free the world, as the children of Babylon believed you would."

Gru hobbled off into the darkness with silence at his back. Free the world? Knick looked at Shade and found her violet eyes trained on him. Suddenly Molly was walking toward him, her collar jingling. She nuzzled his hand and tucked herself under his arm when he lifted it to pet her. She sniffed at his face and licked his hair. Her breath was hot and wet and smelled like shit, but there was something comforting about her presence.

"Your life grows stranger and stranger, friend," Lethan said as Whiskey hopped over to Molly and continued to stroke her fur. The lehn handed the dog another nut, which she gently licked out of the creature's palm then sniffed around for more.

"It's exhausting," Knick agreed. "You know there's no way we're getting to Fiddler's without trouble. We go right through the heart of the Cradle, knee-deep in cog territory."

"We could take the Grey," Lethan began, "but we would lose much time. The roads aren't direct."

"We shouldn't go looking for trouble," Shade agreed, "but we shouldn't lose any more time than necessary. If I have to cut a path through the cogwheelers, I will."

"No, that's not an option," Knick snapped. "I don't want you using your power anymore than you have to."

"If I have to, then I do," she countered. "Don't handle me like glass. Trust in me, not the Shaman."

"I do trust you," he exclaimed, getting to his feet. "But they were your words that bothered me the most—that maybe it was a good idea. That maybe as a shadow you could protect me better than you could as you are now."

"Don't be afraid of things you don't understand!" she shouted as she stood. There was a beat of silence before she continued; her voice was calmer. "Daedalus will be with me. There will be no need to test my limits."

Knick nodded and looked away. "Fine," he said. "Let's go

back. I'm sick of tombs."

Lethan quickly doused the fire, gave them a moment to adjust to the darkness, and then lead them out of the tomb and into the quarry. Bit and Tad were still waiting across the way, lounging on the edge of the ridge and throwing rocks into one of the larger piles in the pit. They stopped what they were doing when they saw them emerge. Molly was wagging her tail at Knick's side, what could've been a smile on her snout as her tongue hung out of her mouth. The boys went back to tossing rocks, content.

When the great doors opened and they were ushered in to see the circulet, Rexis immediately noticed the stench. The chamber, large as it was, smelled of rot so strong that he nearly vomited. Donovan wrinkled his nose, mouth contorting as he struggled to resist his gag reflex. By the time they crossed the wide space to stand in front of the Regent, they had regained composure, but the smell had gotten even stronger. The delegates beside him had remarkable control to sit through this fetor.

The Interim bowed and waited for the order to rise. When it came, Rexis had to do everything in his power to keep from reacting to the Regent's features. His face was rolling waves of skin, corpse white and peppered with black veins and moldy patches. His eyes were so droopy, they were almost closed, but he could still see the milky white orbs glazed over in accelerated age. His thin, white hair had mostly fallen out, leaving a few long hunks and scattered wisps clinging to his scalp.

"You return successfully," he croaked, and the smell of rot grew even stronger. "Good. Malkira will serve you well." He folded his frail hands in his lap. He smiled, showing off his black teeth. "It is time to act. I have jobs for both of you."

"Yes, Regent," Donovan and Rexis answered together.

Fire and darkness. All of her dreams of late had been nothing but fire and darkness. Swirling columns of blazing red heat connecting earth and sky, roaring balls of flame falling from the clouds, and even the rain was liquid fire. All around her, everything burned. And all around her was darkness, darkness that was dissolved by flame and replaced with more darkness. She stood at the heart of the destruction, felt the heat penetrating her skin, her soul, like an oven but she was not cooked. Not her. She was fire, and fire was her. This was form and function in its rawest form. One purpose.

To consume everything.

Vox's eyes slowly opened to bright, white light. Her vision was fuzzy. As she struggled to orient herself, she realized she could not move her arms or legs. Panic overwhelmed her.

"Heart rate rising," a strange voice announced. "Ninety BPM." Feet started shuffling around her. She saw the blurry movements of bodies in her peripheral. She winced, jerked, pulled at her restraints. She felt so weak. "One hundred."

"BIS?" a woman asked.

"Sixty-five, rising," someone replied.

"Blood pressure?"

"One-twenty-five over eighty."

"Get her EEG up on the monitor." After a moment, the woman said, "Sedate her."

Vox tried to shake her head, to lift it, but she couldn't. She was bolted upright, arms pinned at her sides and legs at shoulder width. Someone approached her, white shoes and legs and coat, pristinely clean and pressed to perfection. Where was she? The person reached up to turn her head, wielding a needle poised to bite a vein in her neck. But when their eyes met, he gasped and backed away.

"She's awake," he announced.

"What?"

"That shouldn't be."

"Corto?" the woman asked.

"She is still under heavy anesthesia."

"BIS."

"Sixty-seven, fluctuating."

"She's awake," the man reiterated. More men and women came to look at her. She saw their compassionless faces gazing at her in scientific wonder.

"Call Porter," the woman who had been speaking consistently said. "Tell him the patient is awake."

"Heart rate is still elevated," a man announced. "Fluctuating at one-ten."

"Keep me updated," the woman told him. She took a cautious step toward Vox. "You're safe. Do you understand that?"

Vox just stared at her. Her throat felt clogged, tongue thick. She couldn't speak. But she did not feel safe. She felt trapped. But she knew better than to struggle in her state. If she did, they would only put her back to sleep. The one called Porter may have answers for her. She had to be patient.

Vox closed her eyes to watch the swirling columns of fire spearing into the burning sky, tried to draw strength from it. When she heard a set of doors whiz open, she looked up. The hurried footsteps went right to her. A young man appeared, older than her but too young for such a high station. His face was not unkind, however.

"Operative Flamefang," he began gently, "I am Dr. Alexander Porter and I am your primary care physician and the head of this team. We have created a whole department devoted to your wellbeing. I am sure you are wondering where you are. The answer will upset you but please allow me to explain." He cleared his throat. "You are in Heaven, Operative. You were—"

"Heart rate rising!" the technician exclaimed. "One-forty, rising!"

"Please, calm down," Porter said.

"Still climbing!"

"Sedate her," the woman ordered.

"No," Porter said.

"But sir—"

"I said no."

"One-sixty!"

"Blood pressure one-thirty over ninety."

"We have to sedate her!" the woman exclaimed.

"I said *no*, Dr. Raditz." He looked at Vox calmly. "You have to breathe deeply and calm down."

But she couldn't breathe deeply. She could barely breathe at all. She was trapped in Heaven. She was bound, drugged. Her child was in danger. There was a loud pop and someone shrieked, another cursed. Someone yelled, "Get that fire out!"

"There's going to be another incident," Dr. Raditz told Porter. "We have to sedate her!"

"One-ninety, rising!"

"Listen to me," Porter whispered, ignoring his colleague. He cleared the space between them in spite of the woman's warnings. "You are in danger. If you value your child's life, you must calm down and listen to me."

Vox gaped at him, panic overwhelming her. There was another pop and an alarm started wailing, which only scared her more. Tears were freefalling, chest constricting, airways clogging. Porter reached up and touched her cheek as Dr. Raditz yelled, "No!"

"I promise you, I will save your child's life," he said firmly. "I promise you. I will save your child. But you must calm down."

For a moment, there was nothing but his dark green eyes looking into hers. And then the tech yelled, "One-eighty, dropping." Dr. Porter nodded at her, shushed her in long, soothing sounds. When he withdrew his hand, he shook it as though he had been burned. Dr. Raditz immediately went to him to examine his trembling fingers. He waved her away and mumbled a request. Wet and dry cuts of cloth were brought that he used to clean Vox's face, all the while murmuring kind things. As he worked, she could see the palm he had touched her with was bright red, the skin starting to blister.

"One-forty, dropping."

"Blood pressure stabilized. One-twenty over eighty."

"Turn the alarm off," Porter ordered. Within seconds, it was no longer wailing. The smell of burnt machinery was strong. Ventilators were switched on, oxygen cycled into the room as the smoke was sucked out. By the time Porter finished cleaning her up, Vox could breathe again and the air smelled sterile once more.

"Eighty-five BPM," the tech said with an exhausted sigh, as though he had been monitoring his own heart rate.

"Are you ready to talk now, Operative?" Porter asked her.

"FFvvffv," she sputtered. "Vvvffah…ahx…"

"Vox?" he echoed. She barely managed a twitch of a nod. He smiled genuinely. "Your name is Vox. Good." He brushed the hair away from her face. "Are you ready to talk now, Vox?" She twitched again. "Very good." Dr. Porter removed himself from the intimate space and put his hands behind his back. "No doubt you've experienced great pains during the course of your pregnancy. It was such a pain that caused you to lose consciousness, allowing our agents to secure you and bring you to our facilities.

"There is an enormous energy signature inside your body. All of our data regarding the Keeper Elites suggests a higher energy flux that peaks when the frequency of your bells triggers your weapon artifacts, creating a phenomenon. Energy flows through you at an alarming rate and in exorbitant amounts. You become a conduit of sorts, channeling that energy in bursts. When the gate opens, you bend the elements around you, mutate them, evolve them. When the gate closes, you return to a state of rest, but there is residual extra energy that remains inside of you.

"This child also carries the same energy markers, but magnified. As the child grows, the energy contained expands. Your body cannot contain it. If left alone, it will take you apart. You and your child. We are doing everything we can to stabilize your condition. The effects are debilitating. I apologize for that but it cannot be helped. We've been monitoring your dreams, which no doubt reflect the chaotic state of your subconscious. As you progress through your final trimester, your energy becomes harder to control and to contain. Your body is a conduit, attempting to open itself up to let the energy pass through, but it is so great that you would not be able to control it. And when one gate opens, so would the other, and as energy rushes in, what was already there magnifies. You would become the world's greatest human bomb."

Vox whimpered as despair overwhelmed her. Porter brought more cloth to catch her tears, shushing her again.

"I won't lie to you," he began quietly. "The extraction of a healthy and living Keeper Elite child is of upmost importance to the Tower. A Keeper Angel would be quite the secret weapon." He dabbed at her cheeks as more tears rushed out. She knew that. Of course she had known that. "If we let you go, you would die. Your child would die. You would likely kill thousands in the passing. If you stay with us, we can at least save your baby. Do you understand?"

Vox tried her best to nod but she was too upset to struggle with movement. "Nnyyhnns...nyes..." she blubbered around her swollen tongue.

Dr. Porter nodded. "Good," he whispered, and gently injected her with a sedative. Vox closed her eyes and returned to the firestorm.

The *Toxic Ox* was empty aside from Duke prepping for the evening rush, Cakes drinking at the bar, and the whole of Knick's company gathered around two tables pulled together, eating lunch and planning for the next step. Molly sat beside Knick's chair, wagging her tail and catching scraps he tossed at her. Slot was the only one who wasn't eating; instead, she was curled up behind Molly with her head on the dog's back and her arms wrapped around her, stroking her neck and belly while smiling ear to ear.

"The Dirt Men," Jilk said when Knick told him what they had learned. "You've got to be fucking kidding me. Not only are they hard to find but they're a piece of work. They'd kill you as soon as look at you, unless you got numbers—and we don't got numbers."

"I won't let that happen," Shade said. "The Dirt Men are no match for a Keeper."

"You say that now—"

"I know that," she corrected him.

"You've dealt with them before?"

"I have."

Jilk shrugged. "All right. So how are we going to get there? Kresht is on the other side of the Mine."

"*We* aren't going anywhere," Knick told him. "You guys are staying put. Nothing's changed—we can't afford to draw attention to ourselves and we can't afford to slow down."

"I don't think we should be half a world away from each other, either," Solo piped in.

"We chose this spot because it's remote. You go any closer to the Cradle, you'll have cogs falling on you."

"They'll be falling on you, too," Slot told him. He nudged her with his foot and she swatted at his boot.

"I'm one man," he reminded her, "and well protected. You guys stick out like stains on Heaven's door. Three well-known cogs and," he waved at Otto, Antion, and Isis at the far end of the table, "you three."

"You're all crazy," Cakes shouted from the bar.

"Shut up, Cakes," Jilk hollered. "Hey, you want us to stay out of the heat? I'm not complaining. After what we went through to get here, I got a little more time in me before I'm bored. But I gotta ask, Knick. How much longer are we going to do this?"

"I don't know," he admitted and drew his hand across his face. "There are five tribes. Three down, two to go? Then I guess that means we'll go to Mesopotamia. Your guess is as good as mine."

Jilk watched Knick and Shade exchange glances and had a feeling Knick wasn't telling him everything but he didn't push it in front of everyone. "So we go. And then?" he asked instead.

"I don't know."

"We stop Tiamat from waking," Isis answered. Otto shifted uncomfortably. "That is all that matters."

"What does that even mean?" Jilk exclaimed. "You're asking us to believe in fairy tales without any answers."

"I ask nothing of you. But if I asked for something, it would be that you believe in him." She nodded at Knick. "But you already do. That is why you're here. I ask of Knick only that he believes in her—" everyone knew who she meant "— and she believes in her Enoch, in the teachings that raised her. Her eyes have seen things the rest of yours have not. Shade and Daedalus have fought to protect this world, agents of an order that has done just that for thousands and thousands of years. Belief in fairy tales is not why you are here, nor will it ever be. But belief is why you are here, is why you will continue on this road."

"Sometimes, I don't know if you're a wise woman, a little girl, or a puppet master," Knick muttered.

"Don't speak to her that way!" Antion exclaimed.

"Hush," Isis gently whispered. "He is free to doubt me. My interest is in the protection of the Balance, the preservation of this world. Nothing else matters."

Isis was looking so intensely at him that Knick wondered if she was trying to tell him something, another meaning hidden in her words. Before he could attempt to puzzle it out, Jilk changed the topic.

"Whatever," he mumbled and gave Knick his full attention. "So what's your road?"

"We can't take the Grey," Knick said for certain. "It will take too long."

"Well you can't go through the Cradle," Solo interjected. "It'll be a massacre." He caught Shade's eye and added, "On their part."

"What other choice do we have?" Lethan asked. "Our road is either too long or too bloody. We have to decide."

"Lethan's right," Knick said. "Can we afford to lose that much time?"

"No," Isis answered. "The sands are falling. The King's Road will not wait. We must reach Mesopotamia before the awakening."

"What about the webworks?" Ross asked timidly. All eyes turned to him. He nervously looked around, subconsciously tapping at the table. "The webworks connects half the Mine."

"No," Jilk protested. "No. No fucking way."

"That's near-suicide," Solo agreed.

"It's crazy *and* stupid!" Cakes shouted.

"It is dangerous," Lethan surmised. "Not suicide, but very dangerous."

"I said near," Solo pointed out.

"Yeah, but...so's the cogs, right?" Ross chirped. "The only difference is, well, the spinners aren't looking for you."

"You're talking pitch black, cramped, maze-like caverns," Jilk reminded him. "There's nowhere to hide, more cave and darkness to run to, and you're pitted against creatures that see in the dark, creatures whose hunting grounds are that cramped maze."

"That's actually not a bad idea," Daedalus murmured thoughtfully.

"It's a terrible idea!" Jilk exclaimed.

"For once he's right!" Cakes added.

"No, wait a minute," Knick said, narrowing his gaze on Ross. "You're right. They're not looking for me."

"Knick!"

He looked at Jilk, wide-eyed and prepped to convince him. "Jilk, the webworks will allow us to bypass most of the Cradle in half the time it would take us in the Grey."

"You're crazy!" Cakes blurted. "You're all gonna die!"

"There's no point in risking the shortcut if it means you'll die. Those tunnels are dangerous!" Jilk yelled. "It's one thing to skirt along the edges, but to go days, weeks through the heart of that place? It's insanity!"

"We'll stick to the outside as much as we can," Knick promised. "The spinners never go so close to the cities." He paused then added, "Almost never."

"There's more than just spinners in there, Knick."

"We'll be fine," he insisted.

"Crazy!" Cakes hollered.

"You *are* crazy," Slot mumbled and patted Knick's leg. "But that's always why I liked you, anyways."

"Funny, same to you," Knick said, petting her head. She giggled happily and squeezed Molly tighter. For a moment, he thought Slot reminded him an awful lot of dog. She was easy to please, fiercely loyal, relatively fearless, and extremely dirty. He thought about trying to feed her some table scraps—and she would probably laugh and tilt her head back to catch—but then he saw the jealous look on Jilk's face and decided against it. "Anyway."

"You realize you were the one who navigated us through the works in the first place, don't you?" Lethan asked Ross. He nodded. "Then you also realize that, if we do this, you will be navigating us once more."

Ross' eyes grew as big as silver dinars. "Wait a minute, I—"

"We will protect you," Daedalus interrupted him.

"But I—"

"Ross," Knick said seriously. "We need you." The boy made a face of pure discomfort and guilt then nodded. "Good."

"You need gear as well," Lethan said as Duke came over to pass out more beer bottles. "You can't go stumbling through that nest again without your eyes."

Duke shrugged. "Should be something in the old mining shop. Right down the road. Triggart sells all sorts of mining surplus."

"Thanks, Duke," Knick said.

"You're still gonna die," Cakes said nonchalantly and tipped his bottle back.

Casey was changing Silvo's bandage when she felt the ground shake. Her hands stilled over the wounded arm as she looked around for signs that someone else had noticed it. Everyone seemed absorbed in their task, unaware. Had she imagined it?

"Casey?" the patient asked.

"Did you feel that?" she whispered.

"Feel what?"

"That tremble—"

It came again, stronger. Silvo's eyes widened in surprise. Others began to stir around them, looking to those closest for confirmation. There was a third thump and Casey was among many who suddenly got to their feet. A sickening knot was forming in her stomach. Boom, boom, boom! The sound was coming closer, vibrations growing stronger.

"Get down!" Silvo told her, but Casey's eyes were transfixed on the door. Something was coming right for them. It was going to collide with Sanctuary. BOOM! BOOM! BOOM! All they could do was stare and wait. Something struck the door hard and a shudder of fear ran through the crowd. "Get down!" Silvo hissed and grabbed her ankle, pulling her feet out from under her. Casey went down hard as the door was struck again and split open. Wooden shrapnel and ice shards flew across the room, striking everyone who was standing. Silvo, even with all of his injuries, rolled on top of her. "Keep your head down!" he told her.

Casey covered her head, screaming with every BANG that came. People were screaming, too, but not just in fear. They were screaming in pain. When the noise finally settled down, she slowly lifted her head. Silvo slumped off of her. When she looked at him, she saw a giant shard of ice buried in his back and several smaller ones protruding from his skull. She gasped and tried to push away but her limbs were shaking so badly all she managed to do was flounder. The sound of boots crunching through the wreckage caused her to still, blood running cold in terror. As her eyes went to the gaping hole where a door used to be, she saw just how much damage had been done. The room was in ruins, stone and wood everywhere, people dying or dead. The man who appeared through the debris cloud was tall and slim with spiky blond hair and cold blue eyes. He was grinning ear to ear, showing off sinister fangs. His right arm was encased in vicious-looking ice.

"Knock, knock," he said, gaze sweeping across the room. When he saw her, he stopped and squinted. "You aren't a Keeper," he growled. "I would remember you. So pretty." He took a step toward her. "So fragile."

The Baron ran into the room with the other Interim and several Kur, weapons drawn. More Kur came from another passage as Camilla and her naga appeared from a third, all desperate to know what had happened.

"What have you done?" Eros exclaimed. The intruder hissed as his grin widened.

"It's been so long, Eros. How's the family?" He laughed at his own private joke. "Oooh, that's right. They're all dead." He glared at the Interim. "Or soon to be. I wish I could say this was just a social call, but I'm here on business."

"What do you want, Donovan?" Eros asked. That's when Casey noticed her mother behind the Cleric, looking from her to the intruder and back again. She was thinking, plotting, debating. Casey shook her head but her mother just looked at her with a determined expression.

"No, not what I want. What *he* wants."

Donovan glanced around, saw Camilla, and flicked his sword at her. There was a flash of light and a shock of screams. Casey ducked her head in reflex, heart thumping wildly. When she looked up again, she stopped breathing as she waited for the dust to clear. *Mom,* she thought. *Please, mom!* A pillar of ice had shot out of the ground, capturing Camilla and raising her up on display. The naga and her mother were cowering in the hall but looked to be unharmed.

"What he wants," Donovan reiterated. "Now for what I want. What *I* want is to see you die. Is Shade here? I'll let her watch me kill you…and then I'll gut her, too."

"You don't have that power," Balthazar's deep rumble of a voice declared. "You were always second rate next to her."

For the first time since he had arrived, Casey saw the mask of the one called Donovan slip. Hatred burned in his eyes.

"Not…anymore…" he growled, lifting his right arm. "Not even you can match my power, Eros."

"We will see," Eros murmured.

There was a flash of light as Donovan struck first. His ice exploded around a stone chunk that had been thrown up in front of the Baron so quickly that Casey didn't even see it move. She lay paralyzed on the ground as the three Interim began fighting the intruder, swords clashing. Ice flew everywhere but the Baron and his allies only used their power defensively. The Kur, she noticed, stayed out of their way.

"Get the injured out of here," Kallo ordered the soldiers. They spread out, careful to avoid the Interim, and began searching the dead for survivors. Delia checked Silvo and then reached for Casey.

"I don't think so," Donovan growled, flicking his wrist.

All around them, ice chunks burst out of the group, spearing Kur or freezing them. Delia was thrown back as ice erupted between them. Casey's mother screamed, raced across the room, and pulled Casey to her feet as Keepers rushed around them, trying to clear the danger zone and help those they could. She coughed as dust filled her lungs, stumbling across the room to one of the side tunnels.

"Laura!" her father yelled, drawing their attention. Clara was screaming in his arms. The passageway shook so violently that the ceiling started to collapse, forcing them out into the open room. Casey could barely tell what was happening. She was being pulled along by her mother, stumbling on the unsteady ground, tripping over rubble and corpses. She was having trouble breathing, trouble seeing. And then a force hit her back and threw her into a hallway. Her father was next to her, his side red with fresh blood.

"Dad!" Casey exclaimed, fingers shaking over his abdomen as she tried to think of what she should do. Clara shrieked and Casey looked up just in time to see her mother throw herself in front of her little sister. An ice shard flew right through her chest and stabbed the ground next to Clara's skinned legs. Casey screamed, screamed in horror, screamed in denial, screamed in overwhelming pain. Her mother hit the ground hard, eyes gazing lifelessly upward. Clara laid her head on her mother's stomach, sobbing uncontrollably.

Kallo flashed across the room, picked Clara up by her waist, and darted into the hall as his twin sister appeared and pulled Casey and her father to their feet. A swarm of Kur forced them down the hall, pushing Casey away from her mother. She clawed at them, shrieked, begged them to let her go, to save her mother. They didn't listen. She was swept along in the crowd like a ragdoll in a raging river. She watched ice and stone fly across the mouth of the hallway, watched her mother's body until it disappeared.

It was raining when Knick, Shade, and Lethan packed up to go, this time with a dog, a kid, and a second Interim, and Jilk felt it was a bad omen. He told Knick as much when they were alone but the guy only shrugged and said, "I'd find a good omen more suspicious these days." They smoked side by side on the porch, watching the rain fall. Slot was out there with Molly, rolling in the mud and laughing like a kid.

"Guess it's time for a bath," Solo said as he came through the swinging doors with a cigarette between his lips, sparking a lighter.

"You think?" Knick asked. "I don't know. If dirt builds character, mud's gotta reinforce it or something. Right, Jilk?"

Jilk made a face and laughed sarcastically. Solo's laugh was genuine. They smoked in silence for a few moments, enjoying the rain and the quiet. Jilk lost himself in his thoughts as he watched Slot play in the rain with Molly. He didn't feel good about this. Something wasn't right. And Isis' words bothered him most of all, mostly because they were true, but there was something else in the meaning...some sort of dark control. Could he call it manipulation if it was true? He wouldn't abandon Knick for any reason, no matter what words came out of her mouth. The way she dismissed his need for answers with cold logic—that's what made him feel off, like he was walking into a death trap out of his own insistence and she could save him but wouldn't. *She's done it before*, he remembered as he watched Molly tackle Slot to the ground, the two rolling around in the mud. When he and Knick and the siblings had met Isis for the first time, she had silenced Knick's protests with cold logic. Look where it got them. They were knee-deep in the danger zone.

"Hey, Solo!" Slot yelled, pulling Jilk out of his thoughts. He ducked just in time to avoid being hit by a flying mud ball. It hit Solo's chest and shoulder and the spatter doused his cigarette.

"Oh hell no," he muttered and jumped the railing, chasing after his sister as she squealed and ran. He scooped up mud and flung it at her as Molly loped alongside Slot, barking happily. Jilk wondered if all of this would change after Mesopotamia. He wondered if there would be a future for all of them, or even some of them.

"Why are you doing this?" Jilk wanted to know. "Why are

you *really* doing this, I mean. Is it really just about a girl?"

"Don't lecture me," Knick muttered. "You can't tell me anything I haven't told myself."

"Fair enough."

Both men took drags on their rettes and exhaled clouds of gray.

"Why are *you* doing this?" Knick asked. "I get I'm an idiot, but you have roots in the cogs. It makes no sense for you to ditch them for me, some newbie they stuck in your outfit."

"It didn't take long for you to become one of us, even if you tried hard not to." Jilk took a long drag, watching the siblings play in the rain. "A lot went down when I was under. Maybe it wasn't smart. But I'm here because I trust their judgment."

"Tch," Knick clucked. "You know why they're here, don't you?"

"Yep. Because they trust my judgment."

"That's a bit circular. You'll never go forward that way, just round and round."

"When one of us has a strong gut feeling, we guide the others. About you? We all had a gut feeling. So here we are, in the thick of stupid."

"You can still go home."

"And you'll send me a postcard? Fuck that." Jilk grinned and so did Knick. "Here. Take this." Jilk pulled a .45 ACP from under his jacket and passed it to Knick. "Take it."

Knick stared at it for a long moment before accepting it. Being armed was smart, but the need to be armed was discouraging. It just reinforced how much danger they were all in. It was a sobering thought. Knick tucked the pistol into the back of his pants under his jacket. They smoked quietly for several drags and watched the mud fight.

"I gotta ask," Jilk said, breaking the silence. "Why Gothic?"

"Didn't you ask me once?"

"Yeah, back when you believed you were a better liar."

"Fuck you," Knick said, laughing.

"You going to ask me why her?" he asked, pointing across the yard to where Slot was scooping up more mud.

"Nope."

"No?"

"No. I already know. With Slot, everything on the inside is good. Everything. It makes the outside good, too."

"Yeah," Jilk agreed, quietly regarding his friend. "You had better make it back, Knick. I'm getting emotional with all these goodbyes."

Knick smiled at the joke and nodded that he got the message. Suddenly, a strange man was yelling. They looked up to see Slot at the meat bun cart, still covered in mud, ordering one of the buns. The merchant was trying to wave her away but she grabbed one anyway and raced back to the *Toxic Ox*. Jilk waved at the angry merchant as he glared over at him.

"Knick!" she exclaimed. "Knick! Before you go, you have to try this!" She held it out for him, her muddy hands clutching the wax paper, doing her best to avoid getting any grime on the food. He took a bite, groaned in approval, and ate the rest of it out of her hands, getting a bit of mud on his face. She laughed and tried to wipe it off, muddying up his face even more.

Then they were all laughing, laughing like nothing in the universe was wrong.

When the rain died down and Knick departed with two Keepers, a Krueh-jin, a miner, and a dog caked in mud in tow, Jilk went inside to where Isis, Antion, and Otto were sitting at a private table; Antion was tapping on the computer deck Jilk had scrounged up for him. He intruded on their conversation without any warning or permission. He had changed his mind about not being bored sitting around waiting, and he wasn't about to let Isis watch him walk into the death trap. If he was heading in that direction, he was going to run in screaming.

"How's it coming?" he asked, nodding to the deck Antion was pushing away. "Find anything?"

"As I told my lady Interim when they returned, I have found nothing useful on this digital information wire thing," Antion replied. "I need real information. I need books. I need a Keeper library."

Jilk nodded. "So," he began, "let's talk about Lake Hern."

Gnarly roots sprang out of the ground and spiraled into a helix around Donovan, sprouting thorns as they closed in. As the Ice Sovereign flicked his sword to freeze them, Balthazar sent a wall of stone to crush the frigid thorns into his body. For a moment, there was just a pillar of rock. And then it began to crack, ice crystals leaking through. It fell away. Donovan was panting, pierced through in several places, but the bulk of his body had been encased in ice to protect his most vulnerable places.

He released the ice in a shattering blast. Balthazar used rock as a shield, Sonia used vines. Eros merely swiped his sword in front of him and the shards splintered into a million pieces and swept away from him. He looked to Camilla and was relieved to see she was mostly unharmed, though her skin was deathly pale and her lips were turning blue from the frozen prison she was trapped in.

"You're holding back!" Donovan complained, grinning wickedly. The man was bruised and bloody but still in fighting condition. It wasn't a good sign. He should be dead.

The fight had raged for hours. Sonia and Balthazar were waning, both as injured as their enemy. Even Eros felt exhaustion creeping into him. They had been very spare with the use of their aegis, but Donovan had forced much over the course of the battle. And yet Donovan used his power like he had it in infinite supply. Whatever relic the ex-Regent had dug up for him had made him incredibly powerful.

The evidence was in the ruin all around them. The survivors had long-since evacuated, but there were so many corpses that Eros wondered just how many had actually made it out. He had known Sanctuary would be vulnerable, but where else could they have gone? Muriel knew every secret Eros knew. He had also known that there was no force that Muriel could send against him that could defeat him; Muriel knew it, too. So he borrowed someone else's power. That was the ex-Regent's way. Eros had known that about him long before he had ever betrayed the Order. Perhaps it had been hubris to think he could save the last of the Order from within this vulnerable fortress.

Sanctuary had not been a refuge, just a trap.

Now the last thread of the Order was unraveling. So many were gone, executed by Donovan's hand but dead by the Baron's. But Camilla was still alive. If he could do nothing else, he had to save her. They had once been the three-headed beast that guarded the Order—the Cleric, the High Counselor, and the Baron—with unique minds fueled by the same heart. He had lost the High Counselor. He had lost the Order. He could not lose her, too.

"Do you want to die, Donovan?" Eros asked calmly. The man hissed, idly swinging his sword over the back of his hand.

"You can't kill me. Not anymore. I am more powerful than you ever were, than you ever could be!"

"How powerful can you be?" Eros asked him. "You're bleeding."

"So are you," Donovan growled.

"I'm bleeding because I've cut you," the Baron told him, "not because you've cut me."

That provoked him into action once more. Steel rang out against steel and ice, and all around them the wrath of each aegis roared and flashed. The fought on, even when the rumbling started. They had shaken the very foundations around them. It wouldn't hold forever.

"If you're so powerful, why are we still alive?" Sonia yelled over the noise of combat. "Or is your great power limited to self-preservation?"

Donovan laughed. "You've given it your all. Both of you! You can't beat me. Your nobility counts for nothing!"

"Then defeat me!" Balthazar cried, bearing down on him with brute strength. Donovan barely managed to block the force of the attack. Sonia quickly dove into his vulnerable side, sword glittering like a hungry fang. Donovan saw just in the nick of time. His gauntlet pulsed in a shimmer of blue light and more crystals grew out of it. A force exploded out of him, knocking everyone back. Donovan stood gasping raggedly, pale eyes crazed. The ground shook so violently that a side passage collapsed.

"You need to leave," Eros told his Interim as they got to their feet. "It's time to go. Look for survivors."

"Yes, time to run!" Donovan howled. "Run like the weak cowards you are!"

"What about you?" Sonia asked the Baron.

"Just go. I will join you shortly."

"No!" Donovan boomed as the others departed down the only open passageway. "You stay. You'll fight me! I'll make you fight me!" Suddenly Donovan's pale eyes grew dark, lips pulling into a fang-less grin. "You'll fight me," he said again, "when I destroy the last reason you had for holding back."

Before Eros could react, Donovan reached out with this icy gauntlet and gleaming sword. A spear of ice shot across the room and staked Camilla. She gasped, spit up blood so dark it was almost black. She looked at him, mouthed the words, "I'm sorry," and then life left her.

Donovan's power was not enough to destroy Eros, but it had been enough to destroy the last of the Order. Donovan was a tool, nothing more. It had been Donovan who saw the victory in killing Eros, a task he had failed at. The ex-Regent had known the real victory was in destroying everything the Baron shepherded. So he had unleashed a madman with no qualms about killing those who had once been his brothers and sisters.

Eros had held back. Using the Sword of Scars unleashed terrible power at a very high cost. It required an incredible tolerance for pain and an unwavering amount of patience. It demanded respect of the Balance, for the weapon itself created Balance. Blood for blood. Perhaps he had held back because a traitor like Donovan was not worth his sacrifice. Maybe because he struggled to believe Donovan had fallen so far. Maybe because he did not want to use his power against someone who had once been family. Or because he had felt he didn't have to. Perhaps it was because, deep down inside, he hoped the Ice Sovereign could be saved.

All of those delusions died with Camilla. There was only the Balance. Donovan's betrayal had to be punished, and so did the Baron's hubris.

Eros thrust the Sword of Scars away from his body and a blast of energy ripped across the room, striking the Sovereign in the gut and splintering into a V that carved its way across his chest and exploded out of his shoulders. He slumped to the ground, gasping, choking on blood.

Blood for blood. A red stain in the shape of a V sprouted under Eros' shirt. He hid the pain as he walked over to the body of the kinslayer, chunks of ceiling falling around him. There in the dust and ice and blood was not a wicked man but a trembling boy. Those pale eyes looked at him like a boy to a father who had just slapped him across the face. Innocence betrayed.

"I renounce you," Eros whispered.

Donovan's face contorted with rage and he bore his fangs,

blood coating his teeth. "I hate you!" he screamed. "I hate you! You were supposed to protect us! You used us! You betrayed us! I hate you! *Hate you!*"

Sonia and Balthazar returned to find him standing over the dying man. They said nothing but he felt their sorrow in his bones. When he glanced back at them, he saw in their eyes their message—that there were no survivors. Eros moved into the tunnel leading away from Sanctuary with Sonia and Balthazar trailing quietly behind him. They listened to the crazed screaming until the ceiling collapsed completely.

They turned to the Void, black shooting stars in the darkness, and left the tomb behind.

A few hours of walking and they were back in the webworks, only this time with thermal goggles. They weren't as fancy as the Krueh-jin gear, but they were enough to navigate the tunnels. If Shade focused on the wall or the ground, she could see it, but when she looked away, everything but the people became dark again. She looked at those with her, muted versions of themselves in light. Ross was at the front, tapping nervously, with Lethan by his side. Molly plunged ahead fearlessly, sniffing everything. Occasionally she would bark once, startling everyone. Knick and Shade walked side by side a few meters behind Lethan and Daedalus brought up the rear.

"So you know where we're going," Knick casually said, "but I don't get the feeling you're excited about it."

"I'm not," she admitted. "Serena and I have a history."

"Well," Knick prompted when she didn't immediately continue. "You can't leave it at that or I'll fill in the details myself. Let's see, who could Serena be? Ex-girlfriend?"

Shade rolled her eyes. "Serena was the clan priestess but she had a rebellious youth. Before a priestess becomes a mystic, she trains an acolyte to take her place. When Serena was an acolyte, she decided she didn't want to be priestess and ran away."

"Isn't it normal for kids to rebel?" he asked. "Not that I remember being a kid."

"So they say."

"How was this your problem?"

"Serena had managed to disappear without a trace and

smuggle herself halfway across the Mine. She was using adept spells meant to protect the clan to force people into giving her what she wanted. Anyone who tried to stop her got burned. So Eros sent me to drag the brat back home." Shade shook her head. "She's hated me ever since."

"How long ago did this happen?"

"Eight years."

Knick laughed. "I'm sure she's over it by now."

"Doubtful. Serena is an unbalanced, self-important mageling that never managed to grow up."

Knick laughed even harder. "Wow, I've never seen you so riled up. I can't wait to meet this witch."

"Shade is Serena's ultimate rival," Daedalus explained. "She fought Shade and lost. She was forced back home by an outsider. She was disgraced for her betrayal, her defeat, and her failure. Even though she was just a child, she bore the prodigal shame for the rest of her youth."

"Then why did they even let her become the priestess?" Knick asked.

"She was chosen," Shade replied bitterly. "She will make our mission difficult if she can."

"How much authority does the priestess have?" Knick asked.

"Most of it. She is the acting clan head."

"Whoa, whoa, wait," Knick exclaimed. "Wait. Back up and start over."

"Daedalus," Shade called and looked over her shoulder. "You know more about the clan than I do."

"What do you want to know?" he asked.

"Something. Anything. Everything," Knick answered.

"The Skahradahn are warren-dwellers led by two women, the mystic and her priestess. The mystic, also known as the Rope Woman, is the head of the clan though her role is performed from behind the curtain. The priestess is the acting clan head but will always defer to the mystic's wisdom."

"Why is it always women?" Knick wanted to know. "The crone, the shaman, Red, and now a priestess. Are Typhi tribes all matriarchies?"

"The Krueh-jin do not always have female leaders," Lethan said over his shoulder. "There have been as many men in charge as there have been women."

"The Ataashvatan, too," Daedalus said and looked at Shade. "You asked me if I had heard of them. I had, but not as Ataashvatan. Babylon's immortals, however—that was a name I knew. It was the name of a mercenary band. They had many leaders, mostly men."

"I get it, I get it," Knick said.

"Women are often clan heads," Daedalus explained. "Mothers are the heart of all life. A woman's womb is every man and woman's first home, her milk their first meal, her words their first tutelage. They look to her for shelter, nourishment, love, and guidance."

"So why have men as leaders at all?" Ross asked. Shade could hear the nervousness in his voice. He had been deathly afraid of going deeper into the webworks but had done so with a brave face. She could see how he trembled, each step harder than the last.

"The hard winter," Daedalus replied. "Women may be at the heart of life, but it would not be possible without a man. A balance is needed."

"Aaahhh," Knick groaned, "I knew there was a plug in there somewhere." Shade smiled faintly. "Move on. Where do the Dirt Men figure in?"

"The Dirt Men are the clan warriors who conduct raids for supplies and keep the warren safe. They are the past, present, and future consorts of the priestesses—"

"The *sorcerers*," Lethan spat with dislike. "You call them priestess and mystic, but they are nothing more than sorcerers."

Lethan marched ahead angrily. Shade wondered what conflict between the Krueh-jin and the Dirt Men had transpired to result in such hatred and distrust. Knick jogged after him, yelling, "Wait a minute!" Shade dropped back until she was walking next to Daedalus then slowed her pace and waited for him to match it before speaking.

"I've wanted to ask you about something," she began hesitantly.

"Of course."

"The Sirens," Shade began, pausing only to measure the distance between them and the others. "They mentioned you. What did you do to them to make them so afraid of you?"

"Afraid?" he echoed with a hint of amusement.

"And respect," she added.

"It was a long time ago." He cleared his throat. "You had already come to the Order but I had not yet changed identities. I was sent to investigate a dispute in the Talaos region; the Sirens were involved. When it was settled, they saw me as a...preferred partner. Sometimes they select men they feel will give them the most talented daughters...and they picked me. I refused so they attempted to dominate me. It didn't work. A few of the Sirens might have gotten...singed...in the process."

"When they tried to touch your melody," she guessed.

"That's right," he murmured. "They tried to touch yours? What happened?"

"She fell down in pain. She told me that my shadows shatter everything." Shade frowned at him. "That only Daedalus had such power."

"I was the most powerful Interim once." He smiled at her. "Now that person is you."

"You have had to hide your power."

"I have, but it never left me. I know what I am capable of, Shade. And you are capable of more."

Shade's frown deepened. She had never been considered more powerful than the others. There were no ranks among the Interim. But something had happened to her. She was able to use her power without the bells, which should be impossible, and she had done things she would never have dreamed of being able to do. She had teleported through shadows, directed the shades as if they were sentient, and had even entered their realm. The Shaman warned her that the use of this power could turn her into a shadow forever, opening the door that allowed Shade to believe she had literally become a shadow in those moments.

But there were no teachings on this kind of power. She had been schooled very specifically on what her capabilities would be. She had worked closely with the Baron and her other teachers in developing the manifestations of her aegis. A possibility that there was more to it did not exist. And yet...

The Sirens had said only Daedalus had power like hers. She needed to know if he knew what was happening to her, if it had happened to him. She needed guidance. At the very least, she needed to tell someone who could understand her.

"Eros confiscated one of my bracelets the day I brought

Knick into Asgard," she told him. "The day Knick left, I gave him mine."

"You gave him yours? But then you had none." Realization struck him. "You had no bracelet when you went to Heaven." They both stopped walking. "How? How did you—?"

"I don't know."

"You used the aegis without your bracelet," he muttered in disbelief, as if saying it would make it real. "That's not possible…"

Shade pulled off her goggles and was plunged into darkness. She needed that darkness, the sanctuary of the unseen. In front of Knick, she had to remain brave and confident. Not only because she needed to protect him, but because she needed him to believe she was everything he thought she was. But Daedalus was different. He was an Interim. The Order had been her family, Asgard her home. In the Keepers she had established her safe place. Until Daedalus had found her and told her the truth, she had thought she lost that safe place forever. There was a measure of shame she carried—not for saving Knick, but for failing her family.

This strange power felt a product of that failure, that shame. She couldn't bear to look at him.

"I did more than that. I commanded the shadows. I entered their realm." Her confession was a whisper, "I think I became a shadow." Until now, she had not had the courage to voice it. "What's happening to me, Daedalus?"

He didn't speak for so long that she instinctively looked up. She heard him pull off his goggles. Suddenly, he was embracing her. It was only for a moment, but it was warm and strong. "You are becoming what we were always meant to be," he whispered. When he released her, he gave a shy chuckle. "I don't have answers for you. But you shouldn't be afraid. The child born under the third sign will carry the power of the Old Ones—your prophecy." He put his goggles back on and waited for her to do the same. They started walking again. "Eros may be able to tell you more."

Eros. At the mention of that name, Shade's chest constricted painfully. She regretted the things she had said to him. He had raised her, trained her, guided her. He had never given her a reason not to trust him. He had been firm but kind, gentle but strong, decisive and fair and everything a leader should be. He had always trusted her. She had repaid his kindness with betrayal. Even when he reached out in understanding and forgiveness, she had told him to stay away from her.

"How is he?" she asked.

"He is the Baron. He is the strongest of us, facing this crisis calmly. He is a rock for every Keeper still alive. And he is the one who suffers the most."

Shade nodded. She had expected no less. "I hurt him."

"He forgave you."

"No, not yet. Not until I ask for it. He deserves my apology."

"He deserves your trust. If you give him that, nothing else is needed." Daedalus hummed thoughtfully. "It's strange for you to talk so openly with me. We never spoke like this before. I thought it would be hard for you to stop seeing me as Daelus."

"I had learned enough about the one called Daedalus," she explained, "and how he figured into my life that I felt connected to him even though I didn't know of his existence until I believed he was already dead. When you told me who you were, it was as if the puzzle clicked—the kindness and gentleness of Daelus…the strength and authority of Daedalus. I should have known. I didn't, but I should have."

"Why?" he asked. "There was no reason to suspect I had lied to you."

"You were trying to tell me—"

"I was trying to tell you while trying to *not* tell you. It wasn't fair. I knew it. I wanted you to see more than Daelus but I couldn't show you." He smiled faintly. "I'm glad you could accept Daedalus."

"You saved my life. At the very least, I owe you that much." Before he could say she owed him nothing, she blurted out, "And," she hesitated, "and I needed you. I felt so far away from home. I missed you. All of you. I was trying to be strong on my own, but when I knew you were Daedalus—someone I could rely on—I…" She unburdened herself, let the walls down, acted incredibly selfish. "I depended on you. Because I needed you."

Daedalus nodded solemnly. He opened his mouth to

speak but lost his words. They walked in silence until they caught up to the rest of the group. When Knick saw them, he started toward them.

"It just occurred to me that if you guys know all about these Tribes, why couldn't you just point the way?" he exclaimed as Molly stared whimpering, turning anxious circles. "Why bother with this road show?"

"We know of them," Shade explained, "but we did not know they were the Tribes of Typhi. There are many peoples and clans spread across Lotus Maze, like the Exotics of Razhada or the—" Shade paused when she noticed the dog's nervousness. "Something's not right."

They all froze and strained to hear in the pervasive silence, barely even breathing. Molly padded this way and that, her collar jingling. She whimpered again. Whatever she heard was beyond the humans' senses. Molly stamped her paws, growling and wincing simultaneously. Shade looked at Knick and found him looking at her.

"There's something in these tunnels," he whispered. "And I think it knows we're here."

Lethan began turning his head this way and that. "Wait a minute," he rasped. "Where is Whiskey?"

The lehn was nowhere to be seen.

The Inscriptor smiled at the customer across the counter and passed her the glyph carefully wrapped in tissue paper and tucked inside a gold-colored box. She took it with trembling fingers and tears in her eyes, the tears of a mother's last hope for her child, the tears born of the depravity of turning to sorcery because science had failed her. The Inscriptor knew better. This work was still science, only less likely to kill you. Come morning, her child would open his eyes and ask for a glass of water. In three weeks time, he would be on the fast track to recovery. There would be no souls sold or blood contracts, and the cost of one boy's life would not be paid for by another life, just forints. Lots and lots of forints.

As the woman dug into her purse and pulled out the second half of the payment, someone came through the door. The Inscriptor looked up and froze, blood running cold. Dimitri, Sovereign of the Sword of Seas, walked into the shop with a knit brow and dark circles under his eyes. He looked utterly harassed with pale skin and eyes so dark they were almost black. The sea was caught in a turbulent storm.

Dimitri was dangerous.

The Inscriptor didn't even bother counting the money the woman held out, just took it and waved her away, gaze transfixed on the Keeper's. When they were alone, Dimitri locked the door and strode toward the counter.

"You…"

"Me," Dimitri said. "You're still flapping your lips? I thought you were past that."

"It makes my customers more comfortable… What do you want?" the Inscriptor asked.

"Your help," Dimitri replied, "finding someone."

"It will cost you—"

"Fuck your games, Ichthys," he growled and grabbed the Inscriptor around the throat. "It will cost you if you do not help me."

"What are you going to do?" the Inscriptor choked. "Cut my tongue out again?"

Dimitri pulled the Inscriptor's high collar down to where the glowing yellow glyph was carved into his throat. It was the only reason the Inscriptor had a voice at all; his tongue had been cut out by Dimitri himself on order of the Keepers for threatening to use the inscription power to expose them.

"No," the Keeper said, "but I may cut out this glyph of yours. Perhaps one of your eyes. I'm sure you can scribble up something to help you see. Or maybe I should take them both. If I didn't know any better, I might think you had something to do with the destruction of Asgard."

The Inscriptor had nothing to do with what happened to Asgard, but Dimitri already knew that. It wasn't said in interrogation, just as a threat. A warning.

"A quick death—" the Inscriptor gasped. "Keeper justice must grant me a quick death."

"Keeper justice is busy."

Dimitri was typically loved, calm and gentle and renewing like the waters that flowed into him. But the Inscriptor knew better. Dimitri was more like the sea than most people realized. He was capable of intense violence and mass destruction. He hid coldness and brutality beneath his kind smile. But this level of rage? The Inscriptor had never seen it before.

"Who are you looking for?"

"Vox." Dimitri let go and walked several paces away. "She went missing. I've looked everywhere. I'm out of options. She's in danger. I feel it."

So it was Vox, the fiery butterfly that flapped her wings and created a tsunami. The Inscriptor took a step toward the Keeper.

"I will find her but the crafting is long and complex. It will take time."

"Just do it."

The Inscriptor nodded and pulled the drapes over the windows. In the eerie lowlight, they made eye contact. In one set of eyes was desperate and ruthless turbulence. In the other was cold hatred.

"Just know that it will end. Fire and water will only cancel each other out. Everything you love and everything you are will be gone."

Dimitri did not speak, only glared, like the rising of a great wave about to overtake everything in its path.

It was two days into the journey that Knick realized whatever was in the tunnels was stalking them. Whiskey was still missing and Molly remained a ball of nervousness. When Knick asked how much further, Ross told him he didn't know.

"I've never mapped the webworks," he confessed. "There're so many tunnels, so many paths, I…"

"Guess!" Knick hissed.

"Miles. Miles and miles."

"You mean days."

"I'm doing my best!"

"Try harder!"

Knick felt guilty as soon as he said it but there was no taking it back. They were all riled up, especially Lethan who worried about Whiskey. He wanted to go back to look for him but they convinced him otherwise. It was too dangerous. They didn't know what was after them and he sure as hell didn't know the way back. If Whiskey was still alive—and that was a big if—then the lehn would find them.

They continued on for another two days as Ross

tentatively tapped out their path, avoiding some tunnels on his own and some because of Molly's aggressive reaction to them. The occasional skittering and raspy breathing sound kept them on edge. There were two watchers every time they slept, but the sleepers got nothing more than fitful winks.

Knick couldn't help but think of Jilk and how he was right. What had he been thinking bringing these people into the webworks? At best, they lost the lehn. At worst, they all died. What was stalking them? Needlers? No, needlers were aggressive with no sense of self-preservation. They would have charged them the moment they'd picked up their scent. Spinners? For most people, spinners were a figment of the imagination, a horror story to keep people out of the webworks, except this figment was fact. He had never seen one but the cogwheelers had warned their own against the webworks, which meant the story wasn't a part of their propaganda. The story was real. But spinners this close to the perimeter? Impossible.

Of course, Knick had no idea how close to the perimeter they really were. Maybe, in all of this darkness and uncertainty, they had gone a lot deeper than they meant to. Or maybe the rumor of the spinners not creeping to the edges of the works wasn't true at all. But if either theory was true, where were the webs? There was just rock, no thick and sticky tangles of thread.

Either way, they were being hunted. *No, it's more than that*, Knick decided one dark day as Ross tried to turn them right for the third time that hour and Molly's ears pinned back, teeth baring as she growled. *We're being herded.* Knick's blood ran cold.

"Wait," he whispered. "Stop." He crept toward the tunnel and stared down it. He mostly saw black. Molly slowly backed away as he moved closer. "Wait. Something's down there. Something doesn't want us to go this way."

A soft hissing sound echoed off the walls. It took a moment before they realized it was laughter. Something was snickering at them. All of the hairs on Knick's body stood up as fear rushed through him. A dark lump moved in the back of the tunnel causing Knick to jump back in surprise. Lethan gasped, his face contorting into a raw expression of fear. Down the tunnel, a clicking noise was followed by a breathy purr.

"Wants to sees us?" the creature choked in a high-pitched rasp, forcing every word. "Then sees us."

Shade and Daedalus immediately drew their swords. Molly's growl became more vicious.

A man crept out of the pitch blackness. He was naked. His body was so thin he looked to be all skin and bones. He was hunched over, knees slightly bent and arms hanging limply in front of him. Scars covered his gray skin. Large barbs protruded from his forearms and calves and smaller ones from his hands. His hair was thin, greasy wisps matted to his skull and dangling wetly onto his knobby shoulders. His eyes were completely black and his mouth was a wide, lipless slit across his face. He was grinning, revealing small, crooked teeth filed into points. His black tongue hung out between his teeth.

A second man leaned forward out of the darkness, crouched on the ground. He looked so much like the first that Knick initially thought they were the same. But the second's face was more pinched and he didn't have any hair at all. This man was not smiling; he was staring at them like a shooter would at his target. Serious, calm, focused.

The first man laughed in that hissing way and then made a purring sound. The clicking noise responded from somewhere in the darkness. And then a much larger form emerged between the two mutated men, thick and hairy legs silently slithering forward against the tunnel walls. A giant spider's maw snapped and clicked as eight black eyes focused on these strangers that had wandered into their web, barely contained in this small space.

The first man reached out and lovingly stroked one of the spider's mandibles. "Ixi," he clicked. The rest of the things he said were sounds, not words, but when his garbled speech ended again with, "Ixi," Knick had a feeling he knew what it meant.

Kill.

"You run now," the man said. "We chase."

The spider screeched and lurched forward. Shade lashed out with her sword and a burst of energy struck the creature and threw it back into the blackness. It rolled and flailed, screaming in agony as the aegis dissolved it, squishing the bald man with the pinched face in its thrashing. Eight legs pounded the walls and ceiling, pushing the thick body into circles until one of the legs snapped off. It gave one last screech as it wiggled violently on its back and then died, the remaining legs curling into its half-eaten face and abdomen.

For a moment, the only sound was that of terrified panting. And then there was a scraping noise. The giant, dead bulk of the spider was being dragged back into the tunnel. The remaining man laughed and took two steps towards them. Two more spiders crawled out of the darkness with three humanoids between their massive legs and maws. More enemies arrived from the tunnel behind them.

"You take the lead, I'll cover behind," Daedalus said to Shade. She nodded once.

Then they sprang into action. Shade led the charge forward while Daedalus pushed Lethan and Ross behind her, using flashes of electricity to push the monsters back. Where one fell, another crawled over it and took its place.

"Ross!" Shade called as they came up on a split. Ross screamed, tapping the stone so erratically that he was more or less smacking his hand against it. More creatures filled up the space on the right, forcing them to go left.

We're still being herded, Knick realized as their path veered deeper and deeper into the webworks. The spinners were chasing them, scaring them, but they were holding back. They screeched and kicked their legs in every side tunnel they were not meant to go down, but they didn't outright attack. *We're being moved to the nest,* Knick thought. *There are no webs. No webs because the works is the web. Fuck.*

They dodged this way and that as man-like monsters and giant spiders hounded them. The Keepers attacked but the ones they felled were quickly replaced. Standing and fighting would be pointless. The goal was to get out, and for that all they could do was run. But Ross was lost in a frenzy of fear, so they were following the only path before them—the path spun by the spinners.

The tunnel opened up and they spilled into a giant cavern at least two hundred feet high. The floor was tiered, sloping gradually to a pit in the center. The pit looked fifty feet wide and plummeted into total darkness. A giant, blue glowing stone hung above it. Stalagmites and flowstones crowded the ground amidst massive columns, some incredibly thin, tapered in the middle, and others so wide that it would take twenty people with their arms stretched out and fingertips touching to wrap around it. Stalactites and drapery peppered the ceiling where thousands of giant spiders were crowded together. Sticking to the walls and huddled among the columns and stalagmites were hundreds of spinners, all sneering with their black eyes and lipless smiles.

Molly started barking, dancing around the cavern in a threatening manner. Ross was shaking so bad that Knick had to hold him up. He put his around across the kid's chest and grabbed his shoulder, sagging when his knees started to give out. He hoisted him back up, muttering, "It's gonna be okay," absentmindedly as he gawked at the spiders above them. Some of the spiders were cramped tight between the stalactites, but others were hanging from web, their black legs flicking out and curling in. Several descended halfway. All around, they were hissing and clicking and purring, talking to one another.

Knick thought he might piss his pants. Instead, he pulled out the gun Jilk had given him.

When he looked at Shade, he found her and Daedalus having a private and silent conversation with their eyes. On most days, he envied the male Interim so much he hated him, but right then he was really glad to have him along. At worst, the spiders ate them all. At best, they just ate Daedalus.

"On the far side," Lethan whispered, "there's another tunnel. We might be able to make it."

"Tut tut," scolded the spinner as he emerged from the black cave they had escaped out of. "Homes sweet homes. Dinner times," he choked. "Ixi...insides sticky sweet." His black tongue lapped hungrily at his lipless mouth. "Open your bellies, lets us taste—"

Suddenly, there was a loud screech and a creature flew out of the darkness, landed on the spinner's head, and clawed at his eyes.

"Whiskey!" Lethan exclaimed. The lehn and the spinner danced around, both shrieking until one of the spinner's eyes was blind. Whiskey bounded off his head, darted across the cave, and leapt onto Lethan's shoulder. The Jin embraced the furball protectively and the lehn wrapped his fuzzy arms around Lethan's head.

The half-blinded spinner screamed at them, a deep and guttural and unnatural scream. The spiders and spinners all responded with clicking and screeching, and then they attacked. Several spiders dropped down from the ceiling and jumped out from between columns and stalagmites. The spinners raced toward them, bony limbs swinging wildly.

"Go!" Daedalus exclaimed. "Run!"

They broke into a sprint for the far side of the cave, dodging dropping spiders and lunging spinners. Shade and Daedalus unleashed the power of their aegis. Knick saw flashes of lightning chaining through several creatures, electrocuting them with so many volts that some of the spiders exploded. Out of the corner of his eye, he saw a dragon esper rising up out of the ground and plunging down onto enemies, dissolving them into jade dust. But more than that, however, was the shimmery blackness of the spiders closing in on them.

Lethan slashed at spinners that fell on them with his kukri and sickle to help clear the path. Molly lunged at the humanoids' throats and at the spider's eyes, black fur disappearing into the sea of black bodies only to reemerge with her maw covered in blood that looked like oil. Knick took every clear shot he could while all but carrying Ross, who was so hysterical that he kept trying to curl into a ball.

And then the creatures crowded around them so tightly that they were trapped again. Knick looked for the blue glowstone to map their progress. His heart sank in his chest as he realized they had only moved so far as the middle of the great cavern. As they were pushed tighter together by the snapping maws and dancing legs, Knick reached out to Shade. He grabbed her hand and felt her tighten her fingers around his. She pushed him behind her as if to protect him.

"I'm sorry, Knick. But I have to," she whispered, pulling off her goggles. And the words that left her lips next were hisses and whispers.

The darkness came alive. All around them shadows of men and spiders lunged out of the walls and rose up out of the ground, attacking their enemies with vicious silence. Knick watched as a human-like shadow took a spider by the head. The creature flailed its legs but the shadowman could not be moved. The mandibles snapped down on the shadowman's head, passing right through it and clashing together. Seconds later, the spider's head came off of its body and the shade was moving to the next enemy.

Knick looked at Shade, at her glowing violet eyes and bright glyph. Her whole image was somehow darker, fainter, like an illusion rather than a body. For the first time since he had met her, he felt afraid of her. Even Daedalus was gaping in awe. What scared him the most was the paralyzing thought that if he reached out and touched her, his hand might pass right through her.

"Shade," he said, letting Ross sink to the ground. She didn't look at him. She was looking into the shadow realm.

"Shade!" Daedalus yelled and tried to grab her shoulder. He found no purchase. His hand just slid through her shoulder. The man paled.

More spiders dropped down to confront the shadow versions of themselves, rowdily fighting and dying. It wasn't safe for them to stay there any longer, and it wasn't safe for Shade to remain in the shadow trance. Knick desperately called her name but she didn't respond. And then she was falling forward. Knick lunged instinctively, not even sure he could catch her, and gasped when she fell into his arms. Shade looked up at him, pale and breathing raggedly. She looked as though all of her energy had been drained.

A deeper cry louder and shriller than the rest suddenly erupted from the pit. Knick and his company turned to look as two mammoth legs appeared, followed by two more. So they had disturbed momma. *Fuck*, Knick thought, looking at Shade once more.

"Go," she rasped.

Daedalus hoisted Ross to his feet as Knick helped support Shade and they sprinted across the cavern, Molly loping alongside them and Lethan leading the charge. Spinners and spiders that noticed their flight tried to intercept them but Daedalus' aegis and Lethan's steel intervened. As hairy limbs and oily blood flew across their path and screams and screeches chased them, they closed in on the far tunnel. Knick risked a glance back and saw a titan of a spider creeping out of the pit, her shiny blue eyes sweeping the room as her children were massacred.

A horrifying, unearthly scream chased them into the tunnel.

Lake Hern was a milky pool about a hundred feet

wide and twenty feet deep, fed by dripping stalactites that clustered over it like angry, yellow teeth. The town was no more than shacks and hovels scattered along one side of the chipped and stony shore. Jilk, the siblings, the Keepers, and Otto made their way to the far side of the lake where the cavern sloped downward into a sinkhole and tiny cave mouths sprouted along the base like drainage pipes.

"If what I remember reading is correct," Antion said, leading them toward a rocky outcropping on the edge of the lake, "there's a staircase hidden somewhere near here."

"Who would hide a Keeper stronghold out here?" Jilk asked as they waded through the cloudy water to an alcove nestled amid the cliffs. "It's visible from the town."

"Yes," Antion agreed, "but who would wade out here aside from children at play?"

"Slot," Solo mumbled, eyeing his sister with a playful grin. She splashed him and he yelped. "Hey!"

"As I said," Antion muttered and walked carefully over the rough, orange pumice. He brightened when he found what he was looking for. Hidden between the wall and the lake was a narrow staircase spiraling down around the great bowl that held the lake.

"Well I'll be damned," Jilk muttered. He motioned for Antion to go ahead. "Lead the way."

They climbed single-file down the passageway, using head and wrist lamps to light their path. The air became limited in such cramped quarters, making it hard to breathe. When they reached the stone slab that Antion said was a door, they waited in raspy silence for him to open it, but after ten minutes of dawdling, the group became restless.

"What's the hold up?" Slot asked.

"It won't open. It's barred," Antion explained. "The Keepers would have sealed it, of course, when they relocated. But I should be able to open it being a Keeper myself."

"Only you can't," Solo deduced.

"Exactly," Antion muttered despondently. They turned around and climbed back up. On the shore, they stopped to sit and breathe. "I don't understand."

"Is there another way in?" Jilk asked, looking pointedly at Isis.

"No," Antion answered for her then said, "I don't know."

Jilk sighed. "For being an Oracle and all, you sure don't know much."

"Hey—" the scholar started, but Isis reached out and touched his arm, shook her head, and looked out to the lake.

"What about a back door?" Otto asked.

"A what?" Solo snapped.

"A back door. You know, for waste disposal. There'd be a drainage system somewhere, like that ditch we passed. Could be one of those caves leads to a back door."

Antion and Jilk exchanged glances and nodded to each other, suddenly feeling revived. They trudged back across the lake and slid into the ditch. Halfway down, the earth was dry as dust, but the bottom of the pit was wet and muddy, as though recently used. A fine trickle of water was crawling out of one of the crawlspaces.

"As good a place as any to start," Jilk said quietly and clicked his wrist lamp on. He smiled at Antion. "After you." The scholar rolled his eyes, turned on his headlamp, got down on all fours, and crawled into the pipe. Jilk eyed Solo and Slot. "You two stay with Otto and the princess. We'll be back."

It was a good thing he wasn't claustrophobic, because the tight space would've sent him over the edge had he been. And after an hour of squeezing under low ceilings and around large outcroppings, he was covered in mud and feeling defeated. Then suddenly Antion began excitedly calling his name, voice echoing off the walls.

"Over here, Jilk! Over here."

"Over where?" he groaned agitatedly, craning his neck to look around corners. "This place is a damn maze."

"Where are you?"

"Intersection forty-three," he replied sarcastically.

"Jilk!"

"What do you want me to tell you, kid? I see, uh, rock. Tunnels. More tunnels. A bit of green in the wall there—"

"The malachite!" Antion exclaimed. "Okay, duck under the underpass to your right then take the tunnel to your left."

Jilk obeyed and soon the space the scholar was hiding. He was so excited about the extra head room that he didn't immediately notice Antion was pointing to the small, barely visible rungs of a ladder. He grinned and slapped the kid on the shoulder.

"Good job."

"Thanks."

"Now let's find our way out of this shithole and get the others."

It took the better part of another hour just to navigate the correct path out of the ditch maze, and when they finally did reemerge, they found Otto, Slot, and Solo gathered around Isis, who was sitting on her knees, hands folded in her lap, head tilted upward in prayer, and her eyes wide and transfixed on the ceiling. She was muttering indecipherable words under her breath.

"What happened?" Jilk asked as Antion ran and collapsed at her side.

"I don't know," Solo confessed. "We were just sitting here when all of a sudden she jumped up, said something about seeing someone, and then she knelt down and has been like this ever since."

"She said, 'I see you'," Slot explained, "like she did at Asgard that one time."

"Did you try to snap her out of it?" Jilk asked.

"She won't budge," Otto muttered anxiously, brow wrinkled in concern. "She won't acknowledge me at all."

"Then we move her," Jilk said and started toward her, but Antion leapt between them, throwing his arms out frantically.

"Don't!" he exclaimed. "Don't touch her! She's in the trance… Don't touch her. I don't know what would happen."

The cogwheelers sighed and, one after another, took a seat in the mud to wait it out.

Eros and his remaining Interim met up with the last of the Order washed up on the banks of a drainage ditch on the outskirts of Tamina, one of the larger towns in the Cradle. Dr. Basset was sitting on the ground with his daughters, all of them soaked and leaking onto the concrete. The moment the eldest girl saw him, she jumped to her feet. Her eyes were bloodshot and ringed in angry red circles. Sorrow and pain and tears scarred her youthful face, rage and grief roiling in her gaze.

"You!" she screamed. "You were supposed to protect us! You were supposed to *protect* us!"

"Casey!" Her father jumped up, grasping his side in pain

with one arm, and grabbed her. "Stop it." Dr. Basset's face was etched with age, the death of his wife the final stone of an already heavy load.

"You killed her! You *killed* her! You put us in that cage and promised to protect us and you let that monster kill her! I hate you!"

"Casey!" Basset yelled, his voice breaking with emotion. He pulled his daughter into a restraining hug as she dissolved into tears. "It's okay… It's okay."

"…protect…us…" she wailed between sobs. Her knees buckled and they shrank to the ground.

The little one, Clara, sat staring at them with her knees up to her chin, tears leaking out of her. She was squeezing her pants so hard her knuckles were white and her body was shaking. She looked up at Eros. There wasn't any hatred or anger in her gaze, just sadness and fear.

Eros surveyed the rest of the bank to count the remaining few of his Order. His captains Kallo and Delia had survived along with eight Kur, five naga, and twelve scholars. Too few. When the naga raised their sheltered heads to confirm the absence of Camilla, the loss of the Cleric struck him all over again. For all of his power as Baron, Regent, and Sovereign of the Sword of Scars, he had been useless at saving those he was charged to protect.

"Find us shelter," he told the Interim at either side.

"Yes, Baron," they said together, one in deep bass and the other in soft velvet.

Eros took in the tragedy around him as Sonia and Balthazar departed. He wondered if they would ever forgive him for his failures. He wondered if he deserved forgiveness. He had sworn to protect them, all of them. But their deaths, their wounds, their scars—their blood was on his hands. He was just as much at fault as the Regent was. Donovan was right.

Because long ago, he had betrayed the Balance. And these innocent people were paying for it.

Knick and his friends stumbled through the tunnel as fast as they could. Most of the spinners and spiders feared them enough to stay out of their way and the few that had more balls than brains were easily cut down by the Jin and

Keeper. The spider queen, however, was anything but afraid. She was pissed off. She moved surprisingly quickly and fit into remarkably tight spaces in spite of being so massive.

Her long legs scrabbled through the tunnels, her unearthly screech echoing off the walls and overtaking all other noise. It was impossible to tell which direction she was coming from, but they kept running, kept hoping they would trip over the exit.

"Ross!" Knick yelled over his shoulder, struggling to support Shade. "Ross, you have to get us out of here!" The boy was hysterical, shaking his head, sobbing. "Ross! We're all going to die if you don't focus! You're the only one who can get us out of he—" Another screech cut him off. "*Ross!*"

Daedalus thrust the boy's hand against the wall and held him by his wrist. His fingers instinctively started tapping. It took several lengths of tunnel before Ross finally found his comfort zone but, once he started tapping, his nerves calmed considerably. Soon he was running on his own, eyes focused. He was centered.

"This way!" he exclaimed, dodging to the left. They took a wide tunnel that looped around to the right and started climbing. *Good*, Knick thought. *That's a good sign*. The queen screamed again and sounded closer than before. "Here!" Ross said, taking them right. The tunnel opened up into a smaller cavern with three passageways leading away from it. Ross anxiously bounced on the balls of his feet, rapidly tapping the wall. He looked at each of the tunnels before nodding to himself. "This way."

They broke into a run and cleared half of the cavern when the queen slipped out of the left tunnel and screamed at them. Daedalus immediately flashed his sword and a column of electricity ripped through the ceiling and struck the mammoth creature in the back. She roared and reared, legs flailing in the room. They had to dodge out of the way to avoid being struck.

"I think you just pissed her off," Knick told him.

"Looks like," Daedalus agreed.

"We need the shadows," Lethan began but Knick shook his head.

"No," he yelled as he twisted away from another sweeping leg. "No! She can't handle it!"

The queen recovered, her mandibles snapping angrily and

dripping with venom. She screamed and lunged for Knick but Molly leapt up and bit down on the creatures face. The queen lurched, flinging Molly away. The dog hit the wall and yelped, but quickly shook the blow off and got back to her feet. As Lethan began hacking away at the creatures legs, Whiskey bounded up one long limb to claw at one of the many eyes. Daedalus attacked from a different angle to distract the beast, and between him, the animals, and the Jin, the queen's focus was divided.

Ross and Knick pulled Shade to the far side of the cavern. She fell to one knee, gasping for air, her energy near depleted. Knick knelt at her side and brushed her hair from her face. He checked the pistol chamber and counted two bullets, wondering if it would have any effect where Keeper voodoo had failed. Ross squatted down, toying with the rocks under their feet, his gaze focused on the giant spider thrashing about. For all the damage being inflicted, the spider did not look to be harmed in the slightest.

"You have to call the shadows," Ross whispered.

"No," Knick hissed.

"We're gonna die."

"Shut up!"

Shade lifted her gaze and focused on the battle. "I have to do something," she whispered. "That beast is made from darkness and old things. They can't hurt it."

"How do you know?"

"The shadows told me. They await my orders."

"You don't have any energy left!" Knick yelled. "How do you even know they could make a difference?"

"You cannot kill a shadow."

The ground shook, causing him to flinch. He instinctively moved to cover Shade, glancing over his shoulder. The queen was using her legs to stab at the ground where Molly was nipping at her appendages. When he met Shade's eyes again, they were starting to glow violet.

"No, don't you do it."

"I have to."

"Bullshit!" Knick scrambled to kneel in front of her, took her firmly by the shoulders. "I'm telling you not to!" He watched her eyes brighten, nethergy building up around her. "Shade. Don't. *Please.* I'm begging you! Trust me!"

For a moment, the light wavered. She was hesitating. Then, there was a thunderous rumble and a loud screech. Knick felt something crawl up behind him. The spider must have sensed the energy bloom. Shade's eyes widened and he knew that in a split second that queen would lunge at him and Shade would unleash her power to save him. And in doing so, she would die. She would expend the last of her energy. She would become a shadow. Forever.

Something inside of him changed. A door within opened and a cool sensation flowed through him. As he looked into Shade's eyes, that door widened. Their glyphs began to glow as one, like they had on their first meeting. The nethergy surrounded her spread, licking at his fingers and creeping up his arms. Inside, he felt energy rushing through him like a wind tunnel, coursing through his limbs.

"Knick!" Shade screamed, her eyes filled with fear.

A great flash of light erupted between them and something exploded around them. The spider that tried to fall on them with her dripping, venomous fangs met a barrier made of pure shadow. The sizzling sound was overtaken by a shriek as the creature's face and legs were eaten by nethergy. The beast stumbled back and her behemoth body crashed into the walls and ceiling. As she thrashed about, Lethan, Whiskey, Daedalus, Molly and Ross ran into the tunnel, but Knick and Shade were locked together, surrounded by this globe of power. They stood, hands linked, and watched. Every time the queen threatened to squash them in her violent flailing, the barrier flashed, burning more of her body away.

Knick did not know what impulse made him lift the gun, but he did. He pulled the trigger once and a loud bang momentarily overcame the spider's shrieking. A bullet surrounded by nethergy blasted a hole through the creature's abdomen so large that they could see the queen's inner workings. The bullet exploded, creating a vortex of nethergy that overtook the entirety of the spider. The puncturing and sucking sounds made Knick cringe as the vortex became smaller and smaller. When it dissipated, a jade blue carcass was lying on its back, legs—some missing and some in halves—curled into what remained of its abdomen.

When he looked at Shade, her eyes were normal, the glyph was no longer glowing, and the energy around her was gone. He felt the door inside of him close. He didn't know what happened—neither did she by the look in her eyes—and he didn't care. Shade's hand in his was flesh and blood. Mission accomplished.

He took her goggles out of her hand and fixed them over her eyes. Then, he pulled her into the tunnel to rejoin the others. No one asked what had happened. They just ran. They ran as fast as they could with Ross tapping out their path. They stopped to rest only when Molly quit whimpering and pacing. He didn't know how long they were down there before they saw the light, but it didn't matter once they spilled out of the tunnel and onto the shale plain.

As they lay panting, Molly went to each of them and nudged their heads with her nose. When she got to Knick, she licked his face until he sat up. For a long time, no one said a word. They just sat there in silence, grateful for their lives, grateful to be out of the dark. Knick wished he had listened to Jilk. Knick had made the call like he knew what he was talking about, risked all of their lives. What a shitty leader he turned out to be. Their detour had probably cost them more time than they would have suffered crossing the Grey.

"Where are we?" he asked, depression settling in his core.

"I don't know," Lethan replied. "By the look of the earth, we could be no more than a few miles out from Kresht, but we could be days off course."

Knick scratched at the ground anxiously as he looked around for some sort of territory marker. As his nail scraped the earth, he realized they weren't sitting on shale at all, but mud. Smooth, firm mud streaked with mica and pyrite to look like stone. Knick slowly got to his feet and helped Shade to stand. He brushed her hair out of her face. She looked utterly exhausted, like she was barely able to keep on her own two feet.

"You're mad," she said.

No, he thought, *I'm just glad you're okay.* But what he said was, "Hell yes I'm mad. I told you to trust me."

"I do trust you."

"Why didn't you listen to me?"

"I made a choice, Knick, a choice to save you. You can't accuse me of not trusting you when you don't like my choices. We were all going to die. I couldn't wait for a miracle that would never come." He knew she was right but he didn't like it. He started to walk away but she started talking again. "But we got a miracle. You. You channeled my nethergy..."

Knick turned back to look at her. "How did I do that?"

"I don't know. It shouldn't be possible." She stared at him so intently that he looked away. "Knick. Thank you."

He nodded. All of his fears in the cave caught up to him in full force. He had been so terrified of losing her that he had put their lives at greater risk by trying to stop her from saving them. He was the worst leader of all time. They were all idiots for following him. Her most of all. Didn't she see how crazy he was about her? Didn't she see that losing her was the only thing he wouldn't be able to stand?

He told himself to smile and say, "You're welcome." But he didn't do either. Instead, he grinned and said, "If you wanna thank me, you could kiss me." Shade rolled her eyes and walked away. "What? It's your turn. Come on. Don't be ungrateful. Just on the cheek. Shade!"

She didn't look back, just shook her head and kept walking. Knick watched her go, still with a smirk on his face and uneasiness in his gut. Lethan looked at him.

"Why do you tease her?" he asked. "You had your moment. You could've kissed her yourself and probably gotten away with it."

"Probably," Knick echoed, risking a glance at Daedalus; the man was staring at the ground. "But not with you guys watching."

"You held back because you could be seen?" he asked in disbelief. "Are you a child?"

"Twelve or thirteen, at least," he replied and clapped Lethan's shoulder. "Time to go."

As they moved forward, the ground erupted around them. Hulking figures sprang out of the earth and burst out of the columns. They were surrounded by giant men with bulging muscles covered in dried mud. Their clothes were caked in it, though the majority was bare-chested. Most had a head, at least, over everyone present.

"Dirt Men," Knick guessed and one of the big guys gave a predatory smirk. "Let me guess. You've been waiting for me."

"Skahradhan wait for no one," the largest of the men said, his voice a deep and resounding bass. "You survived the works—makes you lucky or dangerous. You wander too close to the warren. Who are you, strangers?"

"Knick Coltin. The Keepers are Shade and Daedalus. The Jin is Lethan and his lehn is Whiskey. The kid is Ross, our guide. This," he pat the dog's head, "is Molly. And we're here to meet you. The Dirt Men."

The man's slate gray eyes swept across their merry band, his thoughts guarded. "Shade," he grumbled. "Not good." He looked at Knick again. "What would you fools need from the Dirt Men that you would brave the webworks?"

"You're one of the Tribes of Typhi. And, as it turns out, I'm the One."

The man with the slate gray eyes drew back in surprise and narrowed his gaze on Knick, but the others appeared bored.

"Tribe of what?"

"Should that mean something?"

"One what?" another asked.

Knick couldn't believe it. They really didn't know who he was? He glanced at Shade whose brows were knit in confusion. Before he could say anything, however, the Dirt Men's questions and japes were silenced by Gray Eyes. He merely held up his thick arm and all talking ceased. With fingers that looked like sausages, he motioned for them to follow him.

"Come," he said. "There is someone you must meet." To his men, he merely grunted. They formed up a protective wall around Knick and his companions, and then escorted them across the mudflat.

When Isis came out of the trance, it was dark. Nearby, Solo sat slumped, his chin nearly touching his chest, while Slot was curled up next to him with her head on his knee, both sleeping. Antion was farther away with his back to the wall, snoring softly. Otto was next to her, knees to elbows, his head cradled in his arms. Jilk was the only one awake but he looked dead on his feet. He paced back and forth, stretched some, and then paced again. He stopped to look at Slot once, is expression softening. He knelt down in front of her and brushed the hair from her face. When he stood up and turned to pace again, he noticed Isis and his soft expression hardened.

"Finally," he muttered. "You awake?"

"I am." She did not bother to explain what had happened. "Did you find the entrance?"

"Yeah," he replied. "It's not far. I'll wake the others."

"Don't." She gently placed her hand on Otto's shoulder. "Get some sleep. I will watch."

"I don't think—"

"You will be safe here. No one will come looking this far in the nothingness. We are near the edge of our world."

"Sometimes you make no sense."

Isis laughed. "The burden of too much logic."

"Or not enough."

She laughed again. "You are a strong man, Jilk," she told him as he sat next to Slot, catching him off-guard. He looked at her in surprise. "And for your part, you are vital. Never at the heart of a heroic moment, but a consistent hero of invisible battles."

"What are you talking about?"

"Your role in all of this."

Jilk looked like he wanted to throw her prophetic crap back into her face, but he hesitated long enough to let the mask slip. He didn't look at her when he asked the question, too embarrassed or too vulnerable for eye contact.

"Does that mean I'm useful?"

Isis smiled. "More than useful," she said, drawing his eyes. "You are a necessity. Sleep."

Jilk just nodded and rested his head on Slot's thigh. Isis ran her fingers through Otto's hair and closed her eyes. She hummed softly to herself in an attempt to still her mind of the chaotic swirl of human thought. In the trance, she had been Sight. In the trance, she had seen everything. It would do no good to tell the others, for she was no wiser than before. Seeing everything so clearly was not something this tiny mind could sort through outside of the Theatre. The Weave was great and vast. She needed more time in the trance to see the road, to follow it, to know every trap that lay ahead. She needed more time, and that was something Shade could not readily give her. So she had to still her tiny, fragile human mind. She had to clear it of all unnecessary thoughts, block out all sensation, like the sound of Otto's even breathing and the way his hair felt between her fingers.

She was not capable of becoming Sight on her own. She had to *remember* the roads. They were there, locked inside of her mind. All she had to do was remember…

For a long time, there was only darkness. Complete and total darkness. If his eyes were open or closed, he didn't know. If he was conscious, he couldn't say. He didn't even know if he was alive or dead…until they pulled the ceiling off of him. His memory was spotty and blurry, but he remembered the veil being lifted. He remembered white hoods and splotchy faces. They were speaking, but he couldn't hear them. Their voices were distorted…like he was under water.

Or encased in ice.

Everything after that was in and out. Every time he closed his eyes, he was lost in a swirl of darkness and ice. And when he came through the vortex, tundra lay before him. White mountains surrounded him on all sides and beneath his feet stretched pale grass that snapped when he touched it. The sky was like a blank sheet of ice. Everywhere he walked he saw frosted dead things, but he was not cold. He felt warm. He felt at peace. He was bathed in cool clarity. In this tundra, he knew something had happened to him, that he was on the brink of survival. Then he would slip back into the dark vortex and, when he opened his eyes, would see a blur of movement and surroundings he could not recognize. The process repeated, days, weeks, years—he had no concept of time. He only knew that every time he walked the tundra, he was fighting for his life.

And then came the day that he opened his eyes and saw water bubbling in front of him. Ice chunks bounced in and out of his vision. He was floating, surrounded by warm water with the occasional jet of cold. He was in a medical tank. He heard distorted voices beyond the glass and tried to find the speakers but they were just black blurs.

"He's awake," he thought he heard someone say. There was more noise, like footsteps. He tried to speak but a mask covered his mouth and nose and tubes crawled down his throat.

"Donovan," a voice said clearly. His head jerked.

Regent?

"My Priori found you dying in the ruins of Sanctuary. A

great battle took place, they said."

What happened to me? he thought.

"You were severely wounded. Eros tried to kill you. You would have died if not for Malkira. She saved your life."

Donovan suddenly became aware of the gauntlet still locked onto his arm. Flashes of memory returned in a rush. Intense pain flooded his senses—emotional and physical—and loud noises crushed his ear drums. Something was falling, falling right above him—it was going to crush him. He wanted to reach out and stop it but he couldn't move. And then there was a rush of cold and everything went black. Malkira had encased him in ice to stop the ceiling from crushing him, to stop him from bleeding out.

Donovan gently touched his stomach where Eros had struck him. The rippled flesh alarmed him. He looked down and could barely make out the deep, red lines etched into his body. He had expected scars, but these wounds looked raw and angry, as though fresh. That couldn't be. A few hours in a medical tank should have at least closed the wounds.

"Marks made by the Sword of Scars do not heal. You will bear these scars for the rest of your life," the Regent croaked. "A small price to pay for your life. A small price to pay...for insolence and stupidity."

Donovan's gaze snapped up to where the Regent was standing just beyond the tank. He was a blur and mostly concealed by the bubbles, but Donovan could still feel the disappointed eyes glaring at him.

"Camilla is dead," the Regent snapped. "You have failed me for the last time. Fail me again and I will strip you of everything that defines you and finish the job Eros started. Is this clear?"

Donovan barely managed to nod.

"Good."

The Regent swept out of the room. After a moment, the lights dimmed. There were no other voices or movements. He was alone. Alone like he had always been. Donovan strained to touch his scar again, trembling fingers twitching over the rippled flesh, but the pain he felt was not in his gut. It originated in his left breast. His chest tightened and his eyes stung, and he was grateful for the bubbling water and chunks of ice.

They entered the warren through the mud gate, a wide entryway with large mud columns and thick slabs of wood that functioned as the gate, guarded by two hulking giants made of dirt, clay, and stone that towered over even the Dirt Men. As they approached, Knick waited for a signal to open the gate but instead the two statues came to life. His jaw dropped as the golems clacked and rustled, their thick limbs unfolding and their heavy legs slowly stomping as they each took a door and heaved it open enough to let the group through single file. Knick couldn't help but stare up at the golems as they passed by them. They had no eyes but Knick felt as though they were watching him. It gave him the creeps.

"Sorcery," Lethan whispered, his face pulled into grim resolve as they moved into the warren.

The Skahradhan city was a vast network of mud huts and clay and wood buildings protected by the low cavern ceiling. A wall shielded the compound in its vulnerable spots, from what Knick could see, but he couldn't find any other gates. He wondered how deep into the caves the warren stretched.

As they moved into the city, Knick expected to find grubby women and children covered in dust and mud but the stuff they had constructed their homes from was dry. The people he saw wore nicer clothes than he ever had, almost resembling the high-class citizens of Anshar. Red tapestries and banners trimmed in gold and bearing a peculiar insignia decorated columns and archways and streetlamps. The people and their clan colors broke up the monotony of browns in a way that made this mud hole almost...beautiful.

They followed a winding road of orange clay chips that crafted a mosaic through the warren, crossed a wooden bridge floating over a shallow lake of clear water, and walked up a slope to a many-roomed tent made from bright red cotton slashed with gold silk, so large that it hung from the ceiling. The insignia—a gate bound with rope beneath a fiery orb— was embroidered on the central peak of the tent. Great braziers burned in bowls on either side of the entrance and two more golems stood guard, though these were smaller and encrusted with uncut gems that sparkled in the firelight. One of the golems stepped forward to stop their procession while the other opened one of the draping flaps.

A woman burst from the tent wearing a tight, red dress that fanned out into a train and disappeared into the tent. Her hair was the same color as the golden silk and fell all the way to the back of her knees, straight as a board halfway down before spiraling into a chaotic mass of curls. Her skin was like porcelain glass and her large eyes were two fire-bright opals. She was glaring at them with a haughty mixture of anger and superiority. She was beautiful...and young. Knick put her at twenty, tops.

"You are not welcome here," she said while looking at Shade, "nor is any who calls you companion."

As she turned to go, Knick frowned. "Wait, that's it?" he asked. "You're kicking us out now? You brought us all the way here just to tell us to leave?" And then it hit him. She was showing off. She was flexing her power. Young *and* immature. "What's your angle?"

The girl turned an icy glare on him. "My angle?" she repeated in disgust. "I do not have to explain myself to you. You are nothing."

"I'm the One! You're obligated to help me."

For a moment, she just stared at him like she was processing the information. Then, she grinned. "The one what? The one fool? I don't know you. I am obligated to no one. Now leave."

"Okay!" Knick exclaimed before the Dirt Men could throw them out. "Okay. We got off on the wrong foot here. I think—"

"You think *nothing*," she interrupted, her eyes narrowing. "Your charms—whatever you imagine they are—will not work on me. You came all this way to see a door slammed in your face." She nodded to the Dirt Men then looked at Shade once more. "Get out of my sight."

Serena twirled away as Gray Eyes turned to them. He looked at Knick and mouthed two words. Rope Woman. The Dirt Men reached for their unwanted guests, their giant paws locking around arms and shoulders in vice grips.

"Well we didn't come to see you," Knick blurted, eyeing Gray Eyes. The big man stilled. Serena stopped her withdrawal. "We came to see the Rope Woman." She whirled around. The Dirt Men instantly released them. "You can't refuse us," he said, readjusting his jacket. "Can you?"

Serena walked up to him and stood so close that he had to

take a step back. She leaned forward so that their faces were inches apart.

"You want to see the *Rope Woman*?" she asked quietly, dangerously. "Then see her you will." For a moment, her gaze wandered over his shoulder to where Lethan was standing. There was a flicker of change in her demeanor. It would've been impossible to see had Knick not been standing so close. She stiffened, eyes widened, skin paled, lips parted. And then she turned away. "Enge," she said and Gray Eyes stepped forward. "Take them to the retreat. They invoked the Mystic's name. They are our guests." The words she spoke were ground out with considerable effort. "Treat them accordingly."

Enge and his Dirt Men escorted them away from the tent as Serena disappeared inside. They were led to a large one-story compound made of wood and clay and silkscreen sliding doors. A porch wrapped around the entire building and blazing firepots burned every few links apart. Knick spied at least three golems guarding the premises.

"What's happening?" Knick asked Gray Eyes, the one that Serena had called Enge.

"You will be bathed, clothed, fed, and rested. Tomorrow, you will be taken to see the Mystic," he replied.

"I panicked when you mouthed those words."

"You did the right thing. We would have been forced to put you out otherwise."

"But you didn't want that," Knick surmised. "Why?"

"You are the One."

His eyes went wide. "So you do know who I am!"

"I am one of three who know who you are. The rest do not. They were never told. Our priestess does not believe in you."

"But you do."

"Yes. Because our Mystic does." Enge watched the others as they were led into the building before eyeing Knick once more. "Bringing the Keeper woman was not smart."

"Shade and I are a team," Knick said. "Leaving her behind is out of the question."

"It will make your mission more difficult. The hatred runs deep in our priestess. I do not think she will lose this opportunity for revenge."

"You should know that whatever she tries, it won't work.

Shade is more powerful than she ever was. She will tear this place apart. Tell your priestess that."

"The priestess is powerful. She may relish the idea of flexing her magic. But a battle between them would only do harm."

"Agreed. Shade doesn't want a fight."

"It is not Keeper-Shienar's place to restrain herself, but our priestess is young…"

"I get it. I'll talk to her."

Enge nodded and attendants came out to fetch Knick. They ushered him to a private room. The bed was low, only a foot off the ground, and thick with silk blankets and pillows. He was given a towel and the privacy to strip before they took him to a large shower room where Daedalus, Lethan, and Ross were already washing. Ross was in the farthest corner like he was afraid to show his nakedness to anyone else. The others ignored each other and Knick figured that a Jin and a Keeper would probably be used to the lack of privacy.

The shower floor was made of pumice, lightly scratching at the calluses on his feet as he crossed the room and sat on a wooden bench near Lethan. The shower head was connected to a long hose hooked on the wall. He drenched himself and soaped up.

"So," he began awkwardly, his voice echoing in the room. "Why do you hate these people so much?"

"It is not your concern," Lethan replied quietly.

"Maybe. But I'm curious."

"Why?"

Was there ever a reason for curiosity but curiosity itself? He could come up with reasons but they would be bullshit. The truth was that Serena had a private freak-out the moment she saw Lethan. He wanted to know why because he couldn't stand not knowing.

But saying that didn't sound so good, so instead he said, "We already have a rivalry to deal with. I want to make sure there are no more reasons to worry."

"I would never do anything to upset your mission. My feelings will not influence my actions. I swear to you."

Knick instantly felt guilty for pulling that card. He knew Lethan, more so than any of them, had a handle on his self-control. He scrubbed in silence, washed his hair, and rinsed off. Just as he finished, another attendant appeared and showed them to a hot spring. Burgundy clay columns surrounded the bubbling water and beyond them they could see the town lights. There was a strange, cool breeze passing above the steaming pool that caused him to shiver. He eased into it, hissing as he acclimated to the sting, and then groaned quietly as the heat began to soothe his muscles.

The past half year had been a nightmare.

"I'm sorry," Knick said when the four of them had settled in the water. "I know you would never sabotage us. I asked because I want to know. Because Serena knows you. Because there's history there, unresolved history, and you told me you knew her in name only."

Lethan sighed. "I found Serena in the dark tunnels of the Grey. She was lost, crying. I guided her out back to the light. She told me she had run away from her clan, the Skahradhan, because they meant to make her their sacrifice. I began to hate her people. I took her back to the Kada and she was allowed to travel with us for awhile, but Sabal eventually told us she could not stay. By that time, we had already…" He hesitated, his blue eyes transfixed on the churning water. "We had already fallen in love. I told Serena we would run away together, but she saw how important I was to the Kada. I made her promise that we would go together. She promised…and the next day, she disappeared on her own. I never saw her again. When I heard she had become the Skahradhan priestess," his face tightened, "I was furious. She had deceived me. These people are snakes and sorcerers. They have earned my contempt."

Knick nodded absentmindedly but he didn't think Lethan's feelings had anything to do with contempt.

Inside her palace made of silk, Serena paced back and forth. The moment she had heard Shade was at her gates, she was filled to the brim with old hatred. For a moment, fiery rage had consumed her. The charred corner of her attending room was a black reminder of her inability to forget her past. "Turn them away," was her initial reaction, but she had quickly changed her mind. Revenge was what she needed, not to forget. "Bring them," she had told the herald.

But seeing Lethan again…

Serena passed through one silken curtain after another until she found her bedroom. She looked at her expression in the mirror. She couldn't rub the blush out of her cheeks or blink the starry youth from her eyes. She was turning back into a young girl, too young to be the priestess. She looked like an acolyte again. But she couldn't go down that road. She was the priestess. She would be the next mystic. She had accepted it. She didn't want it but she had accepted it. She could not falter now, not when it meant the collapse of the Skahradhan.

She eyed the parted drapes that led to her balcony and passed through. Across the mud cavern she could see the retreat. She didn't mean to look but her gaze went right to the hot spring where the men were just lowering themselves into the water. Lethan's dark body flexed as he climbed in to soak and Serena immediately closed her eyes…and then opened them again. She studied the curve of his shoulders as he stretched his arms on the rim of the pool, watched as he laid his head back in relaxation.

He had grown into such a fine man. Handsome. Strong. But not strong enough for the Skahradhan… She was to take one of the Dirt Men as a consort, as was custom. An outsider, a Jin no less, would never do to father the next priestess. Serena's fingers curled into her palm, her red nails slashing open the soft skin to draw blood. For just a moment in time, she had been free. She had loved the boy who had rescued her in the dark, and she had lived for survival, purposeless except to love and be loved. For one moment in time, she had been happy.

Serena's eyes moved to the other side of the retreat where Shade was entering her hot spring. That woman had stolen her happiness. She had dragged Serena back to Kresht kicking and sobbing. Serena had fought for her freedom and lost. So she had begged. She had thrown away the remnants of her pride and begged Shade to let her go. Shade had been a wall. Not a single tear or scream had moved her.

If Shade had just let her go, Serena's mother would still be alive. With Serena gone, there would be no acolyte to replace the priestess and her mother would not have been sacrificed to the mystic. If Shade had just let her go, she and Lethan could have been together. She could have chosen her own life, could have found happiness.

But she was retrieved like a lost object, returned to the shelf where she would live her life, posed for the passers-by. She would safeguard the warren, choose a consort from the Dirt Men, bear a child, rear an acolyte, pass her powers to the next priestess, and sacrifice herself to the mystic. She had no choices. Not one. Because of Shade.

Serena ripped her nails from the bloody pockets in her palms and felt the magical energy stirring at her fingertips. The blood dripping from her wounds began smoking. The words were in the back of her throat, sneaking toward her tongue. All she had to do was part her lips and speak.

"Priestess," a deep voice said behind her. Serena snapped out of the spell trance and turned around to see Enge looming just behind the curtain.

"There are many of them."

"They are being attended properly," he assured her. Serena nodded. Four courses of food were being prepared as they spoke. When the guests finished their soak in the springs, they would be given fresh clothes and fed like kings. While the rest retired to luxurious apartments to sleep, Knick would undergo a cleansing ceremony to be pure before entering the Garden. Such was the guest right to any seeking audience with the mystic.

"Was it you who gave them the words, I wonder," she mused, "or did they already know them? It doesn't matter now." Her eyes settled on Lethan once more. She watched as he waved his arms in the animated telling of some tale. "They are here now...old acquaintances and new."

"Keeper-Shienar is not alone. Keeper-Alym watches her carefully," Enge said passively, spoken as the chief of the Dirt Men to his precious priestess. It was a calm and detached tone, void of fear and love.

"You warn me against attacking her openly."

"Your feelings toward Keeper-Shienar are well-known."

"I will not risk the safety of the warren," she assured him, "but I will take this opportunity as it has presented itself once more."

Enge's jaw tightened as he considered her words. "This is a new opportunity, priestess, not an old one returned."

Move on. He was asking her to move on. That was impossible. Serena's gaze let go of the man her heart desired and focused fully on her chief.

"Shade took everything from me. I will never forgive her."

"If you must blame someone, blame me," he said. "I was the one who called them."

Serena cleared the distance between them, raised her hand to touch his arm. She would have touched his cheek but he was too tall for her to reach.

"I cannot blame you," she whispered. "You are all I have left. She must bear the burden of my contempt. There is no other."

Enge gave a shallow nod and withdrew from her presence. She watched him go and considered turning around again but she couldn't bring herself to be content at just watching. It was an opportunity—not just for revenge but also for passion. Once the meeting with the mystic was finished, Lethan would walk out of her life forever. She would not spend the remaining years of her life on this balcony, watching an empty hot spring as she mourned his absence.

Serena summoned an attendant to draw a bath and prepare one of her best gowns. When she was clean, her attendant wrapped her in a slinky, ice-blue dress made of the softest cotton and wove crystals in her hair. By the time she was ready, dinner had been served and consumed. The city lamps had gone from gold to blue to signify the shift from day to night.

"Swear your silence," Serena said.

"I so swear," the attendant replied with a deep bow.

Using a hidden passage behind the silk palace, Serena took a winding stone staircase around the great lake bordering the retreat. The compound was silent. She went to Lethan's assigned room and drew aside the sliding door. He was sitting in the dark, head bent and fingers linked. He did not look at her as she entered; he did not even flinch in surprise, as though he almost expected this.

"I thought of a hundred ways I could gain an audience with you," he said quietly. "None of my ideas were..." Lethan didn't finish.

"Look at me."

"You lied to me."

"Never."

"You said they would sacrifice you."

"They will."

"You're the leader of their clan."

"For now. Why are you with the Keeper?"

"I am not. I am with the One."

"Why?"

"He is the One."

There was a moment of stiff silence. Serena stared at him, at the way his pants curled into layers around his bare feet, at the spread of his toes—small details of a man she desperately wanted to remember. Her eyes climbed to his linked fingers, thin and long, to the sharp protrusion of his knuckles and the balls of his joints, and his short nails that had recently been thick with dirt. She looked at his naked torso, slim but strong, at the flexing in his back every time he took a breath, at his chest rippled with so many small bumps of muscles, at his curving shoulders, his collarbone and throat and jaw. And his face...his face was so grown up, childish features replaced with distinctly adult eyes and nose and mouth.

This body had been very different eight years ago. He had been thinner and smaller and less defined, but still beautiful. He was no Dirt Man but she found she trusted him anyway. He had saved her from the darkness, protected her in the Grey, and provided for her amongst his clan. He did not need a hulking body to take care of her, just the right amount of love.

They had been teenagers back then, brimming with passions and beliefs that seemed to drown the whole world. Now they were adults, with clear heads and grim duties but desires just as strong. Why wouldn't he look at her? Now they were adults, capable of so much more than they were before, and what they had been capable of had been like a gift from God. So why wouldn't he look at her? It had been eight years. Didn't he want to see her? Eight years, with eight years of history behind them and no clue as to any of it. Had there been any other woman who had admired his body like she was now? Adolescent promises told her she was the only one he would ever love, but even then she knew it was a beautiful and honest lie. They were adults now. There would be no more pretending, no matter how much she needed it. Why wouldn't he look at her?

"Look at me," she said again.

"I can't."

"Why?"

"You'll bewitch me."

Serena drew back in surprise. "I would never—" she gasped. Could he believe everything between them was the source of her magic? "I have never—"

"Not with sorcery," he confessed bashfully, "with your beauty."

Serena blushed. He had said something similar to her eight years ago. It was kind and sweet and silly and probably another lie but it was everything she needed to hear. She needed his kindness more than anything.

"I hated the Skahradhan for what they were going to do to you. I hate them still. I hated you for lying to me. For using me. For leaving me. But when I saw you on the hill, I couldn't breathe, couldn't blink, couldn't speak... You were so beautiful...I—"

"Lethan," she whispered. "Please. Please, look at me."

He did. He turned his head and those electric blue eyes of his drank her in with awe and adoration. She loved his eyes the most. Lethan bolted up, gawking. For a moment, he just stared at her like she had stared at him, memorizing every detail.

"You are," he choked, "siraiko." It was the word his people used to represent things that were so stunning they could not be described. He came to stand in front of her, reached out, and, without ever making contact, ran his hand along her arm and over her shoulder. "Am I too late? Have you chosen your consort?"

"No. There has only ever been you."

"For me as well."

His palm hovered an inch away from her cheek, careful not to mix his fingers with her hair. He was waiting for her permission. He had done the same eight years ago, when he found her in the dark cave. He asked her, "May I touch you?" and then he led her out of the blackness. Again on the night they first made love, he came to her and reached out and waited for her to come the rest of the way.

Serena reached up and touched the back of his hand, pressed his palm to her cheek. And then he was kissing her, pulling her against him, tangling his fingers in her hair. They clung to each other like they were afraid another eight years would come between them. And as they made love, they did so with the gentle false promise of forever, the kind lie that there was a future for the two of them. And even though she knew it wasn't true, it was exactly what she needed.

Molly barked as she ran to where Knick was sitting on the patio, her tail wagging happily.

"Hey, look at you," he exclaimed. "They fixed you up, too, huh?" Molly's mangy coat had been cut and cleaned and now her black hair was sleek and shiny. She had so much energy for someone whose best friend was twenty-five years dead. He couldn't see any flecks of gray anywhere on her coat. "Weird, huh?"

"What is?" Daedalus asked as he joined him on the patio.

"This dog was Red's best friend, so they said. But Red's been dead for twenty-five years. That means this dog is at least that old. She should be dead but she's not even gray."

Daedalus tipped his head back thoughtfully as he sat down on a bench. "Strange, but not the strangest thing I've ever heard."

"Keeper voodoo?"

The Keeper smiled. "No. Probably Typhi voodoo."

Knick shrugged one shoulder. "Where's Lethan?"

"He retired hours ago, shortly after you slipped out of the feast."

"It was four courses this big around." Knick gestured a wide plate with his hands. "I was stuffed at two."

Daedalus nodded in agreement and silence settled uncomfortably between them. Since meeting in Britz, they had not spoken very directly and never privately. Knick couldn't say he wanted to. The guy was in love with Shade—*his* Shade. He was powerful, smart, and not half-bad looking. He was a Keeper. He understood her in a way Knick never could. And…he held her debts. Sacrificing himself to save her when she was so young? How could Knick compete with that?

But Shade had told Knick that he was the Balance to her, the center of her universe, not Daedalus. As long as he was her Balance, they would never be apart.

Knick cleared his throat. "Thanks," he said. He owed Daedalus that much. "For your help."

"You're the—" He stopped himself. "No, Shade told me

you didn't like that."

Knick grimaced. "You're not really here for me, right? I'm not stupid. You're here for Shade."

"*You're* here for Shade," Daedalus corrected him. "I am here for both of you. But...I think you would rather I wasn't."

"Maybe," Knick admitted. "Sometimes, I'm glad you're here. Other times, I wish you'd fuck off."

"Because of Shade?"

"Because I'm human."

Daedalus nodded and his expression changed. He was serious, somber. "So am I." He stood up. "But I will still serve you, protect you. Shade believes in you so I will put my faith in you as well." He hesitated. "I love her. I have loved her for her entire life. But Keepers are trained to never give in to their feelings. I made peace with this unrequited love a long time ago. So while, at times, I envy you, I won't betray you. You have my word."

Knick just knelt there next to Molly, too stunned to react. Daedalus envied him? He couldn't believe it. "Yeah," he muttered after he realized he was just staring dumbly. "Thanks."

Enge emerged on the patio. "Keeper-Alym," he said and bowed his head. "Knick."

"How's Shade?" Knick asked. She hadn't been present at the feast. He knew she was tired from the webworks but he also knew Serena had a vendetta against her.

"Keeper-Shienar is resting. Her wounds were tended, her stomach filled. They brewed our finest healing tea and she drank deep. Now she sleeps. She will be recovered in the morning."

"Good," Knick said, sitting down on the ground with his back to a column. Molly licked at his hand to prompt more petting.

"Thank you," Daedalus murmured, bowed his head, and withdrew.

"Alym, Shienar," Knick began, "terms of respect?"

"Yes," Enge replied. "Keepers are greatly respected among the Skahradhan. Until our priestess' incident, there was never a word uttered against them."

"You don't agree with her. You know, I get that you have to protect her, but does it really have to go so far?"

"So far?"

"That you defend her even when you know she's wrong."

Enge nodded. "I am just a man," he rumbled, "made from dirt. I am blood and muscle and skin like leather. I move mountains or become one. Dirt has no thoughts, mountains need no feelings. I serve the mystic and protect the priestess. Nothing else matters."

"Nothing? Family, freedom?"

"Duty," he said, "is greater than love. Freedom is an idea defined by perspective."

"I can't live like that."

"Has someone asked you to?"

"No."

"Then why are you bothered by it?"

"It's a cage." Knick rubbed Molly's neck as the animal yawned and laid down, her warm back pressed against his thigh. "I can't stand cages."

"This is my choice."

"We can build our own cages."

"Can we?" Enge wondered. "Then your choices are defined with someone else's definitions."

Knick's jaw tightened as he braced himself against the blow of Enge's words. Spoken so simply, filled with such profundity. The worst part of all was how right he sounded.

"For a man made of dirt," Knick mumbled, "you have a lot of thoughts."

Enge smiled a small and knowing smile.

According to Jilk's pocket watch, it was already late evening by the time everyone was awake and ready to head into the subsystem. Antion led the way while Jilk headed up the rear to keep anyone from getting lost. It took a lot longer to get six people through than it had two, but the worst that happened was getting covered in mud. They climbed the nearly invisible ladder roughly fifty feet into a crawlspace that seemed to go on for hours. As if being on your belly in the dark wasn't freaky enough, the crawlspace opened up to a natural drain at one point. A deep pit loomed beneath them while smooth walls stretched above. Water trickled along the sides, lightly spraying them as they inched across the narrow bridge that spanned the ditch. After that, however, it was more uneventful tunnel.

It was almost midnight by the time they found the hatch that opened up into a gray stone cellar that clearly hadn't been used in a few eternities. Cobwebs had completely taken over the corners of the storeroom and covered most of the ceiling. Wooden boxes and woven baskets were stacked along the walls, broken, chewed, and rotting. The door would have been locked had the frame not been mostly eaten away by termites. All it took was a gentle push to earn their freedom. The cellar was full of similar rooms and a way up so they took the stairs. They swung their wrist lamps from wall to wall as they climbed the wide and winding staircase. Solo tried to light one of the torches bolted to the stone but all he managed to burn was the cobwebs clinging to it.

They wandered lost through another level of empty rooms—staff quarters, Antion guessed—before stumbling into a cold kitchen. The sheer size of it made Jilk's jaw drop. Once upon a time, they had cooked for hundreds at a time on those black stoves. Asgard was mostly ruins when he wandered through it so all he had known was that it was big, but he hadn't really known how big. The Keepers were mysterious; to the common man, they were both omniscient and omnipotent. How many were there? Thousands! That's what they believed. But it was a belief crafted in the unknown, forged out of rumors and whispers. To stand in such a hall and see for himself just how massive the organization had been was both incredible and chilling.

As they ascended to the next floor, they heard the distant sound of voices.

"Squatters?" Solo guessed but Antion vigorously shook his head.

"They would never have gotten past the seals."

"We did," Slot reminded him.

They followed the noise through a servant's passage until it grew louder. For a moment, Jilk wondered if they were hearing echoes from another cavern, but then they turned the corner and saw the light shining through peep holes and he knew they weren't alone. Antion went rigid.

"Ex-Regent," he whispered. "So this is where he ran to."

"That's the bad guy, right?" Slot asked.

"He betrayed the Order," Isis explained with an

unnerving amount of calm. It made Jilk suspicious. He wondered if she had known what was hiding in this not-so-abandoned fortress all along.

They peeked through the holes and saw a host of brown-robed men bustling between hundreds of shelves housing thousands of books.

"They don't look so tough. We could take 'em," Slot said as a matter-of-fact.

"They're just scholars," Antion said, "like me. Of course you could. It's the Priori you have to worry about."

"Who are the Priori?" Otto asked.

"The Regent's personal and elite bodyguards."

"I fought them, too," Slot said, "when they came to kill Knick. They aren't so tough either." She winked at Antion when he gawked at her.

"You have to worry about any Keeper," Jilk said, thoughts wandering to Shade and Daedalus. How many like them did this ex-Regent have under his thumb? "Tough or not, they have numbers. We don't. There's three of us that can hit a target and maybe one that could hit something on accident." Jilk eyed Otto and Antion and wondered which one of them it would be. "This was a bad idea. We shouldn't have come." He backed away from the peep hole. "We're leaving. Adventure over."

"No," Isis said firmly, and even Antion was surprised. "We've come all this way. Antion and I will blend into the collective until we find what we're looking for, and you four can hide out down here. We have seen for ourselves that the lower levels are entirely abandoned. No one will find you here."

"Find us?" Jilk balked. "What about you? You don't even know what it is you're looking for!"

"We have to try."

"How? They're wearing brown robes and you're in a white dress. You'll get caught and get us all killed!"

"They would never hurt the Enoch," Antion insisted with a tightly knit brow.

"Yeah? That won't stop them from plugging *you* with a few bullets, or any of us. Get it?"

"Three days," Isis said. "Give us three days. We'll find some spare robes or take them off of stragglers. No one will suspect us. These men are part of the collective. They're consumed by what is in front of them, not happening around them. And in three days, if we haven't found our answers, we'll leave."

"No way—" he started to protest but Isis reached out and took his arm, her clear green eyes burning through him.

"Three days."

He sighed. "Cakes was right. We're all gonna die." He pulled his arm back. "Three days."

Otto immediately rushed to her side. "I want to go with you."

"I'm sorry, Otto," Isis told him, "but this is not your path."

As Jilk watched Antion and Isis wander down the secret passage to find a hidden door, a bad feeling settled in the pit of his stomach. *This is not your path.* The words echoed over and over in the back of his mind, like warning bells preceding a flood.

Just as the warren lights shifted from blue to orange, Serena sent the attendants to fetch Knick. She had returned to her silken palace that morning to don the white ceremonial wrap she used to escort seekers to the mystic's cave. With her long, blond hair and white outfit, she was a vision of light. So when the attendants brought Knick with Shade at his side, Serena thought, *here comes the vision of night.*

The procession consisted of the priestess, two golem protectors, the seeker, and the Keeper. No others attended the event. There would be some first-time observers on the ridges—everyone watched their first sending—but otherwise no audience would be present. Facing the mystic was done alone.

At the mouth to the cave, Serena stopped walking. The golems continued until they stood attentively on either side of the black opening.

"No one shall go in or out," she explained, "while you attend the mystic. In the presence of the mystic, guard your thoughts and heart and tongue. The juuri cleansed your body of impurity and made you fit to stand before her. The haana cleansed your mind and made you fit to speak with her. If your soul is cleansed, you will be fit to receive her gifts. The Garden will cleanse your soul or destroy it." Serena motioned for him to approach. "Stay vigilant. Mazza's Garden is a treacherous place. Abbil koshca."

Knick nodded that he understood and then he and Shade proceeded to the cave mouth together.

"No!" Serena exclaimed. "Only one of you may enter Mazza's Garden." She looked pointedly at Shade. "You cannot go."

"Why?"

"Because that is my word."

Shade briefly glanced at Knick. "If your word is all, forget it. It's dangerous in there. I'm going."

"Then you put both of you in danger." Serena smiled. "You're a fool."

She watched as Shade plunged into the tunnel first and Knick hurried in after her. She must have stood there nearly half an hour watching and smiling before the sound of footsteps in the dirt pulled her out of her buzzing thoughts of revenge.

"Where are they?" Enge asked.

"Inside."

"Both of them?"

"Yes."

"No..." he whispered and started toward the cave. "We have to stop them!"

"It's too late."

Enge whirled around to face her. "Why? Why didn't you warn them?"

"I tried. Shade would not let the man out of her sight."

"But she will die."

"No," Serena replied, her smile widening. "She went into the tunnel first."

"Then Knick—"

"Yes. He will die. She will realize that she is not so powerful that she can stop Mazza's curse from taking him, that her stubbornness brought about his demise. She should have listened to me." The words were for the past as well as present. "She took everything from me." Serena turned to look at Enge. "And now everything will be taken from her."

Enge stared blankly at the cave mouth and Serena walked away in grim satisfaction.

When Knick and Shade came out of the darkness, they were staring at a large cavern that stretched out beneath them. Cerulean fireflies swarmed around thin membrane sacs hanging from the ceiling and glowing blue, casting an icy glow on everything below. A rope ladder climbed down into a maze-like network of hedges and clay brick walls. In the alcoves were gardens with white benches and bubbling fountains. On the far side, an eerie light called to them like a beacon. They couldn't see what it was but they knew in their gut it was their destination.

"Shall we?" Knick asked.

Shade climbed down the ladder first and inched toward the hedges as though enemies would leap at any moment. The whole garden was covered in a thin, blue haze. Tiny lights winked here and there, reminding Knick of storybook magic. It was so beautiful, it was sure to be dangerous. Like the Sirens.

Shade led the way into the maze, her lithe form moving gracefully between the hedges. Knick wasn't so subtle. His hand brushed against one of the protruding leaves and it sliced through him. He hissed, drawing his hand back. Blood seeped from a long, red lash. Shade hurried to his side.

"What happened?" she asked in alarm.

"The leaves," he told her, "they're sharp as knives."

She cupped his hand in hers and examined the wound but what she was looking for he didn't know. Suddenly, his hand was burning. The severed nerves lit up with pain that quickly spread into his fingers and palm. He screamed and tried to pull away but she held him through his arm's convulsion. And as quickly as it had come, the burning sensation was gone. Pain lingered in his trembling hand but it was no longer unbearable. Gasping for breath, he stared at the wound. It had been cauterized. But how? When he looked at Shade to ask, he saw the retreating glow in her eyes that told him she had called upon the shadows. What he didn't understand was how a shadow could burn flesh but he didn't think she would be able to answer him.

They continued in silence at a slow pace, careful to avoid touching anything. Fatigue settled in their bones by the time they reached the first garden. Fuzzy orbs of blue light made the small space look like a moonlit retreat. The tinkling sound from the fountain was soothing and the grass looked soft and thick. When the thought struck him to take a nap, Knick knew it was a trap. He shook his head as though he could shake away the thoughts.

"This place is a nightmare," he muttered as they turned away from the resting spot.

They wandered through several more enticing gardens and through countless deadly hedges. Knick remembered looking down at the place and seeing for himself that the maze wasn't very big. How could they still be in it? They had yet to stumble upon the same location so how could they be lost?

Knick saw something move out of the corner of his eye and spun around but all he saw was green bush and blue haze.

"Something's following us," Shade said.

"Yeah," Knick agreed, "but what?"

"I don't know," she replied and then added, "Or how many."

They kept walking but Knick was growing nervous. He felt like he was lost in the webworks again, danger all around but no ability to see it. What was hunting them? How long would it stalk their footsteps before it attacked? And how long could they go without stopping? They had been wandering for days. Or had it been longer? His head was so fuzzy. His mind wasn't his own.

There was only one time in his life when his brain felt this thick…and that was when he was an angel. Knick shook his head to clear up his thoughts but he kept feeling the prickle in the back of his skull that had once told him he was connecting with the Hive Mind. What was this place? Was it some sort of MAAR experiment? Had they been tricked into coming here? No good came from talking to strangers, blindly trusting in their words. He should have known better. The angels and cogwheelers both were looking for him. They had eyes and ears everywhere.

Something scurried in his peripherals again and he spun around but lost track of it.

"It's a trap," he whispered, jerking his head this way and that. He rubbed the back of his neck, wondering if there was something he had left behind when he fled Heaven that could allow the Hive Mind to reconnect with him, wondering if there was something still there that allowed MAAR to track him. He thought he had dug out all of their machinery but it wasn't hard to believe he had missed something.

Fear nearly paralyzed him as his fingers slid over something embedded in the base of his skull. No. No no no no no. He had ripped it all out. How had this, this *thing* gotten inside him? His thoughts slurred like drunken words and he struggled to maintain consciousness. He didn't want to do it— to hand over his mind to the Hive Mind. He didn't want to be an angel again.

This time when he saw the image in the corner of his eye, he was too afraid to move. He heard the hissing laughter and realized they were still in the webworks. The spinners were some kind of MAAR mutation gone wrong and they were wandering around their lab. When had an agent planted the chip in his neck? While they were sleeping? Where were Lethan and Whiskey and Ross? Where were Daedalus and Molly? Where was Shade?

"Shade," he called, looking behind and ahead but both ways were empty. "Shade!"

He frantically began running, hissing and grunting as leaves caught him on his arms and legs. He kept calling for her, feeling his consciousness fading. He became aware of black shapes hurrying this way and that. The spiders were closing in. Had they already gotten Shade?

"Shade!" he screamed.

And suddenly she was in front of him, her hands reaching out to hold his head still. Her violet eyes filled up his line of sight and he froze, locked in a staring contest.

"It isn't real," she whispered.

"The angels," he croaked but she shook her head.

"There are no angels here. It isn't real."

"They put something in the back of my neck!" he exclaimed. Her fingers went to the spot to check.

"There's nothing there. The angels are far away. Knick," her thumb gently brushed the hair from his brow, "it's all right. You're safe."

As he took deep breaths and listened to the sound of her voice, the fog in his head abated. Suddenly he felt lighter. He reached back to rub the base of his skull and found nothing but skin and hair. His forehead thunked against hers as relief swept away the tension in his body. She held him up and let him rest against her. His fingers curled into her sleeves and he clung to her. He was the One and this was a test but he had forgotten all of that. Maybe in the grand scheme of things, he was someone important, but right then—in that moment—he was just a man, scared of his past, of who he had been, and scared to lose himself.

"Are you okay?" she asked softly when his breathing evened out. He nodded and composed himself.

"How come you're not affected?"

"I am," she replied. "I keep seeing dead Keepers. I hear their voices. I know it's not real, but there they are, calling to me... And if, for just one moment, I doubt the reality around me, I'll believe what I see."

Knick nodded that he understood. A soft glow began to emanate between them. At first, he thought it was their glyphs. And then he realized it was originating much lower. He jerked back and saw tendrils of blue light playing at his chest, curling in and out like ghostly fingertips. Then the light turned dark purple and something gripped the center of his chest. A shock of pain ripped through him. He couldn't breathe. The light spasmed as he doubled over, stumbling back. Shade called out to him, her arms scrabbling to hold him up, but he could barely hear her. And just when he thought his whole body was filling up with stone, the pressure sucked out of him.

"Knick?" Shade gasped, pulling him up off the ground.

"I don't know," he stammered breathlessly, frantically looking around for any sign of an intruder. As he got back on his feet, he began swatting at his chest, panicking. Shade reached out and stilled him, her violet eyes intensely studying his body. When she was satisfied, she met his gaze and nodded.

Knick took her hand and linked their fingers together. Even though it hurt with how tightly they squeezed, nothing could make them let go. And then they reached the end of the maze and stepped out of the hedges into the mystic's lair.

Torches and braziers burned on either side to light the space and pillows were gathered on the floor. A woman was hanging against the wall. Ropes tied around her wrists, ankles, and throat kept her suspended, pulled taught against the stone. Blood soaked the ropes, and rings of burgundy crust stained the flesh rubbed raw by the binds. A black mask crusted with dried blood covered her eyes. She wore an elegant black robe embroidered with delicate, pearl designs. Her blond hair was so long it touched the floor and her skin was white as snow.

As they approached, she lifted her chin and they both jumped in shock and horror.

"Welcome," she said. "Do not let my appearance trouble you. Come. I have been waiting for you."

"You…know who I am?"

"You think because I am blind, I cannot see. But I see you better than you see yourself." Her red lips smiled. "I see connections, connections between people, the ropes that bind us together. Many people are connected to you, Knick Coltin."

"If you know who I am, why bother with any of this? That maze tried to kill us."

"Mazza knew the only way to protect the mystics would be to set traps. The worthy would prove their worth and the unworthy would succumb to their own fears and desires. That was hundreds of years ago but her designs remain."

"And that light? What was that?"

"My daughter plays with fire. No…not fire. Voidflame. She knows not what she does. Forgive her and forget her. Her part in this is small and soon at an end."

"Your daughter?" Knick echoed. "You mean Serena?"

"Yes." The woman smiled again. "I am Osira, the Mystic. Breathe easy now. You are in no danger here."

"She said only one person could enter to see the mystic."

"It is a centuries' old misunderstanding. Only two may survive in the chamber at any time. That is the nature of the curse. It was set up to protect the mystic, but now this mystic must protect you."

"Then you're the one who—" Knick cut himself off. He inched closer and swallowed hard. "Can I…is there anything I can…"

"Do for me?" Osira finished for him. "No."

"But you're—"

"The Mystic," she said, "and what I am is an honor, even if terrible. And what I have done for you was done in duty as the mystic. It is also an honor. But to explain it to you would be like describing color to the blind. I cannot help you understand."

Knick glanced back at Shade who seemed to share his

thoughts. If this is what Serena was running away from, he couldn't blame her. Shade had dragged her back to hell. No wonder she hated her.

"They all run. I did, too," Osira told them as though she had read their minds. "We run to say goodbye to the last of our fears. But we come back. All but Serena. Serena ran from this fate because she did not want it and she hoped to spare me from it. And yet my own daughter is my assassin." There was a delicate pause where Knick wondered what she meant by that, but she spoke again before he could ask. "But enough of dwelling on meaningless things. Come. Sit. We have little time now."

Knick inched closer and sat on the farthest pillow. Shade remained standing, lingering just behind him.

"You have come for a gift and a direction. I have both for you, and more. The last tribe you know well—the Ka'djai, the Oathkeepers of Assur, or better known as the Bloodsworn."

Knick's eyes grew wide. "The Bloodsworn?" he blurted before he could stop himself.

"They do not seem like one of the Tribes," she agreed, "but they are. You will find Tasavir, King of the Sworn, in the place called Opera."

"I know Opera." He twisted around to look at Shade. "It's in Romulus, major Cradle city. Heavy cogs."

"The cogwheelers have gone to war," Osira told him. "While you were stumbling in the webworks, they broke through to the surface. You will find your path to Opera open."

"How do you know all this?" Knick asked. "Are you like the Shaman?"

"The source of Hecate's power is drawn from the same well, it's true, but ours is a different skill. I see connections. I know of the cogwheeler war because I was told by a handmaiden. But I know you were meant to be delayed in the webworks so that the way to Opera would be clear because I see it."

Knick stared at her dumbfounded. "You're just telling us this? No riddles or anything?"

Osira smiled. "Would you prefer riddles?"

"Hell no," he answered firmly. "Honesty is much better."

"Riddles are honest, too; you just lack knowledge of the

truth they refer to. But my knowledge is not tied up in knots so I will speak as clearly as I can. Ask your questions."

"What is Mesopotamia?"

"The heart of the first civilization, birthplace of the Keepers and the Tribes of Typhi—city of the dead, now. But within beats the heart of a living entity, Tiamat, from which destruction cometh. To face this being, that is your destiny."

"You aren't telling me anything I don't know."

"You asked me what I knew, not what you didn't."

Knick was momentarily taken aback. Was that a joke? As he gazed up at this woman hanging from ropes, blinded by a mask, bloody and regal and terrifying, he almost laughed.

"How do I get there?"

"Your guide will lead you."

"Red was supposed to be my guide but she's dead. No one else knows the way."

"No one?" Osira repeated. "No. There is another. One who accompanied her always."

"Who?"

"A selfless and loyal being is all I can describe; the thread is strong. When I gave up my eyes, I gave up the ability to see the illusions of reality. I see people the way they were meant to be seen. As monsters and heroes, soldiers and cowards. I won't give you riddles but I can't answer all of your questions."

He nodded in thanks. "It's better than riddles."

"No," she said. "I have only black words for you." She paused. "Knick, your threads end in darkness. I cannot see where they lead."

"What does that mean?"

"It means you are going to die," she answered and he went rigid. Shade stepped forward, hand on her sword hilt.

"What do you mean by that?" she asked.

"I cannot say with any certainty, but I do not think the One was meant to survive Mesopotamia. A sacrifice to save us all. It sounds very familiar, doesn't it?"

"Yeah," Knick swallowed hard, "I've read that story a few times."

"Fact and fiction, it's an old tale. But…" Her head tilted ever so slightly. "There is one thread…one thread that moved beyond the darkness. A slim thread."

"So what does that mean?"

"That there is a way to survive. But that is a narrow and precarious path. One wrong step and you will lose it."

"Good. For a second there, I thought it'd be easy," Knick muttered, feeling sick. He stood up and paced back and forth to work out the anxious energy suddenly coursing through him.

"If you have any hope of surviving or succeeding, you two must stay together. Your threads are inexorably tied. Trust in each other." Osira's chin lifted. "The threads are unwinding. Soon, that which tied you to your pasts will be gone, frayed and burned at the ends. You must remain steadfast. Do not look back. If you look back, you are lost." There was a beat of silence before she continued. "Now is the time for you to make a choice."

"What choice?"

"To be the One or not."

"I already made that choice."

"Have you? Then why are you still floundering in the between?"

"Because I don't know what that means!" he exclaimed, annoyed at her accusations. "I'm their hero or something, but that has no power. No one listens to me, anyway."

"Why should they?" she asked seriously and Knick drew back in shock. "You have let others fight your battles for you. You let others make your decisions. You question your ability and your role every day. You regret the choices you have made. You make your position powerless with your words. They follow you because you *are* the One. But you have done nothing to earn their respect and their trust." Osira angled her head so that it was facing him directly, and he could have sworn she was staring right at him beneath that mask. "You have power. You must use it."

"What power?"

"You already know the answer to that question."

Knick instantly thought back to the webworks. "I can tap Keeper power."

"Yes. Their power is yours to command."

"I don't know how I did it…"

"Then you must learn. You must become the One or disappear from us all and be no one. Your choice determines the change we will see, but it must be done. Your time of floundering is at an end. If you continue in this way, you will say goodbye to the ones you love, all of them. You will watch them die, one after another, in service to your confusion." There was another beat of silence as Knick stared at her, his stomach roiling anxiously. "I regret that I have nothing good to tell you. I have only dark words in dark times." Blood began trickling from beneath her mask like red tears. "You must go now. Our time is done."

"But—"

"Go," she said again and suddenly there was a strange vibration in the earth.

"We just got here!" Knick exclaimed.

"And it is time for you to move on."

The ropes tightened around her wrists and ankles, crunching as they gently tugged on her limbs. She took a gasping breath as though she were being choked. Red came in fast rivulets down her cheeks, weeping blood. The ground began shaking. The hedges were yanked aside by some invisible force, a path through the maze made in violent bursts of power. The azure haze became a deep and dark blue.

Shade pulled on Knick. "Let's go."

"Wait," he said.

"Go," Osira commanded.

"No, I'm not going to leave you like this."

"Knick!" Shade hissed. "You have to!"

"I am sorry. We had to protect our own." Osira lifted her head. Blood covered her neck and seeped into her dark and delicate robe. "All of us. Eros especially."

"What did you say?" Shade exclaimed, starting forward. Knick pulled her back just as one of the blue globes dropped from the ceiling. The membrane split open and a thousand fireflies exploded out of it, forcing them back into the hedge.

"This world we lived in and fought for is done. Forgive us for sending you to the darkness."

"What do you mean about Eros?" Shade screamed.

"Go."

"Tell me!"

"Go."

As another globe crashed down, the ground began splitting open. Knick and Shade sprinted through the haphazard path, razors from the hedges ripping at their clothes and flesh. They jumped onto the ladder and climbed as the cavern collapsed behind them. They ducked into the tunnel and ran without looking back. They didn't stop until the vibration could no longer be felt and the crashing no longer heard.

When they reemerged into the warren, the Priestess and the Dirt Men were gone. Lethan and Daedalus were waiting for them with Molly and Ross.

"What happened?" Daedalus wanted to know.

"I'll tell you later," Knick muttered. "We need to leave." He looked pointedly at Lethan. "You okay with that?"

The Krueh-jin nodded. "I will follow you."

Donovan stood on a dead, vacant field and wondered if it was Malkira that showed him this vision or if it was just a product of his aegis. He walked on dead grass that snapped beneath his bare feet and was surrounded by white mountains that rose up all around him and a sky that was a blank sheet of ice. Frosted boulders and dead things lingered here and there. He passed a frozen lake and kept walking, preferring the tundra over the dark, watery world of consciousness. Here he was warm. Here he was at peace.

He wasn't sure how long or far he went—steps that took minutes or hours spent on miles. Time seemed to stand still. There was no cycle of light or changing in the weather. There was just tundra that seemed to stretch on forever.

As he walked, he relived the moments that had brought him to this one. He had once been a useless princeling— twelfth in line to the Brennon throne. Even his mother, one of the president's five wives, saw him as useless. Regardless of his inheritance chances, because he was in line, he was bred for the life. He had the education, the looks, the financial support. He was a rich brat who had everything but what he wanted most—approval. The money or fame never meant anything. He squandered both. And then one night when he was feeling especially worthless, he took down the priceless Kxithica war blade from the family artifact collection and brought it to his room. The Kxithi would cut out the heart of the cowards and weaklings in their ranks then grind them into a paste to use as warpaint for the brave, a slice of redemption for the unworthy. Donovan was a coward and a weakling. He couldn't cut his own heart out but he could at least pierce it.

That's when Eros appeared—as he was holding the knife, twisting it around in his fingers, contemplating going through with his suicide. Eros appeared and told him that he had a destiny. Donovan had told him that he didn't want a useless, weak man like him. Eros had said...

Donovan shut his eyes tight, feeling a pain in his chest. He didn't want to think about those days, the days when he was weak and cowardly and useless. He didn't want to think about Eros' words, the words that had saved him.

"I do want you," Eros had said, "because the Balance chose you—you specifically. Who you are now is who you choose to be. And if you choose to come with me, I will give you a purpose."

Donovan dropped the knife and nodded. He gave up his old life and joined the Keeper ranks. He cast off his weakness and cowardice and trained every day, studied every day, built a new identity and a new life. He wanted to be useful—to the Balance and to Eros and to the Regent who ruled them. He became an expert swordsman, mastered many forms of martial combat, memorized tactics and strategies, excelled in every aspect of his training, and eventually inherited sovereignty of the Sword of Ice.

But he was never as good as Shade. She became his ideal, his goal. He wanted nothing more than to catch her. She worked hard but not as hard as he. Yet she was the prodigal student, Eros' favorite. He felt a twelfth son all over again.

Donovan frowned and stared up at the bleak sky as the memories rushed at him. He remembered feeling lost in her shadow but he had never hated her. When had the hatred started? When had the darkness crawled into his heart? He couldn't remember. All he knew was that he loathed her—with every fiber of his being did he loathe her, her for being better than him and Eros for betraying him. The Regent had opened his eyes to the Order's corruption and weakness and deceit.

And that hate became a dark crystal at his core, freezing everything it touched in bitter ice. He had hardened himself to their false friendships, numbed himself to their feigned love. Nothing they could do could thaw his ice. Nothing they could do could stop him from destroying them, those who pretended to be family, those who looked down on him, those who betrayed him.

Donovan looked back at the tundra and went rigid when he saw a woman standing in front of him. She was tall with golden skin, thick black hair, and blood red eyes. She was dressed neck to toe in black armor and spikes speared off of her spaulders like wings. She stared at him with the fierce eyes of a warrioress, unrelenting and sharp. Those eyes told him she knew him, knew everything about him, every detail of his soul. He felt himself withering under her gaze.

Just when he thought he couldn't take her penetrating stare any longer, her eyes moved to something over his shoulder. Donovan turned to look. An inferno was roaring behind him. He stumbled backward in shock, gaping at the massive columns of fire connecting torched earth and charred sky. And standing amid the blaze was a figure. He squinted, held up his arm to shield his face from the heat. Malkira pulsed and hardened, thickening his icy barrier. As the flames licked this way and that, Donovan was able to identify the figure.

"Vox," he whispered. What was she doing there? How had she gotten there?

But he couldn't ask her. Nothing would be heard over the roar of fire and he dared not cross into the inferno. He backed further into his tundra and stared. Vox's clothes had been burned away, her hair a flowing fall of flame, and her eyes wisps of fire. Though she was not burned, she was being consumed.

But what unsettled him the most was the dead expression on her face.

Serena threw herself through the silk tent flaps where Knick and his party were waiting for her just outside; the Dirt Men, including Enge, followed her out. Every one of them gawked in wide-eyed shock, all except for Enge.

"What happened?" she exclaimed but the question on her face was 'how?'

"We saw the mystic," Knick explained casually. "We got the answers we needed and we'll be out of your way."

The priestess went rigid. "You should be dead. Mazza's Curse allows only one to enter. I warned you—"

"You played with voidflame," Knick countered,

remembering the mystic's words. "And now here we are." He smiled. "Just point out our new friend and we'll be out of your hair."

Serena's face told of pure fury as she shifted her angry gaze to Shade. "You think you are so powerful," she growled. "You think you are above everyone's laws. You think your skills are unmatched, your cause so just!" She cleared the distance between her and the Keeper. "You are as much a tool as the rest of us. You are worse than that. You are a puppet."

"Is that why you hate me?" Shade whispered. "Because you're a puppet who thought she cut her strings...until I dragged you back. A voice screaming in the wind and no one hears you." She closed the distance between them and said so quietly that Knick almost didn't hear, "I am sorry for you."

Shade turned her back on the sorcerer and started walking away. Serena was trembling with rage. Bright globes of red energy appeared in her hands and her opal eyes brightened.

"For me?" she choked. "For *me*? You are beneath me!" she screamed. Shade shadow-stepped and grabbed Serena by her throat. The Dirt Men shifted into fighting stances but did not engage, wary of attacking when their priestess was in such a vulnerable position.

"I should kill you for what you tried to do to Knick," Shade growled, "but that price has been paid." She released her with a small shove into the waiting arms of one of the Dirt Men. "And you are responsible for that as well."

Serena clutched her throat. Her eyes moved from a departing Shade to Lethan, who looked sadly at the ground. She looked utterly abandoned. She pulled out of the Dirt Man's grasp and stood tall, collecting the pieces of her damaged pride.

"You want to leave?" she asked. "Then go. Leave, and don't come back. Any of you!" She narrowed her angry gaze on Knick. "I don't care who you are. I will send no one with you." She smiled triumphantly. "Resolve your quest on your own. No Skahradhan will aid you."

"I'll will," Enge said and stepped forward. "I'll go."

Serena looked as though he had slapped her in the face. "No!" she hissed. "No, you can't. I forbid you!"

"You don't have that authority, priestess," he said and bowed. She looked at him wildly and desperately as she came to the same conclusion Knick had—the mystic had given this order.

Knick nodded solemnly. "Time to go," he said quietly. The group turned to leave. Not even Lethan hesitated with goodbyes.

"No!" Serena shrieked. "You can't go. Enge, stop! I forbid you." She grabbed Enge's arm to stop him but he gently pried her small arms off of him and nodded to a fellow Dirt Man to restrain her. She struggled uselessly against the big man's hold on her. "No, don't go. Please. You can't. The Warren needs you. I need you."

"Goodbye, Serena," he said and began walking away. Panic overwhelmed her.

"Enge!" she cried. "Father! Please! You can't leave me! I need you! Father, don't leave me! Father!"

Knick looked back upon hearing those words, stunned by the revelation. Enge just kept walking. Serena crumbled to the ground, no longer a proud woman but a vulnerable and frightened child. She didn't cry. Knick wondered if she was still capable of tears. She just sat there in the dirt like a broken doll, like a puppet whose strings had been cut...because a puppet was not freed when liberated from their strings, only made useless.

Knick hated her attitude, her blind hatred, her self-righteousness, and her attempt to hurt Shade. But he couldn't hate the woman. He felt sorry for her. She wore the look of a person who was entirely alone in the world, who had always been alone.

He walked over to her and knelt down in front of her. "I'm sorry," he said. She said nothing, only stared at him with fractured sorrow. A single tear appeared in the priestess' opal eyes.

Deep in the bowels of the sanctuary at Lake Hern, the decaying Regent and his fallen delegates were plotting and scheming. The oracle was arranged on a dais not far from the circulet, quiet and unassuming. It read the Weave as the trillions of threads of possible futures broke away or united with the threads of the past. The path the Enoch had deduced as the most plausible future was the most observed, though the others were never neglected. As this path climbed further away from reality and into speculation, the threads thinned and divided. There were many variables, thus many possibilities.

It was on this path that a new thread began to absorb itself into the firm web. The Oracle followed it to a certain outcome. In the gloom of the hall just a few meters away from the circulet, the Oracle began to bubble up. It reached out to the Enoch and projected one word through their telepathic link.

"Run!"

Part Six

"To me *belongeth* vengeance, and recompense; their foot shall slide in due time: for the day of their calamity is at hand, and the things that shall come upon them make haste."

Deuteronomy 32:35

I don't know how the world gets you, but it does. You're born into the system and that's it. Barcode is stamped, and you can't get out. You owe it to them, bringing you into the world like they do. That's what they tell you. That's what they drill in your head day after day, and you're fuckin' grateful they don't know you don't believe it. There are some that do, but most of them just don't know any better. They say ignorance is the only evil, but only because they're ignorant, too. If they weren't, they'd know how lucky the people are that don't know how fucked up the world is. There's no way out, so you just gotta pretend like it doesn't matter. Hate, anger, revenge—it doesn't mean anything. You're in the system, and that's it. Fear and ignorance rule the world. I used to think they were lucky—those in the Mine, I mean. Those sons of bitches are lucky that they have a choice. Not up here. You wake up, and you think life is the opportunity girthing your dreams, and then you realize...the opportunity is the devil and the rut is just a rut. For the rest of your life, you live a life based on mere existence you're only doing 'cause you're too chicken shit to take your own life. Or you work for the devil and hate yourself.

I remember Rosk lookin' at the sky and saying were all fools born under the same stars. I agreed with him. Whatever Rosk said, I agreed with him. Back then, I didn't really listen to him, but now I get it. The only way to change the stars is to change yourself—to go from fool to wise man. I think he'd laugh at me if I told him that now. But I get it, you know? Kid, you got it too, way before any of us.

I'm too old to fight it now, but I think I would've had I known then what I know now. Can't teach an old dog new tricks and can't tell a leopard to change his spots. I'm done, I am the way I am. Unlike the rest of those bald-headed cuntfucks, I know more than I should. I think more than I should.

I wish I didn't.

I'm trapped just like the rest of them. Trapped with this mind that hates the world, hates the system, hates the hierarchy, hates myself, hates everything. Trapped in it and I can't do anything but be, and being blows. I just gotta deal with it, just learn to accept it. Adapt.

Adaptation is really funny. I look out and see the animals adapt to the changing environment. I watch them adapt to the radiated wastelands, the nuked deserts, the stripped seas, the warped sky—and everything is pumped and polluted with anti-agyn toxins, parciphilus gases, microvenoms, contaminates, oxy-pollutants, noxious waste, render eggs, Athena's silent warfare, and all manner of poisons we put there for our god-of-the-machine mentality. They adapt, they learn to live within the hazardous environment. They keep on pushing. So do people. I watch them, I watch the babies born as they grow up to live a wasted existence just like their shit-for-excuse mother and father, watch them toil the dirt, make some more babies, die, and donate their bodies to the see-you-in-hell fund. They had it tattooed on their bodies, inscribed on their tombstone, and it was their dying words. Believe you me.

That's all I have.

And for what? What's the payoff? What's the point of adapting? To put paper in someone else's pocket? They outnumber us by millions but they fear us instead. Fucked up.

I have to beat my head against a wall every time I start to slip up and have a thought like this... I have to strip my mind of all traces of this disease they call knowledge. They don't care if you're self-aware, just so long as you're too down on it to do anything about it.

They rear a world of apathetic worms. That's all people are now. They sit down there and gossip and prattle and at the end of the day their risky words of 'fuck the system' get them killed or beaten by the butt of a rifle to the head. It's just easier to live and not deal with the trouble of rebelling. Fear beats them into submission, schools them in apathy, and that's the legacy of the human race from here on out.

I can't care anymore, that's what I learned.

I wake up and put on the suit and slip on the shades and do my job. I'm jacked into the system, believe it, and I can't pretend to be okay with it... I have to be okay with it. See what I'm saying?

Sure, I have these memories I fought too hard to remember to just let go of. It makes living this life I have to live really hard. Raped my heart so hard I don't know that I feel anything anymore. Of course I still do. That's the problem.

I hate remembering. I hate the way life turns out. I hope it's better for you... I hope the system doesn't get you like it got me and got everyone else. 'Cause that's all I got for you, kid...hope.

I'm not a person anymore. I'm a number. I don't have the face I used to have...I have ITS face. I can't have a mind anymore, kid. My thoughts don't belong to me anymore. Fuck...all I got is hope, kid.

If you break away from this fate, maybe I'll be able to believe in something again.

I'm sorry I couldn't get out.

It just beats you down...so no one can get out alive. I'm just so tired of being forced to live, forced to live in this system, forced to keep going, forced to keep doing what I hate, forced to do what I don't want to do.

My greatest wish is to die…and I can't even do that.

This letter is all I got left of me. At the end of it, I go back to being a number, a faceless agent, one brain of the same mind. After this, I have to erase what's left of my individuality. It's just getting' too hard to hide it from the hive mind.

I just wanted you to know…just wanted someone to know. I used to exist… I used to be a person. Once, a long time ago, before I knew the system had me, had all of us… Once, when I used to be ignorant.

I don't know if you'll ever read this, kid. But if you do, I just want you to know how it is…I just wanted to ask you not to hate me, not to hate him, not to hate what happened…if you hate anyone, hate the heartless bastard that did this to us. The angels, Operations, the company, the cerebrates, the engineers, the mentors, all of them…they didn't start out this way. They're victims of that devil that erected the White Tower. Too late for them, too late for me…kill us all and save us, save the people, save everyone. Give someone out there a future to look forward to. Give them a future without ignorance, without apathy. Give them something they don't have to be afraid of.

And when you come to me, don't hesitate, kid… Please.

I promise I won't hate you. I've just lived too long without having a life. I'm so ready for the end of it.

Don't hesitate, kid.

I promise I won't hate you. I could never hate you. You're all I ever had to believe in.

Rudy

Jilk woke up in a haze and blinked repeatedly as he tiredly scanned the dark room. He yawned and sat up. The old bed creaked under his weight as he threw his legs over the edge and rubbed his eyes. He yawned again and stretched, twisting side-to-side until he heard several cracks, and then he popped his neck. He grunted, still sleepy. His mouth felt like glue. He worked his tongue around his teeth, roof, and walls to build up saliva then spit into the corner.

Day two, he reminded himself as he slipped out of the bunkroom and sought the food store in the next room. He fished a protein bar out of his sack, ripped open the wrapping, and took a large bite. As he chewed, he smelled cigarette smoke and saw a faint light in the hallway. He checked the bunkroom and saw that only Solo was still in bed. Jilk shoved the rest of the bar in his mouth and went in search of the light source.

He found Slot smoking in the kitchen perched on the far counter, a light globe centered on one of the islands. She smiled sheepishly when she saw him. *Busted*, her eyes said. He shrugged to say it was no big deal and lit up, too.

"Couldn't sleep?" she asked.

"Slept enough," he replied. "There's nothing to do but sleep."

"You gave her the days."

"Yeah, I did," he muttered. "Sometimes I can't remember how we wound up here."

"Cause family's more important 'n anything. And Knick is family."

He resisted smiling. "You said cogs were family."

"They were. But more like distant cousins and uncles. They don't count like you and Knick. Y'all are immediate family."

"Solo is your immediate family," Jilk told her, unsure whether he was happy or frustrated by her words. On one hand, she thought of him as family. On the other, family could mean she looked at him like another brother.

"So are you and Knick."

Jilk sighed. "Why are you up anyway?"

"Stomach hurt."

"You sick?" he asked, concerned.

"I'm fine."

He started toward her. "If your stomach hurts, I don't call that fine."

"Cramps, genius."

"Fuck," he cursed and spun around. His face burned with

embarrassment. He knew Slot was a girl but she was so not-girly that he completely failed to consider her having girl problems. He took quick, deep drags on his cigarette and turned back around. "Surprised Solo didn't put a stop to that."

"He did when we were in Thebes. Got me the shots'n'shit. But can't stop it forever unless you stop it forever." She grinned at her nonsensicalness. "But Solo said one day I might want kids so he wasn't gonna go that far."

"Have kids," Jilk muttered in numb awe. "Do you want kids, Slot?"

"Donno. I'm still a kid myself." She ground her cigarette butt into the side of the cabinet and lit another rette. "You always said I had as many brains as a ten-year-old."

He laughed, remembering all the incidents he had yelled that at her. "You're damn right."

"You like me, don't you?"

The question completely caught him off-guard. He choked on his drag and coughed up smoke. He gawked at her wide-eyed. "What?"

"You like me. Kinda like a man likes a woman."

He swallowed the lump in his throat. This wasn't exactly how he had planned to confess but denying it seemed like a waste of an opportunity. His heartbeat was so thunderous in his ears that he barely heard him choke out the word, "Yeah."

"You sure?"

"Am I sure? Of course I'm sure. You think I'd lie about that?"

"No. It's just...I'm not really much like normal girls. Solo says anyone likin' me s'gay."

Jilk wanted to punch her brother in the jaw. "Asshole," he muttered under his breath. "Look," he said louder, "no matter how you dress or how you act, you're a woman to me. But I don't like you 'cause you're a girl. I like you 'cause I think you're amazing." He fidgeted nervously with his cigarette pack, lit a fresh one before he finished his old. "It's okay if you don't like me back. It won't change anything."

"I think I like you, too," she said.

His head snapped up and the cigarette fell out of his mouth. "You do?"

"Yeah. But there's somethin' I gotta do first 'fore I can think 'bout that seriously."

"There is?" he asked nervously.

"Solo gave up his life for me. I can't go forward until I give it back."

Jilk picked up his cigarette. He knew how intensely Solo protected his sister but he didn't know all the details. Trapped in his elation, he barely managed to ask, "What do you mean?"

"There was a girl he once loved. Lana. Was after we joined the cogs, 'fore we were put to your unit. I thought everythin' was cool with her. One night, I'm s'posed to be sleepin' an' Lana'n'Solo's in the next room bein' gross and coupley. She says to him, 'Come live with me.' Princess lived in a big house in Thebes. Daddy was a rich man workin' for *the* man. Solo starts t'get excited when she tells him the offer's just for him. So he turns her down. Next thing you know, they're arguin' and she's yellin' things like 'sister complex' and 'unnatural'. He told her I was family an' he wasn't leavin' me behind. 'You made enough sacrifices for that girl! She can take care of herself. You act like she's your whole life!' S'what she said." Slot pushed on the butt of her cigarette with her thumb, staring at it but looking far away. "He yells, 'She *is* my whole life!' Got real quiet. Then Lana said she was his lover and she wouldn't settle for second. Solo says he guesses its goodbye then."

Jilk raised his eyebrows. He never knew there had been any woman in Solo's life. Since the siblings had been placed under his care, they had been stuck together like glue. He didn't even know if Solo was aware other women existed.

"Just like that?" Jilk asked.

"Just like that."

"What happened?"

"She flipped. It got real ugly. First she was just mad, cursin' and throwin' things. I came out and told her my brother may have problems hittin' girls but I didn't. Then she started cryin'. She begged Solo not to end it, to talk about it, but he threw her out. He told me she was crazy. Said, 'Good riddance.' But he was hurtin'. He loved her a lot. Endin' it like that, it hurt him deep. He thinks I don't know. I'm not as dumb as people think."

"No one thinks you're dumb."

"Yeah, you do. But s'okay." She grinned. "Means I know more'n people think I do." Jilk internally grimaced. They had seriously underestimated her. "And I know he blames himself for hurtin' her. But he never once blamed me. Solo's whole life has been about protectin' me. He's locked in. And I'm not movin' forward without him."

Jilk smiled and, for the first time since they had met, he saw her blush. "Okay," he said, high on happiness. "When that happens, I'll tell you again."

"Deal," she said with that girly expression, tucking her chin in her palm and looking away to hide it. Jilk laughed, entirely forgetting his annoyance at being stuck in that dark place. Slot liked him. She liked him like he liked her.

"Deal," he agreed, unable to stop smiling.

The firestorm swirled in raging heat. Vox stood at the heart of it as great columns of flame sprang out of the earth and speared the sky thick with red and black smoke. Fiery twisters blazed scorched trails across the dry earth. And everywhere she walked, the dust beneath her feet melted. The ground split and magma sprang to the surface. The heat was so intense that her skin felt cooked and her eyes burned. She could barely breathe. But there was no pain. Her eyes worked perfectly. Her skin was soft and smooth. The fire did not burn her. Because she was fire.

Vox listened to the noise of the inferno as it raged inside of and around her. It licked at every last drop of moisture, consumed every last oxygen vapor, and burned... burned...burned... Everything was burned. Outside of the firestorm, there were doctors rushing about her. They were taking care of her, protecting her, keeping the inferno from overtaking her. It had tried. She had almost become the firestorm several times. They had pulled her out of the fire. But they couldn't keep it from happening. Soon, her body would come apart. She would unravel into a great column of all-consuming flame.

Vox wrapped her arms around her stomach. It glowed white hot with the child in her womb. She would never see this child. Her body wasn't strong enough. The inferno was inside of her. When she had first opened her eyes and saw the firestorm, she thought she had come to the place where her aegis drew its power. But now she knew the truth. It was a place she had created. She was looking inside of herself.

Vox closed her eyes and hummed to her child, fingers

gently stroking her belly. She felt the infant stir, responding to her voice and touch. She smiled and continued to hum. Fire raged all around her and lava pooled beneath her toes. And she felt peace.

The doors to the warren slammed shut behind them, the eyeless golems standing witness to their exodus. Molly was leading the charge toward Fiddler's City, sniffing the ground as she zigzagged around. Daedalus and Shade walked side by side. Enge followed them with long strides. Lethan trudged somberly behind him with Whiskey at his heels and Ross beside him. Knick was the last one out. Shade glanced back at him and stopped. There was a strange look on his face. He stared at Enge's back until anger registered in his face.

"Her father?" Knick yelled, storming after Enge. "You're her *father*?"

"Yes," he replied gruffly.

"How could you walk out on her like that?"

"I had no choice."

"She begged you!"

"Begging is beneath her. She is the priestess."

"And you're her father."

"It doesn't matter. My orders come from the mystic!"

"Mystic, yeah, you mean your wife? Serena's mother?" he snapped bitterly.

"She was not my wife," he growled and stopped walking. "I was her chosen consort. They are not the same."

"So you two just had a child and then absolved yourselves of all responsibility?"

"We raised the priestess as she was meant to be raised—without coddling."

"Coddling? You mean love? Discipline? Your priestess is a spoiled brat who begged her father to look at her and all you gave her was your back! Not a hug—not even a goodbye—you just walked out!"

Enge whirled around, his gray eyes flaming angrily. "Maybe where you come from, fathers hug their children," he growled and Shade saw hurt flicker in Knick's eyes, "but in the warren, for the priestess, a strict discipline is tradition. I needed no fatherly hugs. Osira needed no sweet words."

"Serena did!" he shouted. "She ran away!"

"They all run!" Enge boomed. "But they come back!"

"She didn't!" Knick yelled just as loudly. He pointed to Shade. "That's why you called them, isn't it? Because you knew she wasn't coming back."

"It isn't your business."

Knick shook his head in disgust. "You're damn right." He started to walk away then stopped. "And you know what? I didn't even know who my father was. I was raised by angels. And silver lenses show one expression—your own."

Knick stormed past her without looking at her. She wondered if it was the hallucinations in the maze that made him so irritable or if it was something more. They had spoken only once about their heritage. Like her, he had no idea who his father was, though he had suspected his mentor. He had never said anything else about it. He had never even told her how he had escaped from the Hive Mind.

Enge walked up beside her and stopped. "It is none of his business," he said.

"You say that," she began, watching as the others walked ahead of them, "because it is something you do not wish to discuss. But he is the One. The Tribes believe he is destined to deliver them to their lost homeland. But he does not believe in destiny. You put a great burden on him, ask him to care for you and yours, yet you tell him you and yours are none of his business." Shade looked up at the large man. "If you're none of his business, don't ask for his help."

"Some things are because they are. You are a Keeper. You understand prophecy and destiny."

"I understand his prophecy has not worked out the way I thought it would. It makes me wonder if it was true for them all."

"What are you telling me, Keeper-Shienar?"

"If you believe in him, believe in him. Not the prophecy. Him."

Enge bowed his head. "I understand."

With their noses in books, infiltrating the collective had been the single least difficult thing they had done since setting out from the Healing House. Antion and Isis had found musty old robes from the laundry room, slipped among the throng, and were not even recognized as strangers by the scholars who spoke to them.

"When I was a scholar," Antion confessed that first night, "I admit I never saw the faces around me. I knew the High Counselor, Nico—of course—and the Interim. There were a few closer than the others, but men and women I spoke to…for *hours*…I never saw them. I looked but never saw." He felt ashamed at the thought. That's when Isis touched his arm.

"All of us often fail to see what is right in front of us," she told him. "That is the way of humans. You see only through perspective."

Then they found a table to organize their research and began scouring the shelves and nearby stations for books. Isis chose to scrub the other scholars' notes for useful tidbits while Antion picked through the many tomes. Once he had a book in his hands, he felt complete. With his eyes fixed on the inked words, he lost all sense of time and the people around him. Only once when he was trading one book for another did he glimpse Isis studying quietly beside him and remember where he was and what he was doing. He watched how seriously she read, how her delicate brows were pulled together. This information gathering should have been strange to her, for the Enoch who saw all, but she seemed as at home as he did.

Consider me as you consider yourself, she had once told him. *We are equals now.* But he did not feel her equal. She was knowledge. He was merely a scholar. Not having a book between his fingers for so long had been tough. After all, he had been reading since he was just a boy. But Isis…to see everything and not be able to access it within her own mind? It must be torture.

Antion silently vowed to reconnect her with the Weave. He didn't know how to do it or how he would accomplish it, but he understood very well that it was what she wanted. Then he went back to studying and forgot the world once more. But the night proved fruitless for discovery. They slept no more than three hours then went at it again. Antion noted many scholars did not even bother returning to bed. Some napped in their chairs and others refused to sleep altogether. Antion remembered those days well. Once upon a time, he would have been wide awake for days on end, reading. He missed it.

It wasn't until late the second night that they found anything useful.

"This," Isis said suddenly and pointed to the paper in her hands. "This is it. I have been seeing this acronym pop up in all the notes recently. ZZ. Now I understand," she mumbled, almost to herself. "Zerzura."

"What is it?"

"I don't know. But this one man has a note…"

She slid the page across the table so he could take a look at it. The scrawled letters read "Meso?" Antion bolted upright, eyes wide. He looked directly at Isis and they shared a grim stare.

"I'll go find everything I can on it," he told her.

It took hours before he was able to find anything on Zerzura, and it required hijacking a book from another scholar. By sometime in the middle of the night, he came across a useful passage.

"Zerzura," Antion said, "is a mythical white city within a lost oasis. It is said to be the resting place of a great treasure. A wall encompasses the city and the gates are guarded by black giants, who keep any from coming or going."

"Mesopotamia," Isis said as a matter-of-fact.

"Are you sure?"

"Could it be anything else?"

Antion thought hard about every mythical city he had ever read about but quickly dismissed each one as it popped into his head with the recollection of tiny facts that reinforced the impossibility. "No," he said. "But how do you know?"

"I have seen the great wall and the black giants," she confessed.

"How?" he gasped.

"I have seen Shade's dreams. And where she walks in dreams…are places we ought not to go, places that we must go." She looked at the book in his hands. "Tell me more about Zerzura."

"There isn't much," he admitted. "It says…mm…" His finger skimmed the lines quickly as he muttered under his breath. "Ah, and at its heart slumbers the king and queen."

"Without a doubt, Zerzura is Mesopotamia."

"Mesopotamia was lost," Antion said.

"And the Tribes went looking for it," Isis continued the thought.

"When they couldn't find it, they built Etemenanki."

"Their hubris was cursed and they scattered, never to be one people until the coming of the One, who would lead them back to their true home."

"Zerzura," a new voice said. Antion and Isis looked up to see a young scholar no older than Antion standing on the other side of the table. He smiled, showing off crooked teeth, and quickly sat down. "I was on the Malkira project," he told them, "and am catching up on the Zerzura one now. You guys, too, huh?"

"Yes. I'm Antion," he introduced himself. The young man held out his hand and Antion shook it.

"I'm Tate," he said. "That's a nasty scar you got. Was that before Tower life?"

Antion frowned and started to say no but Isis reached out and touched his arm, squeezing gently as if to warn him. "Y-yes," he stuttered.

"How'd it happen?"

"I was attacked by angels. They used these slug-like... things—I don't know what they were. It latched onto my face and..." He didn't feel like explaining anymore. "They ripped it off. I didn't get medical attention until it was too late to do anything about the scar."

"Damn angels," Tate cursed. "I'm sorry, friend. At least nothing like that can happen to you again." Tate looked at Isis and held out his hand. She shook it.

"I'm Isis," she told him.

"Tate," he told her as if she hadn't been present when he announced his name earlier. "This is a huge find. It ties our whole world together."

"What do you mean?" Antion asked.

"The angels refer to the aegis as Dionysian artifacts. Zerzura, in legend, is sometimes called the City of Dionysus."

"Meaning Keeper technology is born of Zerzura," Antion said. Tate snapped.

"Exactly."

"Zerzura is Mesopotamia," Isis said, "the first civilization and the original birthplace of the Keepers and the Tribes."

"The Tribes?" Tate asked. Antion could see his mind racing behind his eyes as he sifted through every bit of data in his brain regarding the subject, making connections and educated guesses. "Tribes of...Typhi?"

"Yes," Antion confirmed. "They are the original people of Mesopotamia. When the city was lost, they tried to rebuild it, starting with Etemenanki—"

"The Tower of Babel," Tate said.

"Yes, but they were cursed and scattered. For thousands of years now, their goal has been to go home."

"And now it's the Keepers' turn to go home as well," Tate muttered as he sifted through the notes scattered around them, "if we can find the way. They have been researching it for years, some of these guys." He nodded to the scholars around them.

"They haven't found it yet?" Antion asked.

"No. The path is well-protected. For awhile, they thought the leylines were the clue...but they couldn't connect the dots."

"Leylines," Isis gasped and the notes between her fingers fluttered across the table. "Of course. Someone, bring me a map! Quickly!"

In Pylos, Caleigh walked through the crowded streets as a nosferatu. They cowed at the sight of her, faces warped in disgust and fear. She was monstrous compared to them, disfigured and unpretty. In this bright and shining world of Anshar, it was not the beautiful that stood out; everyone was beautiful. It was the ugly that people could not look away from. Even by miner standers, she was hideous. It was the grayworm. Growing up in the Mine, every kid caught caveworm. It was treated, beaten, and never contracted again. Grayworm was different. It was a rare, deadly mutation of caveworm. Those that survived were left with horrible, worm-like scars that covered their body.

She had been a nine-year-old monster.

And now she was full grown and walking the streets of Pylos where every man and woman and child jumped out of her path, recoiling as though touching her would twist and deform them as well. Caleigh ignored them and kept her eyes on her destination: a small hovel of a shop smashed between two buildings. There was no name over the door. It was not a place one visited frequently. It was a word-of-mouth business. Inscription.

The curtains were drawn and no light seeped from the small cracks. Either the Inscriptor was divining or out. She pushed her satchel from her side to her back as she reached out to open the door. It was locked. Caleigh frowned and slipped a couple of lock picking tools from her belt. The door clicked open.

"You weren't closed after all," she muttered to herself. "My lucky day."

A loud scream wiped the smile from her face. She pushed open the door and the smell of incense and candles hit her with the sound of gasping and groaning. She paused at the threshold, wondering what she had interrupted, and then crept inside. A man in a long coat was standing in a dark corner and the Inscriptor was pulling himself upright from a secret compartment under the floor. His chest was heaving, limbs trembling, and smoke was rising off of his clothes.

"What happened?" the man in the corner asked. "What did you see?"

The Inscriptor coughed and groaned as he wormed his way out of the hole. The tools in the pit were red hot with heat and the inks he had brewed were on fire. The pool was glowing bright orange, casting an eerie light across their faces. In this bouncing light, the Inscriptor looked as though he might hurl.

"Ichthys! Tell me!" the other man boomed, stepping closer to him. A great wave of dark blue light seemed to crash down upon them. Caleigh felt suddenly drenched in ice water. She peered at him more closely. "Where is she?" he screamed and a symbol on his forehead pulsed.

A Keeper. The man was a Keeper. Caleigh went rigid, her gaze transferring to the cowering man on the ground.

"H-Heaven," he croaked.

The Keeper's fury instantly drained from his face along with all of the color. Pale and awash with fear, he bolted past Caleigh and threw open the door with such force that it cracked. When they were alone, Caleigh dropped onto knees and crawled to the Inscriptor's side.

"Are you alright?" she asked. "What happened?"

"The Keeper," Ichthys rasped, "is in Heaven. Vox," he reached up and clawed at Caleigh's shirt, "is burning."

"What are you saying?" Caleigh asked as flesh bumps sprouted on her arms. "A Keeper was captured?"

The Inscriptor whimpered. "P-please," he stammered,

"help me. I can't see. My eyes... I can't see..." He desperately grabbed at her clothes. "Help me..."

Caleigh looked closer at his face and saw that his eyes were charred. She wrenched out of his grasp and kicked away from him, guilt ripping through her as he reached for her, fingers scraping the ground. He begged her not to leave him, begged her to help him. She thought she was going to vomit. Suddenly all she could smell was burnt flesh. She jumped up and ran out the door, sucking in deep breaths of clean air the moment she had cleared the frame. The Inscriptor's wailing reached her even outside.

Leave him, a voice inside her head told her. *Run. Get as far from here as you can.* Caleigh reached for her satchel straps and held on tight to anchor herself. That's when she remembered her sack was still full. She had a job to do. She must deliver the package. Nothing could break the Bloodsworn's sacred vow.

She crept back into the dark building and slipped the package from her bag. The Inscriptor was lying there motionless. She knelt beside him and tucked the package into one of his hands. She saw that he was weeping blood. His fingers twitched around the package while the other hand weakly grabbed for her clothes but he could not reach.

"Help me..." he whispered. "Please..."

Caleigh couldn't stand it anymore. She stood up and hurried out. "Help!" she cried. "A man has been injured! Someone, please help!"

Most of the crowd gasped and shrank away from her but a few Enforcers broke through the throng and rushed over. She pointed inside and watched them rush in. A few seconds later, an alarm began wailing to signal a block emergency. A medical truck would be summoned, doctors and sanitation officers would be rushed in, and the Inscriptor would be helped. She hoped.

Caleigh disappeared into the crowd and made for the closest Bloodsworn portal to the Mine. A Keeper was captured. What did that mean? What should they do? She had to warn someone. She had to tell Tasavir. He would know what to do.

It was the middle of the night when Knick and his entourage finally reached their destination. Fiddler's City had all the darkness and silence of an OT town but the size and architecture of a Cradle hub. The buildings were tall and crowded together, a wood and brick hodgepodge of misshapen structures. On the highest point in the center of town was the bell tower. It rang for every light change—sunrise, midday, and sunset. It was an old system created for the Mine's first settlements. Most didn't use it anymore but Fiddler's City was old country.

The bell tower's ground floor was the station house where the train ran right through the center of town. A light was still on in the ticket box so the group pooled their rials and bought passage on the next train, which wasn't set to leave until first bell. They waited scattered on the platform. Lethan and Whiskey leaned somberly against the station wall, lost in thought—probably thoughts of a lost love. Enge stood away from the group straight as a board with his arms folded over his chest and Ross sat cross-legged in the middle of the walkway, snacking on geke chips leftover from the Skahradhan banquet. Shade leaned against one of the support beams and looked at the tracks, and Daedalus hovered near her. Knick slumped against the support beam one over from hers and pet Molly. No one said a word to each other and the hours ticked on quietly.

Knick was just starting to snore when Daedalus approached. He snapped his head up and hoped he didn't snort as he came awake. Molly was asleep with her head in his lap. He patted her between the ears and briefly glanced at the Keeper before focusing on the tracks.

"The Keepers function similarly to the Skahradhan," Daedalus said. "We all abandon our families for a higher calling. But it is a choice. That was something Serena did not have."

"Neither did Shade. She was born into the Order."

"Like you were born into the angels," Daedalus noted. "Not every path in life is a choice."

Knick glared at him. "Are you about to feed me more destiny bullshit?"

The Keeper smiled. "No. I'm going to tell you that the real choices we make are not the ones regarding which path to choose, but the ones we make at every pitfall on the path we're put on."

Knick tilted his head back against the column and sighed.

"Sounds a lot better than it is."

"Most things do," Daedalus agreed.

"Were you born into the Order, too?"

"No, but I entered very young."

"How old?"

"Five."

"What happened?"

"My family and I were taking a trip. I don't remember where or why, just that it was storming. Something happened—lightning struck or a transformer blew—and we crashed. I was the only survivor." Daedalus looked at the train tracks, his eyes reflecting nothing as he mentally went back to that time. "I heard the sirens in the distance. Heard the rain on the metal. Everything seemed to be on fire. My parents and my brother were dead.

"And then Eros appeared and offered me his hand. 'Do you know why you have survived, Daedalus?' he asked me. I shook my head. He smiled so kindly. 'You have been chosen by the Balance...and if you likewise choose the Balance, the world will believe you died here with your family and you will never be able to go back to this life. In return, you will be given a new family, a charge to safeguard them, and the power to do so. If you choose to come with me, Daedalus, I will protect you.' Then he held out his hand." Daedalus lifted his eyes to look at Knick "I was only five, but I knew I wanted to be part of his family."

"Eros means a lot to you." He glanced over at Shade. "To both of you."

"Eros has a young face but he is a fourth generation Interim. He is wise and he is strong—and he makes us strong. He knows us better than we know ourselves. He is like a father to us, but also a brother, a friend, a teacher, and a mentor. He is many things, but most of all...he is someone we can trust."

Knick frowned. Hearing Daedalus describe him was a little bit inspiring. He wondered if he hadn't given Eros a fair shot on their brief meeting, but no way in hell was he going to admit it.

"I didn't get that vibe," he muttered just as the tracks started rattling. "Train's coming," he announced and stood up.

The cry of the locomotive drowned out all other noise as smoke flooded the platform and the train rolled into the station. It took two hours to unload and reload, to refuel, and to finish boarding. Knick and his friends had a car to themselves, a transformed cargo hold with a bunk bed bolted to the wall in one corner and a few couches bolted to the floor in the other. Ross went right to sleep while the others settled into a state of catatonia.

When they had been running tracks for at least an hour, Shade came over to sit next to him.

"I want to talk to you," she said, "about what happened in the maze." She paused as if waiting for him to protest or say something smart but he just looked at her. "You were an angel. I've known that since the beginning. I never really gave it much thought. That time in your life was over and no longer mattered. But, in the maze, you were afraid of them, that they had gotten you."

She hadn't asked him a question but she stared at him like she wanted an answer. Knick cleared his throat.

"Yeah, being an angel sticks with you. Even if you want out, you know there's no where you can escape them. Except the Mine. But the Mine is nothing but horror stories. What if it's not even real? What if it's just something they made up to catch you? Because hell sounds good in comparison."

"But you did escape."

"I did. Because once you know, you have to do something. You can't go back to pretending. So you wait until you're at your breaking point, until you know you'd rather die than stay there. Then you run and…and you die or you make it."

"But to get to that point, you had to break the Hive Mind. That's what I don't understand—how you managed to break away from it."

Unbidden, Knick's mind went back to those last days he was an angel, to the events leading up to his escape. He didn't want to think about them. He didn't want to acknowledge them. So he pushed them out, shook his head.

"I don't want to talk about it," he muttered. He expected Shade to get up and walk away but, instead, she laid her head on his shoulder. He froze.

"When you do," was all she said.

He glanced at her face and saw her eyes were closed. He carefully laid his head on top of hers. She didn't move. Slowly, Knick relaxed. He thought of the woman leaning on him—how that meant so much more than her head on his shoulder. He leaned on her, too, in every way imaginable. When he was an angel, there had been no one. He had been surrounded by people but had been utterly alone. But now, for a myriad of reasons, he had a dozen people around him, people for him, people leaning on him. As Knick looked around at their tired faces, he realized that he was leaning on them, too.

The warehouse Sonia and Balthazar had procured as a hideout was cold but housed everyone comfortably. The naga had done their best to treat the wounded while the Kur procured supplies. The Keepers were no more than refugees. All of their power amounted to nothing in the end, not when they had turned on themselves. When Eros counted them, he had twenty-seven Order survivors, not including the Interim, who were so scattered that he could not say for sure who was still a Keeper.

He surveyed them all from the foreman's office, every battered soldier and guideless healer and helpless scholar. When their glyphs had appeared and the representative Primordial came to claim them, they were promised a place in the world—a safe place—and a purpose that would never cease, yet it had been stripped from them in a single night.

When his eyes fell on the Basset family, his frown deepened. The father lay wounded, tended by his eldest daughter, who was so broken with despair that she refused to eat or speak to anyone but her family. The littlest one, Clara, broke his heart to watch her. She wandered from person to person carrying blankets, food, and supplies, offering it to anyone she came across. A child's capacity for love could not be hardened when buffered by ignorance. Ignorance, Eros mused, was more than bliss. It was the secret to paradise.

If only they had all refused to eat the fruit of the tree.

He turned away from the dirty window as Sonia and Balthazar entered the office. Looking at them, he thought of his lost Interim. Of Bartimaeus, who had died saving them. Of Vox, alone and in pain. Of Dimitri, desperate and hurting. Of Rexis and Donovan, the traitors, whose souls had been scarred so deeply by their turning that they could kill their own family. He touched the new scars on his chest and ignored the sharp sting that ripped across his flesh.

"Baron," Sonia greeted him. "We have food and water for the month, if rationed properly. Kallo and Delia are overseeing the distribution."

"We have averted prying eyes," Balthazar explained, "for now. But they will come again. We are not safe here, even with the cogwheelers marching on Anshar."

Eros nodded and glanced back at the window, at those scattered on the warehouse floor.

"Baron," Sonia prompted but he remained silent. "What should we do?" But he had no answer for her. "Baron? What do we do now?"

Eros could not answer her. They had lost. The Order was destroyed. All that remained of their great Order were powerless refugees. The Balance had shifted. What should they do? What *could* they do? He didn't know. He had no answer for her.

Rexis stood before the doors of *The Bright Mermaid* and grit his teeth. Again, he told himself that this wasn't meant to be his job. It had been Donovan's task. And, once again, he reminded himself that if Donovan had been the one to come, he would've killed everyone. It was better this way. At least…that's what he told himself.

Rexis ground his teeth together anxiously. He didn't want to do it but there was no changing course. He stomped to the doors and pushed them open. The waiting room was empty. Across from him was a single, narrow corridor that led to a labyrinth of corridors. He hesitated. Donovan would have simply stormed the place, but the *Mermaid* was full of peaceful women. They did not deserve to die. Like Camilla…

He thought back to the days when the Cleric and her naga healers had patched his wounds after a dangerous mission. They had been beyond kind. Their compassion felt incorruptible. Many of the Obeahani became naga, and Camilla herself had once been the High Healer before she had been chosen by the Balance. He couldn't hurt these women who might have one day been Keepers.

He hoped they wouldn't make him.

Rexis straightened when a young girl appeared, her long skirts swishing around her feet and her hair covered with a white net. Her tiny hands folded in front of her stomach as she bowed respectfully. When she smiled, her eyes were warm and trusting.

"Welcome to *The Bright Mermaid*, traveler," she said in a small voice. "How may we assist you? Are you unwell?"

Rexis tried to tap into his usual charm but he was too anxious. He gave her his best smile but it still felt stiff. "The High Healer," he said. "I can speak with her, ay."

"I will see if she is available," she replied and disappeared down the corridor. It didn't take long for her to return. "I present the High Healer Etrusca," she said and side-stepped to allow the other woman to come through. Etrusca was a giant, nearly filling the threshold. Seven feet, at least, he thought. She smiled at him and gave a shallow bow.

"How might I assist you?" she asked him.

Rexis clenched his jaw, teeth grinding together. "In the interest of keeping peace," he began, "I'll need you to come with me."

She looked taken aback by the threat but all she asked was, "To where?"

"To the Keepers," he answered. "To see the Regent."

"And why might the Regent need the services of the High Healer when he already has those of the Cleric?"

"The Cleric is dead," he admitted. Etrusca and her handmaiden went rigid and pain filled their lovely, gentle eyes. The young one teared up. "You need to come with me."

Etrusca sighed. "I have heard disheartening things. The Keepers are engaged in a civil war. The Regent betrayed the Order and those who remain struggle in vain to delay a war between Anshar and Kishar. The women of the Mermaid take no side in our services. We will heal all who need it...but we will not help your Regent destroy something else. Please give him this message and go with good will."

Rexis' jaw was so tight that his teeth hurt. His fingers flexed against his palm, hesitant to draw his sword. "You're coming with me," he told her, "if I have to force you. Don't be stupid. Think of your girls and come willingly."

Etrusca bowed her head sadly. "I am unwilling."

Rexis drew his sword and swung to angle it at the woman's throat but a bright burst of blue light rebounded his weapon. He stared at the shimmering barrier that split the room in half, watched as it faded and became invisible. He tapped at it cautiously but every time his sword touched it, blue light rippled away from the tip.

So they aren't defenseless, he mused, *but a good defense won't stop me*. He twisted his wrist, heard the bells jingle, but was hit with a blast of energy before he could execute the attack. A great wind knocked him backward, almost threw him on his ass, and began pushing him out the door. He growled, hands grappling for a hold on the doorframe. On the other side of the barrier, Etrusca stared at him passively. *Please leave*, her eyes said. But he couldn't leave. He couldn't return to the Regent in failure and say that a bunch of passive women defeated him. He would be killed for being useless and the Regent would send Donovan, who would slaughter the whole house.

Rexis grit his teeth as he strained to hold onto the frame against such a strong force. He slowly pulled himself inside and around the corner so that he was being pressed against the wall. He struggled to reach the metal sconce on the wall. The moment his fingers touched it, he sent himself through it and appeared on the other side of the barrier where a second sconce was bolted to the wall.

The young Obeahani threw a wisp of paper at him that dissipated in a bright flash of light. He recoiled in pain, his eyes burning in his skull, and stumbled forward. When he managed to open them just a crack, he could see in the blur the women were gone.

"Shit," he cursed and rushed after them. He plunged into the labyrinthine hallway, wary of any other surprises. He had expected the women of the Mermaid to act as passively as they appeared but he his assumptions had cost him. Their actions had been nothing more than defensive but he refused to underestimate them again. "Stop playing games!" he yelled as he rushed along the narrow and empty corridors. There was no answer.

He stopped suddenly when he turned the corner and saw a young woman blocking his path. He thrust his sword at her but she did not flinch. He stopped just short of gutting her but still she stared at him blankly, unafraid. Rexis scoffed, shoved her to the side as easily as a curtain, and tried to move past. She reached out and grabbed his forearm. He turned back to pry her tiny fingers off of him but paused when he felt his skin start to burn. Pain lit up his arm as her acidic touch began to eat his flesh away. He snatched her bony wrist so hard that he felt it break under his strength. She cried out, fell against the wall, and cradled her arm against her chest, but she did not flinch or cry or glare. Rexis looked at the red handprints on his arm, saw his flesh was whole, and realized she had not truly wounded him.

"Don't make me hurt you," he told her. "Don't make me hurt you!" he yelled louder for everyone to hear. His voice faintly echoed down the corridor.

Rexis continued following the path, pushing past every woman who stood in his way. They all reached for him, crowding the way until it was hard to move. They reached for him, touched him, tried to cripple him. He shoved them away but they kept coming. He didn't want to hurt them but a broken wrist, he decided, would heal.

As he raised his hand to slap one of the girls, another flash of light caught him off-guard and sent him stumbling blindly. Hands immediately flew to touch him, their fingers burning his shoulders and arms and stomach. He shoved harder, plowed head-on down the hallway. More light flashes kept him blinded, forced him on the offensive. Their hands came for him again and he cried out in agony. He swung wide, shoved one of his tormentors away, and felt a small head connect with the wall with such force that it cracked.

Rexis did not have time to be mortified by his actions because the tormenting touch of the women of the Mermaid pushed him further into rage. He felt as though he were being eaten alive, dissolved by the digestive acids of some greater monster, blind and cocooned and unable to move.

The bells on his wrist jingled. Rexis threw back his head and screamed as his desperation to survive overrode his moral compass. All at once, the metal framework of the building bent and twisted to his will. He heard the walls around him snap and crumble. When the pain had subsided and his body was left trembling in shock, he lifted his head and looked around.

The Bright Mermaid had been destroyed. Metal pipes and beams had reformed into spikes that had assaulted his attackers. The Obeahani hung lifelessly around him, speared on the reshaped beams, and lay bloody at his feet, eyes wide as their bodies shuddered in their last moments, like wounded butterflies pinned to the ground. He couldn't breathe, choking in shock. As he surveyed what he had done, he saw Etrusca huddled amid her fallen sisters, tears streaming down her cheeks. She looked up at him in crushing grief, lower lip trembling.

Rexis stared at the hair and blood matted on his hands and dropped his sword. *I am a villain*, he realized, *just like Donovan*. Rexis looked at Etrusca once more. His task had been to secure the High Healer. He had to complete his mission. With a shaky hand, Rexis retrieved his sword and, with legs like gelatin, crossed over to his target. He angled the weapon at her throat, not trying to hide how it shook in his unsteady hand.

"I told you not to make me," he whispered.

Etrusca's head dropped in resignation and she nodded.

The maps they had spread across the table were covered in writing and lines as Antion, Isis, and Tate did their best to piece together the secret of the leylines. The voice came on so suddenly that Isis could only freeze in shock.

"Run!" the Oracle screamed in her mind. "RUN!"

The door near the top of the chamber banged open and a dozen Priori spilled into the great library. Isis jumped up as they targeted her and began their quick descent. For a split second, she thought about not running. If they caught her, they would reconnect her to the Weave. If they caught her, she could be Sight once more.

And you will see for the enemy, she scolded herself. The Oracle's chilling shout echoed through her mind once more. Run!

She used the corner of the table to propel her forward, racing between the stunned throng of the collective and the bookshelves, small enough to navigate the crowd with ease. Priori were yelling at the monks to clear away. Isis was afraid to look back and see if they were listening or still standing dumbly in shock.

And then suddenly a wire coiled around her shins and she fell to the ground. She looked up at the wall, at the cracks she knew were there, and mouthed the word, "Run!" to whoever might be watching. And then strong hands were on her, hoisting her up with ease. Her eyes searched wildly for Antion as they carried her through the room, surprised murmurs buzzing about. She found him standing next to Tate, wide-eyed and on the verge of panic. In his fist, he gripped a pen as though he might be stupid enough to use it as a weapon. She gave him a warning glare before averting her eyes to avoid bringing unnecessary attention on him. He had escaped the Regent's gaze and could warn the others.

Isis lifted her head and held her chin high. She would go to this fate without fear.

Romulus was second in size only to Thebes and was one of the greatest cities of the Mine. It was the first planned project when the coal miners moved deeper toward the core and those left behind realized they were going to make a life underground. So dark, steel towers rose to fill the massive cavern, a shadowy reflection of Rashrima Haan above.

The train pulled in at the Kardin Line that divided the inner city from the sprawl—a sort of east meets west, with the sprawl housing the degenerates, the black market's black market, and one hell of a party while the city was all work, no play in the cogwheeler sense of protocol, plus all the richy-living.

Off the platform, they were surprised to find only one cogwheeler patrolling the ramps. The mystic had ensured him they had emptied out but it was hard to believe without seeing it, yet here they were, easily slipping past a one-man patrol. They went west and descended into the sprawl. They walked four blocks through junkies and partiers, thumping music, carts selling foods with strange smells, and stands peddling exotic goods until they came upon a large, ostentatious building that looked more like a gilded sculpture than a place of business. Fluted columns and delicate metalwork reminiscent of lace were the face of the structure. The word OPERA was woven into the lace like letters captured in an artistic spider web. Strange music could be heard through the walls. The door was a solid slab of braided gold, or metal painted to look like it—Knick couldn't tell which. Next to it was a small, golden nameplate no bigger than his big toe. The word OPERA was carved into it. He ran his thumb over it, felt the ridges of the letters, and then pushed.

A screen not previously noticed lit up and an aniform appeared before them; he was mostly human save for the tusks jutting up from his lower mandible, the yellow eyes, and the ridges in his cheeks and jaw that gave his face drastically sharper angles. The aniform didn't say anything, just glared with his thick, spiky eyebrows.

"We're here to see the Bloodsworn King," Knick told him. The aniform grunted and continued to glare. Daedalus stepped up.

"Haze," he said, "enough. Let us in."

When the aniform saw the Keeper, he grunted and nodded but still looked to be glaring. Knick wondered if it was a permanent feature of his mutated face. The screen turned off and a hidden door about ten feet away from the actual door opened up and allowed them inside.

"You guys know everyone, huh?" Knick remarked. Daedalus grinned knowingly.

"Just people with power," he replied as they walked down a narrow, blank corridor.

"Snob," Knick coughed as they came to another golden blockade with a sliding peephole. It clacked open, a pair of yellow eyes assessed them, and then it slammed shut. Molly barked. A second later, the door opened.

They entered a finely decorated waiting room where everyone but Shade and Daedalus was promptly searched by more tusked aniforms while Haze looked on angrily, a fifty pound assault carbine cradled in his arms. When security was satisfied, Haze angled his thumb at the ornate door on the far side of the room, his yellow gaze following Molly as they walked out.

The chamber they entered was massive. The walls were made of wood and ivory, the floor of marble, and fluted columns and sculptures ringed the central floor to support the six stories of balconies above. Display cases ranging in size to display something as small as jewelry and as large as a wild animal were embedded in the walls. Pedestals of varying height were sprinkled around the main floor and at the heart of the room was an ornate wooden stage draped with silk and lace.

All around them, people mingled happily and a gentle hum of conversation filled the open space. The crowd included what one would expect: rich people dressed either extraordinarily or extravagantly; some wore gilded masks, others hats three heads tall, and many with hairpieces that must've weight at least ten pounds or more. Yet there were seemed to be as many grungers and bums, strutting their stuff in dirty layers and tatters. The rich spoke with them as often and as happily as their own, as though there was no class divide. The servants thrust wine glasses and cheese plates at each person fairly.

Ross stepped next to Knick. "What is this place?" he gawked. Knick shook his head. He had heard of Opera when he was a cogwheeler but he had assumed it was a club, not...whatever this was.

"No idea," Knick mumbled.

"It's a trade house," someone behind them said. They turned to see a pink-skinned woman with a mass of curly, magenta hair. Her face was painted with sparkly, sky blue powder and intricate designs were drawn in white across her cheeks and around her cobalt eyes. She wore a white mesh dress. "Welcome to the Exchange. But you are here to see Tasavir. Please, this way."

They followed her around the perimeter of the trade house to a red door. Knick and Ross struggled not to look at her ass, which was more than obviously displayed through the sheer clothing. She led them to a large, oval office where hookahs sat on low tables surrounded by colorful pillows. The people who occupied this space were far more exotic than the ones on the main floor.

One man was covered head-to-toe in an elaborate and perfectly woven series of tattoos that made him look like a tapestry; his body was not just a mishmash of artwork but literally told a story. There was a woman covered with pearlescent scales and a tail as thick as a leg sitting next to a lady with long, peacock feathered hair and dressed in a multitude of purple and blue gems peppered with diamonds embedded in her skin. A man no taller than three feet sported a silver, plaited beard, with orange eyes and pale skin covered in black spines and bony ridges that climbed down his spine and disappeared into harem pants.

Before Knick could take a good look at the others, a tall, slim man with blue skin and chiseled features approached him. The man had wavy, yellow hair that stood up on his head and twisted back into a point like a curved horn. His eyes were two citrines. He was dressed in tight pants and an open vest covered in gems the color of his eyes and slashed with silk. He wore metal cuffs on his upper arms, forearms, and wrists. Every muscle in his body seemed to stand out.

"Welcome," he said. "I am Tasavir, King of the Bloodsworn. Welcome to all of you. "

"I'm—"

"I know who you are," Tasavir interrupted him. "You're Knick Coltin. You are the One, they say." He smiled at the Keepers, nodded to them, then knelt down and reached out. Molly nuzzled his fingers and he stroked her head affectionately. "So she says, and her word carries much weight. When we lost Red, we thought all hope was gone. Yet here you are." He ruffled Molly's ears then stood up and led them through a back door into a private office filled with wood furniture and yellow velvet cushions. The walls were packed tight with books except for a half-column covered in a mosaic of chipped glass protruding on the right.

"I thought you were King of the Bloodsworn. What exactly is the Exchange?" Knick asked.

"It's a trade house," Tasavir answered as he leaned back on his desk, "somewhat inspired by the Bloodsworn work regiment. Bloodsworn only take jobs when they are being paid with something they consider valuable. And so it is here—an exchange of valuables."

"How is that different than any other store?" Ross asked. "You're buying things you want."

"Currency is only valuable because people assign value to it. For patrons of the Exchange, currency holds no value. They are interested in other things. That is what we deal in. What is valuable to some may not be to others. That is where these people come to find the fulfillments of the empty spaces in their lives. Some people trade jewelry, statues, trinkets, and animals. Others trade themselves, their services, their talents."

"A slave trade?" Lethan balked.

"Not at all. We do not deal in such base practices. This is refinement, Jin, not a profit house. What I am talking about is something much more satisfying. I knew a young woman whose singing voice was simply angelic. I knew a man who sought such a voice. The songbird wanted a Torshi pipe, very rare...very unique. The sound is unlike anything I've ever heard and is poorly replicated. But this man had come into a Torshi pipe by inheritance. So he traded the pipe to the songbird in exchange for her voice. She lives with him and sings for him when he requires it, and she plays the Torshi for thousands across Lotus Maze."

"And those people out there?" Knick wondered.

"Yes, colorful, aren't they?" Tasavir smiled. "They are patrons. We attract many kinds of people, especially the eccentric."

"They're incredible," Ross muttered bashfully. "I've never seen anyone like them."

Tasavir smiled. "Would you like to sit with them?" he offered and Ross' eyes lit up. "While we conduct business, of course."

"N-no," he stammered. "They're too—"

"What? Beautiful? They are, but beauty is entirely subjective and nothing if not admired. Melisandraria," he called and the pink-skinned girl poked her head in the office. "Please, take this young man to a table. He admires our guests."

The girl smiled and reached out to Ross, gently pulling him out of the room. "Come," she said. "Come."

"But I—"

"Must have an interesting story," she finished, "to be traveling with such purpose." She bowed to Tasavir. "If I may, the others wish to speak with the big man and the blue-eyed one." She smiled at Enge and Lethan. "If it please you."

Neither man looked eager to move. Tasavir laughed.

"They will not fawn, I promise," the King told them. "They admire you but it is curiosity that prompts them."

"Go ahead," Knick said, "if you want."

Enge and Lethan exchanged glances but neither moved. When everyone continued to stare, they hesitantly withdrew. The door closed and silence pervaded for a long moment. Knick saw the pleasantry leave Tasavir's face, replaced with seriousness.

"I know why you are here. Long ago, Red and I made a trade..." There was a dark shadow that flickered across his face at the mention of it. Knick wondered how precious their trade must have been to invoke such grief. "Do you have the Typhi star?"

Knick pulled the symbol of Etemenenki from his pocket and held it up. "You mean this?"

Tasavir took it and set it on a special pedestal on his desk. The lights dimmed as a laser beam shot through the bronze symbol and projected a glittering white image all around them. They were surrounded by speckles of diamond dust and hard, white lines of flowing energy that crisscrossed across the room.

"What is this?" Knick whispered.

"The King's Way."

That's when he saw it. The white lines all originated in cities he had found a tribe. He was looking at a map of Lotus Maze, both Anshar and Kishar, and ultimately a record of his journey. But the glaring white lines did not connect one tribe to the other in a representation of his path. So what were they?

"What do they mean?" he asked and traced the edge of one of the lines.

"They are the leylines," Tasavir answer.

"And they all connect at one point," Daedalus observed.

"Mesopotamia," Shade whispered and walked up to the glowing intersection.

"Deep underground," Knick added. "Coal mines deep. I guess it makes sense. If it was easy to find, we would have heard of it."

"It's beneath Asgard," Daedalus observed. "Right under it. Look." They traced the path from Asgard in Tonatti Haan down, down to the intersection of the leylines. "It was right under us all this time and we never knew."

"We still don't know how to get there," Knick reminded them. "Red is still dead. All these gifts and guides amount to nothing without her."

"No, this is the King's Way. It has always been there. Red knew the way, handed down for generations, but she made sure the secret did not end with her. There was one other who walked the path with her time after time, one other who never left her side."

"But wh—" Knick's voice stopped in his throat. He looked at Molly, whose tail wagged happily at his attention. "Red's best friend…" Osira's voice echoed in his mind. *There is another. One who accompanied her always…a selfless and loyal being.* "Molly." It was so beautifully absurd that he wanted to laugh. "Molly knows the way."

Shade met his eyes with renewed hope. He almost smiled at her.

"There is bad news," Tasavir said. "The Sworn I trained to be your oathkeeper was Hezara," he explained as he walked behind his desk. "She died during a delivery. But I will not leave the oath unfulfilled. I will go in her stead."

"You?" Daedalus asked. "But the Bloodsworn need their King."

"Nautolom will take my place. He is a good man. He will serve the realm well. Besides," he pushed a button and the mosaic column lowered to reveal a tank that held a frozen woman, "I was part of my promise to her."

Knick's jaw went slack as he stepped up to the tank to finally look at the woman that had set this all in motion. She was tall, robed head to toe in black, and her hair was fire red. Her eyes were stone gray flecked with flying embers. Even dead, she had a formidable presence. Or maybe it was because he was so intimidated by her—this woman he never knew, this woman who had pulled all the strings from beyond the grave, prepared his path before he was even born. He had seen her influence everywhere he went. Twenty-five years later, Roskolniv still grieved her as though she had died that day. Gru, Sabal, Tasavir—all of them.

Molly padded up beside him and whimpered. She turned a few circles, crying, and then howled. No one spoke, just watched. Molly nudged the glass with her nose and then laid down at her dead master's feet. Knick looked back up at the red-headed woman again and thought, *It should have been you here right now.*

Tasavir hung his head. "The Krueh-jin collected the bodies to burn but...I could not let them burn her. So I brought her here."

"To collect her?" Knick balked.

"To preserve her. I could barely believe that she was gone. I couldn't bear to let her be erased." He shook his head and looked up. "But the ends she wove have come together at last. Now that you have met, she can leave this world knowing her life and her death were not in vain. It is your right, Knick Coltin, to burn her."

Knick stared at the Bloodsworn King and then swung his head back to the frozen Red, the leader of Babylon's

Immortals. She looked it—immortal, as though fire would only make her stronger. And yet Tasavir claimed it was his right to burn her. But what had he said? That he couldn't bear to see her erased. What right did he have to erase her?

Just then, the door was thrown open and Caleigh stormed the office.

"Tasavir," she exclaimed. "A Keeper was—" She stopped when she saw them all crowded there and stared wide-eyed.

"What has happened?" Tasavir asked as he removed the Typhi star from the laser. She eyed the guests apprehensively. "Go on. They should know. It is their friend you would speak of."

Caleigh swallowed the lump in her throat. "I delivered a package to the Inscriptor of Pylos. He was servicing a Keeper—tall, dark hair—who sought information on another Keeper called Vox. He said she was taken captive by the angels and was being held in Heaven." Shade and Daedalus immediately stirred. "He said she was burning!"

Knick felt a literal change in the air, a thump in his gut that told him bad things were coming. The two Keepers immediately headed for the door. Knick followed after in a rush. They raced through the oval office, startling the patrons. Enge and Lethan instantly detached themselves from the company and gave chase.

"How could this have happened?" Shade exclaimed.

"I don't know," Daedalus admitted. "I will warn Eros," he said as they crossed the trade hall. "I will gather the rest of the Interim and meet you at Heaven's gates."

"I can't," Shade protested. "I can't leave him."

"Vox needs you. No other Interim can do what you have done!"

"I vowed—"

"Your first vow was to the Balance and to your own," he reminded her as they spilled out onto the street. Shade hesitated only a moment and then nodded.

"You're right. I will meet you."

Daedalus reached out and squeezed her shoulder then disappeared in a burst of black and shot off into the night.

As Isis collapsed on the ground and was surrounded by Priori, Jilk threw himself at Otto and held him back, one hand clamped tight over the boy's mouth. Otto struggled against him but was too weak to put up much of a fight.

"There's nothing we can do!" Jilk hissed in his ear. "Don't be stupid!"

Jilk looked at Isis as the Priori picked her up with ease. Her feet left the ground, blond hair tangled around her face. Those green eyes looked right at him. Run, she mouthed. And then she was gone. Jilk waited until the Priori were gone before releasing Otto. The boy fell to his knees in emotional and physical exhaustion, groaning to himself about his failure.

"We need to leave," Jilk said. "Now."

"What about Antion?" Slot asked.

Jilk's jaw and fist clenched. "I don't know. But it's out of our hands now."

"We have to find Knick," Solo said.

"No, I'm not leaving her," Otto protested. "I'm not going."

Jilk knelt down next to him. "Don't be stupid. She told you to run. Remember what she said? This is not your path. She needs you, Otto, but you can't help her if you throw your life away." Jilk stood up and motioned to Solo. "Get him up. We're leaving. Now."

The Nest was buzzing with electric rest, a steady hum of machines working at minimum output. The brain pulsed, glossy with lubricants and sweat, as parasites crawled purposefully over the sleek and spongy metal. Operations sat quietly locked into their eternal roles, half-fused with the machine, as robotic arms descended to change the stained silk sheets covering their faces.

After hours of steady rain progressively growing more torrential, an unusual weather report flashed through the great data stream and the system flagged it repeatedly. Dark clouds completely covered Rashrima Haan and were rolling outward. Satellite feeds were immediately tapped. The storm was not moving in a typical pattern but originating at a single point and then spreading outward in all directions. Within seconds, Operations confirmed the storm's origin point was right there in the city.

Centrum's electronic eye opened.

"Operations," a voice echoed in the chamber. Centrum screamed angrily as the hive mind accessed Heaven's external cameras. "The Leviathan is at the gates."

The scars of the last Keeper visit were still red and raw. The Hive Mind trembled fearfully within the lubricants as it gazed at the tall, dark form of the Interim standing before Heaven. Clouds so dark they looked black covered the sky in early night. The rain was so heavy, it was flooding the streets.

"Stop him!" Centrum screamed as the Hive Mind quaked in trepidation.

Daedalus knew something was wrong the minute he saw the scars on the tunnel wall that led to Sanctuary's only entrance. There were traces of aegis in every mark. He ran as fast as he could, stopping only when he saw the splintered frame. He slowly walked into the collapsed ruin of the hideaway and a wave of nausea hit him in full force as he spied the mangled bodies of his allies crushed beneath fallen stone and punctured with ice crystals that refused to melt.

What had happened here? Daedalus turned this way and that, studying every bit of destruction as he tried to piece together the event. Donovan had come. He had attacked. But how had he wreaked such havoc? He didn't have the power. Sonia and Balthazar would have held him at bay. Eros would have obliterated him.

Daedalus knelt next to an encasement of ice that covered a massive blood stain. Someone had been frozen as they lay dying, he realized, and someone had come to dig them out. He followed the ice to find the Cleric's corpse and turned painfully. Everywhere he looked, he saw his friends, his comrades—dead. But where were Eros and the others? Where would they have gone?

He crept through the ruins, searching for answers, and came upon the body of Laura Basset. He went rigid with fear. Regret washed over him in debilitating waves. He immediately drew his sword. The bells on his wrist jingled as he sent a pulse through the aegis. It was a call sent into the ether with the hope an Interim would answer.

The signal pinged back to him and he knew where he had to go. He erupted into the voidstar.

The raging firestorm's intensity had grown so immense that Vox was certain it was nearing its apex. The flaming twisters had amassed, fusing until there was only one massive dervish of fire. It tightened around her as the coals beneath her feet gave way to more lava. The magma that gushed between her toes encased her feet like the shallow of a river, steadily climbing higher. Her body was fire, skin alight with flame that did not burn her even as it ate away her flesh to release the fire underneath. There were parts of her she could not tell where she began and the fire ended. Because she was fire. She was flame. She was the firestorm.

The white center of her flame suddenly pulsed.

Vox's eyes shot open wide and an alarm started sounding in the chamber. She gasped for breath, heading for the edge, and suddenly was thrown over it. She screamed as pain hammered her stomach. All around the room, machinery sparked and popped. The doctors and technicians were thrown into chaos, trying desperately to put the fires out.

Dr. Porter rushed up to Vox, his brow pulled into a tight frown. He reached out to touch her but snapped his hand back and cried out. The smell of burnt flesh instantly filled her nostrils. As the team hurried to control the situation, more objects burst into flame until the whole room shifted from sterile white to warning red. An automated voice began calmly instructing the inhabitants of the lab to vacate the premises. Men and women in white coats began frantically filing through the exit, all but Doctor Porter who stood stone still before his patient.

"Go," Vox told Porter through clenched teeth, straining under the pain. The drugs they had pumped her full of had instantly burned out of her system, purged from her veins. The sluggishness, the disorientation, the thick tongue—gone. "You have to leave."

"I can't do that," he protested. "I promised to help you."

Vox closed her eyes and felt liquid heat roll onto her cheeks. "You have to go now, Doctor." She cried out as another spike hit her abdomen. "There is nothing you can do."

"Vox—"

"Go," she begged.

"Vox!"

"Get out!" She screamed and jerked against her restraints as her nerve endings lit up like someone had taken a hot poker and jammed it into a festering wound. "Please!"

Porter looked around then hurried to each console, cursing every time he came to one that was sizzling. When he finally found a machine still on, he hurriedly typed on the keypad but, within seconds, it was sparking and popping. He cursed again, leaping away, and then shouted, startled, as a piece of equipment next to him became a jet of fire. He looked at Vox again, who was rasping as she hung in the restraints.

"Please go," she gasped, the belt across her neck choking her.

"I won't leave."

Porter looked around again then rushed to a cabinet. He snatched up a syringe from a nearby tray then pulled a vial from the storage shelf, filled the chamber with the clear liquid, then rushed to her side. She shook her head, tried to protest, but he attempted the injection anyway. The moment the needle got close to her skin, it melted. The plastic tube bubbled up, spilling the drug onto his hand. He drew back in shock, shaking his head in disbelief.

"Please," she whined. He had tried to help her. She didn't want him to die here with her. "Go."

Porter took one last look at the fires raging angrily in the lab, fear evident on his face, before looking her in the eyes and finding a last surge of bravery and determination. Before Vox could shout, "Don't," he rushed toward her and took hold of the belt around her neck. His hands immediately began sizzling, the stench of burning flesh choking her. He screamed but didn't let go until the belt gave way, freeing her ability to breathe. Porter stumbled back and fell to the ground, hands red and raw. He gaped at his trembling fingers, at how useless they had become, and then met her gaze one more time.

"I'm sorry," he whispered.

"Just run," she begged. "Please run. Run." Another tremor was overtaking her. "Run! Run now! Run!"

Porter scrambled to his feet and rushed toward the door. Vox screamed and a console on the back wall exploded. Fire rushed through the room, primed with raw power. Porter stumbled out of the lab, just barely missing the gush of flame. The door sealed and he stared through the tiny observation window. Vox heaved as she looked at him, was moved by the sorrow in his eyes. He had tried to help her. He had tried to save her child. For that, she would save him, too.

"Run," she whispered.

It was only a matter of time before the firestorm broke out of her.

The Regent's lips pulled back in a rotten smile as Isis was dumped before the circulet. The delegates all gasped and murmured, some even bowed, but Muriel just sneered victoriously at her.

"Welcome home, daughter," he coughed. "It is good you have returned."

"And here sits the king of fools. Muriel." She got to her feet. "Betrayer."

"I confess you were the only anomaly. I could not predict the pattern of a girl who had never lived a life of her own. Would she submit to the events around her? Would she fight them? How much knowledge did she retain?" He bent forward and squinted beady eyes at her. "Or was she merely a doll pulled out of her fragile house?" He leaned back and smiled. "Who you are does not matter. You were foolish enough to defy me and foolish enough to return to me."

"How did you know where to find me? Your power is waning from the poison in your veins."

"I know when my daughter is near. I retain that much."

"The Regent is a seed, nothing more. That taint is purged in the womb."

He chuckled. "Believe what you will, girl. I sired you. I gave you to the Weave. I don't know how you broke free of it but I know you long for that web. The good father that I am, I will give it back to you."

Muriel made a shallow gesture to the Priori and the double doors on the far end cranked open, unrolling a carpet of light across the room. A dark silhouette pushed a freakishly tall figure into the room. As they drew nearer, she recognized Etrusca and her eyes grew wide. There was blood all down her white robe. She looked at the Interim and knew him as Rexis.

"There is your prince of puppets, Regent," Isis said. Rexis flinched. "Sad child, so desperate for a new dawn. You did not have to kill them. Now you will die a puppet."

The Regent's low chuckle grew progressively louder. Isis stared at the Interim until his burnt-orange eyes looked away from her. His vice-grip on Etrusca's arm caused her to wince.

The laughter reached its crescendo and dissolved into a coughing fit but the dark mirth remained in the Regent's black eyes.

"You know the thing you must do now," Muriel told Rexis. "Go and end it." Rexis nodded stiffly and walked out. "Welcome, High Healer. I share sad knowledge that your sister, Camilla, is dead. You are the only one capable now of bridging the gap between woman and Weave."

"I cannot—" she began but he interrupted her.

"You can and you will."

Etrusca looked Isis in the eyes, her brows furrowed in deep sadness. "I *will not*," she insisted. "And if I die, the knowledge is lost forever." The pain Isis saw in her eyes said, *Please kill me.*

The Regent started laughing again, a low and steady chuckle. "No, it won't. Because when I rip the knowledge out of your mind, I will have it forever."

Etrusca lunged for a Prior's weapon but the others reacted too quickly, pouncing her before she could unsheathe it. The wrestled each other for grasp on the weapon. Isis watched in horror as the High Healer was beaten, listened as she grunted and sobbed. Even as blood trickled down her face, she fought them for a weapon, trying desperately to kill herself before they could take her. And then a Prior easily stepped up to Etrusca and injected her with some strange substance that caused her to go still. Isis did not even have time to warn her. Within seconds, Etrusca was slumped in the arms of the nearest Prior. The biggest of them scooped her up and carried her away.

"Shade, hold on," Knick exclaimed as she burst back into Tasavir's office.

"I have to go," she declared. "The Keepers call."

"Then we will watch over the One," Tasavir said with a solemn nod.

"Hold on a minute," Knick protested as Enge and Lethan stepped up beside him.

"Anyone who wants him goes through me," the Dirt Man growled as he folded his arms over his chest.

"I will comeback as soon as I can," she promised. Knick grabbed her arm.

"This is a bad idea," he hissed. "You remember the last time you went to Heaven? You almost died."

"I will have all of my Interim brothers and sisters with me," she explained. A flicker of sadness shadowed her face. "All of them that remain."

Feeling uncomfortable about arguing in front of everyone, he pulled Shade out into the corridor. "Remember what the mystic said? She said we have to stay together. Do you remember that?"

"I remember. I won't be gone long. But I cannot leave Vox there to die."

"So let the others handle it. One Keeper won't make a difference."

"It might. I have been to Heaven before. I single-handedly stormed their tower. I showed them how vulnerable they are. If anything, my presence will scare them."

"Or incite them! Listen to me. I have a really bad feeling about this."

"So do I," she whispered, "that my sister will die while I wait for Eros' signal. That by the time we find her, it will be too late."

"I don't want you to go," he mumbled in a last ditch effort. Shade looked from one eye to the next, her brow wrinkled in distress.

"I know," she said at length, "but I don't want to lose anyone else."

Knick couldn't argue so he punched the wall and walked away.

Daedalus skimmed the ceiling of the cavern until he found the warehouse Eros and the remaining Keepers were holed up in. He dropped out of the sky and hit the ground in a burst of dissipating soot and rushed into the building. Scattered soldiers were being tended by a handful of naga but their numbers were so few that it shocked him. Sonia came out of an upstairs office across the warehouse.

"Daelus!" she exclaimed.

That, too, caught him off-guard. He had almost gotten used to being called by his real name. He hurried across the main floor and took the stairs by two. Inside the office, Eros and Balthazar were waiting for him.

"What happened?" he asked.

Eros shook his head. "Later. Why have you come?"

"Vox was missing," he said, "and Dimitri was looking for her." Their faces confirmed they already knew. "She has been found. She is in Heaven and Dimitri has gone after her."

Eros closed his eyes and took in the information. "Beware the scar on the wall," he whispered. Finally, he nodded and opened his eyes again. "Did you find Shade?"

"I did. She awaits your signal and will meet us at Heaven."

"Prepare to leave. I will inform Kallo and Delia," the Baron told them.

"Yes, sir," Sonia said.

Back out on the warehouse floor, Daedalus spied Casey curled up in a corner and crossed to her. When she saw his shadow fall over her, she looked up and her eyes grew big as a 20-forint coin. In an instant, she was on her feet and in his arms.

"I'm sorry," he whispered in her hair. Her thin frame trembled against him as fresh tears rushed to the surface of her raw eyes. "I'm sorry. I'm sorry I couldn't save her." She squeezed him tighter. Her despair ripped through him. He wished he knew what to say to help ease her suffering, but all he could think of was of a little boy in the rain, clinging to his brother's cold, limp hand and his mother's bloody jacket. "I'm sorry," was all he could say.

Eros, Sonia, and Balthazar crossed the warehouse, ready to depart. She suddenly went very still and stifled her sobs. She leaned back, confusion evident in her brow. She looked at the Baron and the Interim then back at him. She pushed herself way, shaking her head. Her lips twitched between a deep frown and a wry smile.

"Casey—"

"You saved us...so we could die a worse death," she rasped. "I would've chosen the bullet to my head over this slow death." Anger and pain flashed across her face as she screamed, "You should've let them put a bullet in our heads!"

He grabbed her shoulders in an iron grip. "I won't let them hurt you, Casey."

"You're too late!"

"I won't let them take anymore. I promise."

"You promised to protect us but he killed her—he killed all of them. Your promises mean *nothing!*"

He hugged her again. "I'm sorry." She struggled against him but couldn't wriggle out of his hold. After one last fireless punch to his side, she submitted. "I'm sorry."

She clung to his jacket and sobbed. "He killed her. He killed my mom." Her words were choked out between hiccups of breath. "She's dead. He killed her. And they just left her— left her there. I couldn't get to her. I couldn't—they wouldn't let me. I begged them."

"I know," he whispered. Daedalus lowered her to the ground and brushed her hair from her face. "A lot of people died that day…and none of them we wanted to leave behind," he told her. "Not your mother, not Camilla, not the soldiers— none of them. And it hurts. I know it hurts. But if we lose ourselves to our grief, then they've won." She looked at him with round, glassy eyes. "You have to be strong for your sister and your father now. And when I come back, I promise you…we will make them pay for what they've done."

"I don't want payback," she whimpered. "I want my mom."

"I know." He reached out and cupped her cheek in his palm. "I'm so sorry, Casey…"

"You don't get to be sorry," she cried, "when you're leaving again!"

"I will come back."

"I don't believe you!"

"I will."

He held her gaze until she looked away. He forced her eyes back to his. After a moment, her breathing calmed and the tears stopped pouring. She scrubbed her face with her sleeve and sniffled. "I'll believe you again," she said, "under one condition."

"Name it."

"Let me bury her."

"When this is over," he agreed. He glanced at Eros and saw him nod. "It's time."

Casey wiped her face again. "I changed my mind," she rasped. "Make them pay."

Daedalus nodded then crossed over to the waiting Interim. Eros sent a pulse through his sword and the word

Vanguard scrawled down their blades shimmered brightly. Then, they were four shooting stars.

Knick stared up at Red frozen in death. He looked at the way her hair spidered around her face, at the soft ends locked in motion. He stared at her clear skin, at the tiny scars and calluses that marked her pale canvas. At her dark lips, unsmiling. At her gray eyes peppered with embers. She didn't look dead. She looked as though she were on the verge of telling him something important. All he had to do was thaw her out and she would whisper the words that would change everything. The secret to the universe.

"You were supposed to be here," he muttered. "You were supposed to make me believe."

She stared, her silence pregnant with power. He reached up to touch the glass and could have sworn he felt her reach out to him, too. But she was frozen in motion, that delicate pause when even physics defied the universe. She was on the verge of telling him something.

"You had all the answers," he whispered. "You knew what to do. You were supposed to be here."

But she wasn't. She was dead. And Shade was leaving. He was supposed to go to Mesopotamia and do something—he didn't know—face Tiamat, whatever that meant. And he was probably going to die. He was trapped in this prophecy even though he had told Shade he didn't believe in prophecy. And every time he tried to take control, he was swept up in the current, hustled from one place to the next. He felt powerless.

"You were supposed to be here," he said again and Tasavir cleared his throat, startling Knick. He turned around and saw the blue-skinned man enter the office.

"I used to talk to her, too," he confessed, gazing adoringly at the red-haired woman. "I don't know why but it felt more cathartic than talking to a living person. I felt that she somehow knew me, understood me...even though she was dead."

"You loved her," Knick guessed.

Tasavir looked at him and smiled. "Yes. I loved her." He crossed to his desk, opened a drawer, and pulled out a photo. He passed it to Knick. "Do you know what this is?"

Knick stared at the black expanse littered with countless

stars, at the pink aurora, at the faraway galaxies that looked no more than orange and yellow and blue smudges.

"It's space," he replied and handed it back. "It's the universe."

"Yes. And this is how I loved her." He drifted closer to Red's tank, delicately holding the photo in front of him. "Looking at her was like looking at this photograph—in awe and disbelief. That this—" he tapped the image "—is floating above us, around us, infinitely. Far, far away from angels and cogwheelers and Keepers. A great mystery we can only guess at, unknowing of where it ends or begins, existing outside of our will. Something that can only truly be seen from a distance."

"But she was a person," Knick said, "not some clip of space."

"Do you know what she had in common with this photograph?" Tasavir asked. Knick waited for him to tell him. The Bloodsworn King smiled. "Everything." Tasavir reached into his pocket, withdrew a small object, and tossed it to Knick. He caught it, a playback device. "She left that for you before she departed on her final mission." He tucked the image of the universe between two books on his desk so that it stood upright facing Red. "The pyre is prepared...when you're ready." Then he quietly walked out.

Knick watched him go, waited until he was alone, then reached into his jacket, unzipped the inside pocket, and withdrew a delicate piece of paper wrapped in plastic. He peeled away the edges, unfolded the paper, and read again the letter that had forever changed his life. The letter signed Rudy. For a long time, his only thought was to break away from the angels. That was the message here. Get out of the system!

But the system was everywhere. It wasn't just MAAR and it wasn't just the angels and Operations and the Hive Mind. The system was Black Tuesday and the cogwheelers, the system was the Mine and the coal mines and the Grey. It was the Tribes and everyone in every city. It was ignorance and fear.

...kill us all and save us, the letter had read, *save the people, save everyone. Give someone out there a future to look forward to. Give them a future without ignorance, without apathy. Give them something they don't have to be afraid of.*

Ender of all things, that's what the Keepers called him. He didn't know what that meant and neither did they. But maybe the one thing he could do was the one thing Rudy had asked of him all those years ago: to end the system. He had struggled to adapt to his new environment, to *feeling*. He had struggled with the idea of being someone else's puppet, of being responsible for more deaths and more ugly futures. Couldn't knowing the truth and living the way he chose count as freedom? Couldn't it count as breaking out of the system? Wasn't it a start?

But it wasn't a start. It was just another form of apathy. He had been fooling himself from the moment he met Shade, and doing a shit job of it, too. All of his attempts to embrace his destiny—or whatever it was—had been half-assed and he knew it. He had told Jilk and Slot and Solo that they were in or out. They had jumped right in. So what the hell was he waiting for?

Knick fingered the playback device. If he was out, he had to drop everything and walk away right then, no regrets or last-minute-curiosities. Done. Finished. But if he pushed play, there was no going back. He was in, fully committed, no regrets. So what was it gonna be?

Knick walked up to Red, stared at her for a long moment, and pushed the only button on the playback device.

"I know you," a woman's voice came through the tiny speaker. "I don't know your name but I know you. I was waiting for you. The name's Red." Her voice was strong, clear. "I know you have a lot of questions. I know you're unsure. And you're waiting for me to give you answers. I thought about what I would say to you, the advice I could give, the answers I could offer. But, in the end, they don't matter. There's only one thing that matters." He looked into her eyes and held his breath. "Forget prophecy, forget being the *One*. 'Destiny' and 'fate' are just dressed up words for 'future'. And the future comes every second of every day. That's not what matters. What matters is your answer." She paused. "Nobody asked you, did they? Nobody asked you, so I will. And don't fucking tell me what they told you—that you're the One, the Typhi savior, Ender of All Things. Fuck being the One—you didn't give yourself that title. Fuck destiny—this is your life, no one else is gonna live it. Who are we to tell you you're here to save us? Who are we to you? You're gonna throw your life away for someone else, you damn better make the choice on your own. Where you go from here is where you decide to go, what you decide to do. And whatever that is, when you make the choice…it will change this world." Knick reached for the glass once more. "You *can* change this world." She paused again. "They didn't ask you, so I will, and I don't have a right, but I'm asking you anyway." Another pause. "Will you be the One?"

Knick stared at her, floored by the question. It was such a simple thing, to ask. In the grand scheme of things, it probably meant as much as a single grain in a bowl of rice. But to be able to take hold of the sickening shuttle-run that was his life and claim ownership of his choice to ride it was liberating. She wasn't asking him if he accepted the title. She was asking him if he would take it at all. *Will you be the One?*

"Yes," he answered. He thought her heard her smile.

"I was looking for you," she said quietly. "I was wading out to meet you. To see your sky."

The recording ended as Knick stared up her. Wrapped up in that ice, he thought she looked a lot like a piece of frozen universe. He laughed, slid his hand further up the glass.

"The name's Knick," he told her. "And I was waiting for you to say that."

As he looked at her, he changed his mind. She wasn't unsmiling, on the verge of telling him something. She was grinning, everything already said. Knick left Tasavir's office feeling, for the first time since he could remember, at peace, focused. He went outside to see Shade, to apologize. Her sword was shimmering. She looked at him and her eyes said, "It's time."

"Go save your friend," he said. She hesitated at his sudden change in mood, a frown creasing her brow. "Hurry back."

Shade nodded firmly. And then she was gone, a piece of universe in motion. That's when another Keeper with a head full of red hair appeared out of the crowd.

"Are you Knick Coltin?" he asked.

"Who's asking?" Knick replied, feeling uneasy.

"Rexis." His smile widened. "I'm a friend of Shade's."

Water ran in rivers down the streets of Rashrima

Haan and the sky was as dark as the cavern ceilings encasing the Mine. Dimitri stood before Heaven as the rain pounded his back, his rage churning like a violent sea. He knelt down in the river racing around his ankles and sought the source beneath the road, quickened it through pipes it coursed. He felt the tension building, felt the earth begin to tremble, heard the angry whine of metallic stress. Then ground split open, the pipes burst, and geysers of water shot into the sky.

Dimitri twisted his katana and the bells on his wrist jingled. Forming out of the jets of water, dragon-like heads slithered on long necks, rising into the sky. They thrashed about, screeching in earnest. Dimitri pointed his katana at Heaven and the hydra's heads screamed as one. All together, they rushed the tower, smashing their watery maws against the white brick and reflective alloy. Security doors slid out of invisible openings in the walls, locking together to seal off each floor. One set of doors severed the neck of a hydra head that had crashed into the building; from the watery stump, two more heads grew.

Dimitri rushed toward Heaven and let the current beneath him build, carrying him high into the air. It dumped him through a window just seconds before it sealed. Inside, alarms were wailing, sprinklers were flooding the tiles, and an automated voice was calling for an evacuation of the 98th floor and warning against an assault on headquarters by Leviathan. Dimitri assumed he was the Leviathan and that whatever was happening on the 98th floor was somehow related to Vox.

He kicked open the office door and sprinted out into the hallway, racing past corporates cowering in the hallways. The first angel he saw was instantly trapped in a column of water, kicking and gargling as liquid rushed his lungs. Bullets whizzed past Dimitri's head so he summoned a shield to catch then redirect the bullets. Then he was moving again, navigating the white corridors with guesses, killing any angels he encountered, until he found a stairwell. In bold black letters was written '67'. He immediately started climbing.

Around the 75th landing, a thunderous boom caused the whole building to shake and a wave of heat washed over him. Panicked, he took the steps in twos and sometimes threes, vaulting up the stairs on pure adrenaline. When he reached the 98th floor, he was panting in both exhaustion and fear. The door was blown out, the frame wreathed in flame, and the hallway that stretched away from it was burning. He stumbled through the blaze, heart hammering in his chest.

"Vox!" he screamed. "Vox!" A pipe in the wall behind him blew and he threw up his arm to shield his eyes from the steam. "Vox!"

Panic rolled over him in nauseating waves as he blindly hurried on, following the more destructive paths in hope that they would lead to her. And then he found the room, walls charred black except for the angry red cracks spidering away from the lab door, which had melted into a silver pool. He swallowed the lump in his throat, turned the corner, and gasped when he saw her.

She was an angel of flame, suspended upright, head hung in mortal sorrow and pain. The veins beneath her skin had risen to the surface, not blue but fire red. Her clothes had burned away, her hair was a spout of flame, and the swell of her pregnant stomach was glowing like magma churned beneath.

"Vox," he whispered. When she looked at him, her eyes were radioactive yellow.

"Dimitri," she said in a voice unlike her own, layered with elemental energy and raw power, as though she was only partially in the physical world and partially in some metaphysical plane. "It's too late. You must go."

He plunged through the fiery ring and hugged her head to his chest, awed by the power sloughing off of her. He closed his eyes and let the water channeled within lubricate his skin so she would not burn him.

"I will never leave you," he said adamantly. "We will go together. As a family."

Tears of lava dripped out of her eyes and burned holes into his jacket. And when she screamed, the whole building trembled. Her belly steamed with an angry sound like a waking dragon. *The trembles are contractions,* he realized.

Their baby was coming.

Knick lit up a cigarette. "Friend of Shade's?" he echoed. He couldn't recall hearing the name Rexis before. "Aren't you guys supposed to be saving your Keeper pal?"

"Someone has to take care of the One, ay," Rexis replied,

slowly walking toward him. But that didn't ring true, not to his survival instinct or his logic. "So Eros sent me to watch you."

"I don't need a babysitter," Knick told him and turned to head back inside. A voice inside of him suddenly screamed, TURN AROUND! The warning was so abrupt that he instantly obeyed, his skin prickling in fear, just in time to see a sword flying at his chest.

A flash of light erupted between him and the Keeper as Tikal, formed from pink and blue ethergy, lunged out of him and grabbed the blade, stopping it dead in its track. Her eyes like two bright stars flashed angrily. Knick stared at her, dumbfounded. In the moment that he had almost forgotten about the girl called Tikal and the sacrifice she had made for him, she had appeared to save his life, just as she had promised she would. And deep inside, he could hear the soulsong crying out.

"What…what the hell…?" Rexis gaped.

"Inanna's Dirge," Tikal growled in a musical, otherworldly voice. "Death eater. You cannot have him, Betrayer."

She exploded into a second burst of light, creating a force that threw Rexis back, nearly knocking him to the ground. Knick touched the scar on his chest, felt it burning. This was what she had meant when she said she would go with him—to be carried inside, an invisible shield, and save him from the killing blow. She had not died like he thought she had. She had been reborn, just as the Shaman said she would be. Reborn into a death eater for the One.

"I'm sorry I doubted you," he murmured. He didn't even know if she could hear him, but he felt like he needed to say it. He promised himself he would not forget her again. "Thanks."

"That trick won't work twice," Rexis snarled as he recovered from the shock and raised his weapon once more. Knick picked his dropped cigarette up, placed it between his lips, and lifted his fists.

"Let's try that one more time," he mumbled around the rette.

A ball of blackness landed beside them and Shade stepped out of the dissipating energy. Her eyes widened when she saw Rexis, gaze bouncing back and forth between them. Knick's heart jumped to his throat. She wasn't supposed to be here.

She was supposed to be storming Heaven. Why did she come back?

"What's going on?" she asked. "Rexis. Why are you here?"

"To kill me," Knick answered her. "Would have, if not for Tikal. I...I'll explain that part later."

Shade frowned, expression reading disbelief. "Rexis," she said, voice hitching to form a question. He lowered his sword and looked sideways at her, a lopsided grin forming.

"You can't believe that, Shade," he said. "S'just a misunderstanding."

"Your sword flying at my face was a misunderstanding?" Knick wondered aloud, the question dripping with sarcasm. "So is this." He showed Rexis his middle finger.

"See?" Rexis motioned to Knick. "What's credible about that?"

"I believe him," Shade said before anymore arguing could be done. When Rexis stared at her in surprise, she said again, "I believe him."

"You can't be serious," he muttered.

"Tell me why."

"You'll take his word over mine?"

"Tell me why."

"How long is it you known me? Shade. We're best friends."

"Your sword is drawn!" she exclaimed. "Now tell me why!"

Rexis sighed and hung his head in silence. After a long moment, he made a soft tsk-ing sound and said, "You weren't supposed to be here, Shade."

Hurt showed openly on her face. "You," she whispered. "You're the traitor."

"No," he shouted furiously. "No, it was *Eros* who was the traitor! *Muriel* and *Donovan* who betrayed the Balance! I did what I had to do to protect it!"

"Protect it?" she balked. "Protect it how? Asgard was destroyed! Thousands of Keepers died!"

"I didn't want that!" he screamed. "I didn't want any of their deaths! But the Order was sick. It had to be purged! And from the ashes, a new Order will arise."

"How could you?" she hissed.

"I did it for the Order. I did it to end a toxic line of

leadership and ensure a bright future."

"Led by a betrayer?" she uttered in revulsion.

"Led by you," he corrected her. "Once the Baron and the others are destroyed, I will eliminate Muriel and his sycophants! And you will become the new Regent, leading the Order into an era of greatness. I will serve you, a faithful Baron, and together we'll preserve true Balance—not this sham of judgment and equilibrium that has long spoiled these many generations, creating lawless men like Eros and power-starved monarchs like Muriel."

"And Knick?" she asked. "He is the One. Why would you target him?"

Rexis frowned and slid his gaze to Knick, eyeing him like he would a cockroach crawling across the ground. "He changed you," he muttered. "You, who so unerringly walked the tight line between black and white, plunged headlong into the gray because of him. And when he is gone, you can give this up, become the chosen force of Balance once more. He is not the One. Not the real One. You are." He looked at her imploringly. "Let me end it. Let a new era begin."

"You're deluded," she whispered. Rexis flinched as though her words had slapped him. "How could you have fallen so far?" She drew her sword and a dark expression manifested, causing Rexis to shy away in unease. "You were my friend. You were my brother. I don't want to fight you. But if you raise your sword against him one more time, I will kill you."

"No," Rexis mumbled. "You will try to stop me. But you will fail…and then your mind will be free of his influence."

Rexis lunged at Knick.

Eros, Daedalus, Balthazar, and Sonia dropped out of the sky and crashed through Heaven's gate as the watery hydra heads bombarded the reinforced tower. The great drains beneath the complex were vacuuming water as fast as they could but the hydra was not easily defeated. An army of angels was organized on the far side of the zone trying to find a way to deal with these heads that could not be killed with bullets while squads scouted the perimeter for vulnerabilities. Daedalus immediately thrust his sword into the churning water and let loose an electrical current that zapped the angels wading nearby.

"Shade isn't here," Eros observed.

"Something must have happened," Daedalus assessed.

The Baron frowned. "Something is wrong."

"This is different from Shade's assault," Sonia said. "They attacked. They lured her into a trap. But now they are defensive."

"Shade showed them they were not all-powerful," Balthazar reminded her.

"Yes, but it's more than that," Eros told them. "I can feel Vox's ethergy. It's overflowing." His jaw clenched tight. "They are in danger from inside as well. What is the larger threat? Us? Or what they brought into their nest? I don't think they know."

"I've never felt a storm in the ether like this," Sonia murmured. "My aegis is trembling. It feels like fire."

"Will Vox survive this?" Balthazar asked.

Eros had no answer for him. "Balthazar, Daelus, keep the army busy. Take their focus off the hydra and put it onto you. Sonia, hunt the cells organized across the complex, prevent them from gaining an edge. Dimitri has gone inside to save Vox. I will find them and bring them home if I can."

"Yes, Baron," they answered in unison.

"If I give you a signal, get away from the complex as fast as possible. No hesitation. Is that clear?"

"Yes, Baron," they said again.

"Balthazar," Eros called to the dark giant. Normally he would have appointed this task to Rexis. The Keeper's absence was like a hole in his heart. "Open the door for me?"

"And where would you like your door, Baron?" he rumbled.

"Just there." He pointed high up.

Balthazar nodded, twisted his wrist to sound his bells, and bellowed. All around them, the earth trembled with the might of an earthquake. The ground split open and the crack spread, drawing a jagged line from the giant to the building. It climbed up through the great tower of Heaven, collapsing chunks of the internal structure; many of the blast doors crunched inward while some dented as though a force were trying to break out. A churning vibration slithered was both heard and felt. Something was moving beneath them. As Balthazar's roar crescendoed, a great worm made of stone burst out of the building, flashing its razor-sharp teeth made of stone. Angels were thrown from the tower, tiny white dots screaming in the air. The monster lunged for them, twisting, and crushed several in its rocky maw. As it flew out of the tower, it came apart, crumbled into a thousand pieces and dissipated into dirt.

"Your door, Baron," Balthazar said.

And then they scattered—the exotic Sovereign of the Sword of Thorns to decimate the angels around the tower and turn Dimitri's hydra to blood, the Storm and Stone Sovereigns to rip open the earth and call the lightning down on Heaven's army, and the Sovereign of Scars to bleed the tower of wolves and bring home the lost sheep.

Shade appeared in front of Knick and her sword met the enemy's with a loud clack. Rexis dodged right but she intercepted him. He attacked with quick aggression, forcing Knick to shuffle away as the battle pressed closer and closer. The crowd on the street formed a wide circle around the combatants, gasping and cringing, unsure of who to cheer for.

Knick wanted to help her but the look in her eyes told him this was too personal for him to interfere. She had attacked Daedalus because she thought he hunted her for the Balance. But they had quickly resolved all misunderstandings and were allies once more. This was different. Rexis had betrayed the Order, had had a hand in its destruction and the death of her brethren. Rexis had said they were best friends. If it was true, he couldn't imagine the pain she was going through or the anger that was driving her.

So he kept out of her way as best as he could, but he was Rexis' target, not Shade. The Keeper came for him relentlessly, hacking and slashing so viciously that Shade was constantly catching up to him, parrying his attacks. He had seen her fight much more aggressively and wondered why she didn't simply end it. *She doesn't want to kill him*, he realized. *She doesn't want to lose another one of her brothers.* In that moment, Knick understood that his very existence was forcing her to choose between him and her loved ones. Even if Rexis was a traitor, he had been her family, and she had lost too many of her family since meeting him.

Suddenly, Shade flicked her wrist and disappeared. The crowd gasped and took a shuddering step back. She darted out of a shadow behind the Keeper and ripped her sword across his back. He cried out and went down to one knee. She shadowstepped again, appeared in front of him, and held her sword to his throat. At that display, the crowd dispersed in alarm.

"Don't…make me…" Shade growled. But there was more than anger in her voice. There was desperation. There was sorrow.

"Shade," he grunted. "I didn't want this. I didn't want any of it. The Regent came to me, told me of the Order's corruption. He pointed fingers and I believed him, but I also knew he was evil, too. They all were. Everyone but you."

"Bartimaeus wasn't," she hissed. "Nico wasn't! Those innocent collective—they weren't!"

"And the mermaids weren't either?" he shouted, spittle dotting his lips. "But weren't they? *Weren't they*?" He took ragged breaths, eyes wide with fear and confusion. "Sometimes they have to die. Sometimes they make you kill them."

"What have you done, Rexis?" she whispered but he wouldn't answer her. "You were my friend. Let me help you."

Rexis straightened, reached up, and swatted her ponytail. He smiled. "I'm going to help *you*." He flicked his wrist and her bells twisted into awkward knots before flying away from her, ripping the bracelet to pieces.

"Rexis, don't!" she screamed as the Keeper thrust his sword at Knick. The golden metalwork that decorated the front of OPERA suddenly snapped off the building. It twisted into a wall of sharp spikes and raced toward him. Above the jackhammer of his heart, Knick heard Shade scream, "No!"

Knick felt a door open inside of him the same way it had in the webworks against the titan spider. Cool energy rushed through his veins, a wind tunnel of power vacuuming through the widening door. The glyph on Rexis' forehead was glowing brightly and Knick felt his respond, amplifying the light. The other man's glyph brightened as if on command. And then the metal death trap was upon him. There was a swelling of ethergy that surrounded him, padded his body. The spikes slammed into him, absorbed into his body, and then shot back out.

Rexis choked on gasping breaths, run through by eight shards of metal. Blood poured out of his mouth, coughed up in dark clumps. He stumbled back as his trembling fingers hesitantly reached for one of the metal spears as if to pull it out, but he couldn't touch it, didn't know where his wounds began or ended, couldn't comprehend the extent of damage or what actions were needed to save his life. And as that moment of shock rolled away, the fear of knowing he was going to die twisted his face into a pitiable wrinkle of terror.

He opened his mouth to say something but all that came out was a wet hiss. He fell over, his burnt-orange gaze fixed on the black cavern ceiling. His jaw bobbed worthlessly, a breath exhaled in a long, broken rasp. And then the light left his eyes.

Isis knelt on the ground before the circulet, surrounded by Priori who were armed and alert. A compad lay discarded near her, buzzing with electronic snow. It was silent now but half an hour before it had been broadcasting Etrusca's screams as Muriel's men forcibly ripped intel from her mind. He had made her listen, listen as if to say, "This is your fault. You could have prevented this."

Feelings Isis had never before known began to burn under her skin. She guessed the feelings were anger, that they were hatred. Because all she wanted in that moment was to flay the Regent's rotting skin off his frail bones.

His low, raspy chuckle caused her to slowly lift her head. His cloudy eyes were gazing at her, moldy lips curled up in an open smile. She glared at him, her small hands curling into shaking fists. If she lashed out, she would only hurt herself. She was a tiny thing, unimpressive in stature, possessing no strength, without skill or power. Her only talent was in her mind and even that was off-limits so long as she was self-aware.

All she could do was glare at him. All she could do was boil in her rage.

The doors were thrown open, a jarring slam in a quiet room. Isis flinched in surprise, head twitching to the side to hear the footsteps hurrying toward them. Clap, clap, clap. The sound drawing nearer was like a clock counting down to an inevitable event. Her body tensed, eyes flashing as the man swished by her, his white coat whipping about his legs. He stopped to bow to the traitor and then he was moving again, the pause no more than a blip in the countdown.

Isis watched him bend to whisper something to the ex-Regent. The old man's eyes never left hers. He chuckled again and motioned to the Priori. They moved as one, made a collective step toward her. Then hands were on her, hoisting her up. She screamed and kicked, spewing curses. She was not afraid of what was happening or what he planned to do. She merely despised him for what he had done to the High Healer, the kind Etrusca that had gently and respectfully cared for her, and for forcing her to listen to every agonizing second.

Isis shrieked but couldn't hear her own voice, could no longer hear the scuffling of shoes or the crisp commands the Priori shot back and forth. She couldn't hear the betrayer's laughter but she could see his open mouth and bobbing jaw, his spotted skin pulled back in wrinkled mirth. And just as the sound had been vacuumed out of the room, so was all light.

A pulse rocketed through her and suddenly the Priori were jerking their hands back as though seared, crying out as the smell of burning flesh filled her nostrils. Then that sensation was gone, too, and only the scent of ash and flame surrounded her. Isis was filled with fire and light. Just as Shade's power had touched her, now she was overwhelmed with the ethergy of Vox. The Flame Sovereign's mind was engulfed with fire, pain, and raw power.

Isis threw her head back and screamed. Her whole body was floating in the magma, her eyes wreaths of flame, and the unstable elements were vibrating faster and faster. This was not the flow of ancient power that Shade could command. This was chaotic, uncontrolled.

And then suddenly Isis could see everything.

The first several levels Eros climbed were filled with people hurrying this way and that, following the latest evacuation instructions. He met little resistance and, even when he did, it was easily overcome. Then he reached the levels littered with angel corpses, drowned and now steaming from the heat. Dimitri had come through on a rampage. Eros quickened his pace. He knew he was getting closer when he found the thick clouds of black smoke pouring out of an open stairwell and plunged headfirst into the choking fumes. He climbed up, occasionally passing open doorways where he glimpsed more and more damage the higher he went. He followed the charred trail of burned architecture, melted machinery, and exploded electrical units until he came to a spot where a door had once been, now an angry, wide gap of sharp metal shards.

Eros darted into the burning hallway. Charred bodies were tucked in corners or thrown over desks. What had happened? Unintentional flash fires brought out by Vox's instability? Was he too late? No. The destruction was horrific but not nearly as great as he had expected. It was merely a taste of what was to come. He had hoped he could do something for her, maybe even save her. But his hopes were extinguished at the sight before him.

Eros followed the trail of Vox's power until he found the furnace where she dwelt. She was strung up on a vertical table in a cruciform pose. Her skin was glowing red, her stomach a furious ball of white light. She looked at him with bright eyes, barely containing all of that energy inside of her. Dimitri was bathed in blue, shimmering with summoned ethergy just to survive the heat in the room, to survive touching his beloved. He looked at him with eyes like a deep ocean, sad and vast and calm.

"Baron," Vox said. "Eros."

"It has already started," Dimitri muttered in despair. "It is too late."

Eros nodded. "I'm so sorry."

"I am glad to see you one last time, Baron," Vox choked, "father...friend." She cried out as a contraction wracked her body with pain. "You have to go," she screamed between contractions. "You have to get away from me—" her words turned to shrieks.

The Baron looked at the Water Sovereign but the man shook his head. He would never leave her side. They would die together, as a family. The Baron would lose three children that day—a strong daughter, a brave son, and a precious grandchild whose face he would never see.

"May the Great Justiciar usher you into green lands and clear skies, the Balance receive you with great rewards for your exemplary service," he choked on his own words, tears burning hot in his eyes. "And where you go now, my love goes with you. You have made me proud."

"Yes, Baron," Dimitri said, jaw tight with emotion. Vox sobbed liquid fire. And Eros had no choice but to leave.

The blast doors protecting the Hive Mind had sealed the moment the Leviathan approached Heaven, but with the energy readings originating inside the great tower, extra measures had been taken to ensure Operations' protection. The vacuum and fallout doors were locked and all vulnerable access points—ventilation, maintenance and servitor shafts, emergency exits, and elevators—had been collapsed and sealed with trianium foam. Centrum was locked inside the heart of the great machine while a carbon-reinforced cage was lowered over Operations and the brain. Each of the twelve cyborg elements of Operations was braced against the brain with cuffs across their chests and necks and along their arms.

Still, the rumbling was felt in the deep and the Hive Mind screamed in fear. The assault on Heaven was more than a declaration of war or a violation of law. It was an affirmation that they had made a severe miscalculation in harboring the Flamefang. Not for fear of Keepers, but for fear of chaos.

The unstable element was going to detonate. And if their readings touched truth, none of their protective measures would matter. The data was processed over and over again but no matter how many times the computer ran the scenario—hundreds of thousands of times a second—the end result was the same.

Heaven would be obliterated.

The Hive Mind screamed, for that was all a powerless machine could do.

Knick stared at Shade on her knees next to Rexis, looking at him with that delicately stressed expression she wore when she was confused and frustrated at the same time, her eyes and mouth reflecting a tinge of sadness. He had killed her friend and she was sad *for* his death but not sad *by* it. Rexis had betrayed her, violated her trust and her mission, and had left no other alternative to his fate but to die.

But Rexis had been right about one thing: she was not supposed to be here.

"You came back," Knick said. "Why?"

Without looking up or a change in expression, she replied, "I thought of what the mystic said, that we must stay together. Vox has the Interim to support her." She looked at him. "You have me. The place I make a difference is here, by your side." Her frown deepened as some thought crossed her mind. He waited for her to speak it, to make her complex feelings clear to him. "But you didn't need me."

"No, I need you," he said instantly. "I may not always need you to fight for me," he paused to swallow his emotion, "but I need you."

Shade slowly nodded—that she accepted his words, believed them, or was just too tired to argue was beyond his ability to read. And then she looked at Rexis and the moment was over.

"You channeled again. How?"

"I don't know," he admitted. "I just felt his power like I felt yours, and I could touch it, do whatever I wanted with it." He shook his head. "But I didn't want *this* to happen."

"I heard what he said," she began, "but I didn't want to believe it. I should have seen it. I should have helped him. I let him down—"

"No. No, this wasn't you." Knick walked closer and pointed at the corpse. "This happened a long time ago." He knelt down beside her and pulled out his cigarettes. "You asked me how I broke away from the Hive Mind." She gave him eye contact as he slapped the pack against his palm. "I got a letter—a hand-written letter—from the man I told you raised me, my mentor among the angels. He told me to get out, to break away from the system." Knick pulled out a cigarette and placed it between his lips. "He asked me not to blame him or the others, that they were victims, too—victims of the system. And that it was too late for them." He flicked his lighter, held it to the end of the rette, and inhaled. "He asked me not to hesitate when I came to him. He asked me to kill him to save him. Because the system had him and he couldn't get out."

"What happened?"

Knick shrugged and exhaled a cloud of gray. "When I finally became fully aware, I ran. His team met me to stop me. He knew I would run because he had written the letter. He wrote the letter to save me knowing that knowledge would also kill me. It was a risk he thought was worth it." Knick took another drag. "And I killed him. Not because I wanted to...but because he made me. Sometimes the people we love force us to destroy them. For redemption, for penance...or maybe for freedom, because they're in too deep and can't get out."

Shade nodded, closed Rexis' eyes, and then looked at Knick. They stared at each other in silence as he smoked. She reached out and took his hand. He curled his fingers around hers and held on tight.

"Knick," she said. "I need you, too." His cigarette almost fell out of his mouth in shock. "I thought I had lost you."

There were tears in her eyes. She suddenly stood up and went inside. Knick scrambled after her, calling out for her to wait but she hurried on, prompting his pace to quicken. He caught up to her in a small, empty corridor, turned a corner and practically ran into her. She was swiping tears away from her eyes. Knick opened his mouth to say something but he was so shocked that nothing came out.

"I hesitated," she mumbled, pacing back and forth across the hallway, "because I still wanted to trust him. When the steel touched you, I thought—" She stopped pacing, swallowed hard, clenched her jaw. "You asked me why I went to Heaven." She looked at him. "Because I'm crazy about you, too."

Knick cleared the distance between them before he even had time to evaluate the situation. Then he was kissing her, holding her flush against him, and she was kissing him back, arms wrapped tight around his neck. All of the imagined moments couldn't compare with this, with the feel of her pressed against him, holding him, clinging to him, kissing him, wanting him as much as he wanted her. He didn't know where to go next so he shut his brain off, let instinct take over. Instinct held her tightly, explored the curves of her body with the set intention of memorizing every inch. Instinct guided her into an empty room, and she didn't protest when he kicked the door closed.

As he kissed her, intense warmth spread throughout his body. At first, he thought it was because of her, because of the way she made him feel. His nerves were alight, his heart was beating fast and hard, and he was breathing only when their kisses briefly broke. But his body was getting hotter and hotter. He shrugged out of his jacket, but his insides felt like they were melting.

"Knick," Shade gasped when he stumbled away from her. "You're burning up."

He was hunched over, panting. The doorway inside had opened up just like it had with Shade, with Rexis. There was fire inside of him, at his fingertips. He could burn the whole world with the ethergy raging inside of him.

"Something's happening," he rasped and looked at her. "Fire. Heat. It's so intense."

"Vox," she whispered. "Something's wrong. I have to go. I have to—"

"Shade," Knick stopped her. She looked at him in desperation. He shook his head. His words were so quiet, he barely heard himself say, "It's too late." He watched tears slip out of her eyes. She shrank away from him, to isolate herself in grief, but he pulled her against him and hugged her tightly. "From now on, we do this together."

She nodded against his chest and curled her fingers around the folds of his shirt. He rested his cheek on the top of her head, tightened his arms around her, and closed his eyes as the firestorm raged hotter, racing toward an unavoidable climax. Nothing could survive in that heat.

Nothing.

Donovan convulsed as he slipped out of the rejuvenation tank and was dumped onto the cold ground like a hooked fish. Attendants threw towels around him, strong arms scooping him up and forcing him on his feet. The mask over his face was carefully peeled off, removing six inches of tubing from the depths of his throat. He coughed and sputtered as phlegm and saliva dripped out of his mouth. A doctor was examining him but Donovan felt very little but the cold. A light suddenly shown blindingly bright and he squinted bloodshot eyes, recoiling. The voices were garbled bass sounds, like he was still in the tank.

And then someone was walking him out of the room and into a warmer space. He looked down and saw the gauntlet still on his arm, icy and sinister. For a brief moment, he wished it wasn't there. And then he was being dressed in warm, dry clothes and force-fed hot tea. By the time the cup was empty, his hearing had returned and his body was no longer numb.

"I need to see the Regent," he rasped, his voice barely audible. The attendant nodded and helped him to the door. When they approached the audience chamber, he shoved the aide away and continued the journey on his own. Inside, the Priori, a few scientists, and several scholars had crowded before the circulet, all staring at something. Donovan pushed through, still squinting against all forms of light, until he was close enough to see.

The Enoch was glowing.

The Regent, the delegates, and the Priori all gaped in awe as the Enoch's feet left the ground, her thin frame hoisted into the air and encased in a burning aura. Her eyes had taken an orange hue, her pupils no more than pinpricks as she gazed vacantly at the sky. They waited on the edge of fear and wonder for something to happen, but she just floated there, turning slowly like a ballerina in an old music box.

Muriel nodded to one of the Priori and he inched toward her, reaching out to pull her down. Donovan tried to shout, "Wait," but he had no voice to speak with. Before the Prior could touch her, a great force threw him back. The Enoch's eyes flashed brightly and a string of numbers and letters began pouring out of her mouth. At first, it seemed like gibberish, the mutterings of a broken machine. And then someone gasped and said,

"Those are equations. Mathematical equations."

"Meaning?"

"I don't know. I don't even know if they're real."

"They are," Muriel croaked. "It is the language of the universe, the script of existence. The Enoch's mind is the greatest processor to have been created in all our time. Self-aware, the Enoch is no more than a human child. But strip that away—unclog the mind of emotions, free it from the burden of personality and the complexities of perspective—and what you have is raw knowledge."

What? Processor? Donovan thought as he stared at the Enoch. *Knowledge, not wisdom. What does that mean?* The Enoch was being equated with a computer. The heart of the Order was the Enoch and Oracle, sacred vessels of truth, ancient and powerful, mysterious harbingers of fate since the dawn of time. And the Enoch was nothing more…than a computer?

"The Enoch sees every possibility, collates the data

generated by millions of actions a second. She pinpoints the significant events—those actions with far-reaching ripples—and predicts every possible future based upon these choices. She follows every outcome, collecting data from both before and beyond each turning point, until only a handful of futures become the possible projected destinies of the human race."

"But how?" one of the scientists gasped. "The Enoch is a human being. How could she access all that information?"

"Because technology is knowledge, and having knowledge is to be steps ahead of everyone without it," Muriel replied. "And whether you are one step or thousands, it does not matter. All that matters is that you are. In the old days, knowledge was passed orally from one man to the next. Thousands traveled great distances to speak with the Oracle. It only got easier. Now, tens of thousands of satellites circle this planet, connecting every ounce of information across the world, and the nanomachines inside the Enoch's brain can access every electronic device that exists today. There is not a moment unaccounted for."

"But that's not possible," another scientist stammered. "There is no machine in the world capable of organizing such data. You're talking…billions—no trillions of yottabytes processed a second, I…"

"Cannot fathom? No," Muriel sneered, "you cannot."

Suddenly the Oracle flared amidst the Enoch's mathematical rambling. A wraithlike voice hissed, echoing off the domed ceiling and curving walls of the audience chamber, and all voices hushed. No one dared to breathe.

"The sea will part and the mount will erupt. The seed contained, preserved at the cost of the great oceans, dried up, diminished. The spewing of flame to reach Heaven's gates, the foundations crumbled, the bricks returned to the oven. Ruin. Lament the passing of the flame and the sea."

Donovan swallowed a sudden lump in his throat. He instantly thought of the dream world when he was in the tank. He had seen Vox in that world, surrounded by a firestorm, her body coming undone by the flames. What had happened while he had been in the tank? Was what he saw really happening to Vox? Was she being destroyed by her own aegis' power?

As the Enoch slowly spun, her voice grew louder, the equations more complex. The orange glow around her began to brighten. And the Oracle's hissing prophecy continued, mostly in riddles he could not understand, except for the repeated phrase, "Lament the passing of the flame and sea."

Dimitri kissed Vox's brow and his lips chapped from the touch. He knelt down in front of her and gently touched her stomach, the swell of their child, and had to increase the bloom of his ether to stand the searing heat. She looked at him, face riddled with pain and sorrow. He thought back to their happiest moments, to the way she had made him feel when he saw her, thought of her. How beautiful she was to him—then and even now—how bright and full of life. He thought of the warm smiles she gave him, of the first time he kissed her, the first night they made love, to the peace and joy he had felt just by loving her and being loved by her.

Had he known that this was their destiny, this pain and anguish and loss, he would never have touched her. He would have stayed far away from her. He could not regret anything that came after taking that first step, but he regretted taking it. In her, he had found a purpose greater than the Balance. In her, he had found a love deeper than duty. In her, he had found a family stronger than the Keepers. And in that, they had created a wondrous new life that would destroy everything they had, would be destroyed by their transgressions.

The innocent result of their affair would be both the price of their sin and the engineer of their punishment. He couldn't let that happen.

"Vox," he whispered. "I will save our child. I swear to you. I will save our baby."

Vox nodded, her expression twisted up with longing for the end. As a final tide of pain overcame her and she lost herself to screams, Dimitri closed his eyes and sought the source of power inside of him. He removed the lid, allowed it to overflow. The dam broke and water rushed out, flooding his body. Just as Vox was burning up, he began to liquefy. His hands turned to funnels of water, absorbing into her womb. He felt their child, held it in his arms.

As Vox began to rip apart, Dimitri gave all that he was to form a protective bubble in her womb. And as the bounds of human form unraveled into pure energy, there was a single and strong feeling of love. And then the energy reached its apex.

"Lament the passing of the flame and sea," the Oracle exclaimed, louder and louder, as the Enoch's voice rose to a shrill cry. "Lament the passing of the flame and sea! Lament them! Lament!"

The Enoch suddenly gasped, mathematical rambling paused, and the Oracle fell silent. Fate and prophecy and the world seemed to take a deep breath. And as the Enoch turned in the air, Donovan saw golden tears slip out of her wide, orange eyes. Those tears dripped down her cheeks and fell to the ground, burning holes into the rug. She might have looked at him, and in her eyes he saw a column of flame, he saw Vox in a firestorm, and a woman with long, black hair standing before him.

And then she rotated away from him and the aura around her brightened, exploding vertically. Donovan felt his eyes grow hot and he blinked in furious surprise. Tears instantly wet his face.

The whole of Lotus Maze felt the tremble as a pulse of energy rocketed the length of Heaven. There was a swell of silence and then the white tower exploded in a furious column of red light, spearing into the sky and disappearing into the dense clouds and toxic gases. The whole of the complex was overcome in disintegrating fire, blasting deep underground. The earth shook violently to the farthest corners of Anshar and Kishar until, at last, it was over.

As the dust began to settle, the massive compound where Heaven once stood was nothing more than a crater of rubble.

Knick watched in silence as Red was placed on the pyre. Rexis, covered with a white sheet, was arranged below her, and then Knick was handed the torch. He threw it into the kindling. Within moments, the pyre was raging. Shade stood on his right, Tasavir on his left, and Lethan with Whiskey, Enge, and Ross behind him. A cluster of Bloodsworn gathered around in reverent quiet, among them Caleigh with her myriad of scars made more sinister by the bouncing firelight. Molly sat next to the burning pyre of her fallen master and howled. Aside from the popping of the flames, it was the only sound.

Knick turned his hand out and brushed Shade's knuckles, coaxing her fingers to reach for his. She did, lacing their fingers together in a firm grip. He watched the flames in chaotic motion that reminded him of a tribal dance, up and down, limbs flailing, reaching for the sky. Funnels of black smoke swirled upward inside plumes of diaphanous gray clouds. Occasionally a firework of sparks would pop over the pyre, scattering glowing embers on the ground.

"I am the One," Knick said, "and I'll find Mesopotamia." He looked at Shade, looked right into her eyes red from mourning. "I promise."

Shade gave him a small smile and quietly said, "I believe in you."

Eros and the three Interim picked a careful path through the rubble that was the White Tower. Not a soul had survived and most of the architecture had been disintegrated in the blast. All that was left was charred chunks of stone and earth lining the crater. Eros shook his head in despair, hoping in vain that at least one of them had somehow survived. But there was nothing, only black earth, the smell of sulfur, and the taste of ash. He scanned the bleak ruin when he reached the next landing, praying to the Balance for some sign.

And then he saw it, the gleam of light. With utter abandon, Eros raced down the slippery slope of loose debris and stone and sprinted across the massive expanse of the crater's center. He slid to a stop when he came close and took the last slow steps toward it.

Amid the rubble, entirely unharmed, was a sleeping infant, his umbilical cord coiling a few inches away from him, burned at the end. Crisscrossed protectively over the boy were the fang of flame and the sword of seas. Eros knelt in the ashes and burnt chunks as Daedalus, Sonia, and Balthazar rushed to see what he had seen.

The child had survived.

[The Order of the Keepers]

The Order//The Order of the Keepers is the utmost neutral force with one goal in mind: to protect the Balance. The Order exists under a strict hierarchy, with the Regent at the head and twenty-six delegates that act as his council. His personal representative is the Consular. Beneath the Regent are the three Primordials; they are the High Counselor, the Baron, and the Cleric. The High Counselor, the scholar, is head of the collective and Oracle, bearing five priests as consultants. The Baron, the military leader, controls the Interim and the Kur, who are managed by seven generals. And the Cleric, the healer, oversees the naga and the Enoch.

The Collective//A group of monks split into two sects. The first, and the majority, is the scholars that spend day after day in the libraries researching the prophecies. The second is a very small group called the savants that tend to the Oracle, recording all information the Oracle bestows. The savants pass that information to the scholars, who research everything pertaining to the prophecy. The scholars pass their research to the High Counselor, who, aided by his priests, sifts through the research, discarding irrelevant information and organizing the rest to present to the Regent, who will use the research to interpret the prophecy's meaning with the guidance of his delegates.

The Oracle//An unknown force of fate seen through a scrying pool. It reveals glyphs and murmurs prophecy. The Oracle can be invoked but usually only speaks when it wants to. The Oracle is one of two equal parts and forms a synergistic bond with the Enoch. The Oracle resides in a very private chamber called the Seer's Cell; only the savants, the Primordials, and the Regent are allowed to enter.

The Interim and Kur//The Interim is a small sect of elite warriors chosen by the Balance to wield the aegises, weapons of power. They answer to the Baron and the Regent only. The

Kur are the military force who performs everything from small, covert missions to large-scale assaults.

The Naga and Enoch//The naga are the attendants of the Enoch, a very small group that is comprised entirely of females. The Enoch is the dreamweaver and the other half of the Oracle. The naga, the Cleric, and the Regent are the only ones allowed to enter the Enoch's chamber.

Priori//The Regent's personal bodyguards; an individual is called a Prior. They are promoted into the position from the Kur and their command is transferred from the Baron to the Regent.

Elysium//A period of one month out of the year when the collective are not allowed to use the Oracle or the Enoch. It is believed that fate and the future is like a delicate spider web; when the spider web is poked and prodded too much, it breaks. The Keepers declare Elysium as a time when none are allowed to interfere with that delicate web and tamper with fate, allowing the threads to strengthen and fall as they may. It had never before been broken until Ralph Gobol accidentally discovered the prophecy concerning the new glyph. Emergency states of Elysium have been called before, but only in the most strenuous of times when the fate lines are very thin and tangled.

Vanguard//A state of emergency that gives the Baron and his Interim supreme power over all Keeper proceedings, resources, and persons, including the Regent, to solve a problem or problems. Vanguard may only be invoked by the Baron and only under extreme duress. Once the problem is resolved, Vanguard ends and power is immediately restored to the respective authorities.

Circulet//The official assembly of the Regent and his closest delegates, named for the semi-circle arrangement of the thrones.

Ether//Pure energy with mystical properties. Ethergy is positive ether that adds energy to the world; its counterpart is nethergy, the negative ether that takes energy out of it.

[Angels]

The Nest//A chamber in the deepest sub-layer of Heaven that houses Operations.

Operations// A collaboration of three parts. The first is a complex computer motherboard and processor composed of both organic and synthetic material called the cerebrum. The second is twelve men, part-human and part-cyborg, plugged into the cerebrum. Finally, there is Centrum, the mostly-cyborg spokesman who issues the orders to the angels.

Hive Mind//The Operations network that every angel is neurally connected to.

Halo//The DNA archive of every angel, past and present.

[Cogwheelers]

Street Gun//Cogwheeler field operative. There are seven types; the most common are cogger, gunny, heavy, and techy, and the rare ones are sammy, firebug, and longsights.

Cogger//The leader of a cogwheeler cell and tactics master.

Gunny//Weapons specialist is the official job description but that's just code for "uses lots of guns". Gunnies are the most common type of Street Gun.

Heavy//Brute force. Once the gun clips are empty, a Heavy will go straight into a fistfight, utilizing everything they can as a weapon until they are taken out.

Techy//Tech experts, typically hackers.

Sammy//Slang for samurai, which is slang for melee weapons expert. Sammies are rare in that it takes a rare individual to bring a sword to a gun fight and walk away still breathing.

Firebug//Demolitions expert with a penchant for flame-throwers, though there's little need for explosives in the mine, and flamethrowers in tight spaces (like most spaces found underground) typically cause unnecessary collateral damage.

Longsights//Sniper. This type of Street Gun is so rare that each sniper wears his title like a name.

[The Tribes of Typhi]

Krueh-jin//The sons and daughters of Nippur are gypsy nomads who shine their eyes to see in the dark and hunt with creatures called lunalehn. They inhabit the Grey, constantly scavenging for lost treasures, artifacts, and relics. Their survival depends on trade so thievery is punishable by death.

Na Varen//The daughters of Uruk are the spiritual sisters most commonly known as the Sirens. They are a clan of beautiful women who worship the goddess Inanna, and are capable of dominating weak minds. They inhabit the Garden of Souls in the Karnak Sea and the *House of Heaven* in Tarsus. Their charge is to forever sing the Chant of Panghora, though they have forgotten why.

Ataashvatan//The children of Babylon were famously called Babylon's Immortals. Depending on the day and the job, they were pirates, mercenaries, smugglers, and bounty hunters. The tribe is now extinct with the exception of Molly, the dog that belonged to the tribe's leader, Red, who was responsible for preparing the Tribes for the coming of the One and for leading him to Mesopotamia.

Skahradahn//The wizards of Nineveh are warren dwellers ruled by a priestess, guided by a mystic widely known as the Rope Woman, and protected by massive warriors called the Dirt Men. The tribe is mistakenly thought to be all magical, but only the mystic and priestess have powers.

Ka'djai//The oathkeepers of Assur are the renowned dark messengers of Lotus Maze, the Bloodsworn, who transport letters, packages, verbal messages, and much more back and forth between Anshar, Kishar, and even the coal mines near the core. Whatever payment the Sworn accepts is fully his, so being paid with items as well as currency is not uncommon. They have outposts in nearly every city but their headquarters are at a place called Opera in the city of Romulus.

[Other]

The women of the Mermaid//A clan of women who utilize ancient techniques to heal any who require it, though little is known of their practices or history. They are led by the High Healer. Many women of the Mermaid eventually became naga in the Order of Keepers; Camilla the Cleric was once the High Healer before she became a Keeper.

ACKNOWLEDGEMENTS

First and foremost, all credit and gratitude goes to God Almighty for blessing me with the ability and the time to write, and for the opportunity to publish my work.

Thank you to my parents for always being supportive of my passion to write and understanding of my quirks. Thank you Dad for always calling me up to find out if I've written anymore, and for getting excited about every new chapter. Your enthusiasm means so much to me.

Thank you Robert for going above and beyond in every way to make this book a reality. I can't imagine its existence without you.

A gigantic thank you to my amazing friends, family, and fellow authors who have been incredibly supportive and helpful throughout this process. Special thanks to Sill, Fonzi, Aaron, and Mike.

And, as always, GRV—you're the man.

About the Author

Ashley's first great fictional loves were Star Wars, EverQuest, and Nexus Prime. Her greatest passions in life are writing and video games. She has been writing fantasy and science fiction since she was a child and gaming nearly as long, accumulating many obnoxious "in my day, in the snow, uphill both ways" stories of the gamer equivalent. She is obsessed with jesters and tricksters, has wanted to be a Jedi Knight since she was four years old, and is terrified of xenomorphs.

About the Cover Artist

Oksana Kharitonova, also known as Aira Gitt, is an amazing artist from Russia who studied CG and illustration on her own, and draws every single day. Her artwork can be viewed and commissioned at airagitt.deviantart.com and airagitt.tumblr.com.

Working with Oksana was a great experience. She is so talented, was easy to talk to, and focused on capturing my vision. I honestly can't say enough kind things about her.

About *Mesopotamia//Tiamat*

Mesopotamia//Tiamat was originally a short story written in 2008 as an experiment in writing styles, intended to feel like a blur of action rather than fleshed out prose. When it became a short story series, the storytelling method evolved again and again until it became the novel it is today.

While the bulk of *Mesopotamia//Tiamat* is fictional, much of the content concerning Mesopotamia and its mythology is based on the historical cradle of civilization and ancient Mesopotamian religion.

www.ingramcontent.com/pod-product-compliance
Lightning Source LLC
Chambersburg PA
CBHW030545180626
46816CB00005B/1412